A DEEP, THROBBING HUM IRRITATED
SOUSKA'S INNER EAR.

Lukan! Her journeyman called her.

Quickly she looked around the stillroom filled with aromatic herbs and brews and potions. All of the other healer apprentices were busy with their own tasks, trying to finish before the sun fully set lest darkness and unknown qualities invaded their medicines. She crept up the long, narrow staircase against the interior wall toward the journeymen's living quarters. Then past the bedrooms and up another stair to the apprentice dormitories. Finally the ladder to the loft attic appeared, deep in the shadows of the back corner.

At the top, in her own private space, she poured water into a palm-sized ceramic bowl, lit the candle with a snap of her fingers, and dropped her tiny shard of glass into the bowl.

Lukan's face appeared almost immediately.

Souska reached a finger to trace the curve of his cheek but he turned his face away, looking over his shoulder anxiously.

"I have no time. Tell Mistress Maigret that Rejiia is in the city, and I think she's recruiting a new coven."

"What?"

"I'm beached at Sacred Isle, and I can't work magic once I set foot out of my boat," he hissed at her. "Memorize what I said. The Masters need to know this." His face vanished.

Be sure to read these magnificent
DAW Fantasy Novels by
IRENE RADFORD

THE WANDERING DRAGON

Children of the Dragon Nimbus #3

IRENE RADFORD

DAW BOOKS, INC.

DONALD A. WOLLHEIM, FOUNDER

375 Hudson Street, New York, NY 10014

ELIZABETH R. WOLLHEIM
SHEILA E. GILBERT
PUBLISHERS

www.dawbooks.com

First Printing, August 2014
1 2 3 4 5 6 7 8 9

This book is dedicated to all those of my family
with itchy feet who taught me that wandering is valuable.
In all our ramblings you have taught me about the world,
about life, and about love. Thank you.

Acknowledgments:

This book grew out of twelve previous volumes in the world of the Dragon Nimbus. Along the way I have had to thank all those who read the books with a critical eye, those who helped me promote the works, the ones who cooked dinner and planned research trips when I was on deadline, and the readers who bought books so the series could keep going. Rather than bore readers with a long and growing list of names of people they don't know, I ask that all you friends and family, colleagues and mentors, agents and editors, consider yourself thanked and hugged.

PROLOGUE

*C*ORONNAN RESTS QUIET, *but defensive and wary. The people are as wounded as the land after the mage-driven storm that flooded half the fertile fields in the country and ripped up the open prairie with its fearsome winds. The monstrous Krakatrice are mostly destroyed by teams of magicians and dragons. The king works everywhere with his people, rebuilding, restoring, stripping off his fine tunic to lend a strong back where needed. So do his two heirs.*

The people adore King Darville de Draconis. He has forsaken strong drink and regained much of his youthful vigor and charm. No trace of scandal taints him, and the people have forgiven him his bastard son by a witchwoman, fathered before his marriage to his beloved Queen Rossemikka. This kingdom will not rise against him. Not now or for many years to come.

My father has become useless. Fifteen years in prison have taken their toll on his energy and intelligence. He looks old. He acts old, content to sit by the fire in the kitchen and swap tales with his old retainers. He cares not that another, weaker man wears his title, lives in his castle, and sits in the Council of Provinces. My father wants only peace, and has not even introduced himself to the cousin who rules his province. I doubt the vague lord and his even vaguer lady even know their predecessor lives in their castle. He has truly sloughed off the persona of his totem, the tin weasel with flaking gilt paint.

The years of imprisonment were kinder to me. I feel as if time stopped. I look as if time slowed, or even reversed. I made certain of that, when the restoration spell fueling the storm changed us. I stood behind my father and directed things so that . . . some of my aging dumped into him and some of his former youth fed back into me. People mistake my years by ten at least. My beauty is intact.

My powers are not. I need a coven to support my magic. I shall begin recruiting practitioners, men and women who enjoy the inflicting and receiving of pain. Men and women who draw power from the suffering of others.

Pain is the essence of power. That and a few doses of the addictive Tambootie leaf.

A few members here and there I can achieve easily. But for a full thirteen I must search further afield. A new coven, new powers, a new land to rule and subdue. People with a great deal of anger buried deep within.

And no one will suspect my true goals, nor how ruthless I can be when something, someone, stands between me and what I want.

CHAPTER 1

"TOGETHER WE MOURN. Together we bury the dead." The pulsing rhythm of priestly plainsong vibrated through the soles of Lukan's journey boots.

A dragon bellowed in mourning from the sky above.

The journeyman magician looked up, scanning for a flicker of sunlight against nearly invisible, crystalline dragon fur. There! He caught sight of a delicate tracery of fire-green defining a wing.

Why had the dragons come here? Today? They should be at their home deep in the Southern Mountains— towering, jagged peaks trying to pierce the sky with their icy serrated knife tops. Deep ravines lay in shadow most of the year there, hiding treacherous passes and blind snow caves. A safe refuge for dragonkind from the fearful reactions of an ignorant populace. Dragons had always lived separate from humans, intruding occasionally to admonish, to offer wisdom, to celebrate life.

And now to grieve. Matriarch Shayla and her consort Baamin had maintained close ties to Brevelan and Jaylor, Lukan's parents. Upon their deaths, within moments of each other, the dragons had retreated from humankind. The Stargods only knew when, or if, the dragons would once more hover in the back of Lukan's mind. He'd grown up

among them and now their absence left a gnawing emptiness behind his heart. Or was that his own grief?

He paused in indecision as he approached the top of the
latest hill he and the bard, Skeller were climbing. The slopes
were gentle, the footing even. Ten to fifteen miles a day they
covered, easily. He didn't expect the next leg of their journey to be as easy; for reasons more painful than difficult
terrain. Tall grasses, waving bright green in the sun of high
summer. But autumn must follow soon, and already the
plains showed signs of going to seed. The stalks brushed
their knees before bending in their wake, leaving a faint
trail behind. And seeds to be carried farther afield to spread
the bounty.

A bounty sorely needed this year, for though tall, the
grasses should have reached shoulder height, and the seed-
pods should have contained fifteen to twenty seeds each.
He counted only three on each tufted head of the grasses in
his path.

The disastrous floods of early summer had damaged the
wild crops as well as the sown ones.

Once Lukan delivered the cursed letter in his pack to
Crown Prince Glenndon, he and Skeller could set out on
their own individual missions, and depart this damaged
kingdom once and for all. He hoped.

Somewhere deep in his gut he *knew* that leaving Coronnan did not mean he'd leave his problems and anger behind
as well. But his instincts demanded he run far and fast and
forget his friends, the University of Magicians, the untimely
deaths of his parents, and . . . and the love he'd shared with
his brother . . . half brother.

The only person he thought he'd miss would be Souska,
the little apprentice magician he'd been mentoring.

The soft chanting in response to the priest's deep bass
voice echoed around the vale just beyond the hill's ridgeline.

Skeller flung his arm across Lukan's chest, forcing him to
stop. The wood-and-leather harp case on the bard's back

shifted with his movement, thumping lightly. Lukan almost believed the harp—Telynnia—alive and wanting to add her voice to those ahead of them. Skeller's relationship with his music and instrument bordered on magic.

"What?" Lukan mouthed. Then the meaning of the words penetrated his mind.

"Funeral," Skeller said quietly at the same time the word touched the tip of Lukan's tongue. Skeller sounded as if he wanted to add his light baritone to the prayers rising from a great many voices.

"Here?" Lukan asked in surprise. By his calculation they should be approaching Battle Mound, sacred ground, not to be disturbed, plowed, or grazed. Not just anyone could be buried here. Only someone important, someone deeply honored by one and all. And only if the deceased had fallen in battle. Who?

His heart pounded loud in his ears. *Glenndon!*

No. He forced his panic to recede. He'd know if his brother—his *brother*, not just his half brother—had passed. He'd *know*.

He dropped low to the ground and crawled up to the crest where a few scraggly trees offered shade from the hot summer sun as well as shadow to hide him.

"How many?" Skeller asked. His fingers drummed a light tattoo upon his thigh, covered in journey leather trews, in a pattern that took on the cadence of the chant.

"Looks like hundreds," Lukan whispered. He tried spotting individuals in the ring of people holding hands around a wide swath of churned dirt.

Why? Why had they dug up the site of the last great battle in the civil war that had nearly torn Coronnan to pieces three hundred years ago? Only Nimbulan, the greatest magician of all time, had stopped the war by making a covenant with the dragons and establishing a new form of magic that could be controlled by a group, rather than greedy individuals constantly working against each other. The group in charge had evolved into the Magic Circle, twelve master

magicians who could combine their powers to overcome
any single rogue.

Lukan picked out the master magicians who counseled
the twelve lords of the Council of Provinces quite easily,
identified by their deep blue robes. Glenndon was also easy
to spot with his bright golden hair and richly brocaded tunic
in the royal colors, green and gold. (Lukan didn't like to
admit how relieved he felt to see his brother standing tall
and very much alive. He still harbored a great deal of anger
toward him. And toward their Da, Master Magician Jaylor,
dead these two, nearly three moons.) Two small girls, about
twelve and ten, with darker hair but equally rich green and
gold gowns, stood next to him. Those must be Glenndon's
half sisters through his father, the king. Ah, there was King
Darville with his long silver-gilt hair pulled back into a tight
four-strand queue and a heavy glass crown shaped like a
dragon ready to take flight. Next to him was the queen. She
could only be Queen Ròssemikka. Her clothes and demi-
crown didn't matter; she was an older, near duplicate of her
daughter Rosselinda, who had forsaken her royal heritage
to become a magician and was currently first assistant to
Master Maigret, who now ran the Forest University.

"Reports from the capital said only one in ten survived
the mage-driven storm and flooding," Skeller said, his voice
dropping as he gulped back strong emotions. He shuddered,
and the rhythm of his beating fingers slowed to a dirge. "In
a city that boasted twenty thousand souls when I left here
at the beginning of summer . . . I just can't fathom it. They
must be buried here too."

Good reason to further sanctify Battle Mound, a place
to honor the newly dead as well as those lost in battle long
ago.

The citizens had needed nearly three moons to recover
as many bodies as possible, and to rebuild enough that they
could leave their temporary shelters for this day of mourning.

Lukan turned his face away from the mass grave and

looked toward the western horizon, across the River Coronnan, which had receded back within its normal banks. The sun had dipped past its zenith three hours ago. "If we hurry, we can be inside the city before dusk."

"You could give your brother the letter from your father here and we wouldn't have to go into the city at all," Skeller reminded him. He didn't look happy about that solution.

"Not here. Too public. This last meeting between us needs to be private." Lukan looked sadly toward the blond young man in the distance, barely a year older than himself. They'd been incredibly close until a few moons ago. They'd shared everything, wrestled, fought, played tricks on each other, swapped chores in defiance of Da and their masters, and laughed together over everything and nothing. They'd rarely spent more than a few hours apart. Their twin sisters were much the same. But now Lillian and Valeria had gone their separate ways, and it was time for Lukan and Glenndon to do the same. The ties that had bound them were badly frayed last spring when King Darville called Glenndon, his illegitimate son, to the capital to become heir to the dragon crown. Now the time had come to totally sever those ties and find their different destinies.

Lukan only wanted to connect with one person at the University. He wasn't certain how long he could maintain that one connection in good conscience. Souska needed a tutor. Lately, she sounded more interested in becoming a lover.

"I wonder there is any city left," Skeller said. "A mage-cast storm thrusting a wall of water thirty feet high one hundred miles across the Bay and up the river . . . It would have wiped clean every one of the hundreds of river islands making up the city." He shook his head, wanting to deny what the reports had said over and over.

"Of course the city is still there. Glenndon the Magnificent rode a Dragon to the rescue, cast the greatest magic spell of all time, and triumphed over the storm of the millennium," Lukan sneered. "But he left countering the storm to Da and the Circle." Fighting the storm had cost Da his life. His mother had miscarried and hemorrhaged within minutes of Da's passing. She hadn't had the strength or the will to fight for life without him. Lukan gulped back strong emotions.

"All I have to do is deliver this *S'murghin* letter, then we cross to the far side of that mile-wide river and set up camp."

"I was looking forward to a hot meal and a real bed for a change," Skeller sighed wistfully.

"I thought you liked the wandering life, following the caravans, singing for your supper, and sleeping under the stars."

"I do. But I also like the occasional inn with a generous barmaid and an appreciative audience." He looked away, no doubt wishing he could replace the generous barmaid with Lukan's sister Lillian. But despite their love for each other, they needed time apart. They both had things to learn about life and love before they could decide if they wanted to be together.

"I don't know this city. I wasn't invited to come with my sisters last spring to help Da and Glenndon fight the Krakatrice and the civil war," Lukan grumbled. Another time when Da had had no use for him and had forgotten his existence. "But I'm willing to bet the inns and taverns were the first to rebuild, especially close to the port, where aid will have come from King Darville's barons and allies across the sea. I still want to sleep rough and unhindered, but you shall find your beer there. Then tomorrow, we'll search out a berth on the next ship headed to Amazonia, one that leaves after I complete my journeyman's quest."

"And what am I to do alone while you row over to Sacred Isle? Presuming the island and its trees even survived the flood."

"You will sing in whatever bar we can find near the port and listen to the gossip. Listen to the sailors talk while beer loosens their tongues and learn what they know or have heard about your father's prisoner."

The chant soared into a hymn, a familiar and comforting one. Skeller's fingers drumming against his thigh took up the new rhythm, and his entire body took on a straighter and more comfortable posture. He couldn't help lifting his magnificent voice in song, joining with those who mourned and now released their lost loved ones to the beneficence of the Stargods.

Lukan couldn't let go so easily. He held his grief and his grudges tightly in his heart and in his mind, despite the tug of that beautiful hymn, and the dragon flying above. But even he had to add his own voice to the triumphant ending.

Just then, Glenndon lifted his head and scanned the ridge where Lukan crouched. The prince's gaze settled on his half brother.

You came, Glenndon said directly into Lukan's mind with a sigh of relief.

I was sent, Lukan replied.

For the first eighteen years of his life Glenndon had never spoken aloud. His telepathic powers came more easily to him than speech, and even now, five moons after a near-miraculous healing of his throat, he still reverted to mind-speech.

Can you meet me in the palace?

Where in the palace? I hear it's a big place. The twins had been there and reported convoluted passages, wings sprouting at odd angles, twisting staircases, and abandoned sections left over from generations before.

Private parlor, ground floor. I'll have Keerkin, my . . . friend wait for you at the main door. Mentally, Glenndon directed Lukan's gaze to a man of middling height and neutral coloring a few years older than themselves, who stood directly to Glenndon's right.

Lukan nodded his head and grunted an acceptance. Glenndon wouldn't meet him himself, he had to trust that chore to an underling. Just as Lukan was an underling to him. Everyone in Coronnan was an underling to him except the king.

The king. The man who had seduced . . . actually loved . . . their mother before she married Master Magician Jaylor. Mama kept that brief affair secret for eighteen years. The king and Da had been best friends for decades. But the king needed a male heir and had only daughters from his queen, so he'd yanked Glenndon away from his family, and out of his silence, and made him Crown Prince. Now both Mama and Da had passed. Glenndon had his new family, the royal family. Lukan had no one. Even his companion the wandering bard would leave him as soon as they reached his home in Amazonia.

CHAPTER 2

MASTER MAGICIAN ROBB stuffed his aching and swollen hands inside the sleeves of his once-pristine formal robe as he paced. At dawn, damp chill permeated the walls of his small cell. By midday he'd have to shed both the robe and shirt while he sweated in desert heat. If Maigret could see him now, she'd scold him mightily for his disheveled appearance, even as she held his hands and lovingly examined every pore on his body for signs of illness.

She'd also make him shave, two or three times, before his face was smooth enough for her standards. His captors hadn't let him near any kind of blade.

His gut ached from missing his wife and their two young sons. His heart skipped a beat at the thought that he might never see them again, or touch them again, or bear up to Maigret's scoldings again . . .

He yanked his thoughts out of that destructive loop. Again.

His captor had preserved his health. Freedom, light, and dignity had been denied.

Whoever kept him in this benighted cell needed him alive for some reason Robb could not fathom. Of course, it would help if he knew who held him, and why.

Had three moons passed since he'd been whisked out of a transport spell into an alien land? Or was it four? He'd meant to transport to Coronnan City. Had he made a mistake in the tricky and dangerous spell?

Or had a rogue magician manipulated the layers of visualization and precise timing required?

He'd thought and thought through all the permutations—he didn't have much else to do—and drawn the conclusion that a rogue had added an extra layer of images to his own to bring him here. And he thought he knew which rogue was involved. Samlan had a lot to answer for when Robb got out of this *S'murghin* prison. If he didn't go insane first.

To ward off such dangerous thoughts, Robb paced his cell, five steps to a side. He checked the scratches on the wall he'd made to keep track of the days. Had he made one yet since the sun rose?

He didn't think so. His wooden spoon lay on the end of his cot ready for him. He grasped the bowl in his right hand, balanced his left against the wall and scratched hard against the dressed stones with the worn handle. A new line appeared gradually, only slightly lighter than the background. Another fraction of an inch splintered off the handle. His work showed well enough to mark another day. He counted each grouping of five, as he did every morning. One hundred thirty-six.

Surely that couldn't be right. When had thirty days become sixty? Then ninety? Fear broke out in cold sweat down his spine. Praying to the Stargods that he hadn't lost his mind along with time, he counted again, each individual slash against the stone. One hundred thirty-six.

Robb almost wept. "No, no, no," he cried out as loudly as he could, slamming his fist against the wall. "I've cried enough. I've languished enough. I have to get out of here." He looked around at the same four walls he'd addressed every day for the last one hundred and thirty-six days.

"Wizard," a small lisping voice whispered to him from the barred window in the ironbound door of his prison. Iron. Poison to magicians according to myth and legend.

But it wasn't the iron in the door that kept Robb's magic dormant. The iron underground, massive and buried beneath ten feet of stone and dirt, hampered his powers. Only one small window near the ceiling marked the passage of light and dark. Not enough access to the air to gather dragon magic—if any dragons flew the skies of this land—and the floor too thick to tap a ley line—if any of the silvery blue streams of energy ran through here.

"Yes?" he asked wearily. The same voice spoke every morning, making certain he lived before wasting a tray of food on a corpse.

Robb thought it might belong to a beardless boy, perhaps a scullery maid, no one more important.

"His Majesty needs you," the voice said.

Something new!

"What can I do?"

"Follow." A turning key rasped within the lock, iron scratching seldom-used pins into motion.

Robb waited obediently against the far wall, as he did any time his guards brought him food or water rather than thrusting it through a narrow slot in the door, or came to empty the chamber pot when they absolutely had to, and not before. The door opened slowly, revealing a slim female in a sturdy dress, wearing a stained apron. She carried a candle lantern out to the side, not shedding enough light to determine her age, coloring, or degree of beauty. Only a large ring of keys hanging from her belt indicated that she held some authority.

"Follow." She turned around, waving the lantern just enough to indicate she intended to move to the left. After checking to see if armed guards waited to run him through with sword or spear, and finding none—they were all lined up against the corridor walls, stiff and respectful of the woman—Robb followed, shuffling his feet over the uneven stones, breathing deeply of air fresher than that in his cell. Afraid to think beyond the circle of light from the lantern. Afraid to hope for more between one step and the next.

Lily? Where are you!

Lily sighed as her twin, Valeria, burst into her thoughts. Just once she wished that Val would contact her just to check on Lily's well-being and not to solve some problem at home. She had enough problems of her own on the road.

She took her time answering her sister as she tamped down a little soil around the last of the apple tree cuttings she'd brought to plant. Six trees that wouldn't bear fruit for five years. But it was a start at rebuilding the crops for this town on the Dubh River, a major tributary half a mile south of the mighty River Coronnan. The Dubh was still navigable up here, for small boats and flat-bottomed barges to transport produce and livestock downstream. A two-day walk inland from the Great Bay, the town had grown to a substantial size as the only gathering place for the outlying farms. The floods had drowned the crops here, but left most of the houses and barns sodden and only a little damaged. At least the livestock had found higher ground and survived. This place was better off than most. Closer to the big river, nothing remained but layers of mud and corpses.

She signaled the headman to pour a pitcher of water around the cutting. He did so quite reverently. Then the entire village bowed to Lily.

She returned the gesture of respect, then gathered her thoughts to reply to her sister. *Val, I'm somewhere between the river and the Bay in a town called Lower Dubh. What's wrong?* she replied telepathically without breaking her smile and wave of farewell to the devastated farm folk. She'd done what she could to give them hope. Sometimes that was a better cure for despair than a wagonload of food.

You aren't here and that's what's wrong.

I'm not supposed to be there. Though I wish I could stand in the middle of the Clearing and listen to the wind in the everblue tops and absorb the peace of the mountains. She took a deep breath imagining the smells of home. Her heart continued to ache. For many reasons. Loneliness the least of them.

It's not peaceful here at the moment.

Lily caught an echo of childish screams of despair in the background of Val's thoughts.

What did Jule do this time? She asked about their youngest brother, who neared his third naming day.

I don't know, Val wailed. *I've tried everything and he just screams louder.*

Lily had never heard her twin so close to crying, not even when she had worked a long and complex spell, and exhausted her physical strength almost to the point of forgetting to breathe.

Lily waved a last farewell to the town elders and their ladies and turned her steps to the broad path that led to the next village, a day of hard walking to the west, toward the long line of mountains that nearly divided the continent and served as a barrier between Coronnan and their age-old enemy and sometimes ally, SeLennica.

Away from the prying attention of the villagers, she listened more carefully to her twin.

Is he teething? He shouldn't be, not this late. But everyone in the family of Jaylor and Brevelan did everything backward, or sideways, or too fast. Maybe it was Jule's turn to be behind at something.

As Lily was behind her brothers and sisters in magical talent. Her one and only skill seemed to be talking to her twin though separated by a thousand miles or more. And understanding the souls of plants and what they needed to grow best.

Um . . . I don't know. What are the symptoms of teething?

Crying a lot. Drooling a lot. Gnawing on things he's not supposed to.

No. Other than the crying a lot.

Is he constipated?

How should I know?

Lily sighed again. She should be the one at home taking

care of the younger children. Val had no empathy, training, or instincts when it came to nurturing children. She did have a magical talent that she probably thought was being wasted in her current situation.

A journey was about learning. Val needed to learn to take care of others after a lifetime of being an invalid and cared for. Lily needed to learn ... to live, when she should have died with the man she had murdered. *Executed,* she reminded herself. But it still felt as though she'd murdered the rogue magician Samlan when she'd slid a knife between his ribs.

He's out of nappies now so you can't check the soiled ones. Have you taken him to the outhouse today? Lily asked.

I don't usually ...

Then ask your charges, Lady Graciella and Ariiell.

They left for the University early this morning and haven't come back.

Then ask Sharl. Their six-year-old sister had more of a sense of responsibility than Val, Gracie, or Ariiell.

Give him some red fruit and a big glass of water, Val. Then make him sit for as long as necessary. Lily closed down on the communication. Her mind and heart felt empty when the contact vanished. She'd done that too often these last few moons of wandering Coronnan. Grimly she planted her staff of plain hawthorn one step ahead of her and continued her solitary mission. "I should be the one who stayed home, Val. You're the one who deserves a journeyman's journey."

But you wouldn't heal here at home, Val reminded her, despite Lily's barriers.

"We both have a lot to learn, twin. That's why we are both placed in positions that seem so opposite to our natural ways."

Lukan mingled with the crush of people trying to cross a bridge from the mainland over to the maze of islands that made up Coronnan City—five square miles of city with hundreds of islands and connecting bridges, many of them so badly damaged that people had to take longer, convoluted routes to get home. Had everyone still alive in the city trekked out to Battle Mound for the funeral and now returned all at the same time? All these people trying cross at once strained the raw wood of the newly built bridge. He eyed the hinges and latches at either end, freshly crafted but based on the old design, so that in case of invasion, or flood, the bridge could be collapsed as people retreated inward.

He guessed the city had emptied gradually over the course of the day. They'd all lost loved ones. They needed to see the mass grave, sing the songs, pray the prayers, and mourn. Now they could put aside crippling emotions and begin to rebuild in earnest. A determination to survive had pulled them through the disaster, and now it kept the throng moving forward, despite the crowding.

Skeller kept lagging behind, searching faces and postures and patches of newly cut lumber on every single building they passed. Many spaces between houses and shops lay empty, the gaps where buildings ripped from their foundations and now floating out to sea once stood. As crowded as this bridge was, he doubted enough people remained in the city to fill in all of those empty lots.

Those blank places brought home to him, more than the sight of the mass grave and the somber sounds of chants and hymns, just how much the storm, and the mage that had conjured it, had stolen from the heart of Coronnan.

"Thank the Stargods Lily managed to kill the *S'murgin* rogue," he muttered to himself. The fact that his sister had wielded the knife and not Skeller, as they'd planned or at least expected, was a gaping wound between them. Sweet, gentle, Lily, who couldn't bear to eat meat because she felt the death of the animal sacrificed to become food, had executed a man when no one else had had the nerve.

Her empathic talent had exploded outward and engulfed Skeller. He'd shared the moment of death with Samlan as deeply as Lily had.

The fact that the rogue magician was expecting a magical attack and Lily had very little, if any, magic, meant that she'd met no resistance. Lukan didn't think he could have managed the deed, and Skeller had hesitated a moment too long. Lily and only Lily had stopped Samlan before he wreaked any more damage on Coronnan.

Both she and Skeller nursed deep guilt and bruised minds.

"Skeller, keep up." Lukan stopped mid-span to wait for his companion. The tide of people surged around him, mostly silent, shooting him resentful glances but not protesting. They moved more like a stunned herd than people impatient to go about their business. Maybe they'd lost the drive for impatience. They lived. They had the work of survival to do. That was enough.

Except for one. A tall, lanky man hovered at the other end of the bridge. Not hesitant. Waiting. He kept his back to Lukan.

Lukan tamped down his suspicions. No one knew he was coming this way. The man couldn't be waiting for him.

"Sorry. This is all so fascinating, so different from my last visit," Skeller said, still craning his neck to take in everything. As usual, his fingers drummed against his thigh as his mind composed a new song. This one was livelier than the dirge about the funeral. This one was about cherishing life and building something new, fresh, and special, out of the ruins of the old.

Lukan had learned to read Skeller during the moons of their travels together. He could almost hear the melody and lyrics as they formed in the bard's mind.

"Well, I'm going ahead to the palace. I'll meet you at whatever inn you find down on the docks." Lukan started to turn away to join the surge of people flowing inward.

"Wait! How will you know which inn?" Skeller claimed Lukan's arm to delay him.

"I'll know by the number of sailors crowding around to hear you sing. I'll know by the bawdy chorus they take up

in celebration of whatever songs you dredge out of that copious memory of yours."

With that Lukan joined the throng and pressed forward.
Inward toward the largest and highest of the islands, where
the tallest of tall buildings had stood strong against the
flood. His nose wanted him to divert toward a deep concentration of magic—the old University of Magicians. Master
Marcus would be there, ready to officially give Lukan his
right to claim a staff and begin his journey.

Lukan wasn't ready to face the man who had reluctantly
taken Jaylor's place as Chancellor of the Universities, Senior Magician of the Circle, and counselor to the king. "I'll
deliver this *S'murghin* letter to Glenndon, then be free of
family obligations, free to live my own life away from the
shadow of older, more powerful, better respected magicians
that I can't live up to."

Three more bridges and his steps grew heavy, reluctant.
He trudged forward to the pedestrian gate in the palace
wall. The floodwaters had darkened the finely fitted stones
to eight feet above the ground. Lukan looked at the river
flowing around Palace Isle, a good six feet below where he
stood. It ran a bit low in high summer. Still, the clear evidence of just how much water had shifted from the Bay up
the river channels made him pause and gulp.

Glenndon, his brother, had thrown the spell that encased
the acres and acres of palace buildings in a protective bubble, keeping out all of that water; protecting the thousand
or more people who had taken refuge inside the buildings.

Lukan knew he couldn't have done that. Even with a
staff to channel and focus his magic. At the University, on
the adjacent isle, six masters had joined their powers and
thrown a similar spell to protect those buildings and their
refugees.

Still awed and a bit bewildered, he faced the uniformed
guard and identified himself. Apparently Glenndon had
passed word along to expect him. Of course the royal family
had returned before anyone else. They all rode steeds.

Lesser people, like journeymen magicians and wandering bards, had to walk.

A boy of about thirteen, in palace livery of green trews and a gold-and-green tunic, appeared at Lukan's elbow. "Sir, His Highness requested I escort you," the boy said, his burgeoning baritone cracking back to alto at odd moments. He flushed at the way his voice betrayed him, but he did not bow his head in shame.

Lukan nodded and followed, not certain what else to do. At least a servant treated him with respect. At the grand double doors presiding over the twelve steps up to the main floor of the palace, the young servant passed Lukan on to a man wearing normal clothing, a shade richer than Lukan's own, in black and maroon that complemented his hair, dark with just a hint of red in the tip of his queue.

"Journeyman Lukan," the man bowed respectfully. At least he got the title right, even if Lukan didn't wear the medium-blue leather journey clothes that were once considered the uniform of a journeyman on journey. "I am Keerkin, assistant to His Highness."

"Do I know you?" Something familiar in the name and the set of his freshly shaven jaw triggered a faint memory.

"No reason why you should. I only studied at the Forest University for about a year before it became obvious to everyone that I have very little talent. But your father arranged for me to continue my mundane education so that I could become a scribe here at court."

"A spy?"

"You know your father well. My condolences on his passing. He was a great man."

Lukan dipped his head, not certain he shared the country's grief. And yet a niggle of sadness worked out of his heart to remind him that Jaylor had raised him, taught him, and cared for him, even if he did love Glenndon best. And Glenndon wasn't truly Jaylor's son.

"I'd like to see my brother now," he said curtly, not knowing what else to do. Not knowing how else to respond.

"Of course. This way, Journeyman." Keerkin gestured to the left, clearly expecting Lukan to precede him. At last someone showed him respect for who he was. Keerkin, a failed apprentice, owed a journeyman deference, and not just because he was Prince Glenndon's younger half brother.

Lukan tried to memorize the curves and twists of the route, but he kept getting distracted by the fine tapestries depicting the lives and adventures of the Stargods, the trials and triumphs of Nimbulan, the last Battlemage, who made a covenant with the dragons in order to control magic and magicians and thus end the endless civil wars. Such intricate details and brilliant colors! Mama would have loved to add such fine wool embroidery to the clothing she made for her family.

All this grandeur of high ceilings, spacious rooms, sturdy stone walls, and lovely wall hangings could have been Mama's if she'd married the king. Glenndon and Lukan and their sisters could have been raised here, educated here . . . If Mama had become Darville's queen Lukan might not have been born, he might never have developed his magical talent as much as he was able.

He had to remind himself that Mama had loved Jaylor. They'd been happy together for many years. She would have hated the fuss of court life and the press of strangers against her mental shields.

None of the family would have known the dragons. A bit of a wiggle in the back of his mind reminded him that at least one green-tip flew nearby.

Lukan here, he flashed to the unknown dragon in proper dragon protocol.

Verdii here, a juvenile voice replied.

Verdii, please inform the Circle of Magicians that cleanup and recovery of the capital city continue. I don't know what they need most at this moment, but I'm sure they need most everything, including food and untainted water.

A sense of acknowledgment was his only reply, and then

a vacancy at the top of his spine as the dragon closed communication.

He twisted a bit to see if the image of an iridescent, nearly invisible dragon presiding over the scene of Nimbulan's marriage to Myrilandel was accurate. As he drew close enough to reach up and examine the tiny stitches, just to find out how the weaver had made the dragon look so real, his knees and thighs brushed the damp hem and fringe of the tapestry. Mud and dirty water stained the valuable hanging a good three feet off the floor.

Nearly six weeks after the flood, during high summer, the fabric was still damp. How long had water filled this corridor to so thoroughly saturate it?

Curious, he looked away from the images to the mud and water stains.

The letter tucked inside his tunic crackled, reminding of his errand.

If Mama had married the king, Lukan would still be the second son, destined to walk in his older brother's magnificent shadow.

Not anymore. As soon as he delivered the letter, he'd leave, on his own, carving out his own destiny with his own talents and wits.

CHAPTER 3

MARIA D'AMAZONIA WALKED slowly, steadily
along the straight passageways of King Lokeen's castle, careful to make certain she stepped evenly on her
twisted right leg. Each time she paused to change direction,
her hand touched the precious pendant hanging above her
breasts. *Goddess give me strength*. Her keys clanked with
every step, signaling her authority as chatelaine. As they
should. She paused at each right corner and rebalanced herself to make the turn smoothly, but also to make certain the
foreign wizard followed as well as he could. Moons of imprisonment had weakened him, but not dampened his spirit.

Good. She had plans.

But so did her cursed brother-in-law the king.

"If you know what's good for you, do not speak until
spoken to. Offer nothing, give only what you must," she
whispered to the wizard as he passed before her into the
king's private receiving room. She regretted her ill-formed
tongue that made each ess sound like the hissing of the
S'murghin Krakatrice. Another sin Lokeen had inflicted
upon her people—bringing the monsters back to the desert
and nurturing their eggs to export to his enemies.

The stranger looked at her briefly and gave only the barest hint of acknowledgment by blinking his eyes. She
slipped in behind the man in blue, clinging to the shadows

made by the heavy, dark wooden furniture favored by the king. He wouldn't notice her, because he'd never look for her.

"What is your name, Mage?" Lokeen demanded without looking up from the letters strewn across the portable table in front of his throne. Nothing else in the castle was as moveable as that table. The king liked everything fixed in place, never moving a fraction of an inch, even for Maria's maids to clean beneath and around.

Afraid someone might steal his precious possessions as they'd like to steal—should steal—the kingship he'd stolen.

"I am called Master Robb," the wizard said evenly, drawing deep breaths between the few words, not bowing or nodding or giving any indication the king was anything but an equal. The name fit him: tall and spare, nothing fancy about him. Self-assured.

I am called. Not *my name is.* A wily one. He answered the question without answering the question. The old magician, the one who'd been missing since midsummer, had refused to give any name at all. "There is power in knowing another's true name," he'd said. Courtiers and staff alike knew him only as "Sir."

"I'm told mages from Coronnan can all read and write, in many languages."

Master Robb nodded.

Lokeen shoved a worn piece of parchment across the table. It looked like it had been used and reused, each scraping off of old ink making it more fragile. The newest ink looked thin and spidery. From the length of the room away, Maria couldn't make out the words, damn her weak eyes, as weak as her leg.

"What is this?" Lokeen demanded.

Master Robb took one step forward and peered down at the missive. "It appears to be a letter." Robb straightened and stepped back again.

"And what does it say? Who is it from?" Lokeen shouted.

His color rose high on his cheeks as he spluttered, nearly frothing at the mouth in his anger. "I do not recognize the language."

Master Robb reached for the piece of parchment, his hand pausing a scant finger's width away. "May I?" he asked.

"Of course you may touch it. How else will you read it?"

"It appears to be greetings from Lord Laislac of Aporia. It is written in the language of Coronnan, not so different from your own dialect. But the letters are archaic, with extra flourishes and decorations."

Was that an insult, thinly disguised? The wizard appeared to accuse his captor of being illiterate!

"I know that. I know what it says. I need explanations, not lectures."

Something flickered across the mage's face. Maria couldn't tell what, but she enjoyed how he irritated Lokeen.

"Lord Laislac apologizes that his daughter Ariiell refuses the betrothal you so kindly offered her."

"How can she? Women in your country have no rights, no status. Her father makes all decisions for her."

So that was why he looked for a bride from across the sea, now that he'd mourned the required five years for his wife. By all rights he should marry one of his wife's relatives, a woman who had a right to claim the title of queen with or without Lokeen as husband. But no, Lokeen wanted an obedient wife who would not challenge him, who had no right to reclaim the crown in her own name.

"Mistress Ariiell has informed her father that, fifteen years ago, when she was heavily pregnant with her son—who is now second heir to the throne of Coronnan—she submitted to a handfasting with the father of her child."

"Handfasting? What in the name of the Great Mother is that?"

"A form of marriage. Binding to both parties. It legitimatizes the child, binds the couple to the raising of the child for life, but does not require the couple to live together as married. Mistress Ariiell reminds her father that this hand-fasting precludes her from marrying anyone else while the father of her child lives."

Lokeen sat in stunned silence for a long moment as all color drained out of his face. He looked skeletal, nearing death.

Maria watched and waited, did nothing to help him, not calling his body servant or ringing a bell for wine.

"Why didn't Laislac tell me of this before we entered into the marriage treaty?" the king said through gritted teeth.

Master Robb shrugged, saying nothing.

"Did you know of this?" Lokeen returned to screaming, color returning to his face. *Kraks*, he hadn't taken ill or died.

"No."

"Should you have?"

Another shrug. Smart man. He guarded his tongue well.

"By your laws, does Darville have the right to annul this handfasting?"

"I do not know. I've never heard of it being done before. The handfasting is rare enough."

"Then you are useless to me!"

"Only if you do not allow me to write a reply and address it to my king in words he will understand, saying it is necessary that he arrange for permission to annul the handfasting."

But since the child is now second heir to the crown, he's unlikely to do that, Maria thought.

Maria shared a moment of triumph with the wizard. Robb had manipulated Lokeen into letting him tell Darville where he was held hostage. And perhaps giving him coded words to launch a rescue. Perhaps this other king would invade with enough troops to depose Lokeen and put a rightful heir on the throne.

She touched the goddess pendant at her chest, wishing for strength. "Useless sack of sperm, you spawned only sons. Now you will reap the rewards of your failure to pro-

duce a daughter," she said under her breath, almost wishing
he'd hear her.

"Message coming in, Mistress," Apprentice Magician
Souska called to Master Magician Maigret.

"*S'murghit!* How am I supposed to get this potion right
with these constant interruptions?" Maigret cursed as she
stomped away from the long bench, filled with herbs,
crushed minerals, beakers, braziers, mortar and pestle, and
only she knew what else, toward the desk she'd inherited
from Master Marcus in the grand Chancellor's office at the
Forest University.

She cursed and stomped a lot more than she had when
she was merely the potions mistress and foster mother to all
the females at the University.

She also cried a lot more. But Souska thought she was
the only one who heard Maigret weep into her pillow deep
in the night, when she was alone and ever so lonely for her
husband Master Robb.

Maigret picked up her circle of glass, bigger around than
her sturdy work-worn hand and encased in a golden frame,
and dropped it into the ever-present bowl of clear water.
Souska hurried to light the candle beside the bowl. She
didn't have an affinity with fire as she did with plants and
dirt, but she'd learned this one trick through frequent practice over the last two moons. And some thoughtful guidance
from *her* journeyman.

"What do you want *now*, Marcus?" Maigret snapped,
keeping one eye on the distinctive colors swirling in the
glass and the other on a small pot bubbling on the brazier.
Impatiently, she waved for Souska to stir the mixture.

Souska jumped to obey, grateful for the chance to eavesdrop on this conversation. Since she'd lit the candle, her
magic was a part of the summoning spell and therefore she
could hear both sides. Her journeyman had taught her that.
Mistress Maigret may not have known that little spying

trick. Except that Mistress Maigret always knew more than she let other people know she knew.

"I thought you'd like to know that Journeyman Lukan was spotted in the city earlier today." The voice of Marcus came through the glass, loud and clear to Souska's ears.

"He's your journeyman, not mine. Why should I care?" Maigret stretched her chin to peer over Souska's shoulder to make sure she stirred the potion correctly, moving her wooden spoon deasil, along the path of the sun, never widdershins, the opposite.

Souska bristled a bit. She *knew* how to stir, even if she couldn't do much else right. And this potion smelled ready. She grabbed a hot holder and moved the pot off the brazier onto a slice of granite to protect the wooden counter.

Maigret nodded absently in approval.

"You should care where Lukan is because the bard is with him," Marcus said.

"And?" Maigret tapped her foot impatiently.

"Lillian is not with them."

Maigret's attention swung back fully to the glass. "You know where my journeyman isn't. But do you know where she is?"

Souska knew that journeymen on journey, male or female, weren't supposed to contact their masters except in dire emergencies or situations of extreme importance to the entire country. A journey was about learning to cope on one's own with little or no resources. It was about learning your strengths and weaknesses and how to compensate. She guessed it was also about learning what was important to the magician, both as a person and as a member of the community of magicians. *Her* journeyman had a lot of anger to let go of before he'd learn much of anything. But he was a wonderful, thoughtful teacher who immediately saw ways to spark her imagination and make her think through a problem.

She had news for him when he scried for her next. He might feel alone and unhindered by his master, but Marcus kept track of him all the same.

"I had a report this morning, just before we left for the funeral, that Lily was sighted delivering a sack of seeds and cuttings to a walled village on the Dubh River. Only the wall isn't there anymore, so they are open to the punishing winds down the river canyon."

"That's southwest of the city, on a tributary. Did the flood reach that far?" Maigret seemed truly distressed.

"If they didn't flood, then the circling wind wicked the water away and the dust storms clogged the secondary waterways with dirt and plants, even trees ripped from miles away. I've heard reports of villages having to dig new channels for their rivers so they'd return to their village and fields and not wander off in a new direction because of the clogs."

"All the spring growth ended up in those dams," Maigret mused. "Lily's got the right of it, delivering new seeds and cuttings. She can't do it all though. Not alone. Who has surplus I can shift to the flooded areas?" She shoved stuff about looking for parchment and pen.

Souska rushed to the front of the desk just in time to catch loose pages skittering toward the floor. Holding everything together with her left hand, she found a clean page and shoved it toward Maigret. Then she uncovered a flusterhen quill, sharpened the copper nib with a thought, and made sure the inkwell was full.

"Where's Linda?" Maigret finally looked up and found the room empty except for herself and her newest apprentice. "This is her job!"

"You sent her to a class on diplomacy," Souska whispered. She didn't want Marcus to hear her and figure out that she eavesdropped on his conversations.

"Never mind. Time you learned to help me regardless of what I need. The potion needs a pinch more mint. Make sure you don't crush it too hard before adding it. I want the essential oils on the outside of the leaf, not lining the mortar." Maigret sat abruptly and started making lists.

Souska read over her shoulder, smiling that she now had permission to spy for *her* journeyman.

CHAPTER 4

*T*HIS IS RIDICULOUS. *Exhaustion makes strong young men limp and uncaring about power. I have ridden long and far and only found two men and one woman interested in what I can offer them. The rest are concerned only with easing aching muscles and getting a good night's sleep so that tomorrow they may begin again their never-ending labors of rebuilding and replanting. The only mating that concerns them is among their steeds and cattle and sheep to replace their lost herds. But the flusterhens survived. They always do. And they multiply and go wild and are always underfoot.*

I and my followers have offered sex, wine, and magic to every likely person to no avail. Not even a whiff of the Tambootie leaves I carry with me for emergencies entices the people of Coronnan. They turn up their noses in distaste.

Time I quit this land and reap better harvests elsewhere. I have heard rumors and half stories of recent events. I know where I must go. There are no ships leaving the port for days and days. Endless days. I must make certain none of my old contacts recognize me and betray my presence to the king or his minions. The University hunts me actively, reminding all the students and teachers to keep an eye out for me as they help clear and rebuild the city. They will imprison me without bothering with a trial. If I dared, I'd take Crown Prince Glenndon to my bed. He is much among the people and the

*city, lifting with the strength of dragons, designing new roofs
with the arcane knowledge of the ancients, consoling the
grieving with a firm touch, a sorrowful hymn, and a prayer. I
should entice him away for a little privacy and rest in the
comforting arms of a willing woman. He could grant me
much magic. Humiliating him would bring me a tiny bit of
justice against both his fathers: the king and the dead Master
Magician Jaylor.*

   *This one time I shall forsake pleasure for expedience. I
shall hide in plain sight.*

   *But while I must hide, my minion can walk the city, listen-
ing and learning like any good spy. His scarred face and
rope-thin body do not alarm the people. Many of them are
underfed and scarred as well. He knows this city better than
most. He serves me well.*

Lukan held out the folded and sealed parchment he'd carried almost the full length of the country. "Da sent this," he
stated firmly, keeping all his emotions pushed into a tight
knot behind his heart. "With his dying breath he commanded me to deliver this to you. For *me* he had only criti-
cism."

   Not quite the truth, but close enough. Da had used his
last breath to tell Mama he loved her.

   Glenndon, taller than Lukan by half a hand, broader in
the shoulder and slimmer of hip as well, bit his lip and
blinked back tears. His golden hair glinted in the sunlight
streaming through a high window. He didn't need a crown
as symbol of his title and position. His life energy surrounded him with a shining aura that even mundane minds
could see.

   "W . . . were you there?" Glenndon stammered. His
throat worked as he swallowed heavily against a choke.

   Lukan wondered briefly if his brother had taken time to
grieve for the loss of their parents, or if his emotions had
been suppressed by the massive amount of work involved

in rebuilding the city. This little room on the ground floor, designed for greeting visitors and nothing more, showed no evidence of the planning necessary to even begin the task.

Lukan nodded, suddenly finding himself needing to banish tears. He hated revisiting those awful moments when Da's heart gave out after trying to control the massive spell that broke Samlan's control over the storm and unleashed its fury. Then as Da told Mama he loved her with his last breath (Lukan had left the room, but heard and saw much through the open doorway from the front yard) Mama had screamed and clutched her pregnant belly. Within minutes she had miscarried and bled to death. Linda said she'd smiled and held out her hand as if reaching for her husband.

Lukan dropped the letter onto a decorative little table and turned his back on his brother. He almost wished he'd taken the time to summon Souska to collect the latest gossip at the University. Then he'd have something to talk about. He couldn't talk about Mama, not even after the passage of nearly two moons.

"I wanted to be there," Glenndon said defensively. "I was halfway into the transport spell when Father—the king stopped me. He reminded me of my duty here. I had to save as many people as I could and that meant cutting off exits, communication, everything from outside the palace walls. I had no choice."

"There are always choices," Lukan reminded him, getting a firm grip on his emotions. "You made the one that seemed right for you at that time."

"Right for the kingdom! Not right for me."

"I'm leaving. I have my journey. I'll spend tonight on Sacred Isle and leave soon afterward." Lukan aimed his steps toward the door, unable to see clearly through the film of tears covering his eyes.

"Good Journey, little brother," Glenndon said. "The island remains mostly intact. I checked. A few trees fell, mud and silt filled in the pit I was trapped in, the central pond is bigger than it was. But the magic ingrained in the island repulsed a lot of the magic in the storm surge."

"I'm glad to hear it. When I saw that so much had been destroyed, so many of the little islands washed away, I wondered if the sanctity of the place could continue to inspire us."

Lukan allowed a few moments of silence, almost comfortable with Glenndon in their shared concern for Sacred Isle.

Then Glenndon lifted his chin, shook back a few stray hairs that had escaped his queue and fixed a neutral gaze on Lukan. "Greet the trees with respect, meditate deeply, and leave the island a stronger man." That sounded almost like a ritual leave-taking. "I wish you could stay, share a cup of ale, tell me all that has happened since I left home."

"This is your home now. Our family is scattered; there is nothing left at the University for either of us anymore."

"Mama and Da . . ."

"Are dead. Lily is on her own journey taking seeds to where the crops were destroyed. Val is at home taking care of the little ones, along with Lady Ariiell—who is no longer insane—and Lady Graciella, who may very well fall insane before she delivers her child. Especially if her mother takes her in and berates her for . . . well, for being alive." Lukan left before he could take his brother up on the invitation to linger and reforge their fraternal bonds.

"You need to get your instructions from Master Marcus before you row over to Sacred Isle," Glenndon called after him.

"I have my instructions." He'd made them up himself when the rest of the world had abandoned him.

"What is taking so long?" King Lokeen screeched. He paced from window to desk, peered over Robb's shoulder, and paced back again, hands waving wildly about.

"Letters need careful wording, sir," Robb replied. The

man was making him nervous. Would he notice the tiny bits of magic that disguised words to make them seem ordinary but actually held another meaning? Even this tiny spell cost him dearly in strength—as if he were wading through thick mud.

If any dragons ever flew these skies, they hadn't come recently enough to leave behind magical energy. If the ley lines reached across the Bay and the ocean, they spread wide and didn't come near the city. He had only his own diminished physical strength to fuel his attempt to disguise his words. And that energy seemed blocked.

He didn't know if King Darville would know to have a magician read the thing for him. When Robb had left Coronnan, magic and magicians were still disdained and forbidden access to the government. But the king had brought Glenndon into his household as son and heir. Surely Glenndon would smell magic in the letter and take care of it. Surely . . .

Robb licked the pen nib to restore the ink and add his magic to it. Bad habit. Maigret would have his hide, especially when he kissed her with a black tongue. A tiny smile tugged one side of his mouth upward.

And that brought the next phrase to mind, almost as if Maigret gave him the words.

He bent his head closer to the page and set down words:

Because of Lady Ariiell's noble status, allowing her to become available to suitors at home and abroad for the purpose of marriage treaties advantageous to the realm and her family is something Your Grace should consider.

Then his mind went blank again.

"That's good. That's good. Make him understand that when I marry the lady I will be in position to grant him many favors, trade concessions, military aid, and what not," Lokeen said, tapping the parchment and nearly sending the magic disguise skittering across the page by disturbing the words before the spell set.

Robb slid the page out from under that tapping finger, using yet more energy to send the real words back under the written ones where they belonged. Then he had to take three long deep breaths to keep his eyes from glazing over and to return his heart to its natural rhythm.

Thankfully the little chatelaine set a fresh goblet of cold, fresh water near his hand. She looked middle-aged, but she seemed never to have grown beyond the stature of a ten year old. He wondered if her lameness had kept her from growing. Oh, yes, he'd noticed her deformity, hard as she tried to hide it. He also recognized the cause of her lisp and wondered if a real healer with magic fueling the examination could do anything for her.

Not his problem, except she'd been kinder to him than Lokeen, and he felt he owed her something. Kindness in this castle always came with a cost. Maria had not yet made known to him what she expected in return.

"Now tell that other king how archaic and useless that handfasting thing is. Appeal to his sense of logic and justice so he'll do away with the ritual. It's useless and interferes with ... with ..."

"Interferes with the lives and plans of the couple: not married but unable to marry anyone else ..." Robb finished for him. That might be the truth, but Lokeen was only thinking that Ariiell's handfasting interfered with *his* plans, no one else's.

Robb looked at the original letter again while magic still colored his vision. The sharp pen lines, formed with a delicate pressure, had not been written by Lord Laislac. That man, Robb knew, could barely read and write, and when he signed his name, the letters came out fat, with extra globs of half-dried ink distorting the letters. No, Ariiell had written the letter herself and signed her father's name. Ariiell broke the marriage treaty her father had arranged without asking his permission. She wouldn't likely enter into another.

In the moons since Robb had left Coronnan and the University, something must have happened for Ariiell to regain her sanity and her freedom. He knew nothing. He'd gathered gossip from his guards about Amazonia and Lokeen's precarious position on the throne, but he'd heard nothing about his native land. Or his wife and children. He didn't even know if Jaylor and Glenndon had succeeded in the chore they'd needed his help with.

Anything outside of Amazonia held no meaning for the locals. They barely acknowledged the existence of the other city-states up and down the coast of the Big Continent— Mabastion they called it. "My fortress" in one of the ancient tongues.

Depression sank deep into his gut again, making his bones ache and his head spin. Even the slight hope that this letter might win him his freedom vanished.

Biting his lower lip in pain and exhaustion, he completed the letter, sanded it, and handed it to Lokeen for signature, a seal, and direction.

He finished the water in his cup down to the last drop, wishing for more.

Maria appeared at his side. "You'll have more in your room," she said quietly. Hardly an elongated syllable or twisting of any of the words.

He nodded at her subtle reminder that he was still a prisoner and needed to return to his cell. A new cell atop a narrow tower with windows to let in bright sunlight and fresh air. Far above any ley lines that might lurk on the surface of the land. Devoid of any magic anywhere.

How had Samlan worked any magic while here?

Oh, yes, Robb now knew that his kidnapper was the rogue magician who had wormed his way into Lokeen's confidence, becoming a trusted adviser and then ambassador to Coronnan. He'd been in and out of the castle for ten years before staying full-time for a few moons after his exile from the Circle of Magicians. But then he'd disappeared from Amazonia as cleanly as he had from the University.

Maria led the way, slowly, masking her own pain with dignity. When they reached the winding tower steps that led to Robb's new prison—light and aboveground, but still a guarded cell—she paused and took a deep breath, in preparation for the abuse her twisted leg must endure to climb. But climb she must. 'Twas her responsibility as chatelaine to escort him to and from his room, as if he were an honored guest instead of a prisoner—or hostage.

Robb offered her his arm.

She shot him an offended glare.

"No offense meant, my lady. Simply a gentleman offering a lady his arm as escort." He bowed slightly—something he hadn't done for Lokeen.

Maria nodded and slipped her tiny hand around his forearm. Neither of them mentioned how heavily she leaned on him. But he noticed the look of gratitude in her eyes when they reached the top.

"You must rest and eat. Meat and red wine will be brought to you soon."

"And a razor perhaps? I would like to shave."

"We'll see."

Robb paused, waiting for what must come.

"His Majesty will need you to dispatch the letter."

The blood drained out of Robb's head, leaving him a bit dizzy and needing to lean against the wall. He knew Samlan's powers, knew him capable of the spell. He also knew how much energy he would have to command with no ley lines or dragon magic available.

"I do not believe the dispatch spell is any more reliable than a loyal courier sent by ship," Maria said. "Two of the six letters the previous mage dispatched were never answered."

"W . . . who were they addressed to?"

"You do not need to know that."

"If I knew, perhaps I could tell you if the receiver chose not to respond."

Maria dismissed that statement with a wave of her hand.

"The other one, the mage who deserted the king in the end, assured us that a response, even a negative one, would come automatically. He'd know and report to the king the answer."

Not likely, Robb thought. Samlan had told the king what he wanted to hear. Nothing more.

"You will not be given the chance to desert us," Maria reminded him as she unlocked the door to his cell. When she had returned the key to the chain at her belt, her hand went automatically to a pendant hidden from view by her gown and shift. "I cannot afford to lose you. I will send someone to fetch you when the king is ready for your next bit of magic." She smiled knowingly, willing to keep his secrets.

If he kept hers.

She knew he'd embedded magic in the letter he'd just written. How?

CHAPTER 5

LUKAN HALF-RAN FROM the palace, a sour taste in the back of his throat. He'd wanted to grab his brother in a desperate hug and just cling to him, sharing his grief, loneliness, and . . . just missing him.

The knot of anger he harbored in his gut beat back that temporary moment of weakness. The thickness of unshed tears tasted like a bitter poison.

He almost ran into the tall man he'd noticed earlier, just outside the gate. But he ran on, not caring if the stranger noted his path with his one good eye, the other badly scarred and burned.

His sister Valeria had told him of a woody root that shrieked when pulled from the ground and looked like a carved doll. When properly prepared, in tiny doses, mixed with a healing tea that countered some of the poison in the root, it would kill alien growths inside a body. When not properly prepared, or in larger doses, it killed the patient within minutes.

He imagined his emotions tasted like that acidic goo.

"I'll only get rid of it by proving myself as a magician and as a man," he reminded himself. He looked at the lowering sun. If he set off within the hour he could row to Sacred Isle tonight. With luck he'd have his staff by morning and be on his way to Amazonia shortly thereafter.

First things first. He needed to eat and to tell Skeller his plans. His rapid steps had already led him out of the palace and onto the first bridge toward the port. He'd studied the maps and knew the route to Sacred Isle. Presuming the flood had not washed away and altered all of the landmarks.

Should he allow himself another day to prepare for the momentous occasion of earning a staff?

Those thoughts took him most of the way to the port. The long wharf stretching out into the Bay and across a deep channel led him to the mainland spit filled with warehouses, chandler's shops, fishnet menders, and taverns.

Lots and lots of taverns. Every other building had a sign waving in the constant sea breeze. On each he saw an overflowing beer mug.

Lukan paused to stare at the first seven that came into view. New beer wafted the enticing aromas of yeast and fermenting grains. Fresh-baked bread too. With his nose so full of welcoming scents and his stomach reminding him to eat, fully and soon, he had nothing left to sniff for the magic of Skeller's songs.

But he heard that soaringly clear baritone rise above raucous laughter in a song with the chanting refrain of "Drink. Drink. Drink."

A smile cleared his mind and relieved the bitterness within him. He elbowed his way through the throng of merry drinkers. Every few paces a barmaid passed him with laden trays. He exchanged a single coin (gleaned from the joint stash he and Skeller had accumulated from previous singing stints) for a mug of smooth beer liberated from one of those trays. Another coin bought him a slab of meat and half a loaf of bread. Truly satisfied with food for the first time in weeks, he washed it all down with another mug.

Skeller, he noted, kept his hands on his harp and away from the constant offerings from the maids—potable and otherwise. Lukan had learned on their wanderings that Skeller didn't need copious amounts of liquor—even the barely fermented stuff served here—to loosen his throat.

He saved the mind- and body-numbing drink for later, when he could rest without guarding his tongue. Even then he never drank enough to spill his true feelings for Lillian, the girl he'd shared so much with, then had had to leave to give them both time to heal.

On that issue Lukan felt only relief. Lillian and Valeria had barely reached their sixteenth birthday. Much too young to consider marriage, no matter how much love they shared.

Skeller on the other hand was nearly twenty-four, the right age to find a wife and cease his wandering ways.

The song ended on a flourish of rapid notes descending to the lowest pitch the harp could issue. Skeller bowed graciously and grabbed a hunk of bread and cheese as he jumped neatly to the floor beside Lukan. He'd disdained meat since . . . since he had first met and fallen in love with Lily.

"What news, friend?" Skeller shouted over the noise of the crowd.

Men stomped their feet and chanted "More, more, more." "Sing us another one!" and "Don't quit now. We're just getting started." A clatter of coins thrown on the table beside Skeller prompted him to bow to the audience as he scooped the small metal discs into Lukan's pouch.

Skeller shook his head at the patrons, but didn't return Telynnia to her case.

"I've delivered the letter. Now I need to find a boat and row over to . . . to my destiny."

"A little late, boy. The sun is near setting and you don't know the river well. Best wait 'til tomorrow."

"Maybe . . ." Something odd at the edge of his vision demanded he look closer. A cobbled-together square table had been pushed against the far wall with four chairs—not benches, *chairs*—spread around the three remaining sides. Two men and two women sat there. One of the men was long and skinny with a scarred face. Upon closer examination it looked burned.

Uh, oh. Seeing the same man three times in one day did not bode well.

Lukan watched the women. The younger and prettier one didn't so much sit, as . . . preside. She ate daintily, cutting her meat into small pieces, sipping a cup of wine between each bite. She chewed slowly, savoring the red, rare meat.

Her manners made her stand out in this crowd of people who worked hard for a living and played harder at the close of day. Her long black hair with a single streak of white running from left temple to her waist arrested every gaze.

A haze of magic surrounded her head, spreading to include each of her companions. She led, they followed. She had power and granted them a little of it.

Except, maybe the scarred man shared her aura without giving up much of his own to Rejiia.

Rejiia. Sorceress from the outlawed Coven. Recently restored to this gorgeous body after fifteen years imprisoned in her totem cat form.

Lukan had seen her before. Once. On the day he and Skeller had quitted company with the twins and their companions.

A long time ago she'd been the most feared and hated woman in all Coronnan.

What was she doing here in the port tavern?

"Skeller, I'll summon Marcus in the morning, before we leave. But I need to collect my staff tonight. I have a feeling I'm going to need it sooner rather than later."

I knew that Master Magician Jaylor had children. Two boys, when he and his journeymen backlashed that insidious spell that turned both me and my father into our totem animals. I had forgotten that fifteen years have passed. A child of two at that time would be seventeen now. The right age for an apprentice magician to become a journeyman.

The right age to draw magical energy from anger. The right age to be vulnerable to my manipulations. The scowling

*boy who just fled this miserable tavern could only be one of
Jaylor's sons grown up. He is the spitting image of his father,
alike in face and form, still growing into his adult height,
which will be as tall, or taller, than his father. Even his aura
shouts a red and blue magical signature akin to Jaylor's.*

*He wears not the blue leather of a journeyman on jour-
ney. Time was, the blue protected them, demanded respect
and aid. That time passed even before the Leaving, when all
of the magicians withdrew from court, the Council, and all of
the larger cities, towns and villages. For his own safety, considering the mood of the people, this boy wears worn country
clothes in mud brown that won't show dirt or stains. The people here in Coronnan City accept magic and dragons more
now than they did fifteen years ago. Magicians and dragons
help them with the filthy work of cleaning up after the
flood—'twas a rogue magician who lost control of that storm
and loosed it upon the populace, though the core of his spell
was restoring magical order to the kingdom. And restore it
did, not order, but me to my proper body.*

*But ... considering recent events ... I wonder that this
boy travels alone and secretively. My Geon noted his magical
aura and followed him most of the day. I wonder why the
boy skulks around a port tavern and claims friendship with
a bard from foreign parts. Could it be ... ?*

He is ripe. And he is mine.

Puffy white clouds drifted across the magician-blue sky that
deepened toward darkness, casting small temporary shadows on the golden wheat, nearly ready for harvest. Stunted
wheat, barely hip high with tiny and nearly empty seed
heads. The furrows between rows showed more weeds than
spreading crops. The field looked abandoned.

Lily sighed, resting her pack and the extra sack of seeds
on the ground. She'd come to expect as much. But here,
along the upper River Dubh, she thought the village in the
distance—a crowded jumble of round huts that leaned and

sagged at odd angles—beyond the pall of the storm and flood.

"The Dubh is too small and too far west for the storm surge to have flooded more than a foot or two above the banks," she mused, turning a full circle, examining the landscape more closely. The line of matted grasses and uprooted shrubs above the current river level showed exactly how high the waters had been.

Skeller would compose a sad song about this blight on the land. But he'd add a wistful note of hope at the end. A note that his magnificent baritone would hold and swell until the audience smiled in agreement.

A long, nearly straight ridgeline rose away from the village running east to west until it met taller hills that became the mountains. She could just make out a misty purple smudge in the distance that marked the border between Coronnan and SeLennica.

A frisson of trouble ran up and down her spine. The land thrummed against her bare feet in an arrhythmic vibration. Something was wrong with the land and the people. Something about that ridgeline pulled and repelled her.

She shifted her feet and planted her straight hawthorn staff into the ground to center her. She'd seen many a magician do the same. The wood felt comfortable in her grip, conforming to the shape and pressure of her hand. But the grain remained straight and true. She didn't have enough magic to channel through the essential tool to twist it to her pattern of power. "I doubt I even have a pattern, let alone any power."

Still, she persisted, as she waited patiently for the nearest magnetic pole to tug at her. When the faint inclination to lean south finally found her, she cautiously turned her back to it and fixed her gaze north. Then she coaxed her eyes to see more than the obvious. A slight depression running north and south where the ridge sloped downward toward the Great Bay. The Caravan Road. And at the base of the ridge another road split from the main one. It ran past Lake

Aporia and the home of Lord Laislac all the way into the mountains. Ariiell's father had been deposed and imprisoned for his treason of importing Krakatrice eggs in order to wreak havoc in the land and make the king vulnerable to assassination and invasion by the King of Amazonia.

Lily didn't know if the king had appointed a new lord. She didn't really care. Lady Ariiell, Laislac's misused and abused daughter, was safe with Valeria at the University of Magicians. The Council of Provinces, its politics and alliances, held no interest for Lily. The health of the land and the people did. But she'd come too far south in her wandering. The circling winds had not reached much farther than here. This was the far edge of where the dry tornado had spread its funnel, nearly one hundred miles across.

Just the other side of that ridge she and Skeller had hunkered down with a trade caravan. In the aftermath the winds had broken loose the secret crate of Krakatrice eggs from the bottom of Lady Ariiell's litter. The huge amounts of magic in the air had prematurely hatched the black snakes. She shuddered and closed her eyes. But she couldn't blot out the memory of a black mass wriggling and undulating across the land, consuming the blood and meat of any animal that had bolted from the storm or been blown away by it.

The snakes had moved north, toward the center of magic. The village lay south of the hatching ground and had not been a part of the feeding frenzy.

Or had it? She saw no signs of life stirring around the huts in the late afternoon sunshine.

Like it or not, she had to know. She had to stay and help in any way she could.

Tomorrow. Soon the sun would set and she'd not have enough light to trek cross-country without a trail or magelight to guide her steps. She could be of no help if she arrived wounded from a fall, or victim of a predator. Spotted saber cats still roamed these prairies. Tonight she'd make a rough camp with a fire and arrive at the tumbledown village early in the morning.

A deep, throbbing hum irritated Souska's inner ear. *Lukan!* Her journeyman called her.

Quickly she looked around the stillroom filled with aromatic herbs and brews and potions. All of the other healer apprentices were busy with their own tasks, trying to finish before the sun fully set lest darkness and unknown qualities invaded their medicines. She crept up the long, narrow staircase against the interior wall toward the journeymen's living quarters. Then past the bedrooms and up another stair to the apprentice dormitories. Finally the ladder to the loft attic appeared, deep in the shadows of the back corner.

At the top, in her own private space, she poured water into a palm-sized ceramic bowl, lit the candle with a snap of her fingers, and dropped her tiny shard of glass into the bowl.

Lukan's face appeared almost immediately.

Souska reached a finger to trace the curve of his cheek but he turned his face away, looking over his shoulder anxiously.

"I have no time. Tell Mistress Maigret that Rejiia is in the city and I think she's recruiting a new coven."

"What?"

"I'm beached at Sacred Isle and I can't work magic once I set foot out of my boat," he hissed at her. "Memorize what I said. The Masters need to know this." His face vanished. Her glass became inert and sank to the bottom.

The room dimmed and darkness seemed to press tightly against her head. Without knowing what she did, how long she stared at the candle willing Lukan to come back, she knew he could not. Would not.

Rowing to Sacred Isle at twilight and spending a night there by himself, without the comfort of a fire or food or any spells at all, he had to wait, meditating and praying until dawn. Then if the Stargods found him worthy of becoming a true journeyman, one of the trees would sacrifice a branch and drop it where he'd find it and know it for his staff.

A spluttering sound alerted her that the candle guttered. She'd sat too long, lost in the flickers that seemed more important than anything else. Slowly she roused herself. She knew from experience that moving too quickly after one of her spells would trigger a headache that would fell her for days, making the smallest crack of light, or whispers in the rooms beneath her, send pain stabbing through her eyes. She could eat nothing during one of those headaches and vomited every potion Maigret plied her with. All she could do was wait out the pain and endure.

As she'd endured the beating by the men of her home village who tried to force her slight magic to desert her. Ignorant people more afraid of magic than they were of the law that might hang them for murder. The journeyman magician who rescued her—not *her* journeyman, another anonymous one—had called down the law on her village. Because she lived, her persecutors kept their lives, but many lost the hands that had wielded the blows.

Only Maigret knew how much damage the men had done to her. Only she knew that these lapsing spells and the headaches were a result of blows to her head. Everyone in the University knew about her nightmares. She screamed loud enough to wake the dead some nights. Less so since her journeyman had begun helping and tutoring her. Little by little, she regained control of her life and her mind.

Not fast enough.

She didn't know which was worse, the headaches or the nightmares. During one, on the first night she'd spent here in the protection of the University, she'd blackened the eye of her bedmate while she thrashed, trying to protect herself from the dream memories. The next night she slept alone up here away from everyone, where her dreams would not wake or harm any of the other girls.

Solitude suited her. Solitude made it possible for her to scry with Lukan.

Lukan. Scry.

She had to deliver a message. What was it now . . . ?

CHAPTER 6

LUKAN SAT WITH his back against a sturdy tree. He didn't know what kind of tree. He didn't even know if he'd found the central clearing around a pond where the Stargods had first landed on their silver cloud of fire. He smelled water. He sensed open space. The tree's roots offered an almost comfortable seat and the trunk cradled his back nicely.

Neither stars nor moon offered light through the thick cloud cover. So far, the rain held off. He expected it to release a heavy downpour near dawn.

"I should expect better than a cold and uncomfortable return to the port?" he asked himself. "I bet Glenndon had an easier time on this island than I will."

An almost chuckle whispered through the tree canopy. "Lily could understand you," he called up to the rustling leaves. "I haven't her affinity with dirt and growing things."

Another whisper, equally amused.

"Did Glenndon have a . . . an adventure while he was here?" he asked, to hear the sound of his own voice rather than endure any more silent meditation. Sitting still on the ground had never been easy for him.

Another whisper stirred in his mind. Along with a shiver of unease.

Had the tree said "Up"?

That was easy. He'd always gone up when troubled or needing to think. Up a tree, up on the roof, climb up a cliff to a plateau, just so long as he put distance between himself and the ground and got closer to the air where dragons flew. Glenndon sought the hot spring pool at the bottom of the small cascade where he'd bathe and play with Indigo, a juvenile dragon. Lukan just went up, wherever was convenient.

This tree seemed to offer him sanctuary.

So he stood from his cross-legged seat and stretched tall with both hands. Not too far above his head, he found a study branch—oak, he thought, from the texture of the bark and size of the leaves—and pulled himself up by the strength of his arms.

When he got a leg over the branch he paused to rotate his shoulders and figure out what to do next. There were more stout branches within easy reach. His instincts told him to keep going up. He scooched around until he had his balance and stretched one arm up. Grasp, center himself, swing a leg over. Three times he moved higher by almost his height each time.

Just as his fingers brushed the bark on a fourth branch, the wind blew the wood beyond him.

Rest here, the wind, or the tree, or whatever else, suggested.

Legend claimed that sometimes the Stargods or the dragons spoke to the journeyman candidate here on Sacred Isle.

"Rest?" But not sleep. This was a vigil, a time to keep watch through the night, to think, and contemplate. If he slept he'd probably fall out of the tree.

A chuckle of agreement the next time the breeze rustled in the leaves overhead.

"I've done this before," he told his tree as he locked his ankles around each other beneath the branch. "Three years ago when a fox raided Mama's flusterhen coop every night for a week. None of us could catch the predator. So Glenndon and I took turns staying awake and watching. Glenndon fell asleep. I climbed an everblue and stayed awake. I caught the fox and took it far away from the Clearing. Da told me to kill it. But I knew Mama would feel the death and be sad for days. So I gave the fox a good mental shake with magic and told him next time Da would kill him and take his carcass to the University for the cooks to make a meal of him. He never came back."

Lukan settled his back against the wide tree trunk and clasped some narrow side branches. Ah, much more comfortable than on the ground. Mostly because he was up.

Up was all that mattered right now.

He watched tiny pinpoints of light peek through the shifting cloud layer. A north breeze sent them scurrying toward the nearest magnetic pole, way far to the south.

Memories of Mama and her empathic touch with animals and people made him smile. The sadness of losing her faded a little. He had so many good memories of her, including endless arguments about eating meat. So he and Da and Glenndon, and sometimes Valeria, took many meals at the University, where meat was plentiful. The cooks understood that throwing magic, even with the aid of a ley line or gathering of dragon magic, cost a body more energy than it could hold. Magicians ate a *lot* to fuel their bodies. He didn't think he'd ever seen a fat magician. They always burned more than they could possibly consume.

His mind flicked to Skeller, his companion during their wandering away from home, away from Skeller's love for Lily, and away from Lukan's anger toward Da. An anger that here in this tree Lukan was having a hard time remembering where it came from and why he'd nurtured it so long.

"Lily taught Skeller not to eat meat. He still respects her wishes. I wonder . . ." He drifted off into another line of thought that touched on Souska.

He liked the girl well enough, what little he knew of her. They'd only met a couple of times. She seemed so lost and vulnerable he'd felt compelled to give her a smile and a little encouragement. During his long nights on the road when he needed to reach out and talk to someone, anyone, from home, her pinched and pale face, and only her face, came to mind. But instead of growing stronger and more independent with each lesson, he found her clinging to him more and more, forcing him to make decisions for her.

Maybe he should talk to her less frequently.

Mama and Da were gone. Lily had taken to wandering on her own, taking seeds and cuttings where needed, nurturing the land and the people affected by the flood, and healing her soul after executing Samlan with Skeller's dagger. Glenndon lived in the city now, a prince and a strong leader. Valeria and her charges, Ariiell and Lady Graciella, had taken up residence in the Clearing with Sharl and Jule, the youngest of Mama's brood, mothering them and healing their own wounds.

He supposed he could return to the Clearing and call it home. Not yet. Not so soon. Mama's ashes, and Da's too, had hardly had time to settle on the wild slopes below the dragon cave, mingled together and inseparable for all time . . .

A sound, a whistle of rising wind, a crack of something close jerked him out of a light doze. He tilted and had to close his hands on the closest branch to keep from falling.

When his bottom felt firmly anchored and his ankles locked once more, he opened his eyes fully, aware that the sun had just begun to brighten the air around him. A glow lined the eastern horizon. A sleepy bird chirped the universal questions, "Is it time yet? Do I have to wake up now?"

"Stargods, I'm sorry. I fell asleep when I knew I shouldn't." A tear tried to creep out of the corner of his eye.

The wind and the tree laughed at him.

He looked where his hands had clenched a branch right in front of him so he'd know how to balance and shimmy down the trunk.

Across his thighs lay a branch stripped of leaves and side twigs, no longer attached to the tree.

Had the crack he'd heard been the tree breaking the branch free and gifting it to him?

He took a deep breath. Then another as he checked the length of wood. His fingers memorized the knots and straightness of grain—without a single variation—where his magic might twist it. It measured about two heads longer than he was tall and fit his hand as if measured for him.

You'll grow into it, the tree told him. *Take my gift and use it well, with honor, and for the good of many rather than the comfort of a few.*

"Thank you, mother tree." He couldn't think of anything else to say as he hugged his protectoress, knowing instinctively that feminine nurturing ran with her sap. "I'll do my best to honor you."

Remember me during your troublesome journey. You will be sorely tried. Think of me and remember your honor.

The tree fell silent as he scrambled down. Just before he set foot on a game trail headed back toward his rowboat, he turned and bowed to the solid old oak. Then he blew her a kiss and fairly skipped away toward the rest of his life.

There are few tall trees across the Bay. You will have to find yourself when you are down rather than up.

Now what did that mean?

Robb ate half the meat and bread provided him, thought longingly of chewing the moist and sweet third apple. He'd gone so long without hearty food his stomach protested when he ate too much. He had to have a clear head and comfortable body to dredge up enough strength to dispatch that letter. And dispatch it he must. Any hope of rescue depended upon that letter getting into the right hands.

Carefully he wrapped the remains of his meal including the tempting apple in his spare shirt and tucked them beneath his mattress. Oh yes, he now had clean shirts and underlinens and a real bed with sheets and blankets along with enough food to keep him happy and healthy. The cost of these luxuries?

Magic.

He had to work exhausting magic at the king's whim. That was why he'd been allowed to sleep the night through before dispatching the letter. He needed good rest so he could begin increasing his strength again, like rebuilding slack muscles after a long fever.

A tap on his door signaled the arrival of his escort to where he'd send the letter, now that it had been written and signed. He didn't expect it would be Maria making the trek up the stairs again. Not if she could delegate the chore to a healthy male guard loaded with dozens of mundane weapons.

The king himself stepped through the doorway, once the heavy wooden portal had swung inward on its sturdy iron hinges. He carried a swath of black and red cloth over his arm.

"My previous magician required freshly laundered robes to aid his power when he dispatched letters for me," Lokeen said without preamble. He held out the garment for Robb's inspection. "You are taller than he. Lady Maria has seen to the alterations." He frowned at the red border on the hem and cuffs and a stripe of the same fabric at the shoulder seams. The rest of the formal robe, cut to the same design as the blue robe Robb had worn for the transport spell, fell in light swaths of midnight black.

"The robe is welcome, but I'd be more efficient with the spell if I had my staff," Robb said, wrapping the robe around himself and belting it with another length of the red fabric. Richly woven wool, whisper thin. They must have a variety of sheep here with extra-long hair to achieve the fineness in the threads. The merchants of Coronnan would pay dearly for wool of this caliber.

"Your staff is held as hostage for your good behavior," Lokeen replied with a malicious smile. "I allowed your predecessor his staff and he deserted me."

"Tomorrow, when I have recovered from the dispatch spell, I could try scrying for the man. I might not have the power to converse with him, but I'd know if he lives," Robb offered, not at all sure he could scry anything without his staff and master's glass.

"Perhaps. I have the letter, signed and directed. I understand that I cannot seal it until you are ready to send it."

"Correct. The spell must be part of the seal and the direction."

"Then let us begin."

Robb breathed deeply, partly to center his magic and organize his mind. Partly to wonder why he hadn't been summoned to the receiving room downstairs. " 'Twill be easier to send it up here," he mused. "Higher, with more air."

"Your predecessor said that hot air rises. He needed the lift to connect to the dragons."

Robb held back a snort of derision. That bit was all bluff and had nothing to do with logic or magic, since dragons did not fly here.

That last statement also told him a lot about his captor. King Lokeen wanted to control magic and magicians, but knew little about either.

The only way to fully control magic and magicians was for a group of them to join together and gather dragon magic. Their combined powers then increased by orders of magnitude to overcome the transgression of any solitary rogue magician. The Circle could impose ethics and honor on all practitioners.

Something to ponder during the long sleepless nights up here in his remote tower.

"You will begin," Lokeen ordered.

"If you will not allow me my staff, may I at least have my glass?" Robb asked, only partially respectfully.

"Glass? No one ever said anything about a glass!" Lokeen looked toward the brace of guards at the door accusingly.

They remained stoically grim with unchanging expressions.

"A palm-sized piece of glass forged by dragon fire and rimmed in gold," Robb explained, circling his right palm with a finger to describe the size and shape of this most essential tool. "I can do much without a staff. There is very little I can do without a glass. If you want the letter dispatched by magic, I must have it. Surely my predecessor—since you have not named him, I can only guess at his identity—used such a tool."

"Sam . . . Sir, your predecessor, always performed this spell in private. I cannot give you that luxury."

Ah ha! Lokeen had not fully named him, but Robb knew for certain that Samlan had worked for him. Logical, after Samlan left the Circle so unceremoniously, taking with him three masters, two apprentices, and a journeyman. If he'd subverted Robb's journeyman and two apprentices, then he'd have nearly a full Circle to work his nefarious magic against Jaylor and the real Circle of Masters.

He had to get out of here and warn his friend and mentor. Which meant he had to send that letter, with or without the glass.

"My predecessor must have used a glass and kept it hidden from you," Robb said. He forced himself to stand tall and straight, adamant that his glass be returned immediately.

"If I give this tool to you to throw this spell, will you return it to my keeping until next time you need it?" Lokeen asked, eyeing him through squinted eyes, his face a mask of worried furrows.

"I give you my word."

Lokeen snapped his fingers. A third guard appeared in the doorway. "Here is the key to the treasury. Fetch the glass Mage Robb needs. You will find it next to his staff on the long table near the back corner. Mind you, if you touch anything else, let alone spirit it away, I will know and have you punished."

The guard blanched, nodded agreement, and reluctantly took the proffered key from Lokeen's hand.

Stargods! What kind of punishment awaited miscreants in this benighted castle?

CHAPTER 7

MARIA ORDERED THE preparations the mage wanted from the base of the turret stairs. Not a single man among Lokeen's many soldiers and guards offered so much as an assisting arm so that she could climb and oversee the proceedings in the presence of the magician.

She'd hidden her pain too well.

Or perhaps, politeness was not her brother-in-law's strong suit. Lokeen considered manners and courtesy an affectation of the weak.

Her mind took her back twenty-five years. Yolanda had just inherited the crown of Amazonia from their mother. Tall, graceful, beautiful, with thick blonde hair, and barely twenty, the new queen had glided through her ornate coronation and won the hearts of her people. From a distance.

Maria and her deformities had been banished from the ceremonies, even though she'd organized most of them.

In the weeks afterward, Yolanda entertained many suitors. Maria did her best to keep the most unsuitable away, especially Lokeen, who presented a smile to the young and naïve queen and a sneer of displeasure toward everyone else. But Yolanda fell in love with the man's smile, his handsomeness, and his thoughtful manners. She began depending upon his advice and good opinion long before the actual wedding.

There was the day when Maria penned letters for her sister.

"Say something nice about the ambassador's wife and daughters. You know what to say," Yolanda said with a dismissive wave of her hand.

"Of course. We greatly enjoyed taking a cup of chilled wine in the garden with . . ." she spoke the words as she wrote.

"Forget that!" Lokeen roared from the doorway. "He's only an ambassador from a minor city-state, not even a neighbor. Just order him to do what you want. Flattery weakens your position." He turned his attention to the woman, his betrothed, and changed his expression from angry disapproval to ingratiating charm. "You look lovely, my dear, as always. But that pale pink is not the best color for your gown. You need stronger and bolder colors to reflect your position as queen of the strongest and largest of the city-states."

"Excuse me, sir." Maria put down her quill pen and rose from her stool. "You are not yet the queen's consort. It is not your place to criticize her dress. She wears soft colors as a reflection of her virginal status . . ."

"Enough!" he shouted, emphasizing his words with a vigorous backhand across Maria's face.

She lost her balance, precarious at best, stumbled over her stool, wrenched her knee and landed heavily on the stone floor. Her twisted body sent lances of pain in all directions. She couldn't move. Her breathing sounded ragged to her own ears.

"Get up and fetch the queen a better gown," Lokeen ordered.

"Majesty," Maria pleaded to her sister, holding up a hand, needing assistance to get to her feet.

Yolanda laughed.

Ever afterward, Maria's hip and knee protested while climbing stairs.

Even then Lokeen had feared showing any sign of weakness, lest it give his enemies a point of leverage to remove him from his purloined throne.

A throne he should have relinquished to the nearest eligible female relative of his deceased wife and whichever male *she* chose as a consort.

Maria was not eligible because of her deformities. Family and courtiers alike had beaten that concept into her from the day she was born. She did not want the responsibility or power. That belonged to stronger individuals; stronger in both mind and body.

At last the sergeant of the guard, Young Frederico—his father, Senior Frederico had held the position before him—emerged from the cellar door that led to the royal treasury (a different wing with a separate entrance from the dungeons). He cradled in both hands an object covered in costly blue silk, and stepped gingerly as if afraid of tripping and breaking the precious and fragile artifact.

Maria recognized the cloth. The previous mage had taken it from the current mage when he arrived along with the staff. Then Sir demanded that Maria open the treasury—she had one of the two keys, Lokeen had stolen the other from his wife, the other rightful keeper—and hide the magical tools there. "Two more precious items resting among the ancient religious artifacts as well as the gold and silver to run the kingdom," he'd said. "But unlike the rest of the treasury, you, Lady Maria, must never, ever, under any circumstances touch either the glass or the staff with a bare hand. It will burn you to the bone."

The ancient Spearhead of Destiny was like that. No male could touch it unless it was given to him by the woman in charge of it. She hadn't mentioned the Spearhead to Sir. He didn't need to know about it. Neither did Lokeen.

"I will take that to the magician," Maria said firmly to Young Frederico.

He hesitated.

"Would you carry the Spearhead of Destiny into battle against the Krakatrice without me giving it to you with a blessing?"

He held out his cupped hands and bowed his head to her

authority and the conclusion that this artifact fell into the same revered class as the Spearhead of Destiny.

She folded the silk more closely around the round treasure—such a wonderful texture in silk; like free-flowing water over a parched hand—and took the precious object from him. Then she looked up the long and winding stair. Practicality won out over awe, and she pocketed the round glass with a gold rim so that she had two free hands to clutch the railing.

Young Frederico must have more intelligence than his underlings, for he stepped up beside her and held out his arm, silently, politely looking off into the distance, not acknowledging her weakness, just accepting it. Just as the mage Robb had done yesterday. Had Frederico witnessed the mage's behavior and mimicked it?

"How fares your sister, Frella?" Maria asked.

"Well enough," he replied flatly.

"Only 'well enough'? I'd hoped for better for her."

"She works at the stables outside the city walls. She's happy working with steeds day and night. But they aren't of the quality in the royal stables," he said, almost as if reluctant to speak of his sister out loud.

"Please send her my greetings and let her know I am pleased so many of the women warriors have found employment in the city since . . . the king dismissed them from palace duties."

"I'm certain she will appreciate your concern." He ducked his head and allowed a tiny smile to tip the corners of his mouth upward.

With his arm and the railing balancing her steps, and moving slowly, with dignity, as one should in a royal procession, she mounted the stairs without stopping for breath or to ease her pain. Frederico held open the door to the turret cell with deference. Someone had taught him some manners after all.

Maria liked this new order—a renewed order of respect for her. Something she hadn't seen since her sister, the

queen, had danced through life happy and healthy. Before
the birth of her first son which had nearly killed her. The
second son had made her an invalid.

She found Lokeen pacing the circular confines of the
room. Robb sat on a high stool before the window that
overlooked the harbor and the ocean beyond, opposite the
courtyard that looked only upon the dungeon cells where
Lokeen kept his pet Krakatrice, eyes closed, breathing
deeply, and conserving his strength for the work to come.

He'd eaten well, bathed, and shaved. A very handsome
man had emerged from the layers of grime and beard. Maria's heart beat a little faster.

She tamped down on her longing and cleared her head.
She needed to observe the spell closely, learn how it was
done, so that perhaps she could perform it herself in the
future. Surely, if Coronnan had so many magicians that they
filled a University with practitioners, then the myth that
only people born with a special talent could work magic
was just a myth. What people needed was not talent but
training.

"We have brought you a bowl of clear water, an oil candle, a flight feather from a sea bird that we left living, a gold
coin from Coronnan, and your glass," she announced as she
placed the silk-enshrouded glass on the table along with the
other symbolic materials.

Robb exhaled deeply and nodded. But he did not move
from his place.

"Get to it, man!" Lokeen shouted.

Robb took another deep breath, held it on a long count
and exhaled it again before turning to face his captor. A
strange glaze covered his eyes as if he looked far away beyond the limits of the walls, further than the ocean horizon,
and deep within himself at the same time.

"I am ready." His voice echoed deeply, as if it came from
another body, one that was not here. Up in the skies perhaps. Or deep on the ocean bottom.

She backed up, awed and frightened by this alien man.

Her hands instinctively clutched the goddess pendant beneath her clothes. She thought she had gotten to know Robb a bit, thought they were becoming friends. But this ... this was not the Robb she expected.

This man controlled vast powers she could not fathom.

Robb glided off his stool, graceful, barely grounded against the wide wooden planks of the floor. He stood at the table and began rearranging his assembled tools without looking at them. Then he waited, expectantly.

Young Frederico rushed to shove the stool behind the mage. Robb sat, again without looking, as if he knew precisely where everything in the room should be.

A snap of his fingers produced a tiny flamelet on his left pointing finger. He dropped his hand toward the candle, and the ember jumped to the wick where it flared high and eager to burn the waiting oil-soaked linen braid. His right hand did not fumble as he brought the tip of the feather to the flame. It scorched only, sending a column of smoke outward, without pattern or direction. The gold coin touched the smoldering feather, and the smoke organized itself into a circle. When Robb gently placed the coin and the feather into the bowl of water, the smoke spiraled downward, following them, only to be trapped by the glass as he floated it in the water atop them all.

Maria watched every move with her jaw hanging open. How? How could he do this? How many years had he studied just to bring flame out of nothing? The symbolism she understood. The means she could not, not without much more close observation.

She barely noticed as he passed the sealed letter through the flame without burning and dropped it atop the glass with the written destination facing downward.

"Seek, seek the one whose face appears on the coin. Fly free and swift, straight as I send you," he murmured, eyes finally focusing on the letter.

Smoke and flame flared up from the bowl, engulfing the letter in a tight twist of gold and green, then flew out the

window, straight across the harbor toward the ocean. Maria
watched it as it grew smaller with distance but did not dis-
sipate in the constant movement of air over the water.

When she could no longer see it, she looked back toward
Robb and the bowl. He slumped in exhaustion across the
table. Inside the bowl, the letter was gone.

And so was the glass. Its silk protection lay neatly folded
but empty beside his elbow.

She smiled secretly, finally releasing her grip on her talisman. Here was a man she could admire as a leader. If she
could find a way, she'd make him king of Amazonia, consort
to one of her many female cousins, and cheerfully watch
Lokeen die, eaten by his own Krakatrice.

Lily waded across the River Dubh on a string of flat rocks
that looked to be placed by the local people for just this
purpose. Cool water flowed across her toes, and she wiggled
them in delight. A chuckling tune came to mind rounding
out the voice of the river. Skeller had sung that song . . . She
had to stop thinking about Skeller. He was right. They both
needed time to heal from the murder of Samlan and her
deep empathic bond with her victim—a bond she couldn't
help sharing with the man she loved. They'd both endured
the moment of death as if their own. But they'd lived. And
they needed time apart.

But she missed him sorely.

The river continued its joyful path toward the River
Coronnan and thus to the sea, heedless of the human suffering along its path.

Should she take the time to wash up a bit before striding
into a strange village? A quick inspection showed her hands
no dirtier than usual, and she'd splashed her face with water
upon rising. Bare feet were always dirty. Her boots hung
from her pack, barely used. They blocked her connection to
the land. Kardia Hodos, her home. A living, breathing world
that nurtured humans and dragons and everything in be-

tween. One big circle of life that she couldn't join when she wore shoes.

(Krystaal here. Are you looking for excuses to delay?) a female dragon whispered into the back of her mind.

"Lily here," she replied with proper dragon protocol. "And no I'm not looking for excuses. I just want to present myself as friendly and helpful, not ragged and desperate. These people have probably seen too many ragged and desperate people fleeing the devastation of the flood."

(You are not dirty. Go.)

An emptiness at the base of Lily's skull where the dragon's presence had been almost sent her toppling off the ford. Dragons were like that, intruding with unwanted wisdom one second and then completely gone within a heartbeat.

She jumped clear of the rocks and walked a short way up the hill south of the ridge. Not a lot of flat land here, but the hills rolled gently without steep slopes—except for that ridge. Quickly she realized the village only looked abandoned from a distance. Flusterhens and goats meandered among the kitchen gardens in back of the houses. Dogs lazed on doorsteps in the sun, and cats perched here and there observing all.

But where were the people? Children should be running and playing. Women should be hanging the laundry or shelling peas for supper. Men needed to mend some of those fences, or cut firewood in the copse toward the west.

A flicker of movement in her left periphery that might have been a bird caught her attention. She listened closely for merry chirps. Instead, a mournful tune drifted on the wind from the other side of the hilltop.

Lily trod slowly upward, fearful of what she knew she'd find. She'd sung that same song at Mama's and Da's funeral.

To the east and south she found another copse, smaller with slighter trees, a mix of maple and alder with a scattering of oak. Not an everblue in sight. Twenty or so adults and as many children stood in a loose circle around a tiny

mound of dirt. Six stones piled on top of each other formed
a memorial cairn.

Lily's heart caught in her throat. Sadness, loss, grief, hit
her like an emotional wave. She nearly drowned under the
onslaught of her empathic bonds.

The grave could only be for a baby. Six moons old, one
stone in the cairn for each moon of life. Had it died in the
night while Lily rested across the river, safe and snug in her
nest of blankets with a good fire when she should have been
here with her herbs and knowledge and ability to understand the nature of the illness?

Guilt dropped her to her knees and she died a little more
inside.

CHAPTER 8

N EARLY A WEEK I have sat in this filthy inn awaiting a ship—any ship—returning to Amazonia to carry me and my minions away from Coronnan. Minions only. These slackers only want power given to them. They think the Tambootie gives them power. If they had any to begin with, the drug would enhance their talent. As it is, the dried leaves only give them the illusion of power. Addiction has already set in on one of the men. They are not willing to work for magic.

The three idiots serve a purpose. Nothing more. When I have the critical number of twelve followers so that we number thirteen, all working together, my power will be complete again.

And oh, how I will glory in torturing them all, drawing energy from their pain until they either must bring their latent talents alive or die.

They think only of the pleasure they give themselves during our sexual excess. I think beyond. That is why I am their leader. Bette and Geon have some potential. Bit by painful bit I draw out morsels of magic from them. They work better at feeding me power than doing anything on their own.

Unfortunately, Dillip will have to leave our little coven sooner rather than later. He has not a dollop of talent. His only interest lies in the unconventional sexual liaisons we practice. I need both talent and a willingness to step away from cultural strictures.

These meager three have proven useful in garnering information, though. They listen closely and blend into gossiping crowds. Deep in the recesses of the palace servants' quarters Bette, guided by Geon—by the great Simeon, I do not know how he knows the palace as well as the nether parts of the city—has learned that sniveling Lady Ariiell has finally grown a backbone and discarded the marriage offer of Lokeen, the king of Amazonia. He wants a woman of noble lineage, a proven breeder, and with magical talent.

I fit all those categories.

In the meantime I watch the bard. Last night after singing, he cut his hair to fit Amazonian standards. He sings songs of home, of loneliness, and wandering in exile. He also sings of cooling sea breezes in a hot desert. He knows much about the lands across the sea. He has access to the intimate details of their culture that his people do not discuss among aliens. While I listen to him, I dispatch my two men to listen to gossip on the docks. Sailors always talk to other sailors, even if it is just male boasting of conquests among the barmaids. That kind of information says a lot about expectations and attitudes.

At last, an hour after dawn, Jaylor's boy returns. His hair is a loose mess, his clothes stained, he is bright-eyed with the fevers of hunger and fatigue. But there is a new confidence and quiet settling about his shoulders. He has lost some of his anger. He has gained a staff.

I must work quickly if I am to seduce him to my coven. I cannot delay. He must be an active and willing partner in my bed before we sail on today's high tide. I'll take the bard as well. He is quite comely, and the ache in his heart makes him vulnerable.

"Mistress?" Souska asked her teacher.

"Hm?" Maigret replied, her attention on the stack of

missives on her desk and not on her apprentice. Apprentice Linda, Maigret's primary assistant, continued writing another letter in the endless chain of letters required for the operation of the University. Her pen scratched annoyingly against the fresh parchment. Must be an important letter to warrant new parchment rather than one of the many Souska scraped clean every evening.

She'd learned how each scraping thinned the cured animal skin and how each reuse demoted the value of the words written upon it, according to the rank of the recipient.

"Mistress, I've had another spell." Best to get the excuses over with first so understanding of Souska's failure followed. She had orders to report each spell so that Maigret could track her healing, or lack thereof.

"How bad?" Maigret looked up from her reading and restless rearranging, her attention fully on her apprentice now.

"I don't know how long my mind wandered in the void."

"Were you doing anything dangerous when the lapse overcame you?" The furrows across Maigret's brow deepened and her mouth turned into a more aggressive frown than her usual worry and sadness.

"I don't think so. No, not dangerous. But I know there is something important that I forgot."

Linda's pen ceased moving. The lack of noise from her desk sounded much louder in Souska's ears than the scratching had.

"What did you forget?" Linda asked.

"If I knew what I forgot I wouldn't have forgotten it!" Souska nearly screamed.

"But you might be jostled into remembering." Linda smiled slightly and returned to her writing. Such a neat hand, filled with curlicues and flourishes. The recipient must be an important noble who needed written confirmation of something rather than just a message passed along by his attending magician.

"Tell me what you were doing when the spell took you," Maigret said. She fixed her gaze on Souska, worming a trickle of magic into her mind, looking for the trigger to release the memory.

"I received a summons," Souska said reluctantly. Her nightly conversations with her journeyman were special. She needed to keep them close to her heart, private.

Linda's penned stilled, but she didn't look up.

"From whom?" Maigret demanded. The worm of magic became thicker, more insistent.

Instinctively Souska threw up a wall in her mind to keep her mistress from penetrating deeper.

Maigret reared back as if Souska had hit her. "When did you learn to do that?" she demanded, surprise and . . . and respect coloring her voice and posture.

"I . . . I don't know. I just did it."

"Well figure out how to do it again. That is a valuable skill in a magician. But I still expect you to tell me everything. Everything. You understand?"

Souska flicked a glance over to Linda and back to Maigret.

"Don't worry about my private assistant. She knows how to keep secrets and has sworn to do so," Maigret coaxed.

"I . . . I receive a scry most every night from Journeyman Lukan," Souska said quietly, dropping her head so that her words were muffled. "I think he's lonely and uncertain of his journey. He has no one else to talk to."

"His sisters . . ." Linda started but dropped back to silence at a wave of Maigret's hand.

"I don't know how often he speaks to Lillian or Valeria. He's not supposed to speak to anyone from the University except in cases of dire emergency or threat to the kingdom," Maigret prompted.

"I'm his friend," Souska insisted. "And I'm not really part of the University. I'm just an apprentice in . . ."

"You have a magical talent, no matter how minor. You *are* a part of this University. So what did Lukan tell you that was important enough for you to reveal his lapses in observing the rules of his journey?"

Souska bit back the flood of words that wanted out. She knew that every summons from Lukan eased her own loneliness and uncertainty as much as his. He explained her lessons in detail, making her understand the why as well as the how. That was important. She needed to dig deeply into each process and figure out her own way of understanding the reason for each exercise that led to a bigger spell. She could never remember the steps without understanding why she had to do each one of them.

"Close your eyes and don't think about it. You always overthink your lessons and then freeze for having lost the first part in your musings." Maigret's voice took on a musical cadence that needed additional notes to finish.

Souska played and replayed the chant until an ending flitted across her tongue. "Lukan saw someone . . ." she said and then lost the rest of the thought.

"Someone. Someone important. Someone out of place," Maigret continued the chant.

"Someone dangerous," Linda picked up the litany.

"Someone with magic . . ." Half a thought more crept out of Souska's mind.

"Dangerous magic," Maigret said.

"Rogue magic," Linda added.

"Old rogue." Souska fought the words free of her mind.

Maigret and Linda exchanged a glance.

"Lady Graciella said that at the end of the storm, when the magic that created it sought to restore the land and people to a previous condition of respect for dragon magic and magicians, it also restored Lord Krej and Rejiia to their human bodies. She saw it happen," Linda said.

"Unfortunately, Lady Graciella just this morning returned to her mother's household in Saria to await the birth of her child. She cannot tell us more about this transformation until she reaches her destination and we can speak through a local magician," Maigret dismissed the information.

Mistress Maigret must know about that transformation already. Souska had heard it spoken of since teams set out to help clean up after the storm. Everyone was instructed to keep a look out for the strange pair.

"Lady Rejiia!" Souska pounced on the name. "Lukan saw Lady Rejiia."

"Where?" Maigret demanded, rising from her chair and reaching for her scrying bowl and candle.

"I . . . can't remember," Souska said sadly.

"Where was he when he summoned you?" Linda asked.

"I . . . can't remember. Though I think there was water near him. I remember hearing a gentle splash. And he had to cut short our discussion." Souska shrugged. Energy drained from her head, down past her shoulders to her middle and then out her legs and toes. She thought her head had floated free of her body and looked out at the world from high above her, near the darkness of the void. Bright starbursts behind her eyes nearly blinded her.

"Still here I see," Lukan said to Skeller. The bard sat on a bench at the table he'd stood upon while singing last night. Today he slumped over a bowl of mixed grains, boiled to mush and sweetened with goat milk and honey. Just like Mama used to make.

Lukan's mouth watered as he remembered he'd not eaten since last night and had rowed his little boat a considerable distance to this portside tavern.

"Wha . . . where . . . gotta sleep," Skeller mumbled as he lifted his head a few inches from the table.

Lukan caught a glimpse of red-rimmed eyes and several days' growth of beard before the man dropped his head again, just barely missing planting his nose in the cereal. "Well if you aren't going to eat this, I am." Lukan grabbed the bowl with one hand as he fished his wooden spoon out of his pack.

Skeller mumbled something more without moving. His

harp at least was packed into her case and resting farther along the table, safe for the moment. The bard always saw to his harp's well-being before his own.

"Sometimes I think you love that harp more than you ever did my sister," Lukan grumbled around a mouthful of delicious food. Possibly the best-tasting meal he'd had since Mama had died. Since before she died. Brevelan hadn't been well for several moons. Her seventh child, dead before birthing, had killed her as much as losing her beloved husband had. Fitting that she and Jaylor had passed within minutes of each other. Were they together in the void with the dragons? Or some special *other* life promised by the Stargods?

He hoped they were together. Neither one seemed whole without the other. Like the twins. Like he and Glenndon used to be.

He shook off that thought.

"Do we have a ship?" Hunger appeased for the moment, Lukan scanned the big open room. The innkeeper had opened the shutters over broad windows letting in the morning light and revealing all the stains made by generations of spilled drinks and the flood mud not completely cleaned, just covered up with rushes on the plank floor. Two men sat by the open window, enjoying the fresh breeze on a morning that promised to grow hot within an hour, while they consumed their own breakfasts with foaming tankards of ale.

Only Skeller appeared as worn and dreary as the interior of the room.

Another mumble from Skeller that sounded sort of like "Noon tide," but could have been "None today."

Lukan pounded the butt of his staff on the floor. He liked doing that. He'd never handled a magician's staff before—legend had it that if any other person touched a staff it would burn the hand off. Now he had one of his own. And he liked the way energy tingled from the grip into his hand whenever he touched it to the ground. Pounding filled him with renewed confidence. He was a real magician now.

"Must you do that?" Skeller whimpered, pressing his long fingers into his temples. At least he remained upright. Kind of. If leaning his elbows on the table and staring at overlapping beer stains was upright. "You pound that thing louder than a dragon screeching in distress."

"Heard one of those lately?" Lukan tried to remember the last time he heard a dragon call. Yesterday. At the mass funeral on Battle Mound. Three of them: a green-tip and a red-tip, males, and, more important, an all-color/no-color female. A young one. She hadn't looked as big as Shayla, the matriarch. They had roared a bass harmony to the last hymn. Someone like Skeller, who hadn't grown up with dragons, might think their crooning was a screech of distress. Or grief at the loss of so many people during the storm.

"So what ship did you book passage on?" he prodded Skeller with an elbow to keep him from falling asleep again.

"Didn't." He looked the length of the table until he spotted his breakfast bowl in Lukan's hand. "Get your own." He grabbed it back and slurped up a mouthful, drinking directly from the bowl.

"What do you mean? You're the one who was insisting that we have to sail as soon as possible." Lukan signaled the barkeep for another bowl of cereal. And a tankard of new beer.

"No passage to book. Passenger cabins full up."

"So, what did you mean when you said 'noon tide'?"

"You are working the topsails and I am assistant to the cook."

Lukan liked the idea of climbing tall masts and perching on the yardarm or in the crow's nest. "So we're crew, not passengers. Will we get paid or is just getting us from here to there our wages?" He gobbled several bites of his fresh bowl of breakfast, then drank half his flagon. He hadn't realized how taxing last night was. Talking to Madame Oak must have drawn heavily on his magical, and physical, reserves.

"Two silver dragini each," Skeller said. He looked a little more awake and less green around the edges.

"How much did you drink last night?"

"Too much and not enough?"

"What does that mean?"

"I'm still missing Lily."

Before Lukan could reply to that, a flurry of movement from the steep staircase that led to guest rooms abovestairs caught his attention. Rejiia descended. Her long black traveling gown floated around her feet, emphasizing her grace and elegance. She'd bound up her glossy black hair in a fine cowl of silver mesh with sparkling white beads—too bright to be pearls, too much color to be crystal or diamonds. Iridescent. That was the right word. As if she'd woven bits and pieces of dragon fur into the strands. The long white stripe that began at her left temple swirled through the black tresses in an artful pattern.

Lukan stared in wonder at her beauty, enthralled with her aura of power.

"Close your mouth, boy," Skeller whispered. "Remember that she is still more cat than human. She throws rogue magic and discards lovers like broken toys."

He jerked his head toward the tall, scarred man and the plain, older woman who followed Rejiia's every move. The other, rather ordinary and easily overlooked, man was missing from the entourage.

"I've heard the legends," Lukan whispered back. He did remember to close his mouth, but he couldn't remove his gaze from the vision that graced this poor tavern.

Then she turned her head and smiled at him. The world faded away to whispers of background noise and images. He only noticed her sharp cat's teeth in the logical part of his mind. All thought dropped to a more primitive part of his body that reacted keenly to her presence.

CHAPTER 9

*T*HE BOY FELL *into my trap with hardly a second breath of hesitation. I drift toward him, pleased that I have worn the best of my plain traveling gowns. The fine woolen threads will keep me warm aboard ship. Here in this dismal tavern the cloth clings to my curves, and swirls around me like an enchanted mist.*

Once I could have used enchantment to create this illusion on any outfit, no matter how rough. No more. Rather, not yet. I must conserve my strength for important magic.

I hear my father whisper into the back of my mind that bringing a University-trained magician into my coven is important. Enticing a son of Jaylor is more important.

I tell my father to go away. He has chosen a cozy fire, mulled wine, and his stories of olden times. I have chosen to live now, in the world, creating my own adventures rather than reliving someone else's old and boring ones.

Lukan is my adventure. I need time to lure him in slowly so that he thinks the whole thing is his idea. Too much too soon makes for fragile and brittle chains. A constraining leash that he will soon break and free himself. My bonds will be strong and lovely, like a silken braid.

A braid.

As I watch, his aura begins twisting and folding, wrapping him in layers of protection that include his newly won staff.

*There is no pattern or looping in the wood grain yet. I must
get it away from him soon, before it mimics the braid of his
magic, so like his father's. Even his aura carries the same blue
and red lights that used to make Jaylor stand out in any
crowd, magician or mundane.*

*As I approach Lukan, slowly, measuring each step care-
fully so I do not startle him, the bard rears up from his slump
against the table and grabs the boy's shirt collar.*

"Think with your brain and not . . ." *He breaks off his tirade, looking up and down Lukan's body. Then he twists to
look over his shoulder at me. His eyes narrow and he takes
one deliberate step sideways so that he breaks my line of
sight to Lukan's eyes.*

*Immediately Lukan shakes his head, shriveling the thrall
of my beauty.*

"We have a ship's captain to report to," *the bard says,
clearly, distinctly, as if singing his words.*

"Ship. Noon tide," *Lukan mumbles. Then he shakes himself all over and looks out the window toward the street.
Workers and shoppers alike begin to fill the cobbles. They
shout at each other, hawking their wares and ordering others
about. His eyes focus on the jumble of daily activity.*

"That's right. And we have to help ready the ship for passengers and cargo," *the bard says.*

*Noon tide? Passengers and cargo? Bless the great Sim-
eon, they sail on the same ship as I. I will have nigh on a
week to weave my allure around them both.*

*In the old days I'd need only a day. Now I am more cau-
tious. More patient.*

"Innkeeper!" *I call imperiously.* "Bring me meat. Rare
and juicy. I will dine on nothing less."

Robb lay flat on his back on the comfortable bed. The only
thing he lacked was Maigret beside him and the two boys in
their cribs. Instead of wrapping his arm around his wife, he
could only cover his glass with an open hand, letting the

inherent coolness filter through his skin. A slight tingle within the tool, magic left over from all the spells he'd thrown through the glass, still lingered, ready at his command.

"You are lucky I allowed Lokeen to think I sent the glass back to the treasury," Maria said from the doorway. She leaned against the closed portal, making certain he heard the latch click shut.

He knew from routine that the guards outside would not unlock for any but her command. Every day that passed, he suspected more and more that, except for a chosen few, every man in the castle served her first and Lokeen second. Something in their posture reflected their respect for her. They *listened* to her. With the king they stood overly stiff and stared into the distance, barely acknowledging his orders.

The king kept his throne because of the punishment only he and his guard captain controlled.

"What is so vile about Lokeen's punishment that every man quakes in his boots?" Robb asked, not looking up. He kept his free arm draped across his eyes as though he had a headache, while his other hand shielded the glass and the slight residual magic contained within it.

"Do you know the beast called Krakatrice?" she asked.

He heard her prowling the room, inspecting every item, including the empty pottery scrying bowl and the unlit oil candle on the table.

Robb stilled. Even his blood seemed to cease flowing at the dreaded word. "I read in old chronicles that the Stargods and their helpers rid this world of the monster snakes that turn lush land into desert. The beasts looked to a matriarch with six wings on her back."

"Not all of the beasts died at the hands of my ancestors, the first Amazons of Amazonia."

"There have been no reports of the snakes infiltrating civilized lands until recently."

"The eggs," Maria said flatly. "Properly buried just after

laying, deep in cold lands with no moisture, the eggs go dormant for hundreds of years. When they are unearthed and slowly warmed, they revive and hatch."

"That must be how the younglings appeared in Coronnan last spring," Robb mused, thinking hard and not paying much attention to his hostess. "I fought enough of them a-dragonback. But always more came. More killed livestock and people, all the while instinctively trying to dam rivers and divert the water elsewhere . . ."

"You fought the beasts? You killed them?" Maria moved to his side, grabbing the fine fabric of his robe and shaking him with each word.

He'd never seen her move so quickly, not bothering to hide her limp or reduce her pain.

"One of our healers might be able to straighten your leg, permanently. Or at least build you a boot to compensate for the shortness and the twist," he said cautiously, not certain he wanted to tell this woman everything, no matter that she'd been kind to him.

Her kindness had a price. He just didn't know what it was yet.

"They might even find the cause of your lisp and correct it. They removed extra tissue from beneath my eldest son's tongue to help him."

"Enough of your babble! Our healers have tried everything with no success. Now tell me how to kill the beasts!"

"Can't be done without dragon fire and ensorcelled spearheads knapped of obsidian."

Maria rocked back on her heels.

Robb peeked around his arm. She looked off into the distance, fingers caressing something beneath her blouse — a talisman of some sort he guessed. He might as well not be in the room for all her awareness of him.

"Where are the snakes?" he whispered, wondering if his words would penetrate her deep thoughts. "How does Lokeen control them?"

"The Krakatrice survive on fresh meat. They thrive and

grow on fresh blood," she said, blinking rapidly to bring herself back to the world. "He can only feed them so many live prisoners before they outgrow their dungeon cells and must be turned loose and replaced by new hatchlings."

Robb swallowed heavily. The lump in his throat would not dissolve.

"If I tell Lokeen that I have allowed you to keep your glass as well as your robe, he would drop us both into the dry cell." Her smile didn't reach her eyes.

"He can have the black robe back. I prefer the blue, threadbare and worn as it is," he croaked around that persistent lump in his throat.

"Blue? Strange, your predecessor demanded black and red. He shredded and burned the blue. The cloth was fine, I wanted to open the seams and remake the pieces into other garments."

"He had to burn it to separate himself from the University. Though I have never done it, I think Master Magician Jaylor could have found the man through his robe." That was a flat-out lie, but Maria couldn't read his aura to know that for certain.

"You have never told me the name of King Lokeen's previous pet wizard," he prodded. He knew by the simple process of elimination. But he needed confirmation. When he knew for certain, he could scry for the man. Once he found him, Lokeen might, *just might*, grant Robb a little more freedom in return for the favor. Freedom to seek escape.

"I was never told the mage's name," Maria said flatly. "If he told Lokeen, he never said it aloud. We in the palace who were forced to serve him called him 'Sir.' Nothing more, certainly nothing less, though we had other names we called him behind his back. He was the one who devised the scheme to reanimate the eggs and ship them to our spies elsewhere, to bring low *his* enemies. But Lokeen was the one who kept a few and feeds them prisoners."

"Lokeen will do anything to keep his throne," Robb said. "No matter how cruel."

"Or illegal," Maria added. Then she turned slowly, with her usual cautious steps, and left the room, without telling Robb why she had come to begin with.

He had his glass, for now. He knew what he had to do. Quickly, before he too became food for the Krakatrice.

"Breathe deeply, and follow my instructions," Maigret commanded Souska.

"In on three, hold three, out on three, hold three," Souska repeated one of her earliest lessons in magic. She let the familiar ritual of proper breathing fill her with calm until the magnetic pole tugged at her left side, and the wooden floor tingled against her feet through her soft house shoes.

"You figured out that if you light the candle, you are part of another's summons. You can hear both sides of the conversation," Maigret continued as her own breathing deepened and her eyes crossed slightly.

"Yes, ma'am," Souska replied, knowing Maigret would not see a nod of acceptance. How did her mistress go into a trance so deeply and easily? Souska sat on her stool beside Maigret, fully aware of her surroundings with a slightly enhanced sensitivity.

"To participate in the conversation with me and Marcus, you must do more."

Souska took another deep breath, deeper than before, letting the fresh air from the open window fill her lungs, soothe her anxious pulse and bring her closer to alignment with the pole.

"With two fingers hold the rim of my glass."

Souska placed her right thumb and forefinger on the golden rim of the circle of glass, as big around as Maigret's palm.

"Now with your other hand you must bring a flame to your fingertip and set it upon the candle wick."

"Um . . ." Souska had only ever lit a candle with her dominant right hand. Her left was much less dexterous. But her right was now occupied with the glass . . . She reached to replace her grip on the glass with her left hand.

"No."

She froze with her left hand a hair's width away from the rim.

"Once you begin the gathering of energies you must continue as you started. Light the candle with your left hand."

"But . . ."

"Do it! Right or left. Both hands must work equally well no matter which you prefer."

"But . . ."

"Do it properly or ground the spell and leave so that I may start over from the beginning. Alone."

That "alone" meant that Souska would be excluded from more advanced lessons. Possibly forever. She'd be stuck doing nothing more than stirring potions that someone else concocted and scraping parchment free of letters someone else wrote.

"Concentrate," Maigret whispered. She must have noted the moment of Souska's decision. "Concentrate on the fire within your soul. Find it in your blood, in your center, in your love for your journeyman."

That was a bit more perceptive than Souska thought she'd let on.

She did as commanded. Looking deep within herself to the very core of her gentle magic that let her understand how plants worked together, how her simple songs brought out the best of each flower or leaf. And there, somewhere behind her heart she found Lukan's red and blue aura swirling around, pushing her to do more, be better, learn all that she could. Demanding that she *want* more out of life than perfuming soap and freshening bed linens.

She needed to grow into flavoring foods with the extra bits that each person needed to fill the holes in their bodies depleted by hard work. She should extend her knowledge further into medicines that would oust illness and repair damage.

Her magic flared along with her warming emotions. Fire appeared in the midst of Lukan's aura and pushed itself through her blood, igniting her desire to throw this spell with all the accuracy and speed that his years of practice had given him.

"Not much, but enough," Maigret snorted at the pitiful little green ember glowing at the tip of Souska's left forefinger. "Light the candle."

Souska exhaled and moved her finger, only to find the coal fading, flickering, almost dying as she breathed on it. Hastily she gulped and willed the flame back to life. It spluttered a bit.

"Remember the fire within you," Lukan seemed to whisper into the back of her mind. "Remember."

She did so. The flame found a hint of life. Was it enough? She touched her finger to the charred wick before it could die again. Just when she despaired that the flame would never find a life of its own, it bent, sniffed around the wick, and finally crawled over to it, like a cat seeking a new and different lap. The candle burned steady, then stronger and stronger until Souska thought it would hold on its own.

"Breathe," Maigret reminded her, on a chuckle.

Souska choked on her own breath. One cough that laid the flame flat. The second made it waver again. Then she found the control to bring air in and out on a proper cadence, and the flame held.

"Now, together we must place the glass in the bowl of water. Do not drop it. We must set it down gently, without a splash and with as little ripple as possible to keep the glass clear and clean, otherwise, the images will be distorted. You cannot tell truth from lie in a distorted image."

"I doubt Master Marcus would lie to us," Souska grumbled.

"No, he will not. But others might. Best to learn to do this properly the first time. And *every* time."

Thankfully, Maigret had chosen a wide bowl for the spell, wide enough for the two of them to slide their fingers into the depths and loose the glass as it touched the fresh spring water. Never stale water. That much Souska knew. Water that had not been in a vessel anyone had drunk from. Water that had not had a chance to mix with something else. Water as fresh and pure as a free-running mountain stream.

Following Maigret's example, Souska withdrew her touch on the glass and placed both her hands primly in her lap. They tingled from the flow of magic through them. She resisted the urge to clamp them next to her body under her arms and still the vibrations.

"Marcus . . ." Maigret said, circling the rim of the glass in the water until it hummed. Her magical signature color, a reddish brown that mottled together to be one color more often than two separate ones, followed her finger, wavering in and out like waves lapping the shore of glass. "Master Marcus."

Slowly a delicate orange infiltrated the border of color, blending with it, swirling around and around, brightening as the connection grew.

Souska's thoughts circled and circled. Nothing existed but those colors, merging in a friendly dance.

A sharp jab of Maigret's elbow into her belly forced Souska to blink and revive. "You can't afford to lose yourself in the spell," she whispered.

Souska withdrew her mind a bit. Then Marcus' weary face bloomed into the glass.

"What now?" he asked anxiously, blinking rapidly as if banishing sleep. From the lines on his face, that must be a rare commodity of late.

"Souska has had a report from Lukan," Maigret said without preamble. She didn't need to introduce herself. Marcus would know who summoned him by the colors in his own vibrating glass.

"Souska? Who is Souska and why would Lukan summon her?" he asked sharply.

"Lukan has been mentoring and teaching my apprentice

from afar," Maigret said. Her jaw worked, as if she wanted
to be angry with the Chancellor of the Universities and Senior Magician to the king.

"What is Lukan's message? An illogical means of getting
around the prohibition of calling home except in cases of
dire emergency or peril to the kingdom." Marcus leaned his
head heavily on his hand and closed his eyes.

"This might very well imperil the kingdom."

Marcus roused himself from his doze. "Tell me exactly
what the boy said."

Maigret nodded for Souska to supply the answer.

"Lukan said 'Tell Marcus that Rejiia is in the city.'" She
had to think a moment to remember his exact words. So
much was foggy from the last message. Had she lost something important in her memory lapse?

"Rejiia, eh? She is not enough of a threat to warrant
breaking the rules. She has done nothing, thrown no magic,
or recruited new members to her coven."

That sounded familiar. Had Lukan said anything about
the coven?

"Tell me this again when every magician in the city and
half those in the mountains isn't worn to the bone working
from dawn to sunset clearing debris, salvaging building materials, rebuilding, replanting, trying to find enough food
and clean water to continue one more day." He held a hand
over his scrying bowl and clamped his fingers shut, ending
the spell.

But just as his last finger bent, another color shot into
Maigret's bowl. A disembodied voice shouted, "Help me!"

"Robb?" Maigret gasped, and fell to the floor in a dead
faint.

CHAPTER 10

"ROBB!" MAIGRET'S VOICE came through the glass in fading echoes.

"My love," he gasped. He didn't have much time. If Lokeen found out he still had his glass, there would be hell to pay. The spell dissipated back into the water quickly. "I'm a prisoner in Amazonia!" he called back to his wife as loudly as he dared. But the colors and life had faded from the spell before he finished speaking. He had no way of knowing if she heard him or not.

Suddenly Maria flung open the door so hard it bounced against the wall and would have slammed into her face if a tall guard had not held it back.

"What is the meaning of this? Who is it that you call your love?" Anger infused her face with high color bordering on purple. She panted with rapid, shallow breaths and swayed on her feet.

Robb clenched his fist over the water bowl and fished out the glass in one swift movement.

A large hand clamped over his wrist before he could pocket the circle of glass. The nameless guard pried the tool loose from his fingers and passed it to Maria. He juggled it briefly as the golden rim, still ripe with the scrying spell, burned his fingers. Maria finally took it from him with a corner of her apron. The guard blew on his hands, trying to soothe the magical wound.

Robb did not feel inclined to pull the spell back into him. Serve his captors right if a little ungrounded magic went wild and shimmied all over the castle. If he thought long and hard enough about the consequences, they'd happen.

Maria didn't give him time. "How dare you abuse my kindness!" The last word came out on a long uncontrolled hiss, like a snake about to strike. She slapped him hard across the face with her open palm. For all the weakness in her leg and her tongue, her hands and arms were strong.

Robb recoiled from the blow, straining his neck as he turned his face too quickly. Every instinct wanted to flinch and withdraw, push his stool all the way across the room.

Showing fear now could either save him, or condemn him. Maria needed an ally. A strong one. In the end she'd respect strength and come seeking it again.

He hoped.

He met her gaze levelly with silence. She worked for the man who held him prisoner. He owed her no explanation.

"Take him back to the dungeon," Maria ordered. The high color faded from her face, leaving her paler than usual. Her tone and her expression were glacial.

Robb stood as tall as he could, towering over her stunted frame. The top of her head barely reached his breastbone. Against a truly tall man, like Jaylor or the king, she'd appear a dwarf. And yet she ruled the castle, if not the kingdom, with ready authority.

The guards nodded to her with respect. Then one on each side of Robb grabbed his upper arms and a third prodded his back with the sharp end of a spear. He had to move forward or die.

But would Maria truly have him killed? She needed him alive. Subdued and compliant, but alive.

Robb resisted the physical propulsion of the guards, digging in his heels and bending his knees to weaken their grip.

He'd learned a few tricks over the years. He and Maigret had wandered far during their journeys. They couldn't always access magical weapons.

The spearhead pricked his skin through the heavy woolen robe and his linen shirt.

"Cooperate, Wizard!" Maria lisped. Her words always slurred more when strong emotions gripped her.

Ah, that was why she fought so hard to remain calm and controlled. And in control of others. So that she would not reveal her handicap any more than she had to.

"Why? So that you can kill me later rather than right now?" He wasn't sure, but he had to goad her. Force her to do something she would instantly regret. Then she'd have to apologize. Have to give him more freedom to gain his forgiveness.

"There will be no more talk of killing my mage!" Lokeen yelled from the top of the stairs. He crossed the landing and threshold to Robb's cell in three strides, reaching his hands to grab Maria.

"He betrayed you," she said simply, turning to face him.

The guards retained their fierce grip on Robb, but the one with the spear eased the pressure on his back.

"He's a prisoner. He'll betray anyone he has to in order to escape. But he can't. Not while I have my pets in the cellars." Lokeen leaned forward and captured Maria's gaze with his own piercing stare.

"He kept his glass hidden after he dispatched the letter for you."

"I expected him to. How else was he to know when the desert-cursed missive reached its target?" The king adopted a more relaxed pose. Still the cords on his neck strained. His calm was all an act, feigned for the benefit of Maria and the guards. He released Maria from his penetrating glare and let his gaze wander about the room, stopping when he spotted the ceramic bowl and ewer of water. Then he looked again, pausing when he saw the glass held within Maria's plain linen apron, between her two fingers. He whipped out a square of fire-green silk from his sleeve. Casually he scooped up the cloth and draped it across his palm, then lowered it in front of Maria, holding firm until she released the glass into the protective covering.

S'murghit! The silk would negate the wild magic left in the glass and the gold.

"I shall keep this for now." Lokeen tilted his head to study Robb. "Has the letter arrived?"

"I believe so."

"Believe? Only believe?"

"Your . . . um . . . pets emit a protective bubble around themselves which deflects most weapons and spells. That bubble has spread to include most of the castle. They must have grown a lot since hatching for the bubble to be so big. I can barely throw the simplest spells. I sensed a slight vibration a few minutes ago. Barely an acknowledgment. Couldn't have been anything else."

Lokeen tapped his jaw with one finger, still cupping the glass in his other hand. "So, if I need you to scry for your predecessor, find out where he is hiding and how I can bring him back, you will need to leave the castle?"

"Yes." *Yes!*

"Not today. Tomorrow or the next day I will personally escort you to the farm. Along the way we may stop and allow you to work your spell. For now, since Maria is so terribly displeased with you, a stay in the dungeon is called for."

"The same cell?" Maria asked a measure of satisfaction creeping through her disgruntlement.

"No. That cell was too large and comfortable. It had a window, if I remember. Put him two doors west of the containment area."

Robb hadn't heard that term used here. Containment? *Containment!* The place where the king kept his snakes and tortured his prisoners. The area where the protective bubble would be strongest. The cell where it would be all too easy for a guard to grab a small snake by the tail and slip it into Robb's cell without anyone knowing.

His knees turned to water and he sagged against his captors' grip.

"Death stalks this village, Journeyman." Stanil the village headman stared into the cup of hot tea Lily had prepared for him.

She saw how the villagers trudged back to their daily chores directly after burying the baby. Stanil's baby girl, six moons old.

"In the past week we've lost five people, and still the wraith of death lingers. Two more took sick last night," Stanil continued.

Lily sorted her herbs, laying them in a circle around her where she knelt beside the fire pit at the center of the village. She knew the contents of each packet by the color and texture of the wrappings—linen, canvas, silk, and that new fabric from SeLennica, cotton. She'd also invented a system of knots in the drawstrings, clusters of varying numbers and spacings. Finding them by feel inside a larger pouch inside her pack was easy and familiar. Too familiar, and about to become more so judging by the shuffling gait of these villagers.

From the state of the huts, not a chimney among them, smoke holes cut in the thatched roofs, she guessed most meals were cooked and eaten here around a central fire. A community that worked hard together, sharing everything so that no one went hungry, and what little surplus they had was properly stored against a long winter or shriveled harvest.

"The baby's mother?" Lily prompted as Stanil fell into silence. She fingered a packet of betony and one of dried gillieflowers, wondering if she should add more of each to his cup. He needed strength now to keep himself from becoming vulnerable to the sickness. The hollows around his eyes and his gaunt cheeks could be from nursing his family night and day and failing. More than a bit of grief and guilt in his tone. Only time would heal that.

"Death took her first. A week ago. Our village elder died next, leaving me in charge a decade or more before I thought I'd be ready to take on the chore."

"I'm sorry."

He fell into a deep, brooding silence. Each of the villagers cast him a worried glance as they passed. They seemed to pass him more frequently than need be. Were they worried about him or curious about her?

"I've some training as a healer," Lily said, loud enough for all to hear. "I want to stay and help where I can."

"Run away, little girl. Run very far and very fast before Death takes you too."

Lily firmed her chin and settled her shoulders. "If that is my destiny, then so be it. But I will stay and help where I can. Now show me those who are sick." That's what Skeller would tell her to do. Duty came first. He'd finally learned that and returned to his home to fix the problems of an illegal monarch, or take the throne himself. She could only follow his example, since she couldn't follow him.

Stanil downed the last of his tea, knotted his belt through his cup handle and rose from the flat rock he'd chosen for a bench. "We'll start with Old Milla. She's the weakest and most likely to go wandering with Death next."

Lily shuddered at how this man referred to Death so lightly—as if she were an intimate. Maybe she was. But what had drawn her? Didn't she have enough to satisfy her voracious appetite with all the thousands dead after the flood?

CHAPTER 11

LUKAN FIRMED HIS grip on the yardarm of the tallest mast on the deep-sea passenger ship, indulging in a moment of listening to the cold sea breeze playfully biting at his cheeks and chin. Whispers of exotic lands and oddly accented words drifted past him. For an instant he thought he smelled sharp spices and heavy incense.

Then it was gone, and the sailor next to him shouted orders to release this rope, that knot. Lukan wished for his brother's strong telepathic talent. Glenndon always understood what other people wanted because he could reach into their minds and find the true message that sometimes got lost in words. The Crown Prince had had his reasons for not speaking a word until after he went to court to become part of the king's family.

Cautiously, Lukan tried a minor probe into the sailor's mind. Not easy with only a boat and water beneath him. He needed land. And trees he could climb. But he had climbed the mast, a solid mass of wood that had once been a tree. Could he find a trace of the everblue essence beneath the layers of varnish?

His hands tingled. But he couldn't tell if that was from the wood's hidden life or from the cold engulfing all of his senses.

Then he saw it, clear and shining like a beacon in the

dark, the knot he'd clenched when he steadied his balance. He needed to pull the strand to his left and that would . . .

Release the swaying rope he stood on.

A practical joke to test the new man on the crew. To see if he was as experienced as he claimed when he signed on.

Lukan tugged on the strand of a different knot, to his right and watched the mainsail loosen. As each man in turn manipulated the intricate lacework of lines, the heavy canvas dropped and flapped in the strengthening wind. Other men, on the deck below, secured other lines to tighten the fabric and its crossbar where they needed. Taut once more, the sail caught the wind and surged forward, warping the ship out of safe harbor and into the rolling waves of the Great Bay.

Foam on the crests of the waves sparkled in the bright sun. The wind played with the misting water droplets, sending colored prisms shooting forward in the sun's path.

Lukan breathed deeply and flashed a grin at his potential tormentors.

"In the nest w'you," grunted the joker on his left. His gaze traveled upward to the very tip of the mast swaying with the ship's movement, and the tiny platform up there. No railing. No ropes. Nothing to cling to but the mast itself.

A mast that had once been a tree.

Lukan scrambled upward eagerly, letting his bare feet find the notches, only sorry that he'd had to leave his staff wrapped in canvas and tucked into the folds of his hammock belowdecks in the crew quarters.

"Don't laugh so readily, young'n. You'll be up there an entire watch. That's four hours with nothing to anchor your stomach," the sailor warned him.

Lukan nodded a brief acknowledgment. He knew what awaited him. Nothing worse than hiding from his father in the top of an everblue with only a dragon to ease his loneliness.

He settled his butt on the platform and wrapped one arm around the mast.

"Shout if you see aught cap'n needs to be wary of!" the joker called after him.

"Aye, sir," Lukan yelled back, knowing that was the response required; his link to the man's mind hadn't frayed completely yet.

Then the line of experienced sailors scurried down the mast to where Rejiia's minion watched every move Lukan made. Of Rejiia or her maid he saw nothing.

Time passed. Lukan easily matched his body rhythms to the gentle sway of the ship. He noted the slow passage of sun from high above toward the western horizon, deep in the foothills of the mountain range that divided Coronnan and SeLenicca. From up here, the line was clear, dark green mounds reaching upward toward snowcapped peaks. In the city he could see only the next building. He liked the sea view.

To the east he saw only the promontories, north and south, where the land curved in protective arms around the Bay. He guessed that they'd pass through the mouth of the Bay into open ocean about the end of his watch.

Home. This felt like home. His mind reached no farther than his eyes could see, and contentment gathered around him.

A roar of laughter jerked him out of a light doze. Hastily he checked to make certain he hadn't slipped off the nest. Nope. He was firmly in place with one armed wrapped around the mast and the other hand shading his eyes against the sun's glare. Another peek downward showed him all the sailors going about their business, swabbing decks, coiling lines, securing cargo against the bulwark. A few passengers strolled the cramped spaces. None of them Rejiia.

He sighed in disappointment. Or relief. He wasn't certain how he should react to the woman when she was out of sight. And he free of her enthrallment.

That was it. Enthrallment. Was she so captivating that his heart and soul reached out to her naturally, or had she thrown a spell to trap him? He'd heard about such spells from Ariiell. At first Rejiia's spells would only work while in her presence. But with repeated exposure the web of enticement grew stronger until it became a permanent part of a man's mind.

He couldn't let that happen and vowed to keep his distance. Even if he had to spend the entire voyage up here in the crow's nest. No great hardship.

Another roar in the distance, near a line of clouds marring the eastern horizon. A storm brewing?

(Not yet,) a distant voice whispered into his mind. *(Verdii here.)*

"Lukan here," Lukan replied with both his mind and voice.

"What can I do for you, Verdii?"

(You should ask why I was sent to follow you.)

"Um, why were you sent to follow me?" Anger coiled like a tight fist in the middle of his chest, cutting off his breathing. *I'm on journey,* S'murghit*! I'm supposed to do this on my own.*

(And I am supposed to keep secret the reasons of my elders.)

"Did my father put you up to this?"

(No.)

That was a bit of relief. He could well imagine Jaylor consulting with Shayla and Baamin, the matriarch and her favored mate of the dragon nimbus. Jaylor, Senior Magician and Chancellor of the University *and* chief counselor to the king, would feel no shame in asking the dragons to keep track of a son he didn't trust to pull on his own boots or cast a competent summons spell.

But Jaylor was dead. Completely so—as far as he knew. Jaylor had not reanimated into dragon form to complete his destiny as Old Baamin had. No, Da and Mama completed each other. So with one gone into the void, the other followed.

"Then who sent you?"

(A friend. A friend who wishes you well and knows that

you will face trouble beyond the means of the strongest master magicians. I am to watch only, and be your friend as well.)

"Oh." Lukan had to think on that a few moments. "I have often wished for a friend. A true friend, not someone like Skeller who only travels beside me and will part when we reach his destination, never to see me again."

(Friends we are, Lukan!)

"Friends we are."

Verdii broke free of the cloud shadow and soared high, his fire-green wing tips and spinal horns shining bright as if lit from within by a thousand candles. Silver hints in his juvenile fur reflected bright arrows of light back toward Lukan's eyes, nearly blinding him. The dragon dipped and soared, circling the ship in a wild spiral, then dove deep and fast, wings tucked tight against his nearly invisible body.

Out in the ocean, where the waves rolled high before the gathering storm, he plunged into the deep water. Seconds later he rose up, a giant sharkeel fish gripped tightly in his long talons. The monster of the deep wriggled and fought. But the dragon was stronger. Already his claws penetrated the thick skin of his prey and drew blood. The fish's strength waned as the dragon flapped and flew higher before turning toward land.

(I eat well tonight!) Verdii chortled as he disappeared toward the promontory to the north.

"I hope I do."

"Did you see that?" a sailor asked, climbing the mast toward Lukan. "A dragon. A real dragon. I've heard tales, but I've never seen one before." The young man paused, gape-jawed in awe.

"Aye, I saw it. Legend says that dragons bring good weather."

"Let's hope. Not good to have to huddle belowdecks in a gale. Especially on your first voyage." He grinned widely again. "I'm Joe, come to relieve you. The new cook has quite a spread laid out for the passengers. Crew's fare is not quite so grand. But better than the usual dried journey food."

Lukan's mouth watered and his stomach growled. He'd tasted a few of the delicacies Skeller could create out of grass, water, and song. This looked to be a grand beginning of a magnificent journey. Later tonight he'd summon Val and share some of the wonders of sea travel with her. And have her pass on the information that Rejiia was aboard.

Three S'murghin days I have lain in this pitiful excuse for a bed. Flea-ridden, stinking straw covered in a tick so coarse it would chafe me raw had I not brought my own linens, blankets, and down pillows. By the great Simeon, what I wouldn't give for enough power to calm the rocking decks and raise a steady tailwind.

The long rolling waves grow as the sea deepens beneath them and there is no shore for them to break upon. The ship barely plows through them. My minions tell me that we weathered a mild storm.

I don't care. My stomach heaves with every lurch of the deck.

And we wallow, traversing only a few miles each day. I swear I could swim to the Big Continent faster than this scow. If I could swim. The cat in me shudders in extreme distaste at the idea of soaking my fur. But I no longer wear fur. I frequently bathe and enjoy it. Then, too, I am reminded of the sight of a dragon skewering a monster fish the first day at sea.

My stomach rebels at the thought of eating anything. The rancid water in the barrels stinks of stale fish and rotting plants.

"My lady, you would feel better above decks," mincing little Bette says from right beside me.

"No," I reply through clenched teeth. If I open my mouth further I will hurl. If I had anything left in my stomach but burning bile. The image of spewing over her carefully brushed gown with its tidy darns and mended seams lightens my mood.

Then Geon, with his scarred face, muscles his way into the

*tiny cabin, all I could afford for the three of us. Not a prob-
lem until I took ill. He scowls at me—but then the burns on
his face drag his mouth into a perpetual frown. He has
known pain and can draw power from that. And he gives
pain so deliciously.*

*He scoops me up into his deceptively strong arms. He
stands tall and skinny, with overly long arms and legs giving
the impression he has no more strength or stiffness than a
scarecrow.*

*"My lady, you need fresh air. The closeness of the cabin
will poison you if you remain still any longer." He barely
breathes deep as he lifts me and carries me to the steep ladder
they call a stairway. Even my Geon cannot carry me up, but
he pushes and prods and finally with both hands cupping my
bum he shoves me through the hatch.*

*My head emerges through the square hole just as the ship
lurches once more. My stomach follows suit with a lurch of
its own.*

*Laughter surrounds me from the crew. Worst of all, Lu-
kan, the magician's brat, smirks from his seat on a coil of
rope. He makes no derisive sound, but I see it in his eyes and
the flutter of his hands as he mends a line with a fat and
clumsy splice.*

*I send a waning tendril of magic his way, unraveling the
two rope ends so that he must start over.*

*He sighs in frustration. That restores me more than the
fresh air and heightening breeze. He will know more than
frustration before I am through with him. Before I break his
will and make him my slave.*

*"Bette, tonight you will seduce the boy. Take him in the
pile of spare canvas in the stern. Make him beg for more and
more of your attentions. Drag him into our thrall any way
you can."*

CHAPTER 12

ROBB BREATHED THROUGH his mouth, trying not to gag as the stench coming from the cell three doors down grew. *Rotten magic.* That was the only way to describe it. As if a dozen skunks had loosed their stream uncontrollably while sleeping off a drunk from overripe apples fermenting in the sun.

After three days he'd almost gotten used to the stink. Three days of pacing four steps around his cell, of stretching out on a pallet of straw that hadn't been freshened in moons. It stank too, of sweat and urine and other things. And his beard itched with bugs and a rash as well as new growth.

Idly he scratched at the bugbites on his face, chest, and legs. Maigret would slap his hand away from the irritation. He could almost hear her say, "Scratching only makes it worse." But then she'd apply a soothing lotion, letting her hands linger, caress, soothe, and delight.

He sighed and scratched again. Maigret was a long, long way away, and so were her love and her potions.

His throat closed as his stomach rebelled at a new wave of the odor sneaking under and around the warped door. Not warped enough for him to manipulate into opening without a key, though.

A scream of terror and pain.

The derisive laughter of Lokeen enjoying himself.

Another scream that faded into whimpers.

Stumbling footsteps outside his door. One man. Then two. And the distinctive sound of retching.

Robb's imagination filled in the details.

Stargods! The king had fed someone to the Krakatrice. Deliberately. And he watched in glee as a perceived enemy died horribly.

Was he next?

Maria clenched her fists and drove them into her mouth. She bit down hard to keep from screaming in outrage.

"This has to stop, my lady," Frederico whispered as he wormed his way upward from his knees in the dark corner of this side corridor where he'd lost his breakfast.

"What can *I* do? I am but a deformed dwarf, not fit to lead, let alone rule."

The guard and his companion stared at her strangely. As if they expected her—the forgotten younger sister of the late queen—to assume the crown and order the soldiers to seize Lokeen and feed him to his own torturers.

"The high priestess and all of her council decreed at my birth that I may never take the throne," she murmured. "It would be a grave insult to the Great Mother." As if she needed to explain that again. And again.

"There is no one else, lady."

"I have cousins who are hale and hearty—fertile." She wasn't certain she could even mate with a man without a great deal of pain and suffering.

The men said nothing, letting her search her mind for a solution. A relative. Anyone other than Lokeen.

"He is an abomination in the eyes of the Great Mother," a meek voice from the back of the circle of soldiers muttered. "How can She look on you with disfavor when *he* commits heresy every day he breathes?"

"I do not know. I do not *know*." But the idea of taking

responsibility for the entire kingdom frightened her to immobility. Her knees turned to jelly.

"There are dozens, hundreds of men in the city who would willingly become your champion if you would only grant one of them the Spearhead of Destiny."

Maria blanched. She had no right.

The world tilted a bit around her and she feared she'd fall. A strong arm crept around her waist and kept her upright. She cherished the warmth and comfort of the man's touch for a moment. No one ever thought to touch her, hug her, throw an arm around her in friendship. She missed being touched more than anything since her sister, Lokeen's wife, the queen, had died.

Her mind drifted back to the last time Yolanda had hugged her. The day of her wedding.

"Oh, Maria, the dress is perfect!" Yolanda had squealed in delight, more like a twelve year old with a new pony than a woman about to take the crown of an ancient and powerful city-state. She stooped to wrap Maria in a tight hug. Maria returned the embrace.

"The deep green Tambrin lace from SeLennica offsets the white silk nicely, and is symbolic of the fertility of both you and the lands you rule," Maria had said, tweaking one of the soft drapes of fabric that fell from hip to floor like a static waterfall.

"But the white is so stark, with so little contrast with my hair and skin." Yolanda pouted as she surveyed her image in the polished silver mirror.

"White too is an important symbol. You are not yet married, available to name a consort to help uphold your rule."

Yolanda blushed.

And Maria knew that she was no longer virgin, might even be pregnant. That was also suitable. But it also meant that she was still enamored of Lokeen and likely to name him her consort and husband as well as champion.

After that day, all of Yolanda's hugs had been reserved

for her husband and sons. None left over for her sister, who had been dismissed to the servants' quarters by Lokeen within hours of their marriage.

"Bless you," she breathed to Frederico when the world stopped spinning and the breeze ceased to buffet her.

Breeze? Indoors? Half a level above the deepest dungeon?

And then she saw it. A pale square on the floor at her feet.

The guard who had held her upright bent to retrieve it. "A letter, lady," he said quietly. "Addressed to the Queen of Amazonia."

"I am not the queen," she insisted.

The men did not have to say that a letter dispatched by magic would find the intended recipient no matter what.

Quickly she grabbed the precisely folded parchment and inspected the seal. Green encircled by gold. A dragon impressed into the wax. This could only have come from Darville, king by the grace of the dragons, of Coronnan.

"This is a reply to His Majesty's missive of a few days ago," she said simply, sorting her thoughts as she prepared to deliver it by hand. This should divert Lokeen from his grisly pastime.

Maria couldn't save the man who had preached loudly and publicly in the Temple Square against the king. But perhaps she could gain some time for the wizard.

"All five of you, come with me. You must swear to remove me safely from the king's presence if this news displeases him."

They all slapped clenched right fists over their hearts and nodded grimly. Faint reassurance for Maria. And yet, their determined loyalty gave her hope that she could find a way to end Lokeen's tyranny.

Lily stumbled over her own feet. The world tilted and the sun near blinded her. She pressed against her temples with both hands, trying to contain the headache that pounded deeply into her brain and down her neck. "I'm worn out. Three days without sleep while I nursed the sick has left me so tired I'm dizzy," she lied to herself.

The cold sweat on her brow told her the truth.

She leaned against the rough daub-and-wattle wall of the nearest hut, turning her back on the central fire pit where two women listlessly cut parsnips into the communal stew—more like soup than stew. Hopefully none of the villagers saw her moment of weakness. She needn't have worried, they were all weak, weary, and frightened.

A wisp of white along the top of the hill drew her gaze like a lodestone to the pole. Too late in the day for morning mist. Too solid to be fog, and yet too wispy to be more than just air and water. No person could wear white that dazzling while working the land. No animal would sport fur that bright and attention grabbing.

"Are you waiting for me, Death?" she whispered. Her feet trod in that direction without her thinking about it. She couldn't stay put if she wanted.

Each step toward that drifting form eased her headache and cooled her fevered brow.

(I wait for those who need me.) The husky voice spoke into her mind like a dragon. But this was no dragon filled with life and joy and wisdom.

"Haven't you taken enough souls this year? Why are you so hungry?" Lily demanded as she crested the hill.

Death eased toward the copse and the spreading graveyard. In three days, three new cairns marked the graves of elders and young alike.

(I do not decree who dies. I am. That is all I know.)

"You are too greedy! Leave these people alone. They've lost too much already."

(Who are you, to advocate for strangers?)

"I am . . . I am . . ." And suddenly she forgot who she was, how she had made a new home in this village, why she cared.

The white mist reached out a ghostly hand to touch Lily's brow, then jerked it away as if burned. *(You are not for me. Not yet. Though I will come to you eventually. For now, know that you alone in this village are safe from me.)*

Lily fell into darkness, a sharp wind ripped around her. Falling, falling, deeper and deeper into the well of . . . another time and place . . . into . . .

She woke with a jerk, inside the tiny hut assigned to her, the home of an elder who had lived alone and died surrounded by friends. Her fire had dropped to embers and ashes. Sweat cooled on her body.

In the distance a dragon crooned in relief.

But her heart raced as if she had run uphill all the way to the dragon lair.

"Welcome back to life," Mistress Sella croaked. The crone threw a handful of kindling on the fire and placed a small pot of water over the coals. "You'll be needing a bit more of the fairy bells and willow bark a'fore you tend the sick again. I'll be next." The hunchbacked old woman backed out of the hut that was too small for even her to stand upright in.

Lily's heart continued to trip and slide in an odd and too-fast drumbeat. Arrhythmic, not the music of life. She touched her moist forehead and found a cold spot in the center. Death had touched her but left her living. Why?

Only her pounding heart and ragged breathing answered her. Answered her and told her what she needed to do.

She had to find the strength to awaken her minimal magical talent.

Dragons, help me!

Silence rang inside her head.

CHAPTER 13

"LINDA, I NEED to speak with Maigret!" a voice came through the scrying bowl.

Souska paused in grinding feverfew flowers and leaves in the mortar. Mixed with some chamomile and a little honey in a tisane, this concoction should relieve Maigret of the headache that felled her three days ago, when the aborted message from Robb had broken through the summons to Marcus.

She suspected that the University Chancellor suffered more from heartache. Souska didn't know a remedy for that other than bringing home her mistress' husband.

She sent a brief prayer that Lukan would succeed in finding his master and freeing him.

Souska raced to light the candle as Linda leaned over the bowl and informed the caller of the situation, quietly, as if she didn't want to disturb Maigret in the next room, all the while knowing she would. "Lily, how are you able to initiate a summons?" Linda asked. Puzzlement drew deep lines outward from her eyes and down her chin.

Lily? Oh, yes, one of Lukan's sisters. The one who'd gone wandering on her own after some dreadful accident. Lukan had only said that she needed to heal her mind and soul and could only do that by helping replant where the flood had wiped the land clean.

"Because I have to," came the weary reply.

Souska turned her back on her fellow apprentice in politeness. But she still listened.

"Linda, I need a sack of feverfew, another of willow bark, and ... and ... hellebore." The last word came out on a whisper that sent heat and cold flashing up and down from Souska's gut to her head.

"No, no, no, NO!" Linda replied.

Souska searched her memory for her gran's words on the nature of the plant. "Delightful to look at, lovely when left, deadly if used wrong."

"What are you concocting, Lily? I thought you were nurturing and planting, curing the land, playing healer."

"Everywhere the Krakatrice eggs have hatched—even after the magicians and dragons killed the snakes—the land ... There is a miasma that follows where their blood soaks into the dirt. Entire villages are dying. If I can break their fevers and steady their heartbeats, I think I can give them enough time to heal on their own. Until I find a cure. You have to wake Maigret and get her working on it. I don't have the supplies, or the knowledge, or the skills that she does." Lily sounded desperate. And frightened.

"Where are you, Lily," Linda demanded. Her voice sounded calm and controlled, but sweat beaded her brow and her hand shook as she waved to Souska to interrupt their mistress' sleep.

Since the joined summons spell, Souska really only needed a thought to penetrate Maigret's mind with simple communications. *You are needed.* She couldn't phrase her thoughts any more simply.

"No, don't come here. Don't let anyone come. They'll sicken too. Just send me what I ask for. Quickly."

A quick glance over Linda's shoulder showed only a pale blob of a face surrounded by a red-gold mop of unruly curls that might have been as much aura as hair. The fuzziness of the image proved her lack of magical strength. Or was it physical weakness from illness and fatigue that kept her from appearing clearly in the glass?

"And what's to keep you from getting sick too?" Linda asked. The very question Souska needed to put forward.

"I . . . I had a bit of it earlier. I can't get it again." A long pause. "I think Death awakened my magical talent. Not much. Just enough to call for help, and see . . . and see auras so I know which holes in the life spirit to fill."

"Just how sick are you?" Maigret asked, coming in from her private study attached to the workroom. She had a cot in there as well as her books and supplies. Her eyes looked strained and hollow with deep shadows marring their usual liveliness. "Sounds more like a fever dream than . . . a vision of Death. No one sees Death and lives."

Souska handed Maigret a cup of the hot tisane. She nodded her thanks and drank deeply. She sighed in relief, almost immediately.

"My fever broke on its own," Lily said. "My pulse is still rapid, but . . . I can control it with a tisane made from foxglove leaves."

Souska barely heard her admission. She turned her attention to finding the stores of the requested feverfew and willow bark. Common treatments for fever and body aches. Foxglove to steady the heartbeat . . . Why had she asked for hellebore if she used foxglove, a more proper name for fairy bells? Both were dangerous poisons unless used properly and judiciously. Maigret *and* Souska's grandmother had told her never to use foxglove unless there was no other possibility of saving a life, and then only in tiny doses, building up bit by bit until she found the right one for that particular patient.

Maigret never mentioned hellebore, pretended the plant did not exist. The difference between cure and death was tiny, barely a crumb of dried and ground leaves changed the dosage, and a big strong man could be more sensitive than a still-growing teenager. Or the opposite. A healer could never know the difference until too late.

Lily had to have learned much from her mother, Brevelan, and from Maigret. But she was only a new journeyman.
Did she know enough to save her patients and not kill
them?

"Tell me every nuance of every patient," Maigret demanded. She pushed Linda aside and leaned over the bowl,
cupping her hands around the rim, effectively shutting out
her apprentices. "Foxglove is dangerous enough. But it is
safer than hellebore."

"I've tried foxglove. It helps. But it is not enough. I need
to slow the heart rate more and lower the pressure of the
blood within the heart and veins. Hellebore is the only answer," Lily insisted.

Souska strained to hear. Linda joined her by the work-
bench, looking a little disgruntled. After all, she'd answered
the summons for their mistress and for the past three days
deflected other masters from bothering the woman while
she ached and grieved.

"What can we do?" Linda asked. A stray tendril of
brown-gold hair escaped her blue scarf and slipped over
her cheek. The former princess never allowed a hint of less
than precise grooming to show.

"My gran showed me how to use it, how to dilute it so
that it worked without poisoning—if used cautiously,"
Souska whispered. "A long, long time ago, her people suffered an unknown plague from far away. Along with a trace
of hellebore they used a moss growing on leaf litter—not on
a tree or rock—from the north bank of a creek soaked in
algae, and . . . and a mushroom spiking above the moss,
growing with it in sympathy and harmony. All must be dried
on a rack over embers, then crumpled into the willow bark
tea."

She hung her head as if ashamed. Old remedies like that
were held in contempt by magician healers.

"My mother says that sometimes deep magic isn't the
only way to do things," Linda snorted. "Not everyone can
look into an ailing body, find the alien disease and force it

to leave. Why else would we study all the properties of plants and minerals and combinations and such?"

"I know a place where the moss and mushrooms grow together," Souska offered.

"And I know of a still pool where algae grows around the edges, sliming rocks and embankments alike."

Souska looked into the other girl's eyes and saw a twinkle of agreement and amusement there. "Where do we find the hellebore?" she whispered.

"In the far corner of Maigret's own herb garden. She keeps some on hand for emergencies."

"Fresh roots work better than dried."

"Dried is easier to control."

"Let's do it!"

Together, they crept toward the door. "Take clean linen to gather your remedy, and be careful not to touch those mushrooms with bare hands or you'll leech the curative property from them," Maigret called after them, showing that she was aware of their entire conversation. Her face looked more animated and less worried. She had a problem to solve, and solve it she would.

"Souska, when next you summon Lukan, tonight if possible, ask him if he has heard anything about this illness on the Big Continent."

"Yes, ma'am." A tiny glow warmed Souska's heart. She had a reason to try out her new summoning skills. And she could use them to talk to *her* journeyman.

"While you have his attention, ask him if he has located my husband in Amazonia yet." Some of the worry crept back into her face and her voice. "I'll find a dragon who can take you safely to Lily. Can't risk having a master or journeyman transport you. Don't want to risk you either, but I have to. We've had enough witch hunts in the last ten years to last three lifetimes or more. If Lily kills so much as one patient with her remedy, there will be no stopping the hysteria. Now, make certain you wear a mask and wash your hands any time you touch *anything*. You must instruct her properly on how to use the hellebore. You can learn more that is suited to your talent from Lily than you can about big magic from her brother."

Stars shone brighter out at sea, Lukan thought as he lay back in his nest of folded canvas in the stern of the ship. He wasn't sure why, but the tiny points of light in the deep black sky looked larger, scintillating with a kind of amusement at the antics of people on the planet below.

He watched for a long time, not thinking, just breathing. He needed calm in mind as well as body after a hard day of work—no harder than throwing spells right, left, and sideways for his masters, but different. A part of him half-wished he could sleep in the crow's nest, but his crewmates would wonder at that. The highest point on the ship was for watching, not sleeping. They didn't know his affinity for "up." They didn't know his tricks for staying in place.

The stars blurred as his eyes drifted closed. He wanted to keep their beauty in the front of his mind and vision a little longer.

But what was that? He almost sat up with a jolt as his imagination drew silvery blue lines between the stars, connecting them in a giant web of energy. "Just like ley lines," he breathed.

Squinting, he forced his eyes to focus more closely on the lines, just as if he were looking at them beneath the Kardia. "I wonder . . ." Slowly, gently, he cleared his mind with deep breaths, finding the pole along his right side without the aid of the land. Fully centered, he reached up a hand and drew energy into him. A wee tingle against his fingertips, then a full vibration through his hand and arm. He pulled harder and felt his blood sing in renewal.

"Lily? Val? Are you out there? Can you hear me?"

A sleepy hum followed the lines of energy down through his senses. His vision shifted slightly to the left, from blue toward dark purple. "Go back to sleep, Val. You need your rest to grow strong." He clenched his fist to close the communication.

"Reaching for me, sailor boy?" an uneducated female voice rasped against his senses.

His connection to the life energy of the stars shattered. "Who?" He had to fight to shift his focus from the thrall of the ley lines and the warmth of love for his sister to the stars.

"Just me. Saw you giving me the eye earlier on deck." The woman knelt down as if to crawl onto the folded sailcloth beside him.

A flicker of light from the mast lamp showed only her silhouette. A few feminine curves. He only knew of two women on board. Rejiia and her servant.

This wasn't Rejiia. Nothing long and elegant about her. Short, stocky, and old. She must be older than Rejiia—late thirties, the sorceress' real age, not the midtwenties she looked. Lukan remembered blotchy skin and a hooked nose, dull eyes, and lank, mouse-brown hair.

Then he caught a whiff of enticing musk that reminded him of Rejiia. It overlay the scent of garlic and body sweat. That hint of Rejiia in the mix told him all he needed to know. The woman—was her name Bette?—borrowed some of her lady's magic to seduce Lukan.

He'd just filled himself with the ley lines' magical energy. It bolstered his resolve and his ability to resist.

His glass vibrated loudly inside his shirt beneath his heart. He pulled it out just enough to note the golden swirl inside the circle. "Excuse me, miss. I'm needed elsewhere. You can go back to your mistress. Either your imagination ran wild or someone lied to you." He heaved himself up from his nest and headed for the stern.

No candle or bowl of water. But he had the ocean and his finger to conjure a bit of flame for a moment. "Lukan here," he said, leaning over the deck rail, with glass and hands positioned properly above the water.

"Glenndon here," his brother replied on a chuckle. "When did we start speaking like dragons?"

"Too long ago to remember. What is so important you have to disrupt my sleep?" He wasn't truly angry anymore, but the need to goad Glenndon remained deeply seeded.

"I know you need your beauty sleep, little brother, but this is important."

"Important enough to break the rules by summoning a journeyman on journey?"

"Yes. King Lokeen renewed his courtship of Lady Ariiell. He had a letter magically dispatched to King Darville. We think Robb threw the spell. Samlan is dead. All the other master magicians are accounted for."

Lukan loosed a long exhale. "I figured Robb was in Amazonia. I'm headed there now."

"Smart boy. Robb managed a very brief and aborted summons to Maigret begging for help."

"Master Marcus did manage to find him once, in a prison."

"Yes. We do not know what kind of coercion King Lokeen is using but it has to be strong, possibly torturous, if he's forcing Robb to throw magic. Freeing him will not be easy. Master Marcus and I agree, you may call for help if you need it."

Lukan looked upward, wondering if his new friend Verdii followed the ship even at night.

"Thanks, big brother. I'll remember that."

"Lukan, this isn't a competition. If you need help, summon me."

"If the situation becomes so dire that the dragons and I can't handle it, I'll call."

"Promise me you won't try to bull your way through this on your own!"

"I don't . . ."

"You do. Now promise me."

"I promise that if I can't see another way out, I'll summon you."

"All you need is a thought directed toward me. We are bound by blood and by love. And by memory. You are my brother."

Part of Lukan wanted to shout, "Half brother." But another part of his heart swelled with ... emotions he didn't want to acknowledge. "Good night big brother. You need your beauty sleep. I need to think about some things."

Glenndon smiled. "When in doubt, trust the dragons." He closed the communication.

Lukan doused the flame on his fingertip. It was growing a little too hot to hold much longer. Then he pocketed his glass and looked around to make sure Bette didn't linger to interfere again. The deck was open and empty except for the two crewmen on watch and a third in the crow's nest.

A jaunty tune came to his mind. He whistled the first notes of one of Skeller's more ribald bar tunes.

A blast of anger shot from the hatch leading belowdecks to the passenger cabins. He stepped neatly aside and continued on his way, still whistling into the wind.

CHAPTER 14

MARIA GINGERLY HELD between two fingers the thin parchment with the seal of Darville de Draconis, king by the grace of the dragons of Coronnan, as if it might burn her. The worn sheet spoke of the sender's lack of respect for the recipient—for her, since the letter had landed at her feet. She hoped the foreign king meant unconcern for Lokeen, who must eventually receive this letter. The thinness also betrayed a second sealed sheet within the outer layer.

She sat in the padded chair—the one her sister had had made especially to her measure—in her private sitting room adjacent to the kitchen stair, one leg tucked under her and sunshine from the broad window bathing her in gentle warmth.

"You have to open it, my lady. It is addressed to you; dispatched to you by magic," Frederico whispered from the stool at her feet. He had removed her boot and massaged her twisted foot with knowing fingers, easing the cramps out of her arch and toes. Now he hid his face and expression from her by bowing his head and letting his straight black hair fall forward over his swarthy skin.

"But I did not dispatch the first letter that required this reply."

"King Darville wants to talk to you, not to Lokeen.

Looks to me that the foreigner sees what too many people here refuse to: Lokeen is not our rightful king."

"Hush!" Maria looked anxiously around her room, fearful of eavesdroppers and spies.

"Only stating the right of it."

"I know. But this seems so wrong. I am not queen. I have no right to *be* queen."

"More right than him what sits on the throne and wears your sister's crown," Frederico mumbled under his breath.

But Maria heard every word.

"Need me to open that, break the seal?" he continued, letting his fingers go slack on her aching foot.

"Not you. If I commit treason by doing this, then I must do it alone and not transfer any of the crime or guilt to you, my faithful friend."

"Then you'll need a hot knife to slide under the wax without breaking the seal." He released her and reached for a candle and a penknife from her worktable to his right. When he had lit the candle with flint and steel he passed the short-bladed knife through the flame several times.

"It's hot enough," Maria said, anxious to get through this ordeal so she could make decisions on the outcome.

"Not quite." Frederico stalled her by holding up one finger. Three heartbeats later he nodded, as the blade began taking on a reddish tinge.

Maria slid the blade beneath the blob of dark green wax, satisfied that the seal released from the parchment quite easily. She withdrew the blade and handed it back to her coconspirator. The letter unfolded almost of its own volition. Two pages. The one inside was addressed to Lokeen, no title or city, just his name. She read the first sentence of the outside page—the one addressed to the Queen of Amazonia—and gasped.

Handfasting is a sacred and time-honored custom in Coronnan, beneficial to those who have no access to civil or religious marriage ceremonies. At this time we

*have no reason to dissolve the union between Ariiell
and Mardoll. Neither party agrees to such an annul-
ment. Lokeen, who styles himself as King of Amazonia, must seek a bride elsewhere.*

*The daughter of the deposed lord Laislac has re-
nounced her title, all connection to her father, and all
rights as potential regent on behalf of her son. She has
refused to testify on Laislac's behalf at his trial for treason. Her written statement against him is enough evidence to convict him.*

"Styles himself as king? Them's powerful words. Amazonia's most powerful ally and trading partner doesn't recognize Lokeen as rightful ruler." Frederico sat back and
whistled through his teeth.

"I need to think on this," Maria said, letting the parchment flutter to her lap. She broke the seal without a crest on
the second page and scanned it. It said much the same thing
but with less damning words, affirming Lady Ariiell's re-
fusal to annul the handfasting. This was the one meant for
the king to see.

"I think you should burn both pages."

"No, Frederico. I need to hide mine until I make my decision. I may need Darville's words and his intact seal as a
weapon in the coming weeks."

"I know a place neither the usurper nor his guard captain would think to look."

"A place you can access to show to others of like thinking?"

He pushed Maria's boot back on her foot and laced it
tightly. Then he stood straight, tucked the folded parchment
into his tunic, and backed out of the room, clenching his fist
against his heart in silent salute to her.

The sound of keys rattling in the lock of his cell sent Robb's
heart racing in trepidation. Three days Lokeen had left him

alone. Three days to ponder what drove the man to the extremes of torture and hideous execution. Three days to wonder if he would be next.

"Come," said the guard Robb had nicknamed Scurry— so like the little gray animals, with quick darting movements and furtive looks in all directions before and after each dash from here to there.

"Where?" Robb sat up on his pallet but did not rise or proceed any closer to the door. As uncomfortable as it was, the cell was safe. A known place with known dangers. Unlike the cell two doors down the corridor.

"His Majesty has need of you," Scurry replied with his usual jerking of his neck as he scanned every corner and shadow inside and outside of the cell.

"I have no need of him." Robb shifted, as if to lie back down.

"You will come," Badger, Scurry's broad partner, announced in stentorian tones that echoed up and down the corridor. If Lokeen hadn't guessed at Robb's reluctance before, he knew it now.

With a big sigh of resignation he moved stiffly to his feet. As he straightened his back, he groaned, not because he hurt or had weakened much more over the last three days, but because he needed the advantage of his captor underestimating him.

"Where are we going?" Robb asked as he pulled his old blue robe over his head. They'd taken the black and red one from him, fearing that the cloth would grant him power.

It didn't even grant him peace of mind.

"His Majesty does not tell us anything more than that he has need of you," Scurry said. He bobbed as if bowing out of respect to Robb but afraid to acknowledge it. In other words, he tried to please everyone, ever-fearful for his own safety.

Robb shuffled out of his cell and held his breath. The stink of Krakatrice feeding had subsided, but just the thought of it gagged him yet again. He kept his breaths slow

and shallow until they'd mounted the first set of stairs into
the cellars. Once they'd cleared those two levels and he
reached the half-submerged kitchen level he drew a long
breath of the hot air, redolent of cooking meats, roasting
vegetables, and fresh, flowing water.

In the moons he'd been here, it had only rained twice.
His mind and body longed for the sweet moist air of home.

"I thought this land had recovered from its desert ori-
gins," he said idly, not realizing he'd spoken until he heard
his own words. He'd been living inside his head too long.

"Last year or so we're going back to the dryland ways. If
'tweren't for the three rivers coming down off the mountains to the east and the sweet springs popping up out of
nowhere, we'd be dried-out husks," Scurry admitted.

"A year? Um, do you know when my predecessor, the
other mage, began counseling His Majesty?" Robb counted
back. Samlan left the Circle of Magicians last spring. This
was high summer, and Robb had been here half that lapsed
time. How fast had Samlan worked to gain Lokeen's confidence? Or had Samlan's betrayal begun long before his final exile?

"Himself 'as been dropping in and out unannounced for
years. Didn't come to stay 'til last equinox," Badger said, as
quietly as he could, but his voice still carried to the far ends
of the cellar. "Disappeared just before the solstice."

That explained a lot. Samlan had been unhappy with
Jaylor as Senior Magician for a long time. Jaylor dispatching
Glenndon to the court had been the final act to sever the
older magician's confidence in the elected leader. Of course,
Samlan had no way of knowing that Glenndon was King
Darville's son and was needed in the capital as heir. Most of
the Circle thought only that the young magician had been
sent as Jaylor's spy, or possibly to counsel the king on behalf
of the magicians. A situation that spawned a great deal of
jealousy, neither side willing to share information.

"Do you ride?" Lokeen asked abruptly the moment Robb
and his guards moved into the ground floor reception rooms.

"I used to ride dragons into battle against the Krakatrice all the time," Robb replied, almost too tired to guard his tongue.

Lokeen frowned. "Steeds. Do you ride steeds?"

"I've done so, but not for a long time." Not since his journeying days with Maigret.

"As long as you can keep your seat. We aren't going far today." Lokeen marched past Robb toward the grand double doors that opened into a walled courtyard.

Robb had to blink rapidly against the bright sunlight bouncing off the light-colored stone walls and paving stones. He hadn't seen true daylight in so long! He had to stand with his eyes closed, drinking in the air and light, letting it bathe him in hints of freedom.

When he opened his eyes again, he shuddered in fear. This stone-walled courtyard looked so much like another in the center of Coronnan City. The courtyard of the old University of Magicians. He'd been only a boy, a new apprentice, when he'd left that University to join Jaylor in the mountain refuge that became the new University. So when Jaylor summoned him to the city with two apprentices and three journeymen to help defend the city against Krakatrice, a rogue had been able to insert the image, the feel, and the smell of this courtyard in place of Robb's diluted memories.

He'd landed here. In that first moment of confusion that always beset a magician at the end of a long and tricky transport, Lokeen and his armed guards had been waiting for him. He'd shouted for his students to run and hide, get away any way they could.

He had no way of knowing if any of them had.

"Come, the farm awaits us," Lokeen said on a giggle, gesturing eagerly toward the saddled steeds awaiting them. "My farm. My precious farm where they breed my pets!" The king fairly leapt upon his mount, laughing with glee.

"He is insane," Maria whispered, appearing beside Robb. "Power has gone to his head. The power of magic. The delusions fostered by those hideous monsters." Then she re-treated into the shadowy interior, disappearing as if she'd never been there.

"My thoughts exactly," Robb muttered, and warily mounted the placid mare awaiting him.

CHAPTER 15

LUKAN BIT INTO the silver coin the ship's captain handed him, like he'd seen his shipmates do. The metal tasted sharp and made his teeth ache.

His staff, lashed into its canvas cover and strung across his back, remained inert, not warning of deceit.

"Test the other two coins," Skeller hissed in his ear.

Lukan did so. Then he looked at all three together on his palm. King Darville's distinctive profile stood out from the worn and tarnished background. He had to stare a moment as the image blurred a tiny bit and became Glenndon's. He shook his head clear of that little bit of prophecy. "But . . ."

"Accept them and move on," Skeller ordered. He grabbed Lukan's elbow and yanked him away from the line of sailors waiting to collect their pay.

"Do the merchants here accept coins from Coronnan?" Lukan asked as he and the bard negotiated the narrow gangplank reserved for the crew to depart. The passengers had a wider plank with a rope railing to guide them to the dock.

Rejiia followed the scarred man down the plank, with her loathsome maid right behind her. None of them looked his way, but his back itched as if they watched him keenly.

"No, they only want Amazonian coins with the profile of the first Maria stamped into them." Skeller searched the crowded and bustling area for something.

Lukan hoped he looked for a way away from the ship's berth and the stench of dead fish and rotting seaweed beneath the heavy brine of the salt water.

Not to mention Rejiia and her servants counting and organizing their luggage. The man shouldered three large packs and hefted two oversize satchels. Lukan had no desire to confront either of the women again.

With another yank on Lukan's elbow, the pair headed inland, between two featureless stone buildings that were probably warehouses. "It's a common trick. Pay us in dragini so we have to sign on for the return voyage to use the money, then pay us in Amazonian sand dollars when we get there so we have to sign on again." He flashed Lukan a wicked grin.

"But what good are the coins to us? We don't want to go back to Coronnan. At least not yet." Lukan diverted a small part of his attention to scan the skies for a sign of his elusive dragon friend.

(Verdii here. I follow.)

Lukan spared a moment to look more intently for a flip of iridescent wing or a lacework of green.

Nothing.

Verdii chuckled into the back of his mind, and he heard a big splash far out in the ocean, almost to the horizon.

That wasn't close by human standards. But for dragon wings . . .

"Come on," Skeller insisted. "I know a moneychanger. It will cost you half a coin, but it's worth it not to have to argue with merchants about the purity of the silver."

Trust the dragons, Da had always said. Glenndon too. Lukan was a little closer to accepting advice from them both. Only a little, but in this case, he had to.

As Lukan followed his traveling companion through the narrow alleyways of the port into the scrambled openness of the marketplace his magic began to tingle. Every time he turned, the staff banged against a stall, or a shopper, or something. He paused long enough to extract it and let it settle into his left hand. The tool felt warm and welcomed his touch, almost as if every time he held it, the wood molded to his hand. Walking with it, hearing and feeling a satisfying *kerthunk* every time it touched the bleached sandstone walkway, anchored him to the ground. Every step with the staff became more natural. His legs swung forward in an easy stride.

Did the brightly clad people who flowed through the district with sun-darkened faces and white head coverings make way for him? Or was it Skeller they fell back for. Their gazes followed the bard, lingering on the harp case slung across his back. He carried the instrument as comfortably as Lukan carried his staff. No awkwardness. He knew where Telynnia was at any given moment and how to walk so that she didn't touch anything or anyone but Skeller.

The deeper they moved among the striped tents and awnings the more a sense of wrongness crept up Lukan's back.

Finally, when Skeller stopped before a solid white tent with a black pennant atop the center pole, hanging limply in the still, hot air, Lukan realized what made him so uneasy.

No one talked. Even when they jostled each other, or sought to bargain for the same item. Not a word.

He heard a faint susurration in the back of his head, sort of like dragons whispering nonsense words. But ... it must be his telepathy picking up thoughts. Lots of them, all at once so that no one idea or image came through clearly.

The normal sounds of seabirds calling, waves sloshing against the strand, and fabric flapping as people moved had masked the absence of speech.

And the presence of the lad dressed in blacksmith leathers who crept behind them, always just out of sight but still *there*. His thoughts were fully masked, like a magician with complete barriers around his mind.

Skeller gestured Lukan forward and opened his mouth to speak.

Lukan placed a finger against his lips, then passed him his three coins.

Skeller started to protest, then cocked his head as if

listening. His eyes widened in shock. Abruptly he turned
back to the moneychanger—a man in a loose robe of vertical white and black stripes—and completed the transaction
quite quickly with hand gestures. The man's hat, swaths of
alternating black and white wrapped around his brown hair
and trailing down his back, bobbed with every head movement as he looked rapidly between Skeller's harp case and
the coins moving from hand to hand.

When Skeller stepped back and bowed deeply, Lukan
shifted his attention back to the crowd. Hand gestures suddenly took on meaning for him. And the lad, visible only by
his *absence*, felt significant too. Then he followed his companion away from the busy market toward low stone houses
that marched inland toward a tall, fortified building built
upon a slight rise; a sprawling building with a round tower
that dominated the city. Instead of a wide railed platform,
the tower boasted a conical roof with long narrow
windows—and a lacy pattern that was repeated the full
height of the building. A narrow walkway with a decorative
stone parapet encircled the base of the cone.

At last Skeller jogged across an open square filled with
fountains. Tall trees with long fronds instead of branches
with individual leaves swayed in the light breeze created by
the moving water. Thick succulent plants arranged around
pebbled paths—each path a different color of stone—led a
wanderer inward toward the refreshing sparkling water-
drops playing in the air as they fell inevitably toward the
pool where they mingled together. Then Skeller stopped
before a building that could only be a temple, a temple in
miniature. The columns supporting a broad overhang and a
domed roof gave it away. It looked like every temple Lukan
had ever seen, large or small, this one as small as the neigh-
borhood worship places he'd passed in Coronnan City.
When the bard sank onto the top step, within the shade of
the overhang, Lukan did too.

"What was that all about?" Lukan asked. "Are all your
people mute?"

"Not by choice," Skeller said after a long pause.

"Then what?"

"Couldn't you smell it?"

Lukan thought back to the nearly overwhelming wave of hot air laden with exotic spices, roasting meats and vegetables, sea air, fish. Always fish. And . . . and . . .

"Fear," he whispered.

"Fear," Skeller echoed. "They are afraid to talk. I can only guess what atrocity my father has performed to cause it."

A woman laughed loud and long not far away. It sounded like bells chiming in the wind. "Oh, how delicious. Everyone here is afraid. Deathly afraid. My magic feeds on it and infuses my entire body," Rejiia said from where she stood beside the rim of the fountain in the center of the square. She threw up her arms and spun in exultation, splashing her companions playfully.

I see the bard and the magician hiding in the shadows of this obscure temple. It is famous among my kind, yet deliberately forgotten among the populace. The followers of this hidden goddess live for a bizarre philosophy that no one wants to admit.

They believe that at some point in the far future the people of this world will become so numerous, consume so much land, that food will become scarce. Our need to breed will diminish to a rare few and the rest will embrace members of the same gender for love, companionship, life-mates, and sex, rather than succumb to the primitive instinct to procreate.

It really is an excuse for their attraction to their own kind. Some I have encountered do not realize their true preferences until they encounter their one true love, who just happens to be of the same gender. They make whatever excuses they have to in order to survive in a disapproving society.

No one knows where this prophecy or excuse came from,

yet some say it is as old—or older—than the Stargods them-
selves.

They worship the goddess Helvess.

In the meantime, those few who keep this way of life are
shunned, persecuted, and driven into exile. Some are tortured
and mutilated. They know pain and fear. Some even appre-
ciate the giving and receiving of pain. As do I.

I have borne a child—he lives with his father among the
Rover tribes—and see no reason to have another. Children
deprive me of the pleasures of this life, demand time and at-
tention I care not to give them. So in this, I too am like the
followers of Helvess. I don't care if my lovers are male, or
female, or both at the same time, so long as they give me
pleasure and I can give them pain.

That is why I seek out this small temple for my temporary
refuge in a foreign land. I have heard rumors that one among
these people has access to the king. I need the king in order
to gain political as well as magical power in this world with-
out dragons.

I wonder why the bard and the magician have come here.
Could their bonds of friendship extend deeper? Oh, how de-
licious. I can use their humiliation and guilt to expand my
little coven. I know Bette appreciates lovers of both genders,
though she nurses hurts from Lukan's rejection of her atten-
tions.

Will Geon accept two new men into our group? He will
have to, or leave us. Lukan can tap into ten times the power
Geon can, with or without sex or pain as his fuel. With or
without the books about magic Geon hauls around with him.
He's lowborn and has not enough magic to enter the Univer-
sity. How did he even learn to read? He has no right to know
how to read. But he does, and the esoteric things he learns
can be useful to me.

But what is this? I hear something strange and menacing
on the wind. No! It cannot be. A dragon bellows in triumph
to all who will listen. It has hunted and caught something.
Something menacing to people.

This land has never known dragons. I will not have a dragon in this kingdom. I will not!

And so I enter the temple in search of the one who will introduce me to the king. I must convince the king that the dragons must never, ever, under any circumstances, fly here in Amazonia.

CHAPTER 16

"WHY ARE YOU alive?" Stanil asked accusingly as Lily emerged from Sella's hut.

She blinked away sun dazzle as she stood, slowly and carefully, after stooping low to come through the doorway. She had to pause and let her heartbeat return to normal, or as close to normal as it ever was these days. "Because I came from elsewhere, strong and healthy. My body had not gradually weakened as the miasma became more potent, rising from the ground," she replied as calmly as she could.

Stanil, she noted looked frailer, more gaunt, almost skeletal, as his arms and legs appeared too long without a comfortable layer of flesh. If he hadn't succumbed to the disease by now, he probably wouldn't. Lily had seen no new cases in a day and a half. But if the village headman didn't take care of himself, he'd still be vulnerable to a host of other lethal ailments.

"You should have let Death take you. She touched you and still you live. That's not natural." He turned and stumped away. His own guilt at surviving when his wife and child had died washed over her.

She absorbed his emotions, understood them, and pushed them aside. Startled at how easily she removed herself from deep empathy, she turned to look up at the hilltop.

Death's strange white mist still lurked there. "Did you do this to me?" she whispered.

(Death and life are entwined. You cannot have one without the other.)

"I know that." She paused, chewing on her lip. "I *know* that. Now. Not before."

(Death is like the void. A transition between here and there. You are not ready to enter the void, let alone cross it.)

"Did Mama and Da cross the void together?"

The mist drifted away. *(I have marked you. For now it is a blessing. I cannot take you until* you *call me. Later the blessing will seem a yoke.)*

Lily rubbed the cold spot at the center of her forehead. She hadn't dared look in a basin of water to see if the place where Death had touched her was visible. She detected no difference in skin texture, only temperature. Cold. The deep, bone-chilling breath of Death, in a perfect circle the size of a fingertip.

"Mama blesses you, my lady," a little girl just stretching toward womanhood said shyly. She handed a small pot, scrubbed clean, to Maria at the back door of the kitchen.

"Did she eat the chicken and make broth from the bones?" Maria asked, taking the old dented pot and handing it to a scullery boy.

"Yes, my lady. As you instructed, with the healing herbs. And she and the new babe are thriving now." The girl bobbed a curtsy and backed up one step, preparing to flee.

"Jilla was a valuable soldier. She served our late queen well and does not deserve to die of the milk fever when I can help her," Maria said. "Come to me if she sickens again."

"Yes, my lady." This time the girl did not hesitate to flee up the stairs to the kitchen garden.

Maria turned back to her task and carefully filled a lamp, making sure not a single drop spilled on the worktable of the scullery. The oil wasn't expensive, being the residue of a common tree berry. Still, she hated the thought of wasting any of a useful resource. As Lokeen had wasted the useful resource of the women warriors. Soon enough he would waste more and more essential supplies upon his "pets," the hideous snakes that poisoned everything they touched, especially the minds of those they could manipulate.

Satisfied that the lamp would burn as long as she needed, and then some, she dismissed the guards, Jacko and Jimbo, twin brothers as alike in face and form as two dressed stones in the wall who had taken to following her everywhere. "I shall be safe enough in the treasury," she insisted, when they protested.

The two men looked at each other for confirmation — she could almost see a single thought pass between them — then nodded their compliance. She knew well and good that they would slink behind her and station themselves within steps of the locked and windowless room, deep within the castle and two stories up. In a thousand years, no one had managed to steal from the sacred treasures kept there along with tax moneys and family jewels. Twice in their history the crown had been lost to war, one civil, one an invasion. Those new monarchs had assumed the treasury only after defeating the royal family.

She sensed a third war fermenting among the populace. Before the people rose up in revolution against Lokeen, Maria needed to see that no one had disturbed the items in her charge, including Robb's staff. Lokeen had the glass tucked away in his saddlebag, well insulated in silk.

A hook awaited the lamp to the left of the single doorway into the treasury. A tall man could walk through the portal without stooping, but the lintel would brush his hair. A broad man would have to think twice about entering, and turn sideways or get stuck. Painfully she rose up on tiptoe to secure the lamp. She had to bite her lip and push herself beyond her usual limitations. For one hundred heartbeats she wished she'd kept the guards close so they could perform this chore for her. Then the handle caught on the hook, swayed alarmingly for a moment, and settled to shed a soft glow in a half circle. Far enough for her to see what she needed to see.

Maria ignored the orderly collections of jewelry, crowns, fine brocade coronation robes, and glittering gem-encrusted cups and plates and such. These were reserved for special occasions like a royal wedding, coronation, birth of a royal daughter, or funeral. Dust covered them all, as well as the neat shelves where they rested in organized groups. No patterns of disruption in the dust, so no one had touched or moved anything.

Chests filled with gold and silver coins did not entice her. She needed those to pay loyal retainers and servants their annual dues.

At the back of the room stood an altar carved of rare woods and special stone. A single idol of a pregnant woman with pendulous breasts stood at the center. A single square of silk draped around her nudity. Diamonds glinted from her eye sockets, twinkling with joy in the lamplight. A heart-shaped ruby formed her mouth in a perpetual benevolent kiss. Emeralds dangled from her earlobes. Other lovely ornaments strung in chains formed her long hair, flowing to her heels.

Maria wore a miniature replica on a golden chain around her neck. She brought it out from the inner folds of her blouse, kissed it and let it dangle in full view of the statue.

Then she bowed reverently to this symbol of the royal house (whichever family claimed the title). Automatically words in an ancient language caressed her lips, *Maya 'Panish*. Only women knew this tongue with its liquid sounds and lilting cadence. Only women were allowed to gaze upon this nameless goddess who had become known as the Great Mother.

Reverence complete, Maria sought the most precious artifacts from the earliest times. She touched a fingertip to her tongue to moisten it, then ran it around the rim of a fine

marble cauldron rimmed in gold until the stone sang. The
note caught in the back of her throat, and she let it come
forth to match the cauldron of life. The stone walls picked
up the tone and reverberated in perfect harmony.

"I am not worthy," she said, backing away when the most
sacred object in the entire land quieted of its own accord.
"My body is twisted, strung together wrong. I can never
bear children. But I worship you with awe. I revere life and
abhor the loss of any—including traitors and criminals. I
regret only that I cannot remove the usurper who poisons
our land, our culture, our lives. He perverts the laws laid
down by you eons ago."

In the echoes of the Goddess' song still ringing in her
ears, she almost heard words.

(You know what you must do.)

"I cannot. I am too weak. I am deformed. There is no
other woman of my line who can rule!"

(You know what you must do.)

And then her ears heard only silence. The walls lost their
resonance. The cauldron became just an inert bowl.

But the other artifact on the left side of the goddess, the
side of last resort, seemed to absorb and reflect every bit of
light in the room, gathering it into a single ray and project-
ing the beam directly into Maria's eyes.

The Spearhead of Destiny.

Only the obsidian head remained, as the original shaft of
wood had rotted and been replaced many times over the
centuries. No one in recent generations had seen a need to
replace it. Amazonia had not seen war in almost two hundred years. The Krakatrice had remained elusive, almost
extinct and of no danger until . . . until Lokeen had spawned
his despicable plans. Or Sir had fed him the idea to further
his own plans.

"The time is coming soon, when I must either wield the
spear myself or entrust it to a man." For no man could
safely touch the thing unless it was given willingly to him by
a woman warrior.

Maria knew of no man she could trust this with. Not a single one of the guards. Probably not even Robb.

A tear leaked from her right eye. How could she, a twisted and deformed dwarf, ever hope to use the Spearhead in any way that could be useful to the people of Amazonia?

(You know what you must do.)

She removed the letter Frederico had grudgingly given back to her from her bodice and secreted it behind the statue.

(A beginning.)

CHAPTER 17

L UKAN WATCHED REJIIA and her two servants enter the temple. He let one of the wide columns hide him. Another shadowed Skeller.

"We must find you proper attire to present you to the king," Rejiia's female companion whispered. "He must perceive you as royal, more royal than the Lady Ariiell."

"My sources tell me that the lady has sent a final rejection of the king's proposal. He is anxious for a royal bride, any royal female to secure his throne," said the scarred man (Lukan thought he was named Geon).

"You have hinted before that Lokeen's shaky throne depends upon a royal wife to give him authority," Rejiia mused, pausing before the double doors. "Is it possible that this royal wife could indeed rule without a man at her side?" A big grin split her face and hardened her eyes.

All traces of Lukan's lust for her beauty vanished in the face of her ugly plotting.

"That does not happen often," the man replied. "Women are revered for the daughters they can bear. I have heard that if taking an active part in ruling or heading an army interferes with pregnancy, she is encouraged to stay home and spit out baby after baby."

They moved inside, bowing reverently to the two women stationed just inside the door.

"Geon got it wrong. Yes, we revere our women for the new life they bring forth, but they also fight alongside men, can rule with or without a male consort, and be their own champions. But by the Great Mother, she'd make a worse queen than Ariiell, when Ariiell was still insane," Skeller said, blanching as pale as his bleached leather harp case. "We have to follow her. Keep her away from the king." He stepped out of the shadows far enough for the door guardians to raise eyebrows at him questioningly.

"Not today." A lad in black leather, about fifteen and just coming into his full height, barely needing to shave, grabbed one of Skeller's elbows with his right hand, Lukan's with his left, and turned them both back toward the city.

"Chess?" Lukan gasped in surprise, anger, and . . . hope. "Last I saw you, you transported out of the Clearing with Master Robb. How did you get here? Where *is* he?" A dozen more questions needed to spill forth.

"Not here. Not now." Chess looked all around the lovely little garden and then sprinted to the left, to a narrow passageway leading into a warren of alleys.

Lukan matched the boy stride for stride, remembering their youth together when Lukan had always been the taller, and still was, but not by much. No longer did he have the broader and stronger shoulders either. Chess had bulked up, and he kept a firm grip on both of them without trouble.

Skeller stumbled again and again, trying to pull free and keep watch on the temple. "We have to stop her."

"There are other ways, Bard."

"My brother will help. He's . . ."

"Not in the castle and no longer has the ear of the king, though the people love and respect him for the generous gift of healing he gives without question," Chess said with a firm yank on Skeller's arm. "*You* can regain the ear of the king and prevent the witch from marrying him. Not your brother. He is lost to the royal family. Your father cannot see the good in the nursing order the temple of Helvess has taken on. He sees only the perversion of the partner choices."

They turned right and left again. Lukan had a sense that they aimed back toward the castle in the center of the city, but he couldn't be sure their circuitous route would end up there.

"Where are we going?" he finally asked.

"Someplace safe. Can't talk out here."

The silence of the marketplace came to Lukan's mind. He didn't have to ask if the king had spies waiting for one stray word against their ruler. The fear that permeated the city said it all.

A somewhat larger street loomed ahead of them. Chess stopped abruptly. Skeller almost fell face forward into the road at the abrupt change of momentum.

The clop of many shod steed feet dominated the intersection. A dozen riding animals trotted smartly toward them. Two men in front wearing black and red livery cleared the way with thrusting lances. Close behind them rode a short, paunchy man in a richer black robe trimmed in red. A gold circlet sat firmly on his brow with jet and ruby pendants dangling from it all the way around.

"The king," Skeller whispered in disgust.

"Hush," Chess warned him.

Keeping a firm distance behind the king rode another man. Tall and gaunt, wearing faded blue journey leathers. New gray at his temples formed back-sweeping wings.

"Master Robb!" Lukan gasped.

The magician turned to look sharply in his direction. Recognition sprang into his eyes; hope, and then worry swept through, just as quickly.

"We have to free him," Lukan insisted, trying desperately to pull free of Chess' grip.

"Not now. He's safe for now. We'll have the advantage when they return. I can show you where they keep him. But without a plan, without help, I have no chance of freeing him. You two might. One without, one within. Tomorrow or the next day. No later."

"Pray the Stargods help us," Lukan breathed.

"Pray the dragons help us," Chess retorted. "They'll be more useful in tearing the castle apart stone by stone. That's the only way to get in, unless you're the king's long-lost son come home to beg forgiveness." He stared long and hard directly at Skeller.

Robb bit back his gasp at the sight of his apprentice Chess and Lukan. The two together. Lukan with a staff. Surely they'd been sent to rescue him. Surely he need endure this horror only a while longer.

But why hadn't either of them done something, *anything*, to end this nightmare.

The presence of guards riding on either side of him, at the front of the party, and at the rear told him more than he wanted to acknowledge. They'd never get him out alive.

Could they infiltrate the prison to get him out later?

He doubted it.

Hope died in him.

The king urged his steed on, through the city toward the ragged hills and cliffs to the east and north. "We are almost there. We are far enough away from the castle that you can work magic again," Lokeen called over his shoulder. He dug his heels into the steed's flank to urge it to go faster.

The grinding rhythm of Robb's steed already chafed his thighs and pounded his hips and lower back. He wondered if he'd be crippled when they finally dismounted.

"Hurry up! Do I need to have you slung across the saddle and tied hand and foot?" Lokeen giggled again.

Robb loosened the reins to let the animal match its pace to the others' rapid trot.

Another half mile of tortuous riding brought them around a bend in the road and into sight of a neat little manor house. The sandstone bricks rippled in colors ranging from pale cream to deep rust and back again. The tall box of a building—three stories aboveground—sat within a hedge-fenced farmyard where flusterhens pecked at the sandy dirt, two goats nibbled at the dusty green hedge that wove in and out of the stake-and-string boundary, and a lounging dog of indeterminate breed and color perked his floppy ears, lifted his head, and barked once inquisitively.

The party turned into the gate, riding single file through the narrow gap in the hedge. A middle-aged man and woman, dressed in identical loose robes dyed a pale yellow, appeared in the doorway, bowing deeply with hands held out to the sides, open palms showing that they were unarmed.

Robb swallowed a snort of derision. Those robes— certainly a cool advantage in midday heat—could hide a myriad of weapons. This must be a courtesy ingrained in old tradition.

"Food and wine!" the lead guard bellowed. The couple scuttled inward while the party dismounted.

Robb groaned and winced at every tiny movement in his effort to get off the tall steed. Had the animal grown three hands at the shoulder during the ride? Probably not. He just felt that way from the screaming of his own muscles.

"This is my old farm," Lokeen explained. He affected a stately walk up the six stone steps set in a half circle before the door. Bright red stones limned the steps, clearly delineating them in the glaring sun that ricocheted light off every flat surface—vertical and horizontal. Robb longed for a broad-brimmed hat to shade his aching eyes.

He made himself circle his mount three times to loosen his legs before attempting those six steps.

"Gets easier the more you do it," a guard whispered as Robb passed him on the third circuit.

"But when will *he* give me another chance?" Robb muttered back, sotto voce.

"Depends upon how well you please him today. He's not cruel to those who obey him without question."

The shady interior washed soothingly cool air around Robb and beckoned him deeper. The rust-colored shutters had all been closed to keep out the heat. He presumed the stewards would open them again at sunset to regulate the temperature.

After blinking rapidly for several moments, Robb noticed a long passageway toward a small courtyard at the center of the building. A fountain splashed beside a tall tree with sharp fish scale bark and feathery branches at the top. Beneath the second-story balcony Lokeen had claimed a lounge made of woven reeds. Wicker. He'd read somewhere that the hardened reeds were called wicker, and sometimes painted. These retained their natural soft golden color. The king's booted feet plonked against the hard tile flooring. The steward raced to remove those boots and replace them with embroidered slippers.

"You may sit there." Lokeen waved Robb toward an armchair made of the same wicker.

He sat carefully, his thighs protesting the change. A low table carved in delicate spirals and inlaid with iridescent shells rested between them. Before Robb could sit back and rest, the lady scooted forward from the shadows with another pair of slippers for him. He gratefully accepted her help in removing his tight boots from sweaty feet. A shake of her head warned him not to use the table as a footrest. Apparently only the king was allowed to lounge here.

"Here is King Darville's reply to your earlier letter. I need you to decipher it." Lokeen produced a folded parchment from an interior pocket. The forest green wax seal had been broken and torn away, leaving only a stain on the thin and worn parchment. "Maria gave it to me this morning. The seal was broken already. She read it before realizing it needed to come to me. I do not recognize the hand that wrote it."

"King Darville has many clerks. They write. He signs," Robb explained. But he recognized the precise letters formed by his old friend and journey companion Marcus.

Robb took the piece of parchment and laid it flat upon the table. A quick scan showed him hints of a hidden message beneath the written words. He doubted Lokeen or Maria had noticed that. "What makes you think there is code in these words?" he asked.

"Because the words do not give me the answer I need!"

"Lady Ariiell has refused your proposal," Robb said flatly, reading more carefully. He'd need to ground and center himself and go into a half trance to find the magic within the ink. Did he dare?

"Which she can't do," Lokeen said. His mouth twitched in anger. "Your own laws state that such a decision must be made by her father or guardian. Her father signed a marriage treaty with me. What does she truly say?"

Any sense of friendliness or affability evaporated from Lokeen, though he maintained his casual recline.

The steward brought a tray with a wine decanter, two cups, and two plates filled with spiced meat, dates, olives, and a mild goat cheese. The lady brought a second tray piled with fresh, warm flatbread. Delicacies Robb had enjoyed for a few days while in the tower room, but not in the dungeon. He forced himself to wait for Lokeen to select a few morsels before grabbing his own portion.

They ate in silence a few moments.

"Eat more, especially the meat. I know you need fuel to work magic," Lokeen said, his eyes nearly closed as he peered at Robb.

"I do not want to abuse your hospitality."

"Then eat all your stomach can hold. I need you whole and hale to tell me what that letter truly says. There has to be a code or magic or something!"

Robb wrapped several slices of meat and cheese in the bread and ate his meal in small bites, knowing the big gulps that tempted him would upset his stomach and weaken his magic. Then he drained his cup of wine before leaning against the chair back and breathing deeply. He closed his eyes and sought a connection to the Kardia beneath his feet. Slowly he felt the pulse of the land, the tug of the magnetic pole, and an inner sight that made all the objects around him transparent, yet sharp in detail.

Magical strength trickled into him.

And then . . .

And then . . . a flood of the special energy he had craved to gather for moons.

A dragon. A dragon flew nearby, granting him access to magic. All he could gather and store in that special place behind his heart.

Thank you. Robb here.

(Verdii here. You are welcome. Lukan sends greetings and wishes for patience.)

When had Lukan ever been patient about anything?

Then the elusive presence of the dragon withdrew.

But Robb had replenished his strength and soothed his aches. He made himself ready to see what he could see within the letter.

"The lady is most adamant that she is damaged goods and not worthy of the honor you grant her with your proposal," Robb chanted, as if reading between the lines of the letter when he actually invented a new message, one more to the king's liking. "She says that she needs time and quiet to meditate deeply and reevaluate her place in life before she can enter society again. She will not taint Your Majesty and your kingship with her soiled presence. There are other, more worthy ladies closer to you."

He'd seen the true message, the one meant for him, encoded with magic by Marcus. *Help is coming. Learn all that you can, any way that you can.*

He drew a deep breath and opened his eyes fully to face the king.

Strangely Lokeen did not give in to the rage that burned in his cheeks and blazed in his eyes. "Closer to me. Yes, yes, I heard that a lady arrived by ship this morning. Perhaps she is destined to become the new love of my life and my queen. We shall seek her out when we return to the city in two

days. After we have visited my farm. I will introduce you to
my breeding stock. Soon I will have enough Krakatrice to
rule all of Kardia Hodos, not just this little city-state and
Coronnan. All of it. On my own authority and not second-
hand power granted me by a royal wife. Henceforth I shall
be the only royal in the entire world, and my sons will in-
herit. We will not depend upon women anymore."

"If you will not need a strong queen in your future plans,
I wonder that you seek to marry now," Robb said, feeling
his way through this, one word at a time.

"I will need strong sons to follow me. Not the bard who
rejects his princely duties and prefers to wander in poverty
and sing silly songs. And definitely not the son who follows
Helvess."

CHAPTER 18

"STARGODS, I THOUGHT it was hot outside!" Lukan said as he wiped sweat off his brow. Glowing embers in a central raised fire pit showed him the interior of a blacksmith's workplace. Three walls stood open to the street. Tall stone columns supported the slate awning. The fourth wall must be the back of the smith's home. In the shop, heavy tools lined up neatly along the wall, each one on a designated hook. The workspace was filled with buckets of water—from a pump in the corner against the house—a huge bellows to infuse air into the burning coals, and a well-worn anvil set upon a flat stone so that the top reached waist high on the man pounding a piece of metal flat.

The smith turned to face Lukan, Skeller, and Chess as they stepped beneath the slate awning.

Lukan reared back in surprise. A young woman, maybe almost as old as Skeller, but as tall as Lukan himself and broader at hip and shoulder, with thick thighs outlined by her black leather trews, stared back at him. She'd twisted her pale blonde hair into a thick knot atop her head. Soot lined her brow and cheeks. Sun and fire had given her a deep and ruddy tan.

"I see you've found the one you have searched for these many moons, Chess." Her voice was nearly as deep as a man's, probably in the tenor range. "A magician I presume by the staff. A bard as well." Then she peered more fiercely at Skeller. "*The* bard?"

Skeller blinked, looking around warily for eavesdroppers before nodding. His eyes skidded past the shadow in an alley that might or might not be a tall, thin man with a scarred face.

"Gerta, this is Lukan, the journeyman I told you would come, eventually," Chess said as he took a place beside the bellows and peered closely at the fire. He reached up and pulled down the lever. A slight whoosh of air puffed into the embers, sending white flames briefly through the hot coals. "Skeller you seem to know. Friends, this is Gerta, daughter and journeyman to our master smith Gordo."

The proximity of the castle tower told Lukan why his fellow magician had taken refuge here when Robb had told him to run. Close enough to monitor traffic in and out of the castle, as well as gossip, and give him useful employment to keep body and soul together.

"You'll be needing food and drink," Gerta said, thrusting her tongs and the piece of metal she'd been working into a bucket of water. Hissing steam rose up. Only when it had dissipated did she pull out the half-formed hearth hook and examine it. "Can't leave this now. Da's in the marketplace selling the wares. You can provide for your friends. I'll come consult with you when I finish."

"How much does she know?" Lukan asked as they rounded the corner of the smith's home and entered the single ground floor room that served as kitchen and living space. A narrow staircase along the back wall led to a loft that encircled the big room. In the dimness, he thought he saw partitions between sleeping areas, no doors; each "room" opened to the central living area with only lacy ironwork forming a fence. Not a lot of privacy.

"Gerta and her father know everything I know. They don't like King Lokeen any better than the rest of the city. But as long as the bastard controls the guards and the army they can't overthrow him," Chess spat.

"If the king had kept women in his army or palace guard, they'd have the right to overthrow him," Skeller muttered. He eased the harp case off his shoulders and set it reverently in a corner, behind a chair, where it would not get kicked as people moved about the room.

The entire political hierarchy puzzled Lukan. He'd never heard of women holding more power than men. But if more of the women here were as big and strong as Gerta he could understand why. He had to think a moment to remember if the women he'd passed in the marketplace had also equaled men in stature. Some, perhaps. Not all.

Chess pulled up a trapdoor and jumped into a shallow space beneath the floor. He pulled out three tall, capped jugs and just as nimbly hopped back up. Then he set about dishing up some strange foods and familiar-looking soft, white cheese. Goat probably. "Bread's still fresh from this morning," he said, removing the cloth covering several flat disks of the lightly browned delicacy. Lukan's mouth watered. He'd eaten this version of bread aboard ship and learned to love the nutty flavor and light texture. But what they'd had on ship was usually stale, almost moldy, and strictly rationed, as they did not bake while at sea.

"I'll cook properly at sunset and we'll dine on the roof, to catch the cool sea breeze," Chess continued to explain.

"Salty olives, sweet dates, and light bread," Skeller hummed in delight. "I haven't eaten so well since I left here more than six moons ago."

Lukan harrumphed. He knew Lily was an excellent cook. She'd fed the man she loved quite well on caravan. Skeller himself equaled or surpassed Lily in food preparation. Different foods, but still good.

Why was he defending Lily in his own mind? He'd never liked the idea of her and Skeller as a couple. The bard was nearly eight years older than she!

The same difference in age between Mama and Da. And she'd been sixteen when they met and married, the same age as Lily now.

"How long before Robb comes back to the castle?" Lukan asked, to shift his mind away from thoughts of family. He'd determined long before the start of this adventure that he didn't want or need his family any longer.

"Probably not for two days," Gerta said, coming into the room and grabbing a handful of the brown olives, pickled in wine vinegar and sea salt. "Maybe three days. Depends how far Lokeen needed to go. They rode into the pass along the river. My guess is they're headed toward the farm on the high desert plateau. Two days up. A night there, then an easy ride downhill for a day to come back."

"What do we do in the meantime?" Lukan asked, snagging another piece of bread before she ate the last of it.

"Get to know the city, every hidden alley, every road out, and every boat fit to sail the ocean so we can escape once we've freed Robb," Chess said, his chin firming in determination.

"Trust me, riding a dragon is fun," Linda said brightly.

Souska looked at her skeptically. "Why do they have to be so big?" She scanned the sky above the University courtyard, biting her lower lip so it would not tremble. Her knapsack, filled with the remedies Lily had asked for as well as a few others that Maigret thought beneficial, and a single change of clothes for Souska, weighed heavily on her shoulder.

Three days they'd needed to gather and prepare everything. She hoped there were enough people left alive in the village to test these remedies.

Then she heard a new rush of wind that did not disturb the treetops north of the open space. She cringed, reaching for Linda's hand to steady her.

"Always trust the dragons," Maigret said from the other side of Linda. "No matter what your instincts say, trust the dragon. This one is Krystaal, a young female. She needs experience out by herself before she seeks a lair of her own in another decade or so. She has flown with her brothers but never completed a task with humans on her own."

"Krystaal," Souska tried the name on her tongue and in her mind.

"Remember to greet her properly every time she comes to you, even if it is only in the back of your mind," Maigret said, also scanning the skies for a glimpse of a dragon wing. "Once you establish a strong connection to her, she will never be far from your call."

Summer sunlight shimmered in a vague distortion far to the south. Souska gulped and took a step sideways closer to the older apprentice and their mistress.

"Buck up, girl. The dragons have little respect for a coward," Maigret admonished her.

"They won't eat you," Linda added.

"Easy for you to say. You have royal blood. They *can't* hurt you," Souska argued.

Linda chuckled. "No, they can't. By bonds of tradition, blood, and magic, they won't hurt me. By bonds of friendship and trust with the entire community of magicians, they will not harm a human, unless that human is directly trying to destroy something or someone they love."

"And they love the land of Coronnan and all her people," Maigret finished for her. "Actually, I'm not certain they would hurt a human even then. Krej imprisoned Shayla into a statue of glass. After Jaylor freed her, she did not attempt any revenge except to leave Coronnan for a time."

(Krystaal here. I will keep you safe, little magician,) a voice said into the back of Souska's mind. It sounded as light and clear as tiny bells set to dancing by a breeze.

"Souska here," she replied, hoping she'd remembered the proper phrasing.

"Do you hear her?" Linda asked.

Souska could only nod at the tremendous honor. A dragon had spoken to her. *Her.* A simple country girl who had a way with herbs and almost no magic at all.

Then she saw the dragon, for real and true. A scintillating rainbow of colors dropped from above the rooftops, backwinging to guide her descent into a precise landing on hind feet in the middle of a circle described by twelve flat stones, each marked with the sigil of a master magician.

A smile curved Souska's lips before she remembered to be afraid. By then she was too entranced with the way light reflected off the crystalline fur into glorious prisms. A trace of silver still limned Krystaal's wing tips and spinal horns. Other than that, she looked nearly mature.

"You're bigger than Indigo, Krystaal," Souska whispered, remembering the purple-tip dragon who had helped the entire University of Magicians break the mage-driven storm that had nearly destroyed Coronnan.

(Of course I am. He is a litter younger than I.) The dragon shook herself all over and settled her wings against her body. *(And he is merely a purple-tip. Stunted. I am female, destined to become matriarch.)* She dropped her front legs to the ground and turned an eye full of swirling colors to peer directly at Souska. Her spiral forehead horn came within a foot of grazing the girl's hair.

Souska desperately wanted to step away from that horn. It would pierce her through like any warrior's lance or spear.

Linda's firm grip on her hand kept her rooted in place. "I told you she won't hurt you. Though she might try to intimidate you."

A dragon chuckle sounded in the back of Souska's mind. A deeper and more mature voice. *(Shayla here. Don't let her intimidate you. That chore is reserved for me.)*

"Dragon humor is different from ours," Maigret said. "It will take time to learn to appreciate it." She stepped forward, hand outstretched to stroke the dragon's long nose. "Maigret here, Krystaal. May I touch you?"

(Of course. I won't bite. Hard.)

Souska nearly jumped backward.

"Not funny, Krystaal," Linda admonished the young dragon. "Linda here."

(I know you well, Princess Rosselinda, daughter of Ros-

*semikka and Darville. I was among those who flew over
Coronnan City in celebration of your birth.)*

"Princess no longer. I am Apprentice Magician Linda
now." Linda lifted her chin proudly. "I claim my name and
title because I have earned it, not because I inherited it
from my parents."

Krystaal closed her magnificent eyes and bowed her
head an inch or two in respect.

Souska let a tiny bit of awe replace the fear that kept her
knees trembling and sweat streaming down her back and
across her brow.

"Are we ready?" Maigret asked, still stroking the dragon's head in long caresses of her hand.

*(Yes. I am to take the littlest magician upon my back and
fly her to where Journeyman Lily awaits us.)*

"I . . . I'm ready," Souska said quietly.

Linda squeezed her hand. *You must say it with confidence
and believe it, or you'll never climb onto Krystaal's back.*

"I'm ready," Souska said more firmly. And yes, she was
closer to believing it, just by saying it.

Maigret lifted the knapsack from Souska's shoulder and
hung it by the carry-strap around two of Krystaal's neck
horns. "Now place one foot here," she indicated the dragon's forearm. "Grab this horn, and swing your other leg
over her back. Just like mounting a steed."

"I . . . I've never ridden a steed."

"Oh, well. Just do it and appreciate the loving gentleness
of your dragon, because she is much more patient and tol-
erant than any steed I've encountered," Linda said.

Souska bit back a fearful retort and forced her feet to
move forward, one step at a time, only six more of them
until she was close enough to touch the huge beast in front
of her.

"May I pet you first?" Souska asked.

(Of course.)

She reached out tentative fingers until the soft fur tick-
led her. She smiled. "You are as soft as a cat."

Another chuckle from Shayla in the back of her head gave Souska the courage to touch her palm flat and feel the sturdy hide beneath her hand.

(I am strong. I will not fail you.)

"I know that." Then Souska closed her eyes, gulped back her reluctance to encounter something new, and threw her entire body into mounting. She had to stretch her legs longer and wider than she thought possible and strain her shoulders to pull herself upward, but eventually she sat on Krystaal's back between two sharp horns, both hands clasped around the front one, loving the hard, smooth texture that promised not to break. "Stronger than a magician's staff, and warm, but bright as . . . as a star against a velvet black sky!"

(Which is why my name is Krystaal.) Without further ado, the dragon took six running steps across the wide opening in the forest, pumping her long wings, and lifted eagerly into the sky, nose pointed into the wind.

Dragon delight infused Souska even as she clenched tighter with hands and knees to keep from falling off. "I'm riding a dragon," she said. "I'm riding a dragon!"

CHAPTER 19

B EFORE THE SUN rose, Scurry and Badger awakened
Robb and rushed him through a quick wash and gulp
of breakfast. Then they climbed back on the steeds. Robb
groaned, not certain if the pain in his back was worse than
in his thighs, or than the blistering heat and sun glare. Scurry
handed him a straw hat with a wide brim, the kind farmers
wore when in the fields all day. The hat's shade instantly
cooled his face and made the rest of him more comfortable.
But he still hurt from the unaccustomed stretch and jostle
to his entire body.

Lokeen rode quietly, yesterday's affability subdued.
Robb didn't know what had changed with the king, only
that this quieter man seemed more dangerous than the
laughing conversationalist.

The road meandered east by northeast into the sunrise
and alongside a deep river that grew narrower and more
rapid with every turn. The road shifted from a slight upward
incline to a steeper track. On the other side of the river, the
land rose sharply in sheer cliffs punctuated by waterfalls.
Above the ridgeline rose more rounded peaks. Behind
them he caught an occasional glimpse of a sharp point covered in snow.

"Will we be climbing those mountains?" Robb asked

Badger as the line of riders shifted from two abreast to three and back to one.

"Pass climbs high but cuts through the range," Badger said quietly. A brief shake of his head indicated that Robb should ask no more questions about their journey, or their destination.

A ley line beckoned to him from across the river, where it ran halfway up the cliff. An odd place for it. He'd never seen a line anywhere but beneath his feet, even in the up-lifts of the mountains. This one spoke of strange upheavals in the landscape. He didn't care as long as one of its feeder lines gave him a bit of power. He drank it in eagerly, letting it replenish his starving body and mind.

At noon, they changed mounts at a way station, to shorter and sturdier beasts with shaggy coats and a *bless-edly* smoother, plodding gait. Broad pastures stretched quite a way up the slopes. Small specks of movement— grazing steeds—indicated the extreme distance before the land reached for the skies again. The grass was thicker here than anywhere along the road. Robb searched and found a line of trees that bordered a small river that fed into the bigger one they followed. Everything else looked dusty, green fading to brown.

His lungs strained to catch enough of the thin air. A bit of dragon magic filtered into him with each labored breath. He began to feel almost normal and wondered where the dragon was that had left him this gift.

A little farther along the road they passed over a stone bridge single file. Beneath it, the lesser river fell over a cliff into the greater expanse of water. He estimated that they'd climbed to near the peak of the pass.

For another hour they climbed. The bridges in this stretch all spanned dry ravines. A few spiny plants struggled to grow between tumbled rocks along the banks. They'd not see much water until deep winter, when the storms came fast and furious toward the coast and roared through the pass like a wild beast on a rampage. He wondered how deep the water would run in these narrow breaks.

Thunder boomed ahead of them, resonating on Robb's back teeth, without a sign of a cloud in the sky. Mist rose high, swirling in the afternoon breeze, creating a wind of its own and cooling the tired travelers. Then he saw it, on the main river, stretching into a wide curved cliff, a fifty-foot drop—as if the Stargods had taken a cleaver to the rock and cut away the bottom portion. A massive white sheet of water pelted down that sheer precipice, bouncing and roaring among the tumbled rocks at the bottom. A lot of water in the dry season; this must be a major drainage from deep in the interior. When rain swelled all the creeks and tributaries, the falls would spill over the riverbanks and saturate the land for hundreds of feet to each side.

He wanted to stop and stare in awe at the marvel. Nowhere in Coronnan did such a waterfall grace the land. Scrurry's steed nudged his own to move forward into the parched and glaring desert beyond. How could Lokeen even think about turning such a magnificent landscape into a waterless wasteland? For that was what the Krakatrice would do.

The sun had just touched the western horizon when the land leveled out, along with the river. A light breeze sprang up, cooling sweat and relieving tired men and beasts. And then he spotted a cluster of buildings forming three sides of a square. Men and women with broad hats and stooped backs moved listlessly to herd a lowing cow toward the long, low building marking the southern boundary of the compound.

Within seconds of the cow's disappearance into the shadows, Robb smelled the coppery scent of fresh blood and the foulness of loosened bowels. The three people who had led the cow in came running out, slamming the plank door shut and dropping the crossbar with a loud thunk.

But not before the stench of rotten magic overwhelmed

his senses and robbed him of the tendrils of magic he'd been gathering all day.

Every person moved rapidly away from the charnel house.

"Ah, we have arrived at feeding time!" Lokeen exclaimed. Animation creased his face once more after a day of sullen silence. "Such a treat to know that my pets thrive here at the farm."

"Do the followers of Helvess form permanent bonds?" I ask the two women who help me bathe.

"We are encouraged to do so," the shorter one whispers. The taller and more dominant woman pats her shoulder affectionately. The two exchange a fond gaze for so long I could almost believe they forget me and their duties.

"But there are others who have not yet found their lifemate and actively seek them," the slighter woman adds.

I wonder if she regrets her current partner and allows my hand to brush her body as she helps me into the sunken pool. The tiles are the soothing green of a shallow sea, edged in the cream of wave-froth when it breaks upon a shore. The young woman blushes deeply but does not avert her eyes from my body. Her partner firms her grip on a slender shoulder and jerks her away from water's edge.

I sigh deeply as I rest upon a wide ledge that allows my legs to dangle freely in the constantly moving water while the surface laps sensuously upon my breasts, just barely covering the dusky tips.

"Are we alone here?" I ask, feigning innocence. "Bette and Geon need care after our long journey. I am not used to being separated from them."

"Your two servants are cared for in another part of the temple," the big woman says. She pushes her partner out the door, jealousy written all over her face. "They will find comfort among our numbers. Their attendants have not yet found partners."

"Geon has come to find one in particular," I say, eyeing the woman beneath lowered lashes. "The one known as Faelle."

"The king's son has not yet bonded, but he is a highly respected healer and does not aid in baths. He turns his talent toward helping the injured recover their mobility and return to the outside as useful workers instead of beggars."

"And you?"

"Bonding is a sacred ritual among us. It affirms that we are like outsiders; we seek mates and family. We have talents and skills and offer no threat to them. Promiscuity only confirms outsiders' mistaken belief that we are immoral and should be eliminated from normal society by death or banishment." She turns her back on me and fetches towels and soap from a cupboard in the big watery room.

Disappointed, I am not so eager to linger here. There are things I must do, people I must see, and appointments I must make. I wonder if Faelle does indeed have the ear of the king, or if I must move closer to the castle. An inn, perhaps? These people are too quiet, unwilling to draw notice to themselves or their way of life.

And yet I sense a deep undercurrent of anger and hurt in the few I have met. They have all been shunned, ostracized, possibly tortured for their life choices, much as magician children are treated by ignorant villagers when their talents awaken. I can use their anger. If only they will let me. Is it possible that they all try to suppress that anger with good works in nursing the sick and dying? The emotions are there, even if hidden.

I need only a short time with Faelle, to convince him that I can be an advocate for him and the followers of Helvess with the king his father. I think I need to invent a variation of their gentle goddess that is more to the liking of me and my coven. I must convince them that their goddess is not the true one. Yes, I like that. I am now the leader of my own religion. I must learn to swear by the fearsome Helvess, who never existed, instead of the great Simeon. He was only a man. A wonderfully creative man, but still human and mortal.

"I don't know this part of the city," Skeller said quietly, turning in a circle, gaze staying level with ground-floor doorways.

"How could you have grown up in this city and not have learned all the alleys, nooks, and crannies?" Lukan asked in disgust. "King Darville's exploits as a boy are legendary. He and my father were the terror of the marketplace and explored each and every island, even the ones they had to swim to!"

A strange warmth spread through Lukan as he revived the tale. He'd known his father was a living legend and always resented it—resented that he'd never live up to it. Now he wanted to brag about it.

"I had not the freedom," Skeller said flatly. His expression grew stony, devoid of emotion and animation. And the music left his words.

Lukan gave him silence. He'd speak when he needed to.

"My mother was always ill. Especially after Faelle was born. She kept us close. Fa . . . the king didn't care about us. We were not girls, and he'd not be able to rule through us after Mother died."

"That sounds so strange," Lukan admitted. "In Coronnan we almost had a civil war because Darville has only daughters."

"What of your brother Glenndon?"

"Half brother and born on the wrong side of the marriage vows." Disgust roiled through Lukan's gut, then evaporated. He couldn't hold on to it, nurture it, and let it dominate him. He had more important things to worry about now. "The king acknowledged Glenndon and legitimatized him, but he still had to bring Ariiell's son to court as second heir to pacify some of his lords."

"The lords," Skeller mused about that. "Our royal families rule absolutely within their city-states. They appoint advisers—that's how Samlan came to have influence over him—but the nobles report to no one."

"That's dangerous," Lukan mused.

"Very dangerous," a new voice said.

Lukan whirled to face a young man, dressed all in red, just stepping free of a residential doorway. All of his features, in height, weight, and coloring echoed Skeller. Except the pleasant voice carried no music. They could be twins.

"Faelle!" Skeller exclaimed and threw his arms around his younger brother.

"Skeller. I heard you'd returned and hoped to see you before you succumbed to Father." Faelle held his brother at arm's length. The whiteness of his knuckles betrayed the fierceness of his grip.

"Are you well, little brother?"

That phrase echoed in Lukan's mind. Glenndon had used it frequently, though only eleven moons and only an inch or two separated them. The love between these two brothers was obvious in their assessing gazes. Would Lukan ever be able to hug Glenndon again in love with no shade of anger between them?

"I fare well. Life in the Temple suits me. The people accept my gifts, though Father never will." He shifted a little to the side to show the leather satchel slung across his shoulders. A painted sigil in the oldest of languages—it looked like a snake climbing a magician's staff—proclaimed him a healer. "But how are you? I see pain behind your eyes. Why have you returned?"

Skeller drew a deep breath. "My hurts are of the heart, not of my body. I came home to settle matters with the king. Only then can I return to my love, my friends, my new home across the sea."

Faelle closed his eyes and nodded. After a moment his face cleared of emotion. "So be it. Do you have shelter?"

"Yes, with the blacksmith," Lukan said. From the way Skeller's throat apple bobbed, he guessed his friend tried to swallow strong emotions and couldn't get words out for the moment.

"Send for me if you need me," Faelle said, dropping his

grip on his brother. "Most everyone in the city knows my name and where to find me." He took a step backward in preparation for leaving.

"Faelle, Master Healer" Lukan addressed him. "Be warned. There is a woman sheltering in the Temple who is not as she seems."

"Ah, yes, the Lady Rejiia. We suspect her motives do not align with ours. But until she violates our hospitality we are obligated to give her respite." He half-bowed and faded into the shadows of an adjacent alley.

A second shadow, much taller and thinner, followed him. Geon again. He seemed to be everywhere in the city. At least everywhere Lukan was.

Skeller surreptitiously wiped tears from his eyes.

Lukan looked upward and away for landmarks above the doorways while he gave his friend a few moments of privacy. He'd learned to look up when living in the mountains. Landmarks were always up, not in front of him. He spotted the castle tower far to his left. That meant they were facing the port, but outside the silent boundary.

He picked up their previous conversation, as much to hear his own voice as from interest in the topic. "Maybe because your countries are only as big as the city and supporting farmland, you don't give political power to any but the king. We have many provinces with lords looking to one king, the first among equals. Now. Long ago we had all twelve provinces constantly at war with each other, every lord trying to gain power over the others."

He almost felt Skeller shift away from his deep emotions regarding his brother.

"They still are vying for power inside and outside the system," Skeller whispered, as if that were a great secret. "Like Laislac and his alliance with Lokeen."

"We caught and deposed him before he could do any true damage. The rest of our lords now argue in the council chamber, not on the battlefield, where people die."

"Not something I can do anything about," Skeller shrugged.

Because you ran away rather than fight for what is right—and yours. Lukan had to bite his tongue to keep the words at bay.

"So how do we find our way out of here?" Skeller asked, still looking blindly straight ahead or at the cobbles in the road. He hunted the shadows for signs of movement, but Geon had gone, following Faelle.

"We ask someone who knows," Lukan replied. Now he lowered his eyes to street level. A small, open well, surrounded by stones stacked to waist level, sat in the middle of the next intersection. The houses and shops opened up to give the well space rather than crowding tightly toward the corners as he saw other streets doing. An old woman, bent at the shoulders, lifted a jug from atop her head and dipped it into the water.

"Let me help you with that, grandmother," Lukan said, dashing to her side.

Gratefully she relinquished her hold on the fired clay jug with intricate designs painted around the wide shoulder of the vessel.

Lukan had noted similar bright decorations around doorways and . . . and replicated in colorful tiles set into the middle of intersections. Signs, identifiers, as individual as trees. They told people where they stood and where the road led, if only one knew how to read them.

"Bless you, boy," the woman whispered, her voice old and worn rather than silent out of fear like those in the market.

"May I carry this to your home for you?" he returned in the same tone, letting bits and pieces of fear intrude.

"I can manage if you'll just lift the jug for me. But I thank you."

Lukan raised the jug with little effort and helped her balance it atop her head. "Thank you again. May the Great Mother bless you with many daughters." She wandered off down one of the narrow streets.

He noted that the floral design of red and yellow on her

jug matched the tiles at the intersection, and the painting around the doorways of each dwelling on the street, each with progressively fewer flowers in the paintings. Ah, more flowers, closer to the well, and thus more desirable.

"You sound like a native. If I didn't know better, I'd say you were musician trained," Skeller said.

Lukan shrugged. "I was trained to listen and observe. Same as you. Mama sang all the time. I learned to hear her moods in how she held a note."

"There's hope for you yet. Now tell me what you heard and observed so we can find our way back to the blacksmith shop." He started off down the street at a right angle to the old woman.

"Not that way."

Skeller stopped in his tracks. "Then which way. They all look the same to me."

"They aren't. Observe the decorations as if they were a variation on a tune."

Skeller peered where Lukan pointed, at doorways and streets and then toward roofs and the tower visible above them.

"I can find my way across vast expanses following trader roads, but I can't navigate my natal city," Skeller shook his head.

"You never had to wander unknown streets before. You always had a road to follow," Lukan reminded him.

Skeller set off toward the marketplace and a road they'd learned well the day before. "Doesn't that describe our lives since we set off on this journey?" His fingers began tapping out a rhythm against his thigh. A new tune would follow shortly.

"Hey, I'm making this up as I go along," Lukan called after him.

"So am I."

CHAPTER 20

SOUSKA'S HANDS GREW numb from clutching the dragon horn in front of her. Vaguely she knew that a crisp wind flapped her skirt and made the knapsack bounce against Krystaal's side.

If it bothered the dragon she made no mention of it.

Tall stands of everblue trees passed beneath them, tiny spires against a green and brown landscape.

"I will not think about how high we fly," she whispered to herself over and over. And yet she couldn't help staring in dread fascination at the hills and valleys they passed over. A village with a circle of thatched huts, smaller than pebbles along a creekside. The rivers and streams looked like silver lines drawn with a wavering pen, the ink welling up and flowing wider along a meandering path, then straightening out and growing narrower as if the artist gained more control over a quill pen, or sharpened the nib.

The trees grew more sparsely, replaced with greener oak and elm that gathered in clumps. The villages became more frequent, plowed cropland nestled side by side with broad pastures and open grassland. Once she'd memorized those details, Souska realized that the steep hills lay behind them. Nothing in this landscape looked sharp. Everything had a roundish quality with blurred edges as the hills rolled gently and the streams wandered lazily.

Then Krystaal tucked her wings a little and spiraled downward.

"Are we there yet?" Souska dared ask. "I just got used to flying straight."

(Life is full of change and adventure. Sometimes it comes fast. Sometimes slow.) With that, the dragon folded her wings tighter against her body and dove straight down.

Souska yelped and closed her eyes. "Stargods preserve me. At least if I must die in this fall, make my passing quick and painless."

Abruptly Krystaal opened her wings again, caught air beneath them and leveled out. *(I would not be so careless with you, my friend. I have been charged with your safe delivery.)* She sounded chagrined.

"Did my fears disturb you?" Souska cherished the word friend deep inside her. Such a lovely and unfamiliar word. She wasn't certain she'd ever had a true friend before. The children in her home village that she'd thought of as friends had been the first to throw stones at her when the headman had called her witch.

But then Lukan had befriended her, helped her swallow her fears and hang on before the great spell that had broken the mage-born storm. He was a friend. A true friend who kept in touch with her several times a week while on his journey, when he wasn't supposed to make contact with anyone.

(Somewhat.)

"I'm sorry. It's just . . . just that I'm afraid of everything."

(That is why you were sent on this mission. To learn to overcome your fears or to use them.)

"I thought Mistress Maigret sent me because I know how to use the hellebore correctly."

(That too.) Was that a dragon chuckle beneath the words?

"I didn't know dragons could laugh."

She sensed a question without words in the back of her mind.

"I mean, you are so big, so magical, so . . . so important. Laughter seems—I don't know, too trivial for majestic dragons."

With that Krystaal loosed a mighty roar that could only be laughter and set down upon the land in the middle of a fallow field at the edge of a small village, maybe fifteen asymmetrical huts, a communal barn as big as four of the houses, sheep bleating and running away from the dragon, chickens everywhere, and one solitary figure running tiredly toward them.

"Lily!" Souska called as she slipped down off the dragon's back. At the last second before her boots touched the ground she remembered the precious knapsack and grabbed it.

"Did you bring it?" Lily gasped. Her sun-streaked hair of mixed blonde and soft red looked limp and dull, her steps dragged, and her hollow cheeks had taken on a frightening pallor, much like that of her frail twin. Only her grasp upon a staff that held a straight and rigid grain looked firm and solid.

"Yes, I brought everything you asked for. And more," Souska replied, praying that the slightly older girl would not be her first patient. From the lack of activity in the middle of the day she guessed that *all* of the village was either sick or tending the sick. Or dead.

"Thank the Stargods. We are saved." Lily sank to her knees as if she didn't have the strength to remain upright any longer.

Souska bent to hold Lily's elbow and help her up again. A white spot in the center of Lily's forehead stood out like a candle flame at midnight. The skin looked . . . dead. Except that it showed no sign of blistering or sloughing off. She bit her lip in worry, wanting desperately to make a superstitious warding gesture against the evil eye.

"I'm weak, not ill," Lily said as she leaned heavily on Souska's arm and on her staff in order to stand. "And ever so tired. The work never ends . . . I need your help."

"I'll do what . . . what I can." Souska had to either over-come her fears or give in to them and spend the rest of her life running away. She knew what Lily needed and how to do it. She did. She did!

A dragon screech right next to her nearly deafened her. She slapped hands over her ears as she looked away from Lily to the dragon. A friend in distress. How could she hope to heal a dragon?

(This land must be cleansed!) Krystaal bellowed, flap-ping her wings and running until she caught air and lifted. Her flight path took her around and around the village as she rose. *(Fire and salt. Fire and salt to cleanse the land.)*

"S'murghit! I was afraid of that," Lily said sadly and sank back on the cursed dirt.

"If we need fire and salt to cleanse the land of the mi-asma left by the Krakatrice, won't we create a desert, the kind of place that nurtures the black snakes?" Souska asked.

"The ride downhill will be easier," Scurry said quietly to Robb as he finished saddling the steed.

"No ride will seem easy today," Robb muttered. "But I will be grateful to leave this cursed 'farm.'" He rubbed chafed palms together, trying to ease the ache that spread from his fingernails up his arms, across his shoulders, down his back, through his legs to his feet. He'd give a year of his life for a soak in the hot spring back home. Especially if Maigret was there to scrub his back with her lavender soap.

After what he'd seen last night he couldn't trust Lokeen to allow him to live a full year longer. He hadn't slept well; every time he closed his eyes, he saw again the tangle of black snakes, large and small, writhing around a huge corral, the only fence two natural streams, an artificial ditch filled with water, and a sharp drop down to the big river. Acres and acres of black poison and insatiable hunger for blood and flesh.

"Gather whatever magic you can find," Lokeen ordered as he approached. He pulled on long leather gloves, supple but cushioning to his palms. He didn't offer even that minor comfort to Robb. "When we stop to change mounts, you will scry, or summon, or whatever you call it, for your predecessor. He took with him a precious artifact, and I want it back." No other words, no please or thank you, nothing but orders to fulfill his wishes.

"What keeps the workers here?" Robb whispered as much to himself as to Scurry, who now held the reins of the surefooted steed.

"They are slaves. To leave is death, long and slow," the guard muttered back. "To fail in their duty means that their families are fed to the Krakatrice while they are forced to watch."

"What keeps you in His Majesty's service?"

"Loyalty to Lady Maria. Someone has to protect her from *him* since he removed all of the female guards from the castle. He thinks that by doing so he has weeded out her influence."

But he hadn't.

Robb had a feeling that Lady Maria's royal blood—even though she was not qualified to rule because of her physical ailments—was the only thread holding Lokeen on the throne.

Wasn't there anyone else who could supplant him?

"Now if the bard Toskellar would return and marry a princess from another city, he could push his father off the throne. Maybe even into the dungeon," Badger added.

A bard had stood beside Lukan and Chess when he saw them in the street.

Robb allowed a glimmer of hope to blossom in his heart.

You know what you have to do. The words haunted Maria over and over again. What did she have to do?

She pondered her options as she went about her duties

maintaining the castle. As she had always done. Make sure this section of rooms was thoroughly cleaned so that not a single dust mote dared linger. Dispense the proper amount of valuable spices to Cook for the main meal. Air and change bed linens, oversee the week's laundry. Inspect the steeds for signs of neglect or illness and oversee the rotation of guards.

And dozens of other things, including a little matchmaking between a scullery maid and the head groom. And along the way she sent for the midwife to take up residence in the domestic hall to await the birth of Cook's first assistant's first babe.

She also had to avoid the notice of a dozen courtiers who had no occupation but to consume food, demand new clothes, and try to win Lokeen's good notice. In return Lokeen demanded unquestioning loyalty from his leeches. And any armed soldiers they could command or buy. They'd speak ill of her to Lokeen with any excuse.

This was what she had to do.

(Not enough. You know what you must do.)

She had to invoke the law to displace Lokeen from his ill-gotten throne.

But if she did that, who would rule? There was no one left in the family. Removing Lokeen would leave a vacancy, and the rulers of a dozen nearby city-states would all seek to fill it. War. She'd bring war to Amazonia. Her people had not seen war in almost two hundred years.

"My lady," a breathless guard said, bowing deeply as he skidded to a halt in front of her.

"Yes," she replied absently as she glared at the slate steps leading to a small side courtyard. She was certain that discoloration in the shape of bird plop wasn't there yesterday. Whoever had cleaned it hadn't done it properly.

"My lady, a bard has been sighted within the city precincts," the man said, never quite regaining his breath.

Everything inside of Maria froze. Not even her mind worked properly. "Wh . . . where?"

"No one place. He seems to be wandering the city, scouting it."

"Looking for a likely tavern to host his singing, no doubt," she replied. "What makes you so certain this bard is . . . our bard?" She clasped her pendant near her throat. The rounded edges of the Great Mother warmed to her touch, as if reassuring her that this communication was important.

"I do not know, my lady. Sergeant Frederico told me to tell you." He ducked his head.

"Tell your sergeant he did well. Have the bard watched. Followed closely. Do not approach or apprehend. We need to know if this bard is *our* bard before we proceed."

"Yes, my lady. Oh, and the bard was seen with another man, younger than he, carrying a staff, like the king's adviser used to do."

"A staff?" A magician's staff? Mayhap someone sent to rescue Robb?

Did she want that to happen?

"I would know more. Discreetly. Before His Majesty returns. You have proved yourself loyal and trustworthy. I commission you to procure this information and report it back to me and no one else."

"The king?"

"No one save me."

"Yes, my lady. By the Great Mother, my lady, I will do as you command, with honor and pleasure."

"Great Mother, please let this bard be our Toskellar. Please let him return home and take up his duties as prince. If he marries the right princess he can rule in her name. Now which princess is most likely to tempt him into marriage? She must bring with her lucrative trade and a strong army or we'll not oust Lokeen. He won't step aside without a fight."

Quickly she retreated to her private rooms. She had letters to write and dispatch swiftly. If only Robb were here to do that magically! But he wasn't. So she had to depend upon mundane messengers and fleet steeds. Who could she trust?

If only Lokeen had left two or three women among the guard she'd use them. But they had all become blacksmiths and tanners and drovers. Perhaps . . .

As soon as she'd written the letters she threw a light cloak over her, masking face as well as body, and slipped away from the castle. She knew where to find a blacksmith and a tanner.

CHAPTER 21

"BREATHE WITH THE bellows, match the rhythm," Chess coaxed Lukan into the first mystery of the magic of blacksmithing. "Keep it steady. Steady!" The last came out louder, more urgent as the apprentice guided Lukan's hand.

Lukan's arm muscles froze with the bellows handle pulled halfway down.

"Don't stop. Just ease up. You're putting too much air in."

"Okay, okay. Slow and steady. I got it." Lukan forced himself to breathe with the flow of his movements, willing the air pump to infuse greater heat into the coals.

"Use all of your senses, Lukan. Smell the fire, hear the smoke rising, taste the heat."

"Feel the sweat dripping into my eyes."

"That too," Chess chuckled.

"All I can hear is your girlfriend's hammer slamming into the metal over and over again," Lukan grumbled.

"I'm not his girlfriend," Gerta said flatly as she dropped her hammer neatly into its place on the rack and lifted with her heavy tongs the steedshoe she worked. After a brief inspection she grunted and plunged the arch of steel into a bucket of cold water. Steam hissed as it rose around them, carrying the unique odor of the trade.

Lukan's nose was so stuffed with heat and smoke, of burning coals, of hot metal, and he didn't know what all else, he could no longer tell which scent belonged to which component.

"Smith?" A faint whisper at the edge of the awning arrested all movement.

Lukan whipped his head around so quickly his neck cricked.

A tiny woman, draped from head to toe in a cream-colored cloak that fluttered lightly in the breeze, stood just inside the shadow of the overhang.

"My lady," Gerta said reverently, dipping a curtsy, right knee bent to the side with the toe touching the ground behind her left heel, that was at once the epitome of respect and grace and utterly absurd without a skirt to flare.

Chess rapped Lukan's arm free of the bellows sharply and pushed his back so that he bent over in an unplanned bow.

"Who?" he mouthed.

Lady Maria. As if that answered his questions.

"My lady, you honor my humble workplace," Gerta said, retaining her dip.

Lukan's back threatened to cramp in his unplanned and awkward pose. A hasty look around told him he really shouldn't shift so much as an eyelash.

"Blacksmith, I have need of messengers I can trust," Lady Maria said, taking a step closer to the forge.

"My lady, I am but a simple journeyman smith for my father. I no longer perform such services." Gerta straightened and stiffened. She stood tall, at attention, eyes staring into the distance. Like a soldier.

"There are no messengers left in royal service that I trust," Lady Maria replied. "I would reenlist those I've lost."

"My lady, I regret . . ."

"Smith Gerta, please. This is important."

"Aunt?" Skeller appeared on the opposite side of the awning. His harp hung loosely in his arms as he drank in the sight of the woman.

. "Aunt Maria!" He rushed to enfold her in a hug, for once the harp an awkward impediment instead of an extension of his personality.

Lukan ducked in to relieve his friend of the harp.

"Toskellar!" she cried and threw herself unashamedly into his arms.

"It's Skeller now, Aunt Maria. Just Skeller. Prince Toskellar no longer exists."

"I know, I know, my beautiful boy." She caressed his cheek as if memorizing the planes and angles. "I have missed you sorely."

"And I you. Tell me how you fare?" Skeller kept his hands on her shoulders, stepping back just enough to allow him to survey her.

Then Lukan noticed that she stood crookedly, leaning heavily to the left. He wondered if she'd topple should Skeller remove the support of his touch.

"My lady," Gerta interrupted. Her eyes swept back and forth around the streets and passersby, wary. Her hands at her sides clenched and unclenched as if itching for a weapon. "My absence on a messenger mission for you would be noted." Her chin flicked in the direction of two heavily armed men wandering from shop to home to well, keenly observing everything.

And Geon slinking ten paces behind them.

"I have had some luck wandering the streets at will, my lady," Lukan interjected. But he'd have to find a way to lose Geon in the maze of alleyways. "May I be of service?"

Lady Maria looked at Lukan in puzzlement.

"Aunt Maria, my friend, Journeyman Magician Lukan, and Apprentice Magician Chess," Skeller said. "Lukan, Chess, Lady Maria, most royal sister to our late queen who was my mother," he said solemnly.

"The magician boy?" the lady asked. "I see no staff."

"Over there," Lukan inclined his head toward the corner of the house where it stood, ready and waiting for his command.

She sighed and nodded.

"My letters need to go farther abroad than the city. Can you dispatch them?"

"I . . . I am only a journeyman, my lady. I do not know the spell," he admitted. Shame heated his cheeks all the way to the tips of his ears. He should have learned that spell. He knew the principles of it. Any magician could figure *that* out. But he didn't know the particulars. He'd skipped classes that week—he and Glenndon had gone fishing at a lake outside the village at the base of the foothills.

"Magic isn't what you need, my lady," Gerta interrupted. "You need to reestablish your contact with all of the female soldiers who have been removed from the guard. It is a disgrace that Lokeen has exiled the core of our history and culture from the castle. Amazonia was founded by women warriors. We need to return them to places of honor rather than hiding in fear of a mere man." She stood two heads taller than the lady, jaw firm, spine straight, head proud.

Lukan lost his heart to her in a single breath.

"How can *I* contact them?" Lady Maria asked simply. "Lokeen has been most thorough in his purge of anyone previously associated with the queen. I am watched. The guards think I wish a new pot spider-arm specially made for my personal hearth."

"That I can make for you. And I know how to find a few of my troop. I am too well known; my absence would be noted. There are others working the caravans and ships who come and go at will. Give me your letters and I will see that they are dispatched by trustworthy messengers," Gerta said.

The lady nodded and fished three quarter-fold parchment sheets from the interior of her light linen cloak. She placed them into Gerta's outstretched hand with a snap.

"How have we been reduced to this travesty?" Skeller asked shaking his head. "Forsaking our laws, our most honored traditions, for the greed of one man."

"It all happened slowly, Highness," Chess offered. "Very slowly."

"My sister is as much to blame as any," Lady Maria sighed. "She hated making decisions lest she disappoint someone. She gave over all but the most formal of ceremonial duties to her husband. We got so used to turning to him for a decision, accepting his decrees as stemming from her, that we hardly noticed when she died and he should have stepped aside from the throne."

"And I ran away rather than face my responsibilities to marry a suitable princess." Skeller hung his head.

"You escaped certain death at the hands of a monster," Maria reminded him. "And now you are back, you must do your duty."

"I have no love for . . ."

"Love is not part of the equation. It never has been and never will be in royal families."

Lukan had to gulp. He knew there was little chance that Skeller might find happiness with his sister Lily—and not just because of the trauma of murdering Samlan. Eight years separated them, as well as rank and nobility. Lily would never be happy living in a city beyond the first few days of curious exploration. Now he knew for certain that his beloved sister would never have a chance with the man she loved.

And his brother Glenndon, childhood companion in mischief, confidant, and . . . and friend, faced a similar fate. As heir to the dragon crown of Coronnan he was destined to marry for alliance and treaty, not for love.

Sadness swept over Lukan, and he was very glad that he was just a lowly magician journeyman without royal duty and honor.

Lily watched Souska as she carefully measured the hellebore and crumbled it into the mixture of mushrooms and algae. Together they counted the dried leaves: one, two, three, four, five. Each ingredient drifted into the mixture bubbling sluggishly in a ceramic pot over a low fire in their hut.

"No more than five. Ever," Souska warned. "A little less if you are treating a person of small stature or one who is very old."

"How do you know if it's the right amount?" Lily asked her, committing every motion to memory. A number rhyme came to mind, something Mama used to teach her to make potions. The tune made it easier to remember details. Skeller would use the same method.

"You have to trust your experience and the lore handed down from grandmother to granddaughter through many generations," Souska replied.

Lily sat back on her heels. From this perspective, she saw one mushroom cap that hadn't broken into powder completely. She ground it a bit more with her pestle.

"Can you mix it too fine?" Lily persisted with her questions. "Does overgrinding push the essential components out of the plant and into the mortar?" The last words sounded breathy and hesitant.

Souska ran the back of her fingers along Lily's cheek and brow. "Your pulse is rapid and a low-grade fever persists. I think you need the first dose."

"No, no, I'm fine."

"No, you aren't. Your skin is clammy, your hair lank. And your breathing is ragged. You are only days out of your sickbed, and you used up every scrap of strength you had initiating a summons to Maigret. A sloppy summons that had no secrecy built into it."

Lily had the grace to blush. But it didn't warm the spot on her forehead. Death had said that she could not call her. Yet. "I will recover. There are others worse off. They need this precious brew before I do."

"You need it to keep going. I am here to help. You needn't do it all."

"For that I thank you. I'm surprised Mistress Maigret allowed you to stay."

Souska sniffed the concoction and did not answer.

Lily followed suit, concentrating on the separate scents of

each ingredient, as Mama had taught her. She had to understand the heart and soul of each plant. This would be easier,
better, if she'd gathered the components herself, whispering
a prayer of thanks to their voluntary separation from their
growing medium. She had to work hard to banish the odor
of her own sweat, the last meal she had cooked in the tiny
thatched hut assigned to her, and the stale ashes in the fire
pit. Gradually, she isolated the mustiness of the mushroom,
the faint scent of rot in the algae, the sweetness of the hellebore flowers. All there. All in the right proportion. Time to
add it to the infusion of willow bark tea.

She poured the boiling hot tea into the mortar. The brew
sizzled and bubbled as the medicine absorbed the liquid
and the mortar cleansed itself of residual bits, dumping
them into the tea.

A swish with a wooden spoon and it was ready to decant.

Souska pushed the first cup into Lily's hands. "Drink it.
All of it."

"But . . ."

"First rule of the Healer's guild: Never try to treat another with the same ailment as yourself. You and the villagers get well and then we deal with curing the land. I'm going
to the headman's hut to start dispensing this to the ailing."
Decisively she unfolded her legs and rose, lingering until
Lily drank as ordered.

"Now I know why Maigret ordered you to stay and
help," Lily said as she blew a cooling breath across her tea.

"No, you don't. She ordered me to come because I'm the
least valuable apprentice."

"But you've learned so much . . . you know how to handle the hellebore."

"Anyone could have given you a written recipe and left."
Souska shrugged. "Your brother taught me much over the
summer. But it's not enough. Never enough to make up
for . . ." she drifted into silence hanging her head in shame.

"Lukan is good about that. He'll make a fine teacher
someday."

"As will you, if you survive. Now drink. It's best when hot." Souska took the bowl of medicine and walked resolutely toward the largest hut in the village. It stood square and solid in the center of the half circle of dwellings. "It's not that I'm not grateful to the University for taking me in when no one else wanted me. But . . . but now they don't want me either."

A new chill invaded Lily, as if Death's cold mist had wandered by. She peeked out the doorway toward the hilltop. Death still lingered there. Not here.

I have learned not to ask of Geon how he manages what he manages. He waited until the chatelaine of the castle—a pitiful deformed dwarf of a woman I would not allow in my home—left the castle. Then my servant presented my credentials to an underling. She had not the real authority to accept me as a guest in the castle, but neither did she have the authority to decline a visit from the great-granddaughter of a king of Coronnan.

My royal blood is well documented: My father's father was younger brother to old King Darcine—Darville's father. Of my father's legitimate children I am the eldest. My sisters, if they still live, dwell in exile in Hanassa, or maybe Rossemeyer, somewhere disgusting, with our mother.

By the time the dwarf—I am told she would be queen but for her deformity—returns, I have settled in sumptuous quarters conveniently near the king's private suite, the rooms where he actually sleeps and dresses rather than the more formal receiving room in his privy chamber and robing room.

"If we'd known you were coming," the chatelaine says on a sniff, as if I am unwelcome and she would oust me if she could, "we would have made certain that King Lokeen was in residence to receive you. As it is, you must wait upon his convenience."

"And when will that be?" I ask on an equally disdainful sniff.

She shrugs and turns on her heel to make her slow way out of my rooms. "His Majesty comes and goes as His Majesty pleases. We dine one hour after sunset. Be prompt. No one will bring you food if you are not. Your servants may eat with the other servants in their hall belowstairs."

I swear that I will kick that woman into the murky water of the harbor myself as soon as I am entrenched. I must remember that, royal blood or no, I am a guest. I must behave.

That does not mean I can't begin to ensnare the populace with my enticement spells and seductions. Bette and Geon can begin with the servants and administrators. They already scout out the hidden passages and forgotten rooms in the castle. I have my sights set on the captain of the guard. He holds the most powerful position in a castle hierarchy. By the time I win a proposal of marriage from Lokeen, I need to control all those loyal to him.

CHAPTER 22

"MASTER ROBB, YOU will work magic for me here," King Lokeen announced as they dismounted in the forecourt of the manor at the midpoint in the return journey to Amazonia.

Robb groaned as he slung a leg over the saddle and slid to the ground beside his pony. "Thank the Stargods for small blessings," he whispered to the mount, whose strong back was not nearly so broad or far off the ground as the regular riding steeds they'd use to return the rest of the way.

"What spell do you need me to throw?" he asked, pasting an expression on his face he hoped would pass for a smile but felt like a grimace.

"You will locate your predecessor and the ancient artifact I lent him. I must have the artifact back." Lokeen slapped his open palm with his riding crop for emphasis as he marched into the manor house. Clearly he expected Robb to follow obediently.

Robb allowed his reluctance to serve Lokeen to show in his dragging steps. After what he'd witnessed in the charnel house at the farm, he had no desire to do anything to help a king as mad as this one. Insanity was the only explanation for how the man enjoyed the blood thirst of his pet snakes. Or else the Krakatrice had possessed his mind and his morals. Perhaps he was the pet and the snakes made all his decisions for him?

Thank the Stargods he has no matriarch Krakatrice. At least not one I saw. He's getting all his eggs in the wild, dormant for many decades, perhaps centuries, and therefore not as strong or as fresh. There is still a chance that a team of dragons and magicians can take down the tangle, search out and destroy any more eggs, and end the tyranny.

"Sir, I must have either the name of the man you seek or some personal possession," Robb said wearily. "I have told you this before."

"Names are the key to a man's magical power. Your predecessor would not appreciate my giving you his name. He would not want you to have power over him."

Robb ground his teeth. "Then I cannot find him and you will not get your artifact back." Which suited him fine. Anything to thwart this madman.

"Oh, but I have a personal possession," Lokeen said, flopping down upon his lounge in the shade of the interior courtyard. Servants scurried to bring refreshment. "You may sit." Lokeen waved casually toward an adjacent lounge.

Robb eased his butt into contact with the slight padding beneath the upholstery. Not enough to cradle his aching joints. He'd need a few moments to adjust to this new posture before raising his feet as the king did so easily.

Gratefully he sipped the proffered wine and honey-dipped dates and nuts. But he said nothing. The quest was Lokeen's; Robb was only the reluctant servant. Prisoner. Slave.

"Aren't you curious as to what personal possession I hold hostage against the magician's return and good behavior?" Lokeen asked, licking honey drips from his fingers.

Robb lifted his eyebrows but still kept his mouth shut.

Lokeen giggled. Another sign of madness?

"No curiosity?"

Robb remained silently passive.

"Oh, very well. I did so want to surprise you. Now I shall just have to show you." He clapped his hands imperiously.

A black-clad old man with a permanently bowed back emerged from the shadows carrying a wooden box with rich inlays of different colored woods and gemstones. The old man held the ends of the box between his opened palms, as if unwilling to touch it any more than he had to. It fell the last inch to the inlaid table between Robb and the king. He'd dropped it, close enough that Lokeen knew his reluctance but could not chide him for damaging the box.

As long as my hand from wrist to fingertip. As wide as my palm. Suddenly Robb didn't want to know what was in there.

"Go ahead. Open it. Open it. Open it!"

Robb gulped. Then, holding his breath, he reached forward and flipped the top off with one finger. Steeling himself against the worst, he blinked rapidly, daring his eyes to focus and really not wanting to.

Nestled in a soft bed of lamb's wool rested a man's left little finger, neatly severed from the hand at the palm joint. A smudge of dried blood encircled the cut end where a bit of bone protruded.

He gagged.

"My magician left here in a boat with his three masters, two journeymen, and two apprentices just before the solstice," Lokeen said. "He gave this to me willingly and placed a stasis spell on it so that it would not rot."

"Such a spell should have died if your magician died. Therefore I must presume he lives."

"One would think so." Lokeen shrugged on a half smile—as if he were hiding something.

"But you altered the spell."

"Yes! You are smarter than he was. You figured it out."

"You coerced one of the master magicians to extend the stasis, make the deterioration dependent upon time, not the life of the owner of the finger."

"Three moons he's been gone. The stasis will only last another moon. You must find him for me now."

Robb gulped back his distaste. He could do this. He'd

done worse than touch a dead finger. He'd killed Kraka-trice, at close range.

A servant appeared at his side with a silver bowl filled with clean water, a candle, and his glass on a tray.

"A ceramic bowl would be better, closer to the Kardia . . ."

"Silver is mined from the Kardia."

Robb nodded.

"No more stalling. Find my magician and *my* artifact."

Robb drew in a deep breath. He could make it the first stage of entering a trance, or merely the gathering of energy to find a way to postpone this search.

"I said, stop stalling or you will become the next meal for my pets."

Robb breathed again and felt his peripheral vision close in on him. A third breath and his vision burst into a full circle of awareness, individual objects blended together and at the same time stood out starkly delineated. With a thought he brought a flame to his fingertip and touched it to the candlewick.

The easy part. The familiar and routine part of any spell. He could do this in his sleep.

Now for the innovative part. He must engage his intel-lect, his talent, and all of the energies he'd gathered since leaving the city yesterday morning. He must think, while maintaining the detachment of the trance. But he also had to make the process look like a spectacular and supreme effort in case he failed. Lokeen would have no excuse to say he hadn't tried hard enough.

He placed his open hand above the finger and raised it. The finger followed his gesture. He guided it over to the bowl and slowly lowered the grisly bit into the water. It touched the surface, floated a moment and dropped silently to the bottom of the bowl with barely a ripple on the sur-face.

Next Robb positioned the candle so that the flame re-flected on the water, showing endless repetitions of itself between the water and the polished metal bowl, both partial and complete. In this case, perhaps the elegant silver bowl proved better than the simplicity of a container made from the body of the Kardia herself.

Finally he eased his glass to float on the water. The finger shone through it, magnified until he could see individual pores and hairs, every detail of the severed muscle, bone, and blood vessels. Another three breaths to hold the finger in his mind. Gradually he built up layer upon layer of imagery of the man who used to be attached to that finger. He didn't need to know that renegade master magician Samlan had offered it up as hostage. The finger knew, and it showed him the man in full, majestic anger aboard a storm-tossed boat, holding his staff aloft with a bandaged hand while cradling a piece of ancient bone with the other. On either side of him, his magician helpers also held the long bone, so old it had fossilized to stone. A bone so old it had given up its hold on life eons ago.

A bone so long and twisted it could only have come from a Krakatrice. Perhaps the first Krakatrice, a mutant derived from the same stock as dragons, but so deviant it was exiled.

A mutant that should not have lived and reproduced but did.

As he watched the storm rise and rage in front of Samlan he felt the boat shift violently beneath his feet. Rain drenched his face. Wind tore at his hair and threatened to rip the staff and the bone from his hands.

Magic thrummed through him as he chanted words of rage over and over. His words formed an endless circle that whirled around and around him. As did the winds and the rain, drawing air and water from all corners of the Kardia, piling them up, one on top of the other. The winds circled, tighter and tighter, pulling the water of Bay and ocean up into its vortex.

Robb fell into the storm as surely as if he were part of the mix of wind and water. He fought the external and internal forces that bound him to the magic thrown by Samlan. He watched the traitorous magician from below and to the left.

And then, as the chanting spell reached its climax, Samlan and Robb and the others dropped the bone at the same moment, unleashing the storm to wreak havoc upon Coronnan. A tidal wave one hundred feet tall rushed forward to the apex of the Bay, to the heart of Coronnan City.

"No!" Robb screamed.

He felt himself drowning as he became part of the destruction of his homeland.

CHAPTER 23

"DO NOT LEAVE the spell yet," Lokeen commanded.

Robb fought his urge to find oblivion in blackness.

"You have shown me nothing new. I need more," Lokeen insisted.

The firmness of the king's voice gave Robb something to latch onto. A bit of reality to cling to while he sought answers in the spell.

"What happened after they loosed the storm? I had no summons to invade, or to help, and in so doing plant my troops in Coronnan City ready to displace the king. What happened?"

What happened indeed? Something was off in Robb's vision. He saw . . . he *saw* Samlan. If he relived those events through the eyes of the owner of the finger he should have seen . . . Samlan's robes. He should have felt the strain of holding the staff aloft in the horrendous wind. But he saw the weariness in Samlan's face. He had no staff to cling to. He had only the bone.

"You bastard," he yelled at Samlan. "You took the finger of your apprentice Tem. *My* apprentice Tem. You offered him his life if he helped you. Hideous death if he didn't. And still he died."

"How? How did the boy die?" Lokeen coaxed. "Show me what happened aboard that boat."

Robb focused his inner sight on the finger and endured the sharp ache of the fresh wound on the hand. He was grateful when Samlan finally ordered they drop the heavy bone, made doubly heavy and awkward by its eons-long transformation into stone.

The bone dropped heavily toward the water. The waves rose higher to enfold it, welcome it.

But . . .

But at the last second a bolt of lightning crackled out of the sky, speeding toward the bone as a lodestone toward the pole. Faster, sharper, the blazing light formed an arrow and struck the bone dead center a heartbeat before it touched the water. Fragments exploded upward with a great boom of sound that knocked Tem flat on his back.

A huge wave followed, swamping the boat. Tem rolled to his knees, scrabbling to hang onto something, anything as the deck tilted, pushing him to slide closer and closer to the roiling ocean.

"Master!" he yelled, praying desperately for help.

"See to yourself," Samlan snarled as he climbed into the tiny rescue boat lashed to the other side of the deck.

Another wave slammed into Tem, slapping him face first into the deck. Blackness engulfed him.

The vision ended.

Robb slumped sideways against the lounge, too exhausted to remain conscious. Too heartsore to do aught but weep.

"So, the master magician escaped. But he lost my bone. You must find him. You know who he is. You can find him again. You can summon him and get answers."

"Not now. Now I can do nothing. I barely have strength to breathe."

-᪥-

What is that smell? Sort of sweet with an acid undertone and an overlay of stale urine and sweat. It is close to the elixir of life I have found only during the high rituals of sex and torture of an initiation into the coven.

Without waiting for the nicety of taking Bette with me—she is in the laundry seeing to my personal linen—I follow my nose through the meandering rooms and staircases, descending deeper and deeper. I pass the food storage and wine cellars with little interest, though I do note they are comfortably filled if a little lean on fresh vegetables. Geon explored this area earlier and told me the correct corridors to follow. But he went no farther because it was not the way to the library. He carves his own path through this world, guided by his reading and not by me.

That will change soon.

For I find only blank walls when my sense of smell and wave after wave of magical power tells me I should be atop my goal. Power rises through the stones at my feet, making my toes tingle and my thighs itch with the need to move. Like calling to like, bouncing off each other and amplifying at every rebound. This magic is born of pain and blood, as is mine. I feed on it to satiation and still there is more. I must find the source. Now!

Nothing in this castle follows a straight line. A good strategy for defense—confuse the enemy at every turn and withdraw toward a more defensible core by way of hidden passages, secret tunnels, and doors that don't look like doors.

Hmmmmmm. I stare at the dressed stones and crisp mortar. Nothing out of alignment. Nothing unusual. Perhaps I stare at the wrong wall. So I follow the backward logic of the place and search the blank wall on the opposite side of the cellar. The damp one that faces the ocean and the harbor. Not a stable location for a stairway. But then perhaps the damp and black mold on the mortar are merely illusions worthy of the master magicians of Coronnan.

Nothing there either. These cellars are vast. Many, many rooms that lead one into another. The subterranean levels must also cover as many acres in support of the massive stone keep and outbuildings above. What lies below the wine storage? Only a dungeon would go that deep into the foundations. A dungeon with limited access and means of escape.

So I follow the flow of air back the way I have come rather than seek the power and the scent that draws me. And so, at last I find a narrow wooden door bound in iron with freshly oiled hinges. A stout door that will not succumb easily to a battering ram. The lock is intricate and formidable. But I have magic within me. Strong magic generated by fear and pain and spilled blood.

Holding one finger at the edge of the lock I shoot a spell of unbinding directly into the mechanism. Three clicks and the sound of metal scraping metal and the lock releases. The door swings outward at a touch.

I sense openness in the blackness before me. No sunlight has ever penetrated this passage. But I have power and to spare. Power that builds by the moment.

A scream echoes off walls. The terror within the noise fills me so full of magical ecstasy that fire erupts from a torch stuffed awkwardly into a sconce. I can see the steps winding downward. But I don't need the light. My entire body is alight with the fire of magic.

Like to like. Unreal in its strength. Surreal in my affinity with it.

Slowly I make my way down, drinking in the power, the tension building within me as I go. The stairs end and a stone passageway slopes upward. I follow it, finding doors to prison cells on either side. A cross corridor leads inland away from the harbor. What little moisture manages to seep through the foundations evaporates. A little light filters through high windows. My sense of direction tells me that I am now near the central courtyard.

Then I see him. A tall, well-formed man wearing the uniform of the King's Guard with a gold sash crossing his chest from right shoulder to left hip, where a long sword is sheathed. A plain blade, utilitarian rather than ceremonial. I *have found the one I need and quietly come to stand beside him.*

He knows I am there. I can sense it in the flare of his nostril and an edging of his right hand closer to the grip of his blade.

A weak and whimpering moan of despair leaks through the closed door of a large cell with a wide wooden door. No bars. No window with a cover, no way to peek inside. Either the door is open and the contents of the cell fully visible, or it is closed and whatever lurked there could be forgotten.

Except for the smell of blood and death, pain and fear.

Execution.

"What was his crime?" I ask. The tension that leads to ecstatic release leaves me. I am exhilarated but exhausted at the same time. Being present at an execution is almost better than the act of sex itself.

"He failed to notify me that Lady Maria left the castle. He then failed in not reporting the presence of Prince Toskellar in the city." His shoulders relax as he too senses the end of the thrill.

"Then you are indeed the man I seek. I need one who knows everything that happens and is therefore the most powerful."

He nods. "And you are?"

"Do I need an introduction?"

"Confirmation of your purpose, Princess Rejiia."

"My purpose here in this dungeon or my purpose in seeking an audience with your king?"

"Both."

"Does the execution of a criminal bother you, Captain? I had heard that the death penalty was not a part of your culture."

"It is now."

"And do you agree with your king bringing it to Amazonia?"

"It is . . . necessary."

"But you? Are you in favor of it?"

"Not at first."

"But now you glory in it. As do I."

He nods again.

"Then you and I have a common purpose. A common goal. You already sense the power thrumming through the walls. I can show you how to use that power."

He looks interested, urging me to proceed.

I wave a hand and every torch flares to life as if the sun itself broke through the solid walls, revealing the blood leaking out from under one prison door.

"Parlor tricks. I want real power."

"Then come with me. Is there a locked door you have always wanted to look behind? Is there a person you would like struck senseless? Is there a mind you would like to listen to as if to your own thoughts?"

He offers me his arm to escort me out of the charnel house of a dungeon. I have found a new member of my coven.

"I don't like this move," Lukan muttered as he shifted the weight of his pack to a less awkward position.

For once, he caught no glimpse of Geon dogging his heels.

"I don't either," Gerta whispered from slightly behind his left shoulder. "But the lady says it is necessary."

"What can we do from the castle that we can't do from outside?" Lukan asked.

"A lot," Skeller replied. He strode slightly ahead of them with Lady Maria leaning heavily on his arm. Chess walked on the other side of her, also providing support to the tiny woman.

She limped so badly Lukan's hips ached in sympathy. He couldn't imagine going through life with such a debilitating deformity, let alone expending tremendous energy to hide it. When she'd first arrived at the blacksmith shop she'd moved slowly, cautiously. Now she couldn't hide her disability.

At home, the healers would have worked on her until

they'd either corrected the twisted leg or at least given her a brace and built-up shoe so that she could move more normally.

"I can understand Lady Maria wanting you as her personal bodyguard," Lukan continued speaking with Gerta. They both kept their gazes moving, noting and assessing potential dangers—like the idle man leaning casually against a well at the next intersection. He watched the five of them long after they passed beyond his seemingly casual observation.

Gerta nodded to him, acknowledging the man's overly curious gaze.

"Only a little farther, Aunt Maria," Skeller said soothingly.

"We could carry you," Chess offered. Always polite. Always thinking of others. Lukan remembered why he hadn't befriended the boy at the University. He was just too good to be true. He should have been a healer. Lukan didn't know why he'd become Robb's apprentice rather than one of the hospitallers.

"I am not an invalid," Lady Maria insisted. Her next step was bolder. But the effect of asserting her independence was spoiled when her knee buckled. Skeller had to hold her up. They stood rooted in place for many long moments while the lady panted her way through the pain.

Lukan and Gerta moved hastily to stand before and aft. Gerta held a long dagger along her thigh, ready to raise it in defense. Lukan held his staff across his body, preparing a stream of fire to shoot from the tip. He'd always wanted to throw that spectacular spell, even though he knew the fire would be mostly illusion and not dangerous.

He heard the clop of many steeds approaching rapidly from his left. He shifted his staff in that direction.

"Hold," Gerta ordered. "It's the king and his guards."

"How can you tell at this distance?" Lukan squinted into the distance. All he could see was a dozen tall steeds and men riding atop them.

"A dozen steeds with men riding them," Gerta confirmed as if that were answer enough.

Lukan had to think about that. "In all my wanderings I've seen few steeds inside the city and then only dray steeds hauling heavy goods into and out of the market."

Skeller rolled his eyes as if the observation was too obvious to note.

"That's Master Robb, third steed back," Chess gasped, letting go of Lady Maria. He took two running steps before Lukan grabbed his collar and held him fast.

"Are you asking for death?" Lukan hissed into his ear.

"But . . . but we can grab him and hide him in the city!"

"But we can't get him out of the city. We need to plan!"

"That is why you need to be inside the castle," Lady Maria said shakily. "He looks ill. You'll not get far with him today." With more determination than strength she set off down a narrow side street that led to the back of the castle while the steeds continued past them toward the primary entrance.

CHAPTER 24

"YOU'VE DONE ENOUGH for today," Souska said gently.

Lily sorted bundles of herbs in their little round hut—barely tall enough for either of them to stand up at the center ridgepole. "Never enough . . ."

"For today, you have done all you can. You are stronger but you still need more rest and food to rebuild your health."

"I've said that so often to Val, it sounds strange directed at me." Lily sat back on her heels, staring into the distance. Was she speaking to her twin?

Her golden red hair had more body and luster than just a few days ago. Her cheeks were still too pale and drawn, with dark shadows encircling her eyes like purple bruises. She looked more like her fragile twin than ever.

"That's just it, Souska, there isn't enough food. Our patients need it more than I; they succumbed deeper to the miasma. And there will be no food at all after we burn the fields. And we must burn the fields. The dragons said so." She turned bleak eyes up to Souska.

"I've been thinking about that." Souska thrust aside the leather curtain that sufficed as a door. It provided only a little privacy and less protection. Come winter, they needed to move in with one of the other families.

Outside, in the village common, two women threw a bit of grain for the flusterhens. They could eat the grain and let the hens starve, or feed the grain to the hens and at least have eggs, and maybe meat.

Two men released the remaining goats from their pen and drove them toward the far fields, hoping the fallow grasses would provide disease-free forage for the animals.

Three days ago, no one had stirred in the village except Lily.

How many other villages throughout Coronnan suffered the same disease, but without Lily's help?

"There is a plant, we called it fireweed back home because it was always the first thing to grow in a field after a fire," Souska said hesitantly.

"What about this plant?" Lily asked, some enthusiasm returning to her voice. She'd grown up tending a huge vegetable garden, flusterhens, and goats, but knew almost nothing of larger-scale farming.

"It is good forage for animals."

"But will it grow after we salt the fields? Don't forget, the dragons said the miasma needed fire *and* salt to kill it completely."

"I don't know. I'll have to taste the dirt after we burn."

"Taste the dirt?" Lily looked skeptical. The deep shadows within their hut turned her face into a skeletal mask.

A portent?

Souska shuddered.

"I think I need to taste the dirt now."

"No, Souska. No, don't!" Lily's frightened words stopped Souska in the doorway. "The miasma is still there. You'll get sick and I . . . I'm afraid to go on without help."

"Don't be afraid. I only need a grain or two to know what's in there."

"That may be too much. Wait until we burn."

"What if we don't need to burn?"

"The dragons said we do. My parents always taught me to trust the dragons."

"But we only have the word of one dragon. Krystaal. And she's young. She may not have all the wisdom and knowledge of the elder dragons. She may be wrong."

"Dragons are *never* wrong. What one knows, they all know."

Souska doubted that. But who was she to question anyone? She had almost no magic.

But she knew about farms, soil, crops, rotating fields . . . "Perhaps a young dragon could misinterpret what the others know."

She stepped out of the hut and headed for the edge of the far field, beyond the village precincts to the wild prairie.

"Where are you going, Souska?" Lily called after her. She stood in the doorway, holding onto the frame as though she didn't have enough strength to follow.

"I'm going to call a dragon."

Robb stumbled heavily on the upslant of the dungeon corridor. If he took one more step, he thought he might vomit, or pass out from exhaustion.

Lokeen had not believed him when he said he could do nothing more after throwing the spell to find Samlan. He'd barely had the strength to eat, let alone ride another half day into the city.

Now he knew why scrying into the past was considered a spell of last resort. If looking at events only a few moons away from the present cost him this much strength, what would peering at history do to a magician?

He wondered that those commissioned with solving crimes ever tried it. They could see the truth but they might not recover enough to tell others what they'd conjured.

At this moment, Robb didn't care if he lived or died. He just knew he could stand no longer.

His guards threw him into the nearest cell, closer to the stairs and as far away from the Krakatrice pen as possible. His window, high up on the outside wall of the cell was small, barely an air opening. He didn't care. He probably wouldn't live long enough to breathe the freshness of the back courtyard anyway.

He landed on a pallet that smelled fresh, rolled onto his back, and let blackness creep over him.

A sound disturbed him. The light had shifted. He must have slept several hours. Not enough. He groaned as he rolled to his side, every muscle and joint in his body protesting the movement.

"Can you sit?" a woman asked. Not a harsh voice, nor the shy whisper of Maria.

"Who?"

"I'm Gerta. Maria sent me with broth and bread."

He cracked one eye open to see a tall silhouette standing beside him. She gave the impression of long, raw muscle, not an ounce of fat on her body. She wore a version of the palace guard uniform: black trews and tunic with red piping at the collar, cuff, and down the outside leg seam, and a red sash around her waist. He thought the sash might hide pockets and sheaths for weapons. Even if she hadn't discarded weapons before entering the cell—as all of the male guards did—he didn't have the mental or physical strength to steal one. He doubted he'd best this woman in a wrestling match even in his prime.

"Can you sit?" she asked again, patient and withdrawn, showing no concern.

"With help," he choked out.

She knelt, placing a fragrant tray on the floor as she thrust one well-muscled arm beneath his shoulders and grabbed his left arm above the elbow with the other. He didn't add much help to maneuvering him up enough to lean against the wall, panting from the effort of moving at all.

"Must I feed you too?" Now impatience worked its way into her voice.

"Give me a moment to breathe."

"You've had three hours."

"I need about forty-five more."

"You don't have it." She thrust a morsel of bread into his mouth.

It tasted like . . . the aftermath of the best sex ever, sweet, aromatic, light but full of seeds and texture.

"Don't swallow it whole, you'll be sick. Take time to chew."

He obeyed, savoring the wonder of fresh-baked bread while he tried to remember how to swallow. That accomplished, she held a bowl of warm liquid to his lips, salty, rich broth. He swished it around his mouth letting some of the moisture penetrate before forcing himself to swallow. It came easier this time, like an old skill he hadn't practiced in a long, long time.

More broth, more bread. By the third dose of each he was able to hold the bowl himself.

"Finish it, then sleep a bit more. Friends will come to your window at midnight."

Only the click of the latch on the outside of the door and the presence of more of his meal told him he hadn't dreamed her. She reminded him a lot of his Maigret when they were young and carefree, wandering the world without plan.

"Maggie, I miss you." He fell asleep and dreamed of his wife.

Lukan paced the opulent suite Lady Maria had assigned Skeller. Plenty of room for the bard and Lukan and Chess to share. Lukan had appropriated the valet's closet—an alcove with a normal-sized bed and built-in cupboards for his own meager possessions and a full wardrobe for the prince's. And he had a door to close for privacy. His parents' bedroom back home was smaller.

Chess found another closet on the other side of the master bedroom for his own use. That left Skeller alone in the center room with a bed big enough to sleep all three of them, and a couple more. He had to use a set of three portable steps to climb onto the down mattress. *No thank you!* Lukan thought to himself.

At the moment, all three of them waited in the front room or parlor. Waited for what, Lukan didn't know.

Then he wondered if Glenndon had a similar suite at the palace in Coronnan City. He didn't envy his older brother the lack of privacy, or the necessity of maintaining a large wardrobe, or . . . much of anything at this moment.

At least this suite was up, on the third story. Lukan *really* wanted to find a way to the top of the massive tower, to stand outside and let the wind wash him clean of the confining toxins of living in a city. He hadn't been higher than the two-story rooftop of the blacksmith shop since leaving the ship. The entire city seemed to move onto their flat roofs the moment the sun touched the horizon in summer. He understood the need and liked the idea. A lot.

"What are we waiting for?" Chess finally asked.

Skeller looked up from tuning his harp, something he did a lot, especially to fill idle hours, a familiar ritual to ease his thought process. If he were truly troubled, he'd be plucking random chords from the instrument. "Aunt Maria said we must stay here until summoned. I presume she's waiting for the king to find out we're here."

"If the population of this castle is anything like the University, someone informed him before he dismounted in the courtyard," Lukan muttered. He snapped his fingers to light a candle against the growing darkness. Nothing happened. He tried again. This was a truly simple spell, one of the first taught to new apprentices.

He tried a third time. Not even smoke left his fingertips. In frustration he slapped the candle and its pewter holder with the back of his hand.

"I've heard rumors that there is something in the castle that prohibits magic of any kind," Chess offered meekly.

"Then how did my father dispatch letters to me?" Skeller asked.

"You'll have to ask him yourself," Gerta said, appearing at the door. She closed the door behind her and leaned heavily against the solid barrier. With her eyes closed, she breathed deeply and her posture relaxed.

"You look different in uniform," Lukan said in sympathy. He wouldn't like the stiff fabric of her tunic and trews, or the red piping that had to lie in straight lines no matter how weary she was.

"I'd forgotten how tense everyone is, how wary. No one trusts anyone else, and I hate it. But Lady Maria needs me to protect her and to reach out to the other women soldiers and rebuild our unit." She heaved a big sigh and lurched straight once more. "His Majesty has demanded you present yourself and explain your unannounced return, Your Highness," she addressed Skeller formally.

"And so the dance begins," he muttered. Reluctantly he slipped the harp into her case, staring at it a long time.

"I don't think the king will appreciate your bringing the harp to a formal audience," Gerta said.

"Then bring her I must." Skeller fitted his arms through the straps and turned to face the door, grim determination firming his jaw. "And I do believe I shall play a spritely dance for him. He hates dancing."

Lukan groaned. He'd played similar games with his father and masters, doing his best to unsettle and challenge them because . . . well, because he could.

Somehow, he sensed that Skeller played a much more dangerous game. The scent of fear still permeated the city.

"Um . . . Lukan, you can't bring your staff," Gerta said, staring straight into his eyes with deadly determination.

CHAPTER 25

"I AM A magician. My staff stays with me," Lukan insisted, clutching the precious instrument with pride.

"Precisely. It brands you as a magician. Lokeen already has one magician in his dungeon. He'll throw you and Chess there as well at the first whiff of magic. And believe me, you do not want to be a prisoner in his dungeon," she returned, standing squarely in front of him. "The Great Mother only knows why he hasn't imprisoned Princess Rejiia. She reeks of magic, and I have no talent for recognizing it!"

"Rejiia's magic is designed to cast a veil over the eyes of her victims so that they see only her allure and not her purpose. She will present obstacles if she recognizes us." Lukan met Gerta's gaze, realizing once again that he topped her by only an inch, and he was headed toward being as tall as his father and brother. Her muscles, honed by years of working the forge, and weapons training before that, probably gave her strength well beyond his, and he couldn't work any magic within the castle to compensate for the difference.

"If I may offer a compromise?" Skeller asked. A half smile played around his mouth, as if he knew something they didn't and found it amusing.

"Such as?" Lukan and Gerta replied together, still staring at each other and still snarling.

"Gerta, will you lend me your dagger? I'd use mine, but

then I'd have no weapon at all and I know you have at least a dozen others," Skeller continued. He sauntered over to the bed, threw off the coverlet and stripped the top sheet from the mattress.

"What for?" she demanded, finally breaking eye contact with Lukan.

"An old trick used by scallywags and scoundrels on the caravan circuit." He attacked the sheet with his knife, tearing off several long strips of fabric, each about as wide as his palm.

Cautiously, Gerta drew her long knife from its sheath.

"No, the whole thing, sheath too, but not the belt."

She unbuckled the belt and slid the sheath's loop along its length until it was free, and then handed it to him.

Quickly, Skeller wrapped one strip of fine linen—so fine Lukan had thought it silk at first—around and around the sheath until all but the very tip of the pommel was covered. "Lukan, your arm?"

Lukan proffered his right arm, the one that wasn't holding his staff.

"Your left arm. You want the right free for defending yourself, or whatever."

Lukan shifted his grip on the staff from left to right and stuck out his arm. Skeller placed the wrapped dagger on the outside of his forearm so that the pommel rested just above the elbow and bound it in place with a few light wraps at wrist and middle arm. The he returned the staff to the crook of Lukan's elbow and wrapped some more.

"This is very awkward," Lukan complained.

"It looks like a crutch," Chess offered.

"Exactly," Skeller confirmed. "Now, a few sharp bits of gravel, I keep on hand for throwing in the eyes of attackers, wrapped in more linen and bound to your bent knee." He stooped to finish his disguise.

"That's going to hurt like . . . an unlanced boil," Gerta said.

"Only if he straightens the leg. Limp a lot, Lukan. It

makes the crutch more plausible. You are now a homeless cripple and not worth noticing. I doubt even Rejiia will recognize you."

Chess began giggling.

"What?" Lukan said a little too loudly. He liked the idea of a disguise, but this . . . this was humiliating.

"You need an eye patch. Then you'll look even more helpless."

"He's right," Gerta agreed.

Skeller dug in his pack, the one he hadn't bothered unpacking because the wardrobe held more of what he'd need in the castle than his wandering essentials. "I really like this shirt. But it's so threadbare with ingrained dirt Aunt Maria won't let me wear it in her presence." Grimly he ripped the hem off the garment and tied it diagonally around Lukan's head so that his left eye was covered.

"I can still see daylight and some outlines through it," Lukan said.

"Good. Then you aren't as blind as people will think and you can still defend yourself with the staff on that side."

Lukan experimented with lashing to the left and behind with the staff. He had control.

"And you, Gerta, can extract the dagger if you must just by pulling on the pommel. But leave it in there as long as possible, not only to hide just how well armed we are, but to give the arm brace a bit more stability." Skeller pulled the dagger free of its double sheath about an inch to demonstrate.

"I guess we're ready then," Chess said. He sounded disappointed that he didn't have a weapon or a disguise.

"Not quite yet." Skeller returned to his pack and withdrew a thick canvas sack smaller than his palm with a tight drawstring. "Pepper powder. A pinch blown into the eyes is guaranteed to temporarily blind anyone getting too close."

Chess smiled hugely. And they trooped out the door, Lukan trailing behind as he discovered just how much star gravel on the back of his knee hurt.

"You will not punish the boy!" Maria screamed at her brother-in-law. She didn't know where she found the courage to defy him.

"My son is no longer a boy. He must take responsibility for his actions," King Lokeen said lazily, lounging in his throne, nibbling on honey-dipped walnuts imported from Coronnan.

"He spent some time exploring the world, furthering his education. You dispatched letters to him, he returned. He has proven himself responsible and loyal," Maria argued.

"I have indeed returned," Toskellar drawled from the doorway, leaning on the frame indolently. He looked as lazy and uninterested in the mob of courtiers gathered to watch the show of discipline that might end in bloodshed as he had when a rebellious teenager.

But in the years since, Maria had learned much about observing posture and the way a man's gaze flitted here and there, weighing, assessing. Within three flicks of his eyelids, she knew that her beloved nephew had noted every means of escape, including some she might not consider.

"Introduce me to your friends, son," Lokeen demanded. He scowled as Gerta took a place next to Maria, half a step behind her left shoulder.

"Unnecessary. Waifs I encountered on the road and brought along for companionship." Toskellar lurched upright from his slouch. He retained the lazy, arrogant posture.

"Necessary," Lokeen spat. "If they leech hospitality from me, then I will know them."

Maria took one painful step forward and spread her hands, palm up in an image of abject innocence. "A homeless teenager, a crippled beggar, and a female warrior who was exiled from this place two years ago; of what possible use can they be?"

"You'd be surprised." Lokeen glared at her.

"Why did you expend a great deal of money and energy

to pay a magician to summon me home?" Still looking in-
dolent and only mildly curious, Skeller examined his fingernails rather than look his father in the eye.

"I have found you a bride. We can hold the ceremony in
a matter of weeks. Get her pregnant with a daughter, then
you will be free to wander the world again and I shall continue as regent for your queen."

"No," said a tall, black-haired woman emerging from behind Lokeen.

All the little murmurings and shuffling of a crowded
room grew silent.

Toskellar and his crippled companion—who hadn't been
crippled a few hours ago—started and reached for weapons.
Gerta was only a heartbeat behind in placing one large, cal-
lused hand on her sword grip and the other beneath Maria's
elbow to assist in their escape.

Lukan stood almost frozen in place, gaze glued to Rejiia
and the servants who lingered behind her. How could he
look anywhere but at her magnificent beauty?

He blinked and swallowed, knowing full well that she
cast a magical allure around her. From the stillness around
him, he suspected most of the men in the room had also
fallen victim to her enchantment.

(*Knowledge is power.*) The dragon voice in the back of
his head crept around the edges of his need to move closer
to Rejiia, touch her, kiss her, make her his own. He gripped
his staff with his right hand, in an awkward cross-arm pose.
He needed his essential tool in his hand, not cradled in the
crook of his offside elbow.

The staff tingled in his hand. *Knowledge is power. I know
what she's doing, therefore I can break her spell.* Another
blink and a deep swallow and his eyes cleared. No longer did
he gaze lustfully through a veil of softer colors and misty
emotions. The sharp contrasts and straight lines of real vision jarred him the rest of the way back into control of his

mind and body. *I am stronger than she. She can only build
upon existing lust. I know her for what she is and therefore
have no lust, so her spell upon me is weak. I can break it.*

But he didn't want to let her know that. So he modified
his expression and continued to follow her movements with
his eyes.

King Lokeen almost drooled.

Lady Maria and Gerta frowned. Good. They were im-
mune, no lust or admiration to build the spell upon. For
some reason Lukan couldn't imagine, the magic bubble of
enticement extended to the other court ladies in the room,
but not to these two. Rejiia dismissed them as unimportant.

Bad mistake.

Gerta inched her long sword half-free of its sheath.
"Who are you and why are you here?" she demanded.

A tall man wearing the house colors of black with red
trim and a gold sash from right shoulder to left hip stepped
between Rejiia and Gerta. He too drew his sword an equal
length from its sheath.

Geon melted away and reappeared on the opposite side
of the room.

Lukan now had enemies on two fronts. He poked Chess
with the tip of his staff, urging him to turn around and take
note.

The newcomer must be the captain of the guard, with
that gold sash, the only person normally allowed to bear
arms in the presence of the king. Gerta got away with her
own weapons because she captained Lady Maria's guard. In
the old days she would have taken precedence over any
male in the household, including the king.

King Lokeen continued to gaze fixedly upon Rejiia and
gape. Then he roused himself enough to address the dozen
couples milling about the room. "Lords and ladies of Amazonia, I present to you Princess Rejiia, granddaughter to the
royal house of Coronnan."

"Works fast, doesn't she," Skeller muttered out of the
side of his mouth.

So, he too was not included in Rejiia's need to subdue her audience with lust. Or his own musical magic saw through her spells and rejected them. But how had she drawn enough magic *inside* the castle to throw even this minor spell, where Lukan could find none?

Rejiia drew in a deep breath, as if savoring the taste of the air, and released it. The fuzziness around the edges of Lukan's vision returned along with a need to reach out and touch her. But he was not worthy. His hands were ingrained with dirt and his nails broken . . .

(Knowledge is power,) the dragon voice insisted. It felt like a kick in the head.

"Her tongue flicks in and out like a snake," Skeller whispered.

"Snakes?" Lukan asked himself and his friend. "Are there any of the giant snakes in or near the castle?" That would explain his inability to gather dragon magic or draw ley line magic from the Kardia. But it didn't explain why Rejiia could.

Or did it?

"Princess Rejiia has come from Coronnan to be my new bride," Lokeen said. His words came out a little like he was reading from a text and not quite certain what words came next. "I negotiated in secret with her father, Lord Laislac. The marriage treaty is signed. We marry as soon as the bridal clothes can be made."

"Isn't Laislac Ariiell's father?" Skeller asked, again out of the side of his mouth.

"Yes. That's who the king negotiated with, but she's not the bride he negotiated *for*," Lukan muttered under his breath. "Half the truth is more plausible than a full lie."

Rejiia beamed a huge smile at the court. But her tongue continued to flick in and out very quickly as if tasting the air. Tasting the air like a snake. The captain of the guard returned a sly smirk to her, also tasting the air, quickly, only the very tip of his tongue clearing his teeth.

Geon remained stolid and silent in his corner.

"She's drinking in the smell of fear and gaining power from it." Lukan kept his head down and his gaze averted. He'd heard tales about snakes. He'd trained to hunt the Krakatrice before Robb disappeared. If she had aligned herself with the monsters, then her gaze would be hypnotic, ensnaring the unwary. Paralyzing them.

"If Lokeen started with baby Krakatrice, their bubble of protection would be small, growing with them. Three moons ago they wouldn't interfere with magic. Today they block it completely," Lukan continued thinking half-aloud. "The bubble only goes ten, maybe twenty feet up, depending on the number and their size. I'm betting the fourth floor and above are outside the bubble."

"I have found a royal bride to succeed my late wife as your queen. She is young and healthy and will give us daughters to continue the line," Lokeen continued.

"Young and healthy, my foot," Lukan snorted, continuing to whisper. "She's only a few years younger than my mother. They were half sisters. Lord Krej was Mama's father, but her mother was a peasant girl, not worth marrying." He looked frankly at Skeller, the prince who'd just been thrust aside from the succession. "My sister Lily is nearly as royal as Rejiia and you love her already."

Skeller's head whipped around to stare at Lukan. "Why didn't you tell me this last spring when there was still a chance that Lily and I could make a life together?"

"The subject never came up." Lukan flashed him a grin. "We don't talk about Grandfather Krej as anything but the enemy; we don't want to acknowledge him, or Rejiia, as relatives."

"I thought Lady Ariiell in her raging insanity would make a bad queen for my father. Even after she crawled out of her guilt and grief and pain, she's too stubborn and independent. Rejiia is worse," Skeller spat.

"So what are you going to do about it?"

"I wish I knew."

CHAPTER 26

ROBB SHIVERED IN the cold night air. He wasn't cer-tain whether he'd slept. He hadn't been this tired since his apprentice days, right after the Leaving: the day that the twelve Master Magicians had walked out the Council of Provinces and moved with all their possessions to the mountains, depriving Coronnan of magic and advice and clerical skills. With the entire country angry and suspicious of magic and magicians (thanks in large part to Lord Krej's manipulation of the royal family and council through magic), Master Jaylor had ordered all-day and all-night watches. More than once Robb and his best friend Marcus had gone two nights and three days without sleep.

But they had been young, then, healthy, well fed, and resilient.

He'd aged more than fifteen years since then and suf-fered moons of privation in this filthy dungeon. He'd need a lot longer than half of one night's good sleep in a comfort-able bed, and more meals of fresh bread and salty broth to recover his strength.

All that he knew at this moment was that he needed food and sleep. And an extra blanket. The last he dared not hope for. The first would come because Lokeen still needed him alive. The second he hoped for after the next meal.

Had he dreamed the woman in house livery who had

given him his meal? The bowl rattled next to his pallet every time he rolled over. Therefore, someone had brought him sustenance. He hoped her message that friends would come for him at midnight had been real as well.

His eyes drifted closed then snapped open as a night breeze worked through the tiny window and reawakened the flusterbumps on his arms, legs, and back.

Was that a scraping at the bars and rockwork around the window? He opened his eyes only to slam them shut again in the too bright light at the opening. After the stygian darkness of the dungeon, any light near blinded him.

"Master Robb," a voice filtered through his brain. "Master Robb, wake up."

"If you aren't here to rescue me, then go away and let me sleep."

Something blocked the light for a moment. Then a whisper of wool brushed his nose. He sneezed. Violently. The top of his head felt ready to drop off.

And he shivered again, deeply, from his skin into his bones and back out again.

The wool weighed heavy on his chest, and he realized that whoever crouched at the window had dropped him a blanket. A wonderfully warm and soft blanket. Well, it scratched his face, but it was softer than the straw he lay upon. Quickly he spread the blanket over his entire length. A modicum of relief crept outward from his body core. "Bless you, young man."

"It's me, Master Robb, Chess."

"Chess?" Surprise and delight warmed him even more. "You're alive?"

"And well, sir. I hid and ran as you instructed. I don't know what happened to the others."

"They are dead," Robb said flatly. "Samlan recruited them—upon pain of death if they rebelled—and they died anyway. He left them to die in the storm he'd used them to conjure. When I get out of here, the first thing I will do is kill him."

"He's dead, sir," said a slightly older voice, richer in timbre as if trained to speak or sing publicly.

"Are you certain?" Maybe he could just tell Lokeen that his pet magician had died and not have to scry into the past again.

But he sincerely hoped he would never see Lokeen again.

"I watched the light of life fade from his eyes as . . . as my knife slid into his heart," the rich voice said. He nearly choked on the last words. Not a trained warrior used to death in battle, then.

Robb heard some scrapes and scuffles among the crouchers at his window.

"After I ran from the castle I found refuge with a blacksmith nearby," Chess continued. "I watched and listened as best I could, hoping to hear about you. I've brought Lukan with me."

"Thank the Stargods. How fast can you get me out of here? Lokeen has a farm dedicated to raising Krakatrice. We have to burn them out, salt the land, and bring hard, drenching rain to kill them. We have to stop the king's madness, thinking he can rule the world through the terror of the snakes."

"I know the snakes grant an illusion of power to the ones they bond with," Lukan said. He sounded older, more self-assured than when Robb had left him at the University. "But it is only an illusion. The snakes are in control. Especially if it is a matriarch forming the bond."

"I saw no matriarch at the farm. Just lots of eggs and juvenile males. I think Lokeen's followers steal them from wild nests. Dormant and kept near freezing, but not quite," Robb added. Small hope that the absence of a matriarch would lessen the king's insanity.

"The farm," a woman said on a whispered exhale. He thought it might be the same woman who had brought him food and helped him eat the first few crucial bites.

"What do you know, Gerta?" That perpetually angry voice could only belong to Lukan.

"Whispers of fear. Slavery, drudgery, working to death, having your family executed if you do not obey." Her voice shook. A woman as tall and strong as she, who wore a soldier's uniform as a second skin, needed grave news to crack her demeanor.

"You have to get me out of here so we can destroy the farm. Only then can we begin to bring down the king's tyranny." Robb forced himself to stand so that he was closer to eye level with the window. The top of his head brushed the bottom sill. He made sure he brought the blanket with him and draped it around his shoulders.

"No, sir, we can't break you free," the richly trained voice said.

"This place is killing me!" Robb screamed, no longer caring if anyone else heard him. No longer caring for anything but the possibility of getting away from Lokeen, the monster snakes, and this dungeon.

"Sir, think carefully, logically, please." Could that really be Lukan speaking? He'd never been careful or logical in his life.

"If we break you out now, your absence will be noted," the woman said. "We'd never get out of the city, let alone as far as the farm."

"She's right, sir," Chess added hesitantly. "Can you persevere a bit longer?"

Robb sank back onto his pallet, more weary in his mind and body than he had been when dumped here this afternoon. "I can die in peace if I know that you have destroyed the farm."

"That won't be necessary. I think I can convince the king to move you back to the tower." That was the older, unknown young man. "Lady Maria will see that you are cared for. She likes you. She needs you."

"That . . . that would be helpful," Robb sighed.

"How do we find the farm, sir?" the woman asked.

"I could take you there."

"No, sir. We have to go without you this time. But we will be back. As soon as we can. And when we return we will get you out of here and I'll transport you back to Coronnan as fast as possible." Lukan sounded so sure of himself, Robb didn't doubt him.

"How do we find the farm?" the woman asked again.

Robb told her of the road that followed the river toward the east.

"That road forks three times. Which do we take?"

"Stay beside the river until you reach the plateau. Then turn right, away from the river. Follow the track even though it narrows to nearly nothing. In the next vale you'll find the farm. The road widens, straightens, and is free of ruts and potholes from there."

"Three days," the woman confirmed.

"We were only gone two!" Robb insisted, disappointment cramping his gut.

"You only stayed there one night, sir. We might need longer to torch the place and conjure a storm," Lukan said. He didn't sound reassuring. "I want to make sure the slaves get free before we destroy everything."

"You'll have to stay here at the castle, Bard," the woman said. "You have to do what you can to protect Master Robb and prevent the king from ruining Amazonia any further."

"Three days to observe and rally forces," Lukan added.

Maria suppressed a yawn despite the sprightly music Toskellar plucked from his harp while sitting beside her at the base of the dais. Her nephew worked his jaw as if he too longed for his bed. But Lokeen had commanded dancing, and dancing the court would do. Even Frederico had been enlisted to shuffle his feet beside gaily dressed ladies who tried to imitate Rejiia. He did not look enticed or interested, or anything but embarrassed.

But the lady's servant, Geon, lurked in the shadows,

watching everything, noting every conversation. Maria almost sympathized with him. His scarred face and missing eye put him among the deformed, like herself. People looked the other way rather than acknowledge ugliness intruding into their pretty world of music and dancing and drinking too much wine and beta arrack.

At this moment the black-haired witch pranced with the captain of the guard, revealing an immodest amount of leg as she lifted her skirts to kick and twirl and shake her enticing bottom. The king couldn't take his eyes off her.

Disgusting.

She had to end this farce of a betrothal before it led to marriage. Toskellar's fingers slowed on the strings of his harp—the same instrument he'd loved and maintained since his early teens.

"Play something akin to a dirge," she whispered to him. She knew his talent, knew how he controlled crowds with his music.

He grinned at her, though his eyes drooped with fatigue. With a quick flick of his fingers he adjusted the tuning of his harp. His next chord came out a low and guttural moan that lingered and droned while individual notes dragged themselves free of the strings. Her heart grew heavy and her eyes moistened. She remembered the day of her sister's death and wept genuine tears of grief and fear. Fear of what Lokeen would do to Amazonia without the restraining influence of his queen. Well, not much restraint. He did what he wanted in her name, only maintaining the illusion of being her consort. If he broke too many traditions, alienated too many rich merchants while Yolanda lived, the people could depose him in her name.

The moment she died, he no longer had to bow to any tradition or custom.

One by one the simpering courtiers dropped out of the dance, rubbing their eyes and feet stumbling, as if they had not enough energy left to step above the rush-strewn floor.

Rejiia and her captain carried on for a few steps more.

Then abruptly the witch stamped her foot and swung all of her attention on the bard.

"You displease me!" she wailed. "When I am queen, I will have your head."

Geon moved out of the shadows toward his lady.

"But you are not queen yet," Maria said boldly. More boldly than she thought she dared. "You know that you threaten the king's son with your displeasure. A true king would send you to the dungeon with his pet snakes for such an affront."

"Aunt Maria?" Toskellar stopped playing and stilled the strings with the flat of his hand.

Instantly the courtiers blinked and shook their heads, the music no longer dictating their emotions. Frederico drifted off to Maria's right, more keenly interested in the crowd now that he was free of them.

"Enough!" Lokeen shouted, rising from his throne to loom over the grumbling courtiers and his intended bride. "I will have no animosity within the family. Come, my dear son, my darling Rejiia, kiss and make up. 'Tis time we retired for the night." He held his arms out to both Rejiia and Toskellar, palms up in a magnanimous gesture of good will.

Unheard of. What kind of spell had the witch placed on the surly, selfish, inconsiderate bully?

Toskellar made a great deal of fuss over stowing his harp safely. As he turned back to face the room, he pitched his voice so that only Maria could hear. "The magician is ill. If you value his health and his life, move him to the tower. Tonight. Take him his glass. His staff too, if you can manage it. They will help him regain enough strength to fight off the miasma that plagues him."

Then he smiled brightly and hugged the witch, seemingly falling under her spell, as Lokeen clearly was already, and thoroughly.

But this manipulative bard was not the same man her nephew had been when he ran away to follow the caravan roads while still a teenager. This was a man, fully grown into his personal strength. He'd always wielded music as a weapon to control others through their emotions. Had he now mastered more mundane weapons like sword and ax?

Was he now the warrior who could receive the Spearhead of Destiny to save all of Amazonia?

CHAPTER 27

"DO WE HAVE to do this now?" Lukan asked around a yawn. The moon had set over the harbor, and the wheel of stars overhead circled toward dawn. And still he wore the uncomfortable beggar disguise.

He cast around him with as many senses as he could manage within the dampening field emitted by the Krakatrice. No trace of Geon lurking behind them or around the next corner. The man was everywhere. Not acting, not intruding, or interfering. Just there. Annoyingly *there*.

But for the moment he seemed to be elsewhere.

"We have to have people I trust in place before we leave for the farm," Gerta whispered back. She nudged him forward with the tip of her dagger against the small of his back.

Lukan stumbled and limped, cursing loudly. When he'd found his balance again, he took a long drink from the wineskin slung over his right shoulder on a braided thong, spilling more on his shirt than got into his mouth. He reeked of cheap wine. What guard in his right mind would think him dangerous?

He wobbled and lurched, rebounding from the parapet around the curtain wall of the castle into the body of the nearest guard. "Hey, watch yourself!" the man in red and black shouted. "This walkway is dangerously narrow for a sober man."

"Nah so loud," Lukan slurred, holding his wineskin against his temple. "Hurrs m'ears."

The guard's eyes followed the movement of the hand with the drink.

Lukan unclenched his left fist from his makeshift crutch, revealing a pinch of ground red pepper—the toxically hot kind grown only in the northernmost city on the continent, nearly at the equator. He exhaled, blowing the irritant directly into those distracted eyes. Before the man could scream in pain, Lukan whipped his staff across the back of the man's knees. He fell into Gerta's waiting arms. She clubbed him over the back of his head with something . . . heavy. Maybe a rock. Maybe the pommel of that wicked dagger. Something non-lethal anyway, she'd promised him that. The guard sagged heavily with one last painful moan as he sank into unconsciousness.

Chess slunk out from the shadows and helped Gerta drag the guard away.

While Lukan watched them, a woman guard slipped into place, watching the courtyard within and the city without as she paced an assigned route. A magnificent woman built much like Gerta. Hardly three heartbeats had passed between the first guard and the new one exchanging places. The tall silhouette with broad shoulders remained for any observers from down below.

"One down, six to go. That should be enough for tonight," Gerta said. "My people will continue while we're away."

Lukan could almost hear the smirk on her face. "Teamwork," Lukan whispered, wishing he could lose the gravel at the back of his knee. A painful bruise throbbed around each of the chunks and he swore they grew and multiplied with each limping step.

"Buck up, man. We'll travel faster knowing this job is under control." Gerta prodded him again into stumbling toward the next hapless man who had pledged allegiance to King Lokeen and his pet Krakatrice.

—≫—

"Krystaal!" Souska called as loudly as she dared. The villagers who could stand and walk wound slowly through their day, not far off. If they knew she called a dragon, they could easily take fright and send their fragile, illness-ravaged hearts fluttering uncontrollably and undo all the precious healing she and Lily had given them.

She'd tried calling yesterday at twilight. But . . . but she'd tried too hard after a long day and lost hours of time to one of her spells. Only Lily asking her if she'd talked to a dragon had reminded her of what she needed to do. If Lukan had summoned her, she might have awakened earlier, but she had not heard from him in days . . . or was it weeks. She couldn't tell how much time she lost each time she brewed a new batch of hellebore tea.

So now that dawn had come, she tried again to call a dragon. Only not so hard.

She scanned the skies seeking sight of an elusive transparent wing. Males were easier to spot with vivid colors showing through their wing veins, tips, and spinal horns. A female boasted an all-color/no-color swirl of iridescence and thus was harder to see, unless she wanted to be seen. Krystaal was the only female Souska had seen, other than Shayla, the aging matriarch. Perhaps females were only born when a matriarch reached an age when she knew she'd need a replacement.

"Krystaal!" she shouted again, a little louder in case the dragon was too far away to hear. "You said to call you if we needed your help. We need your help."

Still no answer, no bugle call of greeting, no sight of a wing glistening in the sunlight. Not even the stirring in the back of Souska's mind like a rustle of dry leaves before a telepathic message came through.

Telepathy. One of Souska's many failings. She could hear a message directed to her, but she could not initiate mind-to-mind communication. Just as Lily could receive a scry but not initiate one. Except . . . Lily had found the energy to call Maigret for help.

"Is calling a dragon like a summons or scrying spell?" she wondered. For a long, long time she could only respond to Lukan's spells. Now she could send and even eavesdrop when she had to. But it was hard work, leaving her more tired and hungry than she could afford—and prone to one of her forgetful spells. Maybe she'd tried too hard without focusing properly.

She couldn't afford to succumb to losing time now. The entire village depended upon her for healing and help with everyday chores. And Lily needed her to be vigorous and . . . and confident. Or at least give the appearance of confidence. Lily had recovered somewhat from her ordeal with the miasma. She was not fully well yet, needing daily doses of foxglove and willow bark to keep her stable.

"Oh, Krystaal, please answer me. I really, really, need you." This time she put the force of her mind into her plea, as if she were looking through her tiny shard of glass into a bowl of water lit by a candle flame.

Focus, she heard Lukan's lesson. *Narrow your vision to the candle reflected in the glass, just the flame, nothing else.*

Just the flame. Souska imagined pushing herself into a scrying spell. Just a routine scrying spell. Only she called a dragon instead of Lukan.

Souska here. Krystaal, we need your help.

(Krystaal here.)

The words popped into Souska's mind as if they were dormant seeds suddenly blossoming into life. They'd been there all along. She just needed to . . . to water and nourish them with the force of her will.

"Krystaal, we need food. Enough to get us through the winter. If we have to burn the fields and sow them with salt, they will produce nothing, not even weeds. The animals will have nothing to browse. Please, can you talk to Mistress Maigret or Master Marcus, or someone who can help us?"

(There are many suffering from this illness. They all need

help. Those that survive.) The warmth and humor of friendship seemed missing from her voice.

"I know that. And I will take medicine to them when I
can leave. But I am here and I see these people suffering.
Lily and I saved some of them. But why give them life only
to watch them die slowly of starvation? Please. Help us."

(Burn the fields.)

"What of the few crops . . . ?"

*(Tainted. You must treat them with fire and salt to destroy
all trace of the miasma.)* Was that a morsel of hesitation in
the dragon's proclamation?

"We will. When we have enough people on their feet to
contain the fire. But they will resist unless there is food to
replace what we destroy."

(Much of Coronnan will go hungry this winter.)

"There's a difference between hunger and starvation.
I've faced both as a child. Hunger is better than starvation.
Can you take a few stores from one place, a few more from
another? Deprive each place of only a little, but enough to
give this village life."

Something like a squeak of surprise, the kind a child
made when discovered by a parent playing with something
dangerous.

(We will discuss this. Shayla must speak to the king.) That
was a different voice. Deeper, older. Male?

"Hurry. Please."

A mental shrug terminated the conversation.

Tears pricked the back of Souska's eyes with disappointment. Half an answer and delay was almost worse than no
answer at all.

Breathing deeply, she gathered what was left of her courage to face the next chore. Tomorrow at dawn, they must
burn the fields and use the last of the salt to sterilize the
ground.

Tomorrow at dawn the villagers must face the choice of
never-ending sickness or a year of privation.

A memory of a hungry year at the farm where she'd

grown up—until she was beaten and thrown out because she *might* have a magical talent. Her gran had whispered in her ear: *always taste the dirt before plowing. The Kardia will tell you what it needs: more compost, a year to lie fallow, beans or wheat. The Kardia knows.*

"Sickness or no, I have to taste the dirt."

"This walkway is too narrow. Not enough maneuvering room to defend you," Gerta grumbled as she paced the giddy heights of the tallest tower in the castle.

Finally free of the crippled beggar costume, Lukan measured the space between stone parapet and the base of the conical roof with a different purpose. Up here he had a chance of working a summons. Fatigue dragged at him. He needed sleep. But he'd eaten well, so he should have the strength to throw a simple summons spell—though the bubble of magical protection around the Krakatrice tugged at him, draining the magic from the air and the ground. He had only his own reserves, and not for long.

Something had changed. The bubble grew by the hour, almost visible as a distortion in the moonlight. He wondered if a female had hatched at the farm. Even as a tiny baby, her presence would fuel the weakened males with purpose. He had to finish this spell quickly.

A line of phosphorescent foam told him where the waves broke outside the harbor. That was west. He faced south and concentrated on reestablishing his orientation to the magnetic pole.

Gerta made another circuit of the roof—useless piece of decoration, not even spyholes or rafters inside to allow a guard to shelter while on watch during inclement weather or siege. Her restlessness reminded him too much of his own need to keep moving to avoid confrontation with yet another guard. Magnificent woman. He'd much rather watch her move in the starlight.

A slight tingle in his belly settled and centered him. He'd

found the pole. Now that he knew where and when he was in relation to the rest of Kardia Hodos, he could begin. He stooped below the level of the parapet and fiddled with his bowl of water and tiny candle. When everything was placed just so, he blanked his thoughts of all distractions. Especially Gerta.

A flame leaped from his fingertip to the candle. His glass settled in the water and invited him to look through it far beyond normal sight.

"Glenndon," he willed his own blue and red aura to find the gold in his brother's energy.

Then he waited. The hardest part of a summons, waiting for the other person to respond. He counted to one hundred to the rhythm of Gerta's footfalls. Then counted backward from one hundred, just to keep his mind in the spell.

At last a tinge of gold swirled around the edges of his glass, spiraled inward and leaped back toward him in the image of his brother.

"This had better be important," Glenndon growled. "I only got to bed an hour ago, and I have to be up again in three more."

Lukan longed to fall back into the old teasing routine of awakening his brother. They'd done it often just a few years ago. A prank to keep each other alert and wary. "Sorry, but this is important. King Darville has to stop any ships from Amazonia from landing or offloading cargo. Today. Search every vendor in every port for signs of Krakatrice eggs."

Glenndon's eyes opened fully in the magical image. "Again?"

"Still. I know the magicians and dragons are stretched thin rebuilding and replanting after the flood, but they have to keep an eye out for new hatchings. Especially if any are females. So far Lokeen has no females." Would the hatching of a female invigorate the existing males to make the bubble grow so quickly? "The males are weak without a matriarch. I have a hope of killing them as long as there is no female to guide them and to take full possession of the king's mind. Though he is close to total insanity already. He plans to marry Rejiia."

"Stargods preserve us!"

"Keep that in mind. I'm headed to the Krakatrice farm at dawn." Lukan suppressed a yawn.

"Have you found Master Robb? He can help."

"I found him. But he's ill and weak, a prisoner closely guarded. This is up to me and Chess." Gerta loomed over him, frowning. "And the help of a friend. Just do what you have to do to embargo anything coming from Amazonia."

"Hard to do. Every ship brings much-needed grain and livestock." Did Glenndon look a little gaunt?

That made Lukan's heart stutter. "Do what you have to do. Maybe if you run every load of grain through a sifter? Slaughter the beasts and check their innards?"

Glenndon chuckled a bit. "I'll see what I can do. In the morning. Get some sleep yourself, little brother."

"Val and Lily? Are they well?"

"Linda says that Val is thriving,"

Interesting that he talked to the half sister he'd known less than a year and not to the half sister he'd grown up with.

"Linda knows politics and helps me through the maze of conflicting agendas," Glenndon responded to Lukan's un-spoken surmise. "The Univeristy is helping Lily as they can. She says beware of a plague left behind by the snakes."

Plague? Chills ran up and down Lukan's spine. "Plague. Master Robb has been to the farm, and he's deathly ill."

"Lily is working on a cure. We'll let you know as soon as we know." Glenndon's image faded as sleep called him.

Lukan made his farewells and closed his fist to end the spell.

"The guards are changing and the servants are stirring. We can't get back to your room unseen," Gerta said bluntly.

"Fine with me. I'm happy to sleep up here. As long as I'm up. The stars will keep me company."

With a grunt, Gerta lay down beside him, hands behind her head.

"There's the Wanderer, due east at dawn, north at sunset. Our guide on the journey." Lukan mumbled as he automatically named and sorted the stars.

He fell asleep before he could find two more.

CHAPTER 28

THE SUN HAD just touched the tops of the hills. Red-gold streaks set them aglow with the promise of a new day, a new beginning, a chore that must be completed. Lukan looked his steed in the eye and wondered what mischief the beast had in mind for him. He didn't like riding, but today, with the back of his knee bruised from the star gravel that made him limp, Lukan needed to ride. He was limping for real now.

"It's just a docile hire-steed," Gerta sneered. She swung into the saddle easily. She had chosen the animal with the broadest back, to support her magnificent height and weight, and the longest legs, to eat up the miles between the edge of the city and their high plateau destination. Her mount also stamped restlessly, tossing its head and twitching its mouth around the bit. He'd need a firm hand to keep him from bolting and throwing his rider.

Chess shrugged and swung his leg over the back of a quiet mare.

Another tall and strong woman held the bridle of Lukan's mount. "Hurry up, I've orders to join my troop inside the castle," she said.

"Report to your brother Frederico, Frella. He's our liaison to Lady Maria," Gerta said, walking her steed in a wide circle to keep him from bounding off on his own.

Lukan made note of the complex relationships among the women exiled from the castle. It didn't make the idea of climbing atop his steed any more desirable. "It would be easier to transport you all there by magic," he said to himself.

"But then you'd be too tired to fight the Krakatrice," Chess reminded him. "Besides, you've never been there before, and the image Master Robb gave you was blurred and uncertain because of his fever. I do hope Skeller is able to get him better conditions and a healer." The boy worried his lower lip, looking back to the castle where it loomed over the lowlands and harbor.

"We need to get going, Lukan. Mount now, before the guards at the city gates wake up and detain us with too many questions we dare not answer. We haven't had time to replace them yet." Gerta kicked her steed into an easy stride out of the stable yard.

Lukan checked to make sure his staff rested snugly in a loop of leather tack affixed to the saddle. Frella had assured him that guards used such an arrangement to anchor banner poles or spears during parades or while escorting a noble here and there.

With no more reasons to stall, Lukan hoisted himself ungracefully atop the steed. It sidled and stamped but did not unseat him. He was glad that Gerta had not seen his clumsy effort. Gritting his teeth, he set himself to enduring an uneven gait. "At least I'm not walking. But even with a limp that might be easier."

The steed broke into a jouncing gallop, eager to catch up with his stall mates.

Lukan held on for dear life.

Eventually the steed grew tired of tormenting his rider and settled into a steady gait. At that point Lukan began to enjoy the freedom of traversing long distances on something else's leg power. The scenery told him a lot about how Amazonia had developed. A relatively lush but narrow lowland beside the sea. As they climbed, the farmland grew more productive from both irrigation and the way the first mountains trapped the rain. But this was high summer. Few storms crashed into the land. It looked to him like the entire western edge of the continent had suffered from a lack of storms. Was this a normal cycle of a dry year?

Long ago Coronnan had adopted the practice of storing grain against drought years. They came quite regularly in seven- and eleven-year cycles. They were due either next year or the year after. From what he'd heard on his journey across Coronnan with Skeller, King Darville might have to dip into those stores *this* year to make up for the low harvest after the mage-driven storm. Certainly he would if he had to cease accepting all grain shipments from Amazonia. Not that Amazonia looked as if it could spare those shipments.

If King Darville used up the stored grain, would he have enough left for the next drought?

"Gerta, do you have droughts on a routine basis?" he called ahead of him. She rode her steed easily, as if from long practice.

She slowed her mount on the narrow trail, as if she needed to divert her attention from controlling the head-strong beast to matters of weather and crop management. "I don't know."

"Someone in town said the people had to revert to dry-land ways this year, as if they knew how to cope with drought but hadn't expected it."

She shrugged. Such things were not her concern.

"One of the first things I learned when my Da trained me to hunt stray Krakatrice was that they instinctively dam rivers and streams, diverting water away from their territory. Water is their enemy as much as enchanted obsidian spearheads. If left to their own devices, the snakes will eventually change the climate from lush farmland to desert." He swept his arm wide to indicate the stunted vines and cabbages on the south side of the trail.

"History tells us that when the Stargods first came to Coronnan the Big Continent was nearly all desert, except for a very narrow strip along the coastline," Chess said, eyes brightening because he remembered something important and could contribute more to the journey than just an extra pair of hands. "It took nearly a thousand years after the defeat of the Krakatrice to recover the land."

"Are you saying that the monster snakes are more of a threat to Amazonia, to all of Mabastion, than just the king's hideous need to watch them *kill* people?" Gerta pulled hard on the reins, forcing her steed to stop in midtrail. The beast stamped, snorted, and half reared in protest.

"Yes. That is why the magicians and dragons of Coronnan went hunting as soon as the eggs and snakes began to appear," Lukan affirmed.

"Does the king know this?" Chess asked.

"I heard ... we had a ... situation in Coronnan City early this year when a man thought a Krakatrice was his pet. It had taken over his mind and free will until he obeyed only the snake's need for blood, and more blood. Eventually he led a rebellion in order to give his 'pet' magical and royal blood to allow her to grow bigger and stronger. Meanwhile, her consorts started damming the rivers. The mighty River Coronnan, more than a mile wide in places, slowed to a trickle."

"The king has lost his mind," Gerta said quietly, obviously aghast at the situation. Then she shivered all over, blinked her eyes rapidly and firmed her chin in determination. "We have got to end this. Now." She kicked her steed into a fast trot and headed uphill toward the plateau and the snakes.

-*≫-

Maria curled up in the padded chair in her private parlor that her sister had had made for her many years ago, when the young queen was still vibrant and listened. Before she fell under Lokeen's spell, before she'd succumbed to two difficult pregnancies and dangerous deliveries that produced only disappointing male children.

The privacy of her parlor remained sacrosanct among the servants. Even Rejiia's man Geon would not get past the kitchen staff to listen at her door.

"You look comfortable," Toskellar said. He tapped at the sole of her boot with an oversized hammer—the only one he could find—and tiny little nails. "That doesn't happen often. I remember you telling me and Faelle stories about the glorious past of Amazonia from that chair. We felt loved, and like we belonged somewhere, when you did that." He kept his eyes lowered to the repair of her boot.

"I do love you and your brother. Despite his choice to join the cult of Helvess. But he is a talented healer and found the people who gave him the training he deserves."

"We know how much you love us. More than our father ever did. Or our mother could."

"If you knew you were loved, why did you run away, Toskellar?"

"I go by Skeller now," he said.

"Please answer my question, nephew."

"I ran away because I was young and I didn't know how to counter my father's gradual but determined undermining of our laws, our trade alliances. Our traditions."

"But you are back now. Why?"

"I've seen enough, learned enough, been hurt enough to know that I have to do something before he ruins Amazonia and the rest of Mabastion."

"We have no heir to my sister's crown," Maria repeated the litany that had kept her from running away herself. "The only way to remove your father from the throne is for you to marry a suitable princess and rule in her name. I have sent five letters to our neighboring city-states begging for a . . ."

"I will not have the princess Lokeen arranged for me to marry."

"He is your father. You should call him what he is."

"Then I call him Tyrant."

Finally Toskellar raised his face to her, resolute as she

had never seen him before. He had indeed matured these last five years.

"What is wrong with the Princess Bettina?" Maria broke the staring match by turning her face away as well as changing the subject.

"Before Lokeen married my mother, we had no crime worthy of execution. Exile to the desert was the worst sentence for criminals. We had little crime at all. Oh, we had the occasional assassination, small, sporadic wars, but nothing long lasting and we always, *always* returned to peace with our neighbors as well as among ourselves. Now the king publicly executes criminals. What is their crime? They incurred the king's displeasure."

Maria swallowed deeply. "I . . . knew this, but I did not want to know. I pretended . . ."

"You pretended it didn't matter. But it does matter. And now his bloodlust, his insanity, has spread to our neighbors. Princess Bettina among them. She not only countenances public execution. She avidly watches."

"Is there anyone else you would find suitable?"

"The woman I love." He turned away from her again, letting the hammer dangle idly from his right hand. "She is a natural empath. She won't even eat meat because she shares in the death of the animal that gave its life to feed others."

"If you love her so deeply, why did you leave her?"

"I made an excuse so she wouldn't know how I pushed her away when I should have embraced her and helped her weather the emotional storm of . . . of . . . doing what I did not have the stomach . . . the courage to do. She killed the man who conjured the storm that nearly destroyed Coronnan. She used my knife because she knew I could not do it."

He paused a long time, looking into the distance, his throat working as if he choked back tears. "I felt the man's death. Lily and I had developed a bond. A strong bond born of companionship—friendship—and then love. Her empathy forced her to share in the man's death, and I . . . I felt it too. We both died a little bit in those moments, when his eyes glazed and his spirit passed beyond." He gulped and firmed his jaw. "We both needed time apart to heal. Every day I stay here and see what he and my father have done to Amazonia, I heal. I no longer regret the man's death. I'd do it again even if it cost me my own life."

"Who did she kill?" Maria covered her face with her hands, knowing.

"We knew him as 'Sir.'"

"The magician who came and went on his own schedule for nearly ten years. The man who advised your father . . ."

"The man who introduced the king to the Krakatrice. The man who exported Krakatrice eggs to Coronnan to destroy that kingdom for whatever reason he thought valid. Samlan, a master magician and teacher at the University of Magicians in Coronnan until he defied their ruling council and was exiled."

"He took up permanent residence here in the castle last spring."

"Until midsummer when he conjured the storm with his other exiled masters and apprentices. He diverted Master Robb's transport spell here so that he couldn't help destroy the Krakatrice in Coronnan. Then he coerced Robb's journeymen and apprentices to help him. But he is dead now. They are all dead. My Lily killed him, and I deserted her so that we could both learn to accept that sometimes such a death is necessary. That gentlest, most nurturing woman in all of Kardia Hodos was braver and stronger than I." He gulped convulsively.

Maria watched his throat apple convulse as he choked back strong emotions.

"I would marry her in an instant if I knew how to get her back. The princesses you parade before me would pale in contrast to her. I would go into such a marriage reluctantly, and only if I knew for certain Lily would never have me."

"If you will not marry, we are lost."

"We have you, Aunt Maria."

"No. I cannot. I am . . ." She waved vaguely at her twisted hip. It ached suddenly, despite the carefully placed pillows and padding.

"Long ago our queens led warriors into battle. They commanded armies of men and women. But they ruled with the loving and nurturing perspective of a mother. Not all of our queens have been warriors," he said.

"But they were all mothers of daughters."

"Not all of them. Remember the history you taught me, Aunt Maria. The first Maria never married. She never bore children. In fact, she loved another woman; I believe her name was Helvess. And then there was Joanna III, she married and bore one son who died young of a wasting sickness. In both cases a natural heir rose from the ranks of women warriors."

"Your father disbanded the troops of women warriors."

"Because he was afraid one of them would displace him."

"Afraid?" Maria nearly choked on her snort of derision. "Your father was never afraid of anything."

"He's afraid of you."

"Nonsense."

"Why do you think he has allowed you to live? He has kept you here safe and secure and believing that you are unworthy to rule because he knows that any threat to you will bring down the wrath of every female who ever thought of becoming a warrior as well as the ordinary women who run businesses and manage families."

"I am invisible. No one remembers me."

"You'd be surprised. Here, I've fixed your boot so that you can walk more comfortably." He held up her shoe, showing how he'd added an extra inch to the sole. Then he knelt in front of her and slipped it over her stunted foot. Gently he tightened the lacings and tied them in a neat bow.

"You wear long skirts to cover the unevenness in your legs. You work hard to disguise your limp. This will make the limp even less noticeable, put less strain on your body.

You are strong, Aunt Maria. I think the time has come to show that strength and take back what is your right."

"But I have no heir unless you marry."

"You can give us time to find the right bride for me. You can give us time to heal from Lokeen's tyranny."

"Leave me. I can't do what you ask."

"But will you do what the women warriors sneaking back to their posts demand of you? Gerta's friends bring one or two every half day, displacing men who blindly follow the king. I do not ask where those men disappear to." He rose with that musical grace he'd always had, bowed respectfully, and sauntered out of her private parlor whistling a martial tune composed by the first Maria nearly a thousand years before.

CHAPTER 29

"WHY, WHY, WHY did I let the boys convince me to remain here?" Robb asked the ether through chattering teeth. Cold sweat poured off his brow and across his chest. The tiny stone cell spun every time he turned his head. His heart beat double time and so loudly he could hear little else but his pulse hammering into his head like a long iron spike. "Must be a fever," he said aloud, just to hear his own voice and presume he wasn't hallucinating.

Was that the grating of a key in the lock? He couldn't be certain. Liquid filled the cavity behind his ears and refused to shift or drain, muting all of his senses except the cold and aching joints and racing heart.

"He'll need to be carried, my lady," a man said. It sounded like Badger, but Robb couldn't be sure. Maybe he only dreamed the presence of three men and the tiny woman inside his cell. If he dreamed, then he must be asleep, and sleep healed. Maigret had told him that often over their years together.

"Wrap him in more blankets, like a litter. We have to get him out of this place," Lady Maria said sternly.

"Who are you to order the moving of my prisoner?" a newcomer demanded.

"I am chatelaine," Lady Maria said sternly.

"And I am captain of the guard. All of the prisoners are my responsibility, and I say he remains."

"Everything and everyone within the castle walls are my responsibility," she insisted. Good for her. She'd been so meek and accepting of other people's decisions he'd doubted her capable of holding to a decision. Robb wondered what had given her the courage to defy the captain— the king's right-hand man.

"Not me and my prisoners."

"Would you care to dispute that with the Great Mother?"

The men who had come in with her all gasped.

"I will take this up with the king," the captain said. He turned abruptly on his heel and started to leave.

"The king is in bed with Princess Rejiia. Do you care to disturb him over something so trivial as the welfare of one prisoner? The one prisoner he has ordered you to keep alive?"

Rejiia! No. It couldn't be. For the past fifteen years the daughter of Lord Krej of Saria and the leader of the dreaded magical Coven had been enscorcelled into her to- tem animal body: a black cat with one white ear.

What had restored her? Or did an imposter claim the lady's name and rank?

"I have to . . . to . . ." Robb tried to roll over and leverage himself up. His head spun so rapidly he had to drop it back onto the pallet to find himself again. Bad idea. The pallet offered little cushioning, and now this headache throbbed through his entire body. Maybe if his eyes bled the pain would ease.

"He don't look well, my lady," Scurry said.

"We need a healer, Lady Maria," Badger added.

"He's nearly dead already," the captain sneered. "Leave him overnight and he'll no longer be a problem, or a source of dispute."

"Take him to the tower now. Third story," Lady Maria snapped. High enough for the air to be cleaner but not so high she couldn't climb too many stairs to tend him. "And you, Captain, go into the city *now*. Do not come back until you have Levi and his apprentices. I know of no other healer who can deal with this."

"Maigret. Send for Maigret," Robb mumbled. If he died tonight, he wanted to see his wife one more time. He wanted to loose the bonds of life in her arms. "Maigret is the wisest healer in Coronnan," he added. "Summon Maigret, please."

Lily did not look well. Much of the color she'd regained drained out of her face as she surveyed the line of grim farmers standing around the edges of the fields that should be nearing harvest. Instead, they all held torches. Lily held her staff up as a symbol of her authority as well as her unity with the villagers in this painful task. Tears streaked the faces of the farmwives as they hoed the land clear of weeds and other greenery, making firebreaks on the periphery.

Dawn just touched the tops of the trees that marked the barrier between the undulating prairie and the road that skirted the Great Bay. Rapidly evaporating dew caught the light and sent it back out in an array of colors; tiny rainbows arced from plant to plant, turning the entire landscape into a delightful promise of a warm and clear day. New hope for today. And maybe tomorrow.

A perfect day for beginning the grain harvest.

A harvest that could not happen. Every plant and root was tainted with illness left behind by the hatching of the monster Krakatrice.

"I asked the dragons to bring us food enough to get through the winter," Souska reminded them all. She didn't add that Krystaal had given ambivalent answers. She didn't *know* that her plea would be answered. But she had to give these people hope.

"The dragons brought us the cure. They will not abandon us now," Lily said in a voice that projected to the far corners of the cultivated land.

"Not even forage for the animals," the man next to Souska grumbled.

"We can take them farther afield. Away from anything the snakes may have touched," Souska said, trying desperately to soothe him and herself.

"Might as well move the whole village," an old woman said. "Chickens and goats will walk off all their meat going from here to safe grazing." She mumbled something more that sounded like curses.

"That may be helpful," Lily agreed, chewing her lower lip. "Once we've built new houses on the next ridge, we can burn these too, get totally away from any residual miasma."

"What will be left to build with? Turf?" Stanil, the village headman, asked.

Souska couldn't be sure of his name. Names and position and relationship held less importance to her than how each reacted to her treatment of the illness. She thought that he'd begun recovering on his own—or possibly had an immunity to the disease—and had helped Lily tend the desperately ill and dying before Souska arrived. He'd been the only one strong enough to dig graves.

Bitter anger rose in Souska, flaming her cheeks and drying her tears. It was not right that these people should lose everything, their lives, their land, their very future.

Burning she could understand. Her gran had told of a time long ago when blight hit the rye and they had to burn the crop. But must they then sow the land with salt? That would render it sterile for many years to come. Nothing would grow. Not even fireweed that would at least offer forage for the animals.

Crying heavily, Lily lowered her staff, the grain in the length of wood not twisted or knotted at all from the little bit of magic she might have pushed through the primary tool of a magician. One by one the men stationed around the edges followed her example and lowered their torches. They did not touch flame to the plants. Not yet. Delay as long as possible and retain some small hope of reprieve.

"Wait!" Souska yelled. She gripped Lily's arm with fierce fingers digging into the muscle.

"What?" Lily asked, dazed and confused. She looked like once she'd set her mind to torching the fields, she could think of nothing else.

The others with torches straightened, relief written all over their faces and in their posture. They understood the necessity, but clearly did not want to burn the fields.

"I have to taste the dirt. I have to know that this is the right thing to do."

"You don't trust the dragons? Krystaal said most firmly that we must cleanse the land with fire and salt to erase all trace of the Krakatrice."

"I trust the Kardia to know what it needs to bring it back into balance." Souska fixed a determined gaze on the other healer. Then, without waiting for permission she knelt on the verge and loosened a handful of dirt with trembling fingers. She hesitated. Sickness had come from the land. She'd be the next victim.

One breath and hold; release and hold. Repeat. She focused inward, clearing her mind of all but the need to separate and examine each component of the dirt. She knew what should be there. It was her responsibility to determine what should not be there and find what was missing or in too much abundance to balance it.

Her gran had never trusted the dragons. "They knows what they knows. They needs what they needs. But they don't always know what we know. Or what we need," the old woman had said when Souska was five and they'd caught a rare glimpse of a blue-tipped wing and horns soaring across the sky.

"What the dragons need is not necessarily what we need," she said quietly to bolster her courage.

"My da always told us to trust the dragons," Lily insisted. But she held her staff away from the grain, not touching anything flammable.

"Your da knew magic. For that you must trust the dragons, creatures of magic. My gran knew the land. I trust her wisdom in this matter." Souska touched three grains of dirt to her tongue.

Gritty sand and smooth clay. Damp. Mold. Something acrid. A hint of the barley growing now. A whiff of the beans that had grown here last year. The sickness was there, but faint, nearly overwhelmed by the damp and the . . . and the . . . salt. She licked a bit more dirt off her fingertip. "Salt. Loads and loads of salt!"

"Of course, we are supposed to sow salt into the Kardia once we've burned . . ." Lily said. She sounded uncertain.

"No. The dirt is already laden with salt. Much too much salt." More curious than concerned, Souska entered the field, where the grains grew thickest. She tasted the dirt again. Just a couple of grains. The gritty taste of loam dominated, more damp and mold, less of the acrid sickness (it seemed to be evaporating), all of it filtered through her senses. Then the overwhelming sharpness of too much salt. Her tongue wanted to shrink and curl in upon itself. More salt here than at the edge.

Rising from her crouch she faced Lily and the village elder. "I don't think we should burn everything."

A sigh of relief worked all around the edge of the fields.

"There's barely any sickness left in the ground. But there is too much salt. So much salt that little will grow here next season. This whole area needs to lay fallow with a season of fireweed, letting the animals browse that, and then two seasons of legumes."

"But the dragons . . ." Lily protested.

"The dragons got it backward." Souska stood firm. "The snakes try to kill the land with lack of moisture and salt. The salt is so thick it burns anything that tries to grow. That is how they create a desert out of lush farmland. They kill the land even as they remove the water. Where they live, they leave behind salt and more salt."

"Can we safely eat the grain?" the elder asked. He held

his torch down, like he wanted to grind it into the dirt to extinguish the flames.

Souska raked a few kernels into her palm and examined them closely, turning them over and over again with a questing finger. They looked whole, ripe, and unblemished. A little small, and not as many as should be on each stalk, but then this was the second planting, after the storm winds stripped a lot of new growth from the first planting. Resolutely she brought her hand to her mouth and sucked up three kernels. Nutty, sweet, raw, and salty. No trace of the malaise that had felled nearly the entire village. Maybe soaking would rid them of some of the salt. Maybe they'd just have to learn to cook without adding any more salt. "They taste clean," she said on a long exhale.

"I'm scrying for Maigret," Lily said. "This decision is beyond my journeyman skills and your apprentice prejudices." She marched back to the hut she shared with Souska. "No one goes against the orders of the dragons!" When she ducked beneath the low lintel she threw Souska's pack back out.

"I will defy the dragons if they are wrong," Souska whispered. "That's why I'll never make a good magician."

CHAPTER 30

FURIOUSLY LILY TOSSED pot after pot aside looking for the right one. It had to be ceramic. It had to be bigger around than her piece of glass, and deep enough to hold reflective water. She sorted as she examined and cast aside each one. "The dragons are never wrong," she insisted. "Both Mama and Da said . . . They said to trust the dragons." She choked on a sob. Her parents were dead. Her twin at home forging new friendships and alliances without her. She wandered in self-imposed exile. Skeller, the man she loved, had taken himself across the sea to a foreign land.

She had no one to help her with this crucial decision. She had only herself. And Death.

"If we do not burn the fields and salt the land, then we can't kill the miasma. It will come again and again. It will take everyone here. We are too few. Too weak. Too . . . Alone."

She dropped to her knees and buried her face in her hands. Alone.

Her fingers brushed the cold spot on her forehead. The touch of Death.

Before she could think through her actions and change her mind, she bolted out of the hut, around the field Souska had saved, and up hill toward . . .

Empty. No mist. No hovering presence. Nothing. Death no longer haunted this village. She'd moved on.

"You took no more of the patients I begged you to leave behind," she whispered to herself. And in the speaking she knew that she had become a conduit between life and death. Death would take only those patients of Lily's that she begged to be granted release from pain and illness. If Lily touched a patient and begged for life, then the patient would live, so long as Lily gave proper treatment.

The village was safe now.

Had Death taken the miasma with her?

Maybe . . . just maybe Souska had the right of it. Maybe . . . maybe Lily should start making her own decisions and stop relying on the dragons.

Trust the dragons. She almost heard her mother and her father, voices blended into one.

"Trust them, but rely upon myself. That's why you forced Val and me to follow separate journeys. We had to learn to rely upon ourselves, not each other. And not the dragons."

She let her gaze linger on all the grave cairns in the local cemetery. There were as many new ones as all the old ones combined. But she hadn't sung the funeral hymns in three days.

"The time has come to follow Death to the next village."

(Perhaps. Perhaps not.)

"What is that supposed to mean?" she shouted to the four winds.

Nothing. No whisper of a presence in the back of her mind, either of Death or the dragons.

The cold spot on her forehead suddenly warmed.

Bored. I am bored. King Lokeen has very old-fashioned ideas about what is proper for a princess and what is proper in bed. No imagination. Less stamina.

But if this is my only path to power, then I will tolerate him. But only long enough for him to say his wedding vows and crown me queen. He'll make vows to rule Amazonia in my name. He probably won't live long enough to issue a single decree.

I shan't be bored when I feed him to his own snakes. My guard captain and I shall watch and enjoy each other while the old king screams himself to death.

In the meantime, I need to learn the ways of this castle, who will serve me, who will not. Geon has learned much, but he spends his free time in the library now. Always with his long nose in a book. One cannot learn magic from books! He replies most calmly that he learns other things, like history, culture, law, and how to read what a person is thinking by "tells" in their posture and eye blinks.

Bah. I learned all that at my father's knee. And more. Except for the intricacies of the law. That could be useful information in the days to come.

Now I personally must learn, and not from any book, who is most loyal to the hideous dwarf. Those must find employment elsewhere or die. I cannot have a household of divided loyalties.

My father tried that and look at him now. He's an old man who sits by the fire and daydreams about past greatness now lost. I will not lose my greatness or my power. Not now, not ever.

Lukan lay flat among the withering grasses on the slight ridge surrounding the farm. He could see all activity in the open compound, but he doubted anyone moving from house, to barn, to slave dormitory, to snake house could see him. Even if they bothered to look slightly up and directly toward him. None of them did. Few thought to look up for intruders. They all seemed weighed down, diminished, shuffling as if walking upright required too much energy.

He'd feel safer if he had a place to climb up, away from the ground. But there weren't any higher hills on this wide and dry plateau. And he hadn't spotted a free-flying dragon all day. Not even a light chuckle in the back of his mind. Trees were scarce, spindly, and too far away.

"Fifteen guards by my count," Gerta said. She stretched out beside him, watching the movements with keenly trained eyes.

"Fifty or sixty slaves, all adults, I see no children," Lukan returned, barely moving his lips. He liked working with Gerta. She didn't flirt, didn't dissemble, and didn't defer to him. She knew what had to be done and who was best qualified to do it. No nonsense. Just raw strength. Unusual.

Attractive.

Well, maybe not unusual in Amazonia where women used to rule and fight. In Coronnan he expected women to defer to their men. He'd seen it often enough. Except for Maigret. She stood up to Robb, fought with him, conferred with him, made plans with him. And loved with him.

He hated to think that failure here at the farm might keep his mentor apart from his beloved wife any longer.

"There isn't much water in those creeks," Chess mused. He stretched out on his belly a little way off, surveying from a slightly different perspective. "Not enough water to stop the snakes if they really wanted to get away."

Lukan had a sense of waiting. Waiting for what?

His mind harkened back to the growing bubble of magic around the castle snakes. *Stargods, I hope there isn't a female here that is giving them strength and guidance.*

"What about the pond on the far side, where the livestock are kept?" Lukan asked, jerking his mind away from the possibility of a matriarch. Fire and water. He needed both, lots of both to kill the monsters. Fire he could conjure. Chess could control it better than he.

For water? They both needed help.

What he really needed was a storm. A huge storm that would dump rain, a lot of rain, over the entire plateau. Thoroughly wet, deep mud would be better. Mud would burn the snakes' bellies all the way to their spines.

"The pond looks like it is drying up," Chess said. "The

banks are shrinking. Whatever it is that the snakes do to
turn a land into a desert, it's working here."

"So what's the plan?" Gerta asked, looking to Lukan for
answers he didn't have.

"If we throw firebombs onto the roof of the farmhouse,
that will drive all the guards outside . . ." he said, more
thinking out loud than knowing what they should do.

"The slave quarters look more flammable," Gerta added.

"Guards are the enemy. Slaves are potential allies," Lukan insisted. "We do our best to keep them from harm.
Lokeen has harmed them enough already. Look at them!
Walking skeletons, dispirited, almost ready to give up. Saving them is as important as killing the snakes."

"Fine," Gerta held up her hands in mock surrender. "I
was just noting conditions. Did you notice that the roof of
the snake barn is slate? It won't burn."

"But the walls are dry wood. Very dry wood. A few tiny
gaps between the planks. If we set fire to that building, then
the only route of escape the snakes have is through the door
to the courtyard."

"Where they'll start a feeding frenzy on the slaves,"
Chess said flatly.

"*S'murghit!* I wish I was up," he muttered.

"Sleeping on the roof of the castle tower wasn't high
enough for you?" Gerta asked.

"You were up there with me, studying the stars, looking
for dragon shadows," he reminded her. Though he wished
they'd done more *together* up there away from prying eyes
and keen ears. "Right now I need to be able to see the entire farm from a better perspective. And there isn't a high
hill or a dragonback to help."

"Then we need to circle around and look from different
angles," Gerta said, rising to her knees and scooting backward below the ridgeline before standing.

"We need to see if there is a back entrance to the slave
quarters." Lukan said. He craned his neck to look, but it was
at the wrong angle.

"Unlikely," Gerta said. "Back entrance invites escape."

"Let's go see," Chess said. He flashed his teeth in a grimace that might have been grim humor. "If I can open the back door, or rip some of the siding off, we give the slaves an avenue of escape." He too scooted backward and joined Gerta in stretching stiff muscles.

"Then we fire the farmhouse first, and the snake barn second."

"Where are you going to get enough water to kill the snakes?" Gerta pointed out the one flaw in the plan.

Lukan scanned the sky. Not a cloud in sight. Nor a dragon on the wing.

"In the really old legends, dragons are supposed to control weather," Chess offered hopefully.

"Let's hunt up a ley line while we scout the back," Lukan said. "I think you and I are going to have to do this the hard way."

Maria dipped a clean rag into a basin of cool water, wrung it free of drips and placed it on Robb's brow. His fever continued to burn so high his skin felt as dry and crackling as ancient parchment. He tossed restlessly, calling out in agony for the woman Maigret. Who was she that her name was the only one on his lips?

She guessed the woman was a healer, but more than that to Robb. A lover?

She wiped away a tear in her own grief. More likely Maigret was spouse to this strong and proud man. He demonstrated fierce loyalties. He'd only give his love to the woman he married. He would never merely keep a lover, or love outside his marriage bond.

For that she respected him. For that she regretted having dared dream that he could care for her misshapen form. She'd been cast out of the line of succession because of her twisted limp and shrunken body. She'd been relegated to being housekeeper for her sister, and then her sister's husband. She hoped to remain as housekeep to her nephew's spouse. Even as she dreamed of exchanged affection with Robb, she knew he couldn't give her more.

But he had suggested he could bring a magical healer to her. He offered a chance at straightening her leg so she could grow stronger, walk without a limp. For that she must save his life. He wouldn't have offered her that tiny bit of hope if he didn't care for her a little bit. He'd never love her, not like he did this Maigret. But he could care for her as a friend.

She hadn't hoped for much more. Not really. Only wistful dreams that scattered in sunlight like dew rising to the hot sun.

"My lady, the healers will not come," her under-chatelaine said from the doorway. She scrutinized the wooden planks in the flooring most thoroughly.

"What do you mean, they won't come. One of them at least must respond to royal orders from the castle." Maria trembled and grew cold on the inside. This was unprecedented betrayal from the heart of the city. Dared she petition the followers of Helvess?

"They all said that once they set foot within the castle, they might as well be dead. If they try to cure the magician and fail, His Majesty will execute them for that failure. If they cure the magician, His Majesty will execute them to keep their method a secret, or for allowing him to get sick in the first place."

The crushing weight of conflicting emotions sent a sinking blackness through Maria. They were right. Lokeen had begun to invent excuses to execute anyone. So had the captain of the guard.

Soon, she predicted, Princess Rejiia would as well. How long before the entire city rose up in total rebellion? Or deserted the city in the middle of the night to seek out new lives among Amazonia's rivals? The healers had already begun.

She had to do something and quickly. But what? She couldn't rule because . . .

Robb had promised to bring a healer to her. If she walked without a limp, perhaps she could hold the throne until Toskellar married and begat a daughter. Robb had to be alive, healthy, strong, and in command of his magic to summon a magical healer. She did not know this terrible fever with a racing heart. But she had herbs to treat the symptoms.

"Bathe his face and hands frequently. Give him as much water to drink as he will take," she said to her under-chatelaine. The young woman hovered by the doorway, wringing her hands, not entering the room by a single step. "I do not think you will catch this illness," Maria added sharply. "You have never been into the bowels of the dungeon. The miasma lingers in the air and the ground but does not rise to this level."

"Where . . . where . . ." the girl stammered. "May I fetch something for you so that you need not leave his side?" She finally raised hopeful eyes.

"No. Only I have the keys to the cupboards in the still-room."

"Oh!"

"Yes, I fetch dangerous herbs that if misused will kill the patient. I know how to use them properly, mix them, dilute them. You do not."

"Perhaps it is time I learned."

"Not yet. You do not add empathy for the patient into the work."

"Magic? What good is magic, except for lighting candles and sending letters, things just as easily accomplished without waiting for a magician to do them?"

"You'd be surprised. Until you understand the need to love in the planning and preparing a cure, you cannot do it right. That is why the followers of Helvess succeed where others fail." Unless she loved the patient, even as a friend, she doubted she'd have the courage to blend foxglove with arnica. Ardently she wished they'd had more rain this year to replenish the withering willow along the riverbanks. Willow bark worked better on fever than arnica. She'd do the best she could.

Maybe if she bathed Robb's entire body with beta arrack from Rossemeyer, the distilled spirits would wick away more heat than just cool water.

Maria gathered her skirts, making sure her keys jangled authoritatively from her belt, and swept out of the room as gracefully as she could manage. She might limp—less so with the new lift in her boot—but she had dignity and royal heritage to keep her head high and her back rigid. But her hand reached automatically for the goddess pendant hidden beneath her bodice.

CHAPTER 31

"LILY?" SOUSKA ASKED hesitantly from the doorway to their hut. She held the leather curtain aside,
peering into the dark interior. She spotted a hunched figure
outlined against the glowing embers of their banked fire at
the center, just below the smoke hole. Her companion and
fellow healer shuddered and sobbed. Her skirts couldn't
muffle her cries. The staff she didn't always remember to
carry with her lay on the far side of her pallet at an odd
angle. She must have tossed it there upon entering.

"Lily, what's wrong?" Souska closed the physical distance between them in three strides. She knelt to hug her
friend.

"Go away," Lily choked out.

"I can't."

"Just leave me alone."

"Why?" Souska searched her mind and the dim interior
for inspiration, something, anything that might have caused
this collapse.

Ah, the clay bowl of water and an unlit candle sat on the
floor between Lily and the hearth ring. Souska couldn't see
a sign of Lily's shard of glass, the third ingredient to a correct summoning spell.

"Because ... because ... I can't do it! I can't talk to anyone through ... through this." She waved vaguely at the

bowl as she gulped, trying to control her breathing and her crying.

There was something else she kept hidden. Souska didn't know how she knew, only that she did. "You managed the spell when you called Maigret for help."

"I was desperate. I used every scrap of energy I had and I still did a piss poor job of it. Linda answered the call, and you eavesdropped."

Souska kept her mouth shut. That spell had actually worked best by being scattered so that anyone in the University could have answered. Maigret had not been well and wouldn't have answered without Linda's prodding her out of bed.

"I'm not very good at the spell, but I can do it if I have to," Souska said instead. "Usually I only call Lukan when I know he's going to be available to answer. And he's hasn't been answering me much at all. I'm not sure I can get through to Maigret or Linda." Heat rose to Souska's cheeks.

"You love my brother," Lily said flatly.

"I ... um ... he was a friend to me when no one else even knew I was in the room." Her face continued to burn with embarrassment.

"You love him. And I think he cares for you if he's been summoning you while he's on journey."

"He's not supposed to call the University or his masters. But there are no rules about easing his loneliness on the road by talking to a friend each night."

Lily swallowed a smile, no longer absorbed in her own misery. "Even if we don't salt the fields I think we should burn them so the fireweed will sow itself."

"Harvest first, then burn the stubble," Souska confirmed. "Burning will draw some of the extra salt to the surface. Maybe we can scrape it off, screen the dirt out of it and—I don't know, do something with it other than poison the fields. Krystaal didn't sound interested in sending food stores here. It will be a lean winter with only eggs and rationed grain, but the village should survive."

"We can forage out on the plains. I've seen oaks fat with acorns and nut trees south of here, beyond the ravages of the storm," Lily offered.

"Do you still need to contact Maigret?" Souska asked tentatively.

"Not yet. I'm a journeyman on journey. It is my task to do what I must on my own. I just ... I've never met anyone before who didn't trust the dragons completely and without question." *And who sowed the seeds of distrust in me.*

Souska heard the last unspoken words. Heard them in the back of her mind where the dragons lurked sometimes.

"I think part of being a journeyman is learning to trust yourself. Relying on the dragons *all* of the time is almost like calling for help when you should make your own decisions based on information you have at hand."

"When did you get so wise, little Susu?"

"Susu? That's what my gran called me when I was little."

"Did your gran teach you this wisdom?"

"I don't know. But sometimes I hear her words, almost as if she's still standing behind my left shoulder, but I know she can't because she died nigh on four years ago."

"You'd be surprised who stands beside you," Lily said softly. Her gaze grew unfocused as she stared at Souska's left ear. As though she examined Souska's aura. Or something beyond normal vision.

"Death hides behind a left shoulder." Souska shuddered in apprehension. Chills climbed her spine and spread to her fingers and toes.

"No. Death lurks wherever she wants, usually on the hill. Your gran has settled behind your left shoulder, clinging to you as she can no longer cling to life. She's not ready to go with Death. Not yet. Her love lets her ghost linger with you. Her love tells you what you need to know when you are too uncertain of yourself to make a decision. Don't doubt your gran, even if you do doubt the dragons." The white spot on Lily's forehead glowed like sunlight through ice.

"Are Gran and the dragons one and the same?" Or was

the ghost of her grandmother a harbinger of death yet to
come. Death already walked heavily through the village.
Souska didn't think she'd left yet, even if she had retreated
for a while.

Breathe in, hold. Breathe out, hold. Lukan reminded himself.
All on a count of three. Glenndon only needed three
breaths to ground his body and bring forth his magic. Lukan
always, *always*, needed more. Out here on the semiarid plateau he had little magic to tap. He'd found a thin ley line
running deep beneath his feet. That fed him a little bit of
magic in fits and starts. He and Chess needed to alternate
tapping the energy within the Kardia or they'd drain it for
sure and certain.

What was wrong with this place that the lines, which ran
thick and prevalent everywhere in Coronnan, seemed
blocked and uncooperative here?

Earlier this year Glenndon and Da had discovered a disruption in the flow of energy from the Well of Life throughout the planet. They'd released the blockage and recapped
the well with porous clay rather than poisonous iron. Maybe
the recovery just hadn't reached this far yet.

Or maybe the snakes disrupted the flow as badly as the
iron flagpole rammed deep into the well.

"This would be easier if a dragon came flying by and
spread magic like a gentle rainfall," Chess grumbled. He
looked almost as tired from the effort of drawing energy in
as if he'd worked magic without the aid of the ley line.

"We have to do the best we can with what we've got.
Now, I think I'll forego trying to FarSee into the back of the
buildings. Save everything you've got for conjuring and
throwing fire," Lukan advised. He rammed his staff partway
into the turf right over the ley line. Then he braced himself
against it, trusting the natural wood to align with the Kardia.

A faint vibration ran through the staff to his hands. Then

his toes tingled. He breathed easier, in rhythm with the land. That helped.

Chess stood slightly behind him, feet planted on either side of the line. He clenched his fists and gritted his teeth.

"Um ... Chess, shift your feet inward and relax your shoulders. This is a natural process, not a wrestling match."

"Oh." The boy grimaced in chagrin. "This isn't easy. I can gather dragon magic right, left, and sideways, if there's any about. But I can't even see the line, let alone feel it."

Lukan wanted to roll his eyes. No wonder Chess was still an apprentice.

"Just, ah, place one foot before the other right there." He pointed to a place where he thought the ley line seemed a bit brighter than where he stood. "A finger's width to your right," he corrected Chess when the boy moved.

"Here?"

"Yes, right there. Your feet are in alignment with the line. Not either side of it. What does it feel like?"

Chess shrugged.

"Maybe if you take off your boots."

"Huh?"

"Just do it. And wiggle your toes against the dirt. Feel the land with your bare skin."

Chess didn't look happy. "I have to get my feet dirty?"

"No dirtier than standing over the fire controlling the bellows and breathing soot all day," Gerta said coming up behind them. "I've scanned the back of the buildings and think I found a route in that will keep us hidden."

Lukan nodded in agreement with her, mostly concentrating on Chess' grumbles as he plunked heavily onto the ground and tugged at his worn footgear. The soles were so thin he should feel every pebble and imperfection in the land.

But he didn't.

Surreptitiously, Lukan examined the boy's feet. Blisters on the balls of his feet had healed into thick calluses. Same with the back of his heels. He'd needed new boots a long time ago. He probably hurt so much just walking that he couldn't pay attention to the ground. First order of business was to get him footgear that fit. As soon as they returned to the city.

Which they couldn't do until they finished their job here at the farm. Which they couldn't do without magic.

He shook himself free of the self-defeating loop.

Then he repeated his instructions to Chess, and to himself at the same time:

"Align yourself with the nearest magnetic pole, feel the tug on your back. Place your feet directly over the line. Breathe deeply, again and again. Wiggle your toes in the dirt. Feel the life within the Kardia. Thank it. Draw it deeply inside. Let it fill your lungs and your heart anew. Feed it into every crevice of your body and let it renew your energy."

Peace, calm, and firm resolve filled Lukan. His heart beat a lilting counterpoint to his breathing. He found the rhythm of the land and his life.

"And finally, open your eyes and see the world from a different perspective." He did so himself. Every tuft of grass and scraggly shrub took on keener definition. His world tilted slightly left. Colors brightened and blended shifting to the left of the spectrum as well.

"Wow," Chess breathed. "Is this what magic always feels like?"

Lukan half-smiled. "When you do it right, yeah." He continued breathing deeply in the slow rhythm of life in this foreign land. "Let your eyes cross a little, as if you are searching for an aura around a person."

Chess did so. He'd been taught well, but he didn't always practice skills outside his talent with controlling fire. "Now drop your gaze to the ground. You are searching for the aura of the Kardia. A silvery blue aura that forms a complex web . . ."

"Stargods, I didn't know it could be so beautiful. Why didn't anyone ever explain it to me like that before?"

Lukan shrugged and continued to drink in the power of the land.

"Wonderboys, it's time to get to work. All of the guards are gathered at the farmhouse for the evening meal," Gerta prodded them toward their purpose.

Keeping his eyes slightly crossed and his focus on the ley line, Lukan followed the enticing bit of silvery blue as far as he could on a straight path behind the farm buildings. It seemed to define a depression where water had run—long enough ago that the mud was dry as a brick and cracked like ancient mortar. When he could delay no further, he veered off to approach the slight rise behind the barns. At the top of the rise he dropped to the ground again and turned his enhanced sight toward the wooden buildings.

"By my calculations, the snake barn should be dead center," Gerta whispered. "Storage to the right and left. Slave quarters to our right on the corner, right angle to the barn."

Lukan nodded, not willing to waste the energy of words. Chess added his own silent agreement.

"The sequence should go like this," Gerta said, eyes constantly shifting, wary and alert. Lukan remembered she was more than a blacksmith's daughter. She'd trained as a soldier, part of the queen's elite guard.

Maybe this mission wasn't as hopeless as he thought.

"Chess, can you conjure fire as easily as you control it?" Lukan remembered how easily the boy kept cool and calm while minding the bellows and coals in the smithy. Lukan could do it, but he hadn't the affinity. He was . . . a generalist, with a broad understanding and ability to work with each of the four elements but no real talent with any one of them.

Unlike Glenndon, who commanded everything in the universe to do his bidding.

"Of course." Chess didn't roll his eyes, but the disdain in his voice conveyed his opinion that anyone who couldn't bring fire to his fingertips and order it about was an idiot.

"Good. You stay here. I will let you know when to loose a fireball directly into that back wall, and maybe smaller fires into the storerooms. Gerta, you're with me. If you can find a stick to leverage the planks apart all the better." He dropped back behind the hillcrest, into a dry creekbed, and made his way along the ley line a bit before approaching the other side of the farm's quadrangle.

Slowly, carefully, he and Gerta moved from shrub to shrub, zigzagging their way around the hill, and approached the back of the slave quarters.

"This is too easy," he muttered. "It's still daylight and there's no one watching."

"As if they have dropped their guard because they fear nothing. The snakes are their defense. Who'd dare come here?"

"Us." Lukan flashed her a grin. "Let's hope they remain complacent a little longer."

"Time to get this over with. I see a gap in the wall to start our escape hatch."

Lukan gestured a finger across his lips. They needed silence.

Gerta pulled her dagger—the one that had helped transform his staff into a crutch—and slid the blade between two planks. The wood groaned loud enough to wake the soundest sleeper.

Lukan quickly stuck his staff into the opening and leaned on it. "Give me a place to stand and a long enough stick and I can move mountains," he grunted.

The wooden plank splintered vertically and hung drunkenly from a single supporting peg where it met the roof.

Questioning whispers greeted them from the inside.

Gerta returned reassuring words in the rapid patois of Amazonia—mostly the same language that Lukan spoke but more clipped with short vowels and dropped endings. Then she moved to the next plank. Pressure from the inside released that board more quickly. And a third.

Then a horror-filled shriek from the people inside. They shrank back from the hole in the wall.

"What?" Lukan demanded.

Gerta pointed behind him.

He whirled to face the open maw of a black snake twice as long as himself and as thick as his thigh. Its eyes gleamed a bright, sparkling red. Venom dripped from its hand-length fangs.

CHAPTER 32

MARIA DIPPED A clean rag into the bowl of beta arrack. She dribbled the amber liquor onto Robb's brow, his wrists, his chest, and his feet, trying to bring down the fever that burned within him. The spirits evaporated almost immediately with little effect on the magician's body temperature. When she wiped his skin with another rag doused in water, the cloth came away stained a dark brown.

Something strange was happening. She'd never encountered this illness before. Where did it come from? Was it contagious? The guards and servants stayed away from this room, making superstitious warding gestures if they had to linger at the doorway to hand her a cask of spirits or a pitcher of water.

For once, Geon and Bette found other errands than to watch the sickroom door closely.

No longer embarrassed at the sight of a man's naked body—he wasn't a man anymore, merely a patient in dire straits—she moved her wet cloths farther up Robb's legs to his knees. Someone had told her once that the back of a person's knees held a core of heat. If so, she needed to cool that part of him as well as the more obvious points.

As she twisted his left leg to reach the back of the knee she stilled. Long streaks of brilliant red edged in black stretched up to nearly his groin. A closer look showed chafing on his inner thighs, right where a saddle would rub him raw, nearly pulsed with malignant fire.

She spread beta arrack across the streaks.

Instantly Robb eased his thrashing. Almost a sigh of relief.

"We went to the farm, my lady," the short and skinny guard, Bobbeh, the one Robb called Scurry, said from the doorway. Nervously he rubbed his hands together. "He was alone with the king when they inspected the barns."

"No," she gasped. "He wouldn't."

Scurry said, "He was fine when we mounted up a few moments later. By the time we left the halfway stable, he was limp with fever. I had to help him into the saddle. He could barely hold onto the reins."

"Was . . . was the saddle leather stained?"

Den shrugged, making him look more than ever like a bulky badger full of determination and obstinacy. "Maybe. 'Twas an old saddle, dark and worn."

"Thank you for telling me that. This disease is not contagious. It comes from close contact with the snakes, not from touching another sick person. Will you sit with him a short while? I must speak to His Majesty."

"Don't know what I can do to help." Bobbeh moved a few steps inward. His partner Den remained on the landing.

"Bathe as much of him as you can, with the spirits first and then clear fresh water. If he rouses at all, make him drink three sips from this mug. No more. He can have water if he can take more drink. But only three sips of the medicine every hour."

Bobbeh nodded and took her place on the stool beside the bed. Maria hurried as fast as she could to the king's private courtyard. He'd left orders not to be disturbed while he entertained Princess Rejiia there. Maria wanted to disturb that arrangement.

"Your magician is dying," she said quite loudly the moment she spotted Lokeen sitting on a stone bench, leaning against the back idly. In front of him, Rejiia pranced and sang a wistful tune, kicking at flower heads and flicking water droplets at the king from a decorative fountain.

Her servants puttered in the dirt in a back corner of the yard, by the wall. Maria noted how they always remained out of Lokeen's line of sight. Their constant watchful presence bothered her more than she wanted to admit.

Lokeen jerked more upright. Rejiia kept dancing as if she hadn't heard. Or didn't care. Her servants crept closer, no longer pretending to be occupied. "He can't be dying. I still need him."

"He burns with a mysterious fever. I have tried everything I know, and he does not respond." There was one other thing, but far too dangerous. She'd never prepared hellebore before. Maria faced her brother-in-law, not bothering to hide her contempt. "The chafing on his inner thighs allowed the miasma to poison his blood. I think the saddle was painted with venom."

"Of course it wasn't. Who would dare try such a thing?" Lokeen dismissed her with a vague wave and returned his attention to his betrothed. He was hiding something.

Maria tuned out Rejiia's efforts at enticement. The melody was almost visible as a swirling cloud of dark mist sparkling redly from within. It engulfed the king but did not spread to Maria. She thought she heard a whisper beneath the melody: *You don't need the magician, you have me. Let him die. Let him die.*

Maria turned too quickly. She stumbled. Her twisted left leg nearly collapsed. She caught her balance on the nearest branch. A long thorn in the shape of a spearhead stabbed her palm and she squealed. Dark red blood welled up quickly. She could only stare at the painful wound blankly.

Geon steadied her with a strong arm and handed her a clean handkerchief. He grimaced. Or was that his attempt at a smile?

For a brief moment she suspected he offered her sympathy as well as support.

Whose side did he defend, in truth?

A voice in the back of her head whispered *(You know what you have to do.)*

Fire. Now. Chess, burn that building now! Lukan screamed with his mind, hoping against hope that Chess was mentally receptive.

Nothing happened.

He sensed Gerta moving, guessed she'd backed away, if she was smart. Instead he felt the prod of a dagger grip in his right hand. Staff to his left. Knife to his right. This felt familiar.

He'd trained with both Robb and Marcus to ride a dragon to do battle with the snakes. Though he'd never actually gone hunting with them, he knew the principles.

The snakes carried a bubble of magic around them, preventing mundane weapons from penetrating their bodies. Or their eyes.

But the dagger was mundane. He needed enchanted obsidian, knapped so sharp it almost didn't need magic to slice through the bubble.

> *"Knife blade good and true*
> *accept my power through and through*
> *fly fast and free*
> *stab deep and clean*
> *Stargods make it be."*

Not much of a spell, but with ley line magic held deep in his body and mind he prayed it would work.

It had to work or he died.

Before he could think about it, he flung the knife straight at the open mouth, seeing it sail between fangs and embed in the soft tissue of the throat before it actually did.

The Krakatrice screamed around the long blade, a sound to split eardrums and drive the mind into paralysis. A sound that grabbed his heart and tried to crush it.

Lukan wanted to sink to his knees and bury himself into the Kardia to escape the sound.

And the sight of the great snake undulating toward him. It flung its head back and forth trying desperately to dislodge the knife. Venom sprayed all around with each movement of its head.

Then the back wall of the barn erupted in flame. Long shafts of green and gold streaked along the dry wooden planks, hungry for more, diving inward and upward. It stopped abruptly when it met the slate roof. Resenting the confinement, fire dove back down and through the wood, gobbling chunks whole and turning them into nurseries for more flames.

A second fireball arced overhead toward the roof of the farmhouse, a full story taller than the barn.

Chaotic voices erupted from the center of the compound as guards and snakes fled toward each other.

Lukan didn't want to think of how the fire-maddened and frightened snakes would greet their captors. Their instincts demanded blood. They'd take it from whoever was nearest.

The wounded snake screeched again. It shrank away from the fire. It rammed its head against the ground trying to rid itself of the knife, only driving it deeper and deeper into the brain. Its skin crisped and crackled in the heat of elemental fire turned loose upon the world.

Holding the staff before him as a ward, Lukan backed away.

Fire leaped from barn to storage and over to the slave quarters in two blinks of the eye.

Ragged men and women broke through the hole in the back wall, more willing to brave a few flames and one wounded snake than a bevy of angry and bloodthirsty ones in the forecourt.

Gerta fell face first beneath the onslaught of trampling, fleeing feet. Lukan thrashed and beat the mob away from her with his staff.

One man, about his own age, paused to help him keep the frightened and confused from stepping on the felled woman. Lukan didn't care where the slaves took themselves. He needed only to make sure Gerta lived.

"Verdii! If ever you wanted to help me, now would be a good time. Now would be the right time for a storm," he called desperately into the air, the ether, and into his heart. "The fire and the creek won't contain the Krakatrice long. A little rain would be nice."

"How about a lot of rain?" Gerta asked, spitting dirt and rubbing her ribs as she rolled and sat up without assistance.

(A little rain?) Verdii's voice came into the back of Lukan's mind. *(A little rain is easy. You need more? I'll need the help of my siblings.)*

Lukan nearly cried in relief. He just might survive this day.

A long, searing stab of fiery pain raked the back of his calf.

In its death throes, the Krakatrice impaled his calf with a long venom-spouting fang.

CHAPTER 33

SOUSKA DROPPED A tiny spoonful of the fever medicine between the lips of the headman—Stanil, she had to remember his name. He thrashed and fought swallowing. Lily reached over and pinched his nose closed. Souska tried again to get a few more drops into his mouth. Lily massaged his throat. At last the precious brew slid into him.

"We have to do more," Souska cried. "He was the only one who didn't sicken. The rest of the village is getting well. Why now?"

"Why indeed?" Lily chewed her lip as she dribbled cool water on his brow. "Mistress Maigret taught me that if you let your eyes cross a bit and go out of focus, then look behind the left ear, you can see a person's aura. The color gives clues to emotions and signature colors."

"I know how to find an aura," Souska grumbled.

"Did you know that it can be visible around the entire body, and the color and intensity changes around wounds and the core of illness?"

"That makes sense. Can you do it?"

"I was hoping you could. I have little practice and do not trust what I see yet." She hung her head in shame. In a family full of strong magicians, she was the one failure—not really a failure, just a pale shadow in the wake of the rest of her family.

Souska rapidly reviewed every magical lesson she'd ever had. It was all a blur. What had Lukan said? Something. He'd tried to instruct her through the process. His words touched her more than anyone else's ever had. She learned more in one short scrying conversation with him than in hours and hours in the classroom. She knew how. But could she do it?

"When I first came here, you worked some magic. Not much. But you at least tried. Why not now?"

Lily looked away, swallowed deeply. "Death enhanced my talent. I'm afraid that if I use her gifts, it will bring me closer to her. Too close. I may invite her to take my patient. Now breathe, Susu. Breath deep." She ran a moist cloth over the sick man's face. It came away a dark rusty brown.

Why was he sweating old blood?

Stargods, this disease was different. And yet the same.

She didn't have much time to lose.

She counted her inhale, hold, exhale, hold. Slowly, deeply. Repeat. Her anxiety calmed. She could do this. She had to. A bubble of panic again.

"Don't think, just breathe," Lily coached. She frowned in worry as her clean cloth showed even darker than the previous one. The white spot on her forehead pulsed pure white. Was that the touch of Death?

"Breathe with me, Lily. Breathe as if your life depended upon finding a trance. Death is near."

Lily looked shocked. Her hand reached tentatively toward the touch of Death, but at the last second she jerked it away. "On my count: in on three. That's it. Slow and smooth. Let me worry about the count. Breathe. Feel the air. Find the Kardia. *Breathe*."

Souska breathed. She let her mind and her gaze drift. The world titled slightly to the left. Colors brightened. The headman's aura snapped into view. Pale yellow and brown all over. And . . . and . . . and a big black splotch on his left foot.

She ripped the seam of his trews from the knee down.

He wore tightly knitted woolen stockings. The work of a loving wife. She almost wept that whoever had made those lovely socks was dead, along with a dozen others. She took more care rolling down the stocking and tugging it off his cold feet.

"There!" Lily gasped. "That gash on his foot."

"From the ox-shoulder shovel he used to dig a firebreak around the field. The shovel was covered with tainted dirt when it slipped and cut him."

"That's the source of his infection. But how do we cure it?" Lily asked, staring up at Souska with bewildered eyes.

"We make him bleed. Cut the gash anew, a little longer and wider, but along the exact same line. Then we squeeze out the infection."

"That won't be enough."

"It's a start."

Lukan's breath came rapid and shallow. The pain faded in importance along with his fear. He'd been bitten by a Krakatrice. How long did he have to live?

(Death is neither the end or the beginning. It is between. It is.) The voice sounded like a lecture rather than reassurance. No dragon introduced himself. But the voice sounded very similar in cadence and resonated in the same place in the back of his mind as a dragon.

The world tilted and spun around Lukan. His senses scattered, aware of bits and pieces of everything and none of it made sense. Like trying to piece together bits of broken shell from a dozen eggs to make one whole one before the yolk spilled out.

A flutter of green remained steady, as steady as it could, moving up and down. Up and down. He fixed his mind on that one bit of color in an all white world. Up and down.

Why wasn't there a breeze?

(Because you are a part of the wing.)

Up and down.

Where was he?

(Where you belong. For now.)

"Am I in the void?" Up and down. Iridescent shimmers against the white. Blue, red, yellow flirted with the shifting light. Now here. Now not.

A sense of movement came into play. He soared between the green that beat up and down. The muscles of his back worked to create the strong push down followed by an easing as air drove him back up. Down and up. Or was it up and down.

His direction shifted. Around and around. A huge circle. A flash of colored wings. Circling and circling again, high up. Very high up. Circling, creating a vacancy. Air rushing to fill the center of the circle.

Cool air. Refreshing air.

Moist air.

Wetness to counter the streaks of flame. Fire aimed at the center of the circle. Men running and screaming. Fire attached to their backs and gnawing inward. Writhing black lines, thick and thin, long and short, twisting and turning, avoiding the fire, working against . . . pain. What would cause their pain?

So akin to his own. Something sharp and burning demanded his attention. *If I can feel the bite wound, I am not dead.*

Pain, writhing forms. Fire and rain . . .

Rain that shriveled the blackness into knotted contortions.

"I'm not ready to die. There are things I must do!"

(Death or Life?)

"I can't let the Krakatrice win!"

(Then do not die. Your choice.)

He tumbled down and down and down, the churning air buffeting him in all directions at once.

And then he landed. Breath whooshed out of him. His head hurt, and blackness crowded inward.

-꘏-

"What do you mean there are no matriarchs!" King Lokeen yells at his much beleaguered guard captain.

I cease my dancing. I have woven all the spells I know to bind the king to me with lust. Besides, my feet hurt in these ridiculous hard slippers with the pointed toes and heavy jewel crusts. They force my feet to conform to them rather than supporting and soothing. I have blisters already. By morning I won't be able to wear any shoes at all.

If the power Lokeen promises me were not so great, I would not bother with him.

The captain—my captain now—turns red-faced with a mixture of exasperation and fear and . . . deceit. I can read him very well now. I know what he feels, just as I'm sure he knows my own reaction to the king's desperation.

There is a matriarch, but he doesn't want Lokeen to have her. He wants me, me and my coven, to bond with the Krakatrice through the newborn female. Yes!

"There has to be a matriarch somewhere. Otherwise we'd not have any eggs," the king continues his tirade. "Go hunting yourself. I must have a matriarch to keep my clutches coming."

"Your Majesty, I have sent my most trusted hunters to the far reaches of Mabastion and the interior that no one claims but all wish to harvest. All the nests they have found are ancient, the eggs dormant. We bring them back to life when exposed to sunlight and warmth. The matriarch that laid those eggs did so a thousand years ago," my captain says. He sounds meek but I know the defiant stiffness in his bow.

"That cannot be. It cannot be!" The king begins foaming at the mouth as he jumps up and begins beating his fists upon my captain's chest. "I'll feed you to the males in the dungeons. The matriarch is in hiding until my pets mature enough. Your blood will help them grow."

"I think not," I sneer at my fiancé. As much as I gain power from hearing the death screams within the dungeon, I need my captain. Let the king sacrifice another. "The dwarf has royal blood. Feed her to the Krakatrice. Your son as well. He has magic in his music. Your pets will relish his blood . . ."

"Never!" Lokeen gasps, totally appalled at my suggestion. "The people will rebel and tear down this castle stone by stone if I harm a royal woman in any way. She is sacred. As for my son . . . he remains useful."

"But I shall give you daughters. Many daughters. Daughters who can marry into the royal families of all Kardia Hodos. You will rule the entire world through them. You have no need of a wastrel son." I half-sing those words, lulling him into accepting my alternative.

He says nothing, only gapes at me, drool sliding down his chin. "May the Great Mother forgive you," he whispers.

I have important things to do, Lukan said, not sure if he thought the words or spoke them. His ears roared so loudly he heard nothing else.

The young slave knelt beside him and ripped his trews from ankle to knee along the seam line. "I need a clean knife and water. Beta arrack if you have it!" he shouted to Gerta.

Chess appeared out of nowhere, running full tilt up the slight slope from the creek. "My knife is clean. I ran it through a white flame," he panted, proffering the hilt of his small eating knife.

The slave nodded and examined the keenness of the blade with his thumb. A bit of red welled up. He sucked it a moment until the tiny wound closed.

"Before . . ." Lukan swallowed around a very dry mouth. "Before I lose my senses, promise me that you will report this incident to my brother. Summon him. If you can't get through, you will carry this news to Prince Glenndon of Coronnan. If you can't get to him directly, his bodyguard is Frank. Frank's father is Fred who is bodyguard to the king. Their family has a house on Green Lane behind the palace. Glenndon has to know what is truly happening here. He's the only one who can fix this."

"You aren't going to die," the slave said with a determined glint in his eye.

"But I'll be sick. Too sick to finish this. Glenndon can finish this, if not himself, then he knows who can. Promise you will summon him, Chess!"

Chess and the slave nodded. "This is going to hurt."

"Then, best he clamp his teeth on this," Gerta said. She pressed her dagger sheath against his mouth.

"My staff," Lukan choked out. Darkness crowded his vision and the faces around him blurred.

"Fine. Chew on your staff, but bite hard." Gerta guided his left hand that clutched the staff already so that his essential tool of magic rested across his teeth. Her hand never touched the wood. Smart girl. The grain had begun to twist into a smooth braid, his magical signature. No one else could touch his staff without burning to the bone.

He opened his mouth until his jaw cracked and then got as many of his teeth into the wood as possible.

At the same instant the knife flashed along his left leg. He needed to scream. Gerta held his hands where they held the staff, pressing tightly so that he almost gagged.

The darkness came closer. He felt as if he viewed his body, his friends, and this stranger with a full magical aura of dark brown and bright blue, who might or might not be saving his life, from the top of the slate roof.

A breath of cool air revived him. He opened his eyes to a gray sky filled with lightning flashes that moved around and around. Everything seemed covered in dim mist. Was his sight dying first, before the rest of his body?

"Thank the Great Mother?" Gerta gasped staring upward.

"Thank the dragons," Chess added.

"Couldn't come at a better time," the slave added. "I've bled out the black crud. The wound is clean now, fresh red blood. The rain will wash away any lingering poison on the surface."

"The dragons?" Lukan whispered. He still felt strangely

detached and floating, but at least he was back in his own body. He knew that for certain as fat drops of water splashed against his face and fire lanced his leg. Soothing water. Blessed water in a parched land.

"Aye," Chess said, still looking upward with an awe-filled grin. "There's a green dragon leading five or six others around and around this vale. The whole vale. They're flapping up a wind and pulling the clouds and rain in from the ocean."

Pain-maddened screeches rose from the center of the compound—human and Krakatrice. The fires in the barn and slave quarters sizzled and spat under the onslaught of water.

Lukan dared look at the dead snake stretched across the rise. As he watched, the rain turned the fire-crisped skin into scummy ashes.

"Bless you, young magician. You have saved me and my people from the wrath of those monsters." The slave bowed his head and touched three fingers to his brow, his mouth, and his heart in solemn salute and prayer.

"Thank you for saving my life." As much as he hurt, Lukan was almost positive he'd survive. But he wasn't walking anywhere anytime soon. "May I have your name to remember in my prayers?"

"Juan," he said simply. His swarthy skin beneath his ragged shirt raised flusterbumps in the new chill from a fresh gust of sodden wind. He didn't ask for Lukan's name. Was this a holdover from his time in slavery?

"I am Journeyman Magician Lukan. And this is Apprentice Magician Chess. The lady is Gerta."

"You honor me with the gift of your name."

"I request that you fulfill the mission I gave you. I can see by your aura that you have magic. Help Chess summon my brother. Then get to the port. Here's a coin to buy passage on the first ship headed for Coronnan City. Please find a way to talk to Prince Glenndon personally. You may have only enough time in a summons to give him the barest facts.

The Krakatrice's bubble against magic may not die with them, at least not right away, and that will block your summons. I trust Glenndon to find a remedy for the troubles in Amazonia and to reward you for this service."

That speech cost Lukan all his strength. He closed his eyes and took a deep breath. When he opened his eyes again, the sun had shifted, dropping fast toward the horizon.

"What?" he choked out around a very dry and thick throat. Gerta dribbled a few drops of moisture onto his lips. The she held a cup to his mouth. He sucked fresh rainwater greedily.

Then he focused on Chess and Juan. "Did you summon my brother?"

"Aye. He's starting preparations for . . . something. But he wants us to bring you there quickly. Your father, Master Jaylor, would expect nothing less from one of his spies." Juan flashed Lukan a big grin.

"One of Da's spies. I should have known. More reason you need to get home, and quickly. Report to Glenndon and then to Master Marcus."

Juan nodded. "Don't let him move. Not for another day or two," he said, hanging his head in fatigue. "You have to keep the wound open, and don't move around much until it is truly clear of the venom."

"Transport," Lukan said.

"I . . . I don't know the spell. And I'd be afraid to use it. Last time . . ." Chess said, looking everywhere but at Lukan.

"Last time, Samlan diverted the spell and you ended up here, and Robb in prison," Lukan confirmed. He looked hopefully to Juan. The spy shook his head.

Chess shrugged out of his pack and thrust it at Juan. "Food, better clothing. This will see you to the city and beyond. Take one of our steeds; we tethered them over there." He pointed to the far ridge with a clump of trees and three browsing mounts.

Strange none of the fleeing slaves had stolen them.

Juan clutched the pack to his chest and rose in one

graceful movement. "Bandage the wound loosely so that it can breathe, but thick enough so the miasma from the snakes can't penetrate. I honor the trust you place in me and will speak to Prince Glenndon or die trying." He bowed, turned and ran toward the steeds.

Lukan cringed away from a new cacophony of screams, human and snake. He wanted to run away and leave the monsters with their monstrous human masters to their fate. He didn't think his leg would support his weight.

"Now what do we do?"

A dragon loosed a spate of flame at a snake trying to flee.

(Trust the dragons,) Verdii chortled. He sounded a lot like Da.

CHAPTER 34

ALONE IN ROBB'S room, with no witnesses other than her unconscious patient, Maria balanced the heavy obsidian Spearhead in her right hand. The Spearhead of Destiny. No man could handle it without having it burn his hand to the bone. If a woman of royal blood or a recognized female warrior handed it to the male champion of her choice, then he was safe to use it to defend Amazonia. Upon completion of the challenge, he must return it to the same royal woman's hands. Neither Maria nor her older sister had felt they needed a champion and so had never entrusted it to the king. That was the only reason Lokeen had left it undisturbed in the treasury. She wondered if the next chore he assigned to Robb would be to find a way to strip the Spearhead of the spell, or curse.

Now she held it as she faced a challenge of her own. The magic embedded in the rare volcanic glass tingled against her palm, almost an invitation to use it. She could not argue with one of the most sacred artifacts in all of Mabastion. The Great Mother had blessed this stone.

The time was coming when she would need to give this to a man . . . or possibly one of the women infiltrating the Palace Guard. But not yet. First she had to cure the wizard.

"Frederico!" she called. The sergeant peered into the room cautiously, still uncertain how safe he was from contagion. "I need a bathtub full of seawater, warmed to body temperature. No colder, not much warmer. And dissolve a third of a cake of salt in the water."

"My lady?"

"Do it. No questions. And hurry." Over the next hour she bathed Robb with more beta arrack and dosed him again. This time she had prepared the hellebore, a very dilute mixture. The magician's heart strained too much. Any attempt to control the rapid beat had to come slowly, gently, a little bit at a time.

Sooner that she thought possible, Bobbeh and Den wrestled a metal tub into the center of the room, followed by three androgynous figures clothed in red—followers of Helvess who nursed the injured and sick when no one else would tend them. The tub was an old design, copied over and over from the time of the first Amazon. A grown man could sit in it, back resting at a slight angle, knees drawn up. Deep enough to cover her patient up to the neck in water.

Behind the tub came Frederico marshaling a bevy of more nurses of Helvess, each carrying two full and steaming buckets of water that smelled of fish and seaweed. He handed Maria the third of a cake of salt. By the time the tub filled and the extra salt dissolved, the water had cooled to the proper temperature.

"Move him into the water, cautiously. The change in temperature may provide too much of a shock."

Frederico stripped Robb of all of his clothing, throwing the sweat-soaked underthings, shirt and threadbare blue robe into a corner. A nurse gathered them with long-handled tongs. "These must burn, on the open shore where the winds will take the smoke and ashes out to sea." He scurried out. Maria only suspected him to be male by the timbre of his voice.

The young female nurse turned wide and frightened eyes on her.

"Make sure you stay upwind. Do not breathe any of the

smoke. May the Great Mother bless you and all of your order," Maria said and bowed deeply.

"When we finish, all of the bathwater and the tub must be taken out to sea. I'll have a boat standing by," the male nurse said.

"Good idea," Maria replied and turned her attention to her patient. Their patient. She had help from the least expected place.

And then, miracle of miracles, Faelle walked into the room, clad in red tunic and trews, the red dot of a physician painted at the center of his brow. Tall and blond, he looked like a pale, thinner version of his older brother Toskellar. And yet, he'd added a new assurance and maturing to his posture. He knew his place in the world and did not cringe away. He carried strange metal instruments from long ago for monitoring heart rate and fever and breathing. Maria clutched the goddess pendant beneath her bodice and sent prayers to any goddess who might listen. Working together, they just might save Robb after all.

Maria hugged her nephew tightly, too grateful for his return to speak around her tears. He rested his cheek briefly on the top of her head, then turned to the business at hand. A patient in need of his skills.

Eyes closed, Robb thrashed weakly as the nurses lowered him into the water. The moment the salty water sloshed over the original wound he roused and screamed in pain.

Bobbeh and Den hesitated.

"Immerse him fully," Maria commanded. The nurses obeyed, keeping hands on Robb's shoulders and knees to keep him from bolting, even as the fearful guards backed away.

The noxious odor of burning sulfur, rotten fruit, and a diseased skunk rose up from the water to engulf them all.

Maria needed to run away to save herself.

(You know what you have to do.)

She had a duty to Robb, to Amazonia, to herself to follow through. She tied a kerchief over her face, much as the desert dwellers used gauze veils to protect themselves from flying sand. All of the nurses had already done so.

Holding her breath, she scooped out a bucket full of water. It stained the bucket dark rusty red. A nurse took it from her and handed it to another waiting on the landing, ready for transport to the boat. Faelle added a fresh bucket of clean seawater and let it mix fully with the old. She wondered if the poison would eat through the metal of the bucket. Or ever come clean.

All of the followers of Helvess wore several layers of tight gloves, another protection she had not considered necessary. Until now.

Robb thrashed some more as Faelle tested his pulse with the strange devices. Maria had to lean against the wall by the window in empathic pain.

Toskellar appeared at her elbow. "The guards should . . ."

"They need to stay ready but out of the way unless called by the nurses. Strong men wearing those gloves must hold Robb in the water. The poison will make him fight against the leeching process," she said, forcing herself to stand upright again.

"Then let me stay and help. I'm the one who summoned the healers."

"I won't take a chance on the poison touching you, Toskellar."

"I'll make sure my brother is careful," Faelle said. "As we all must be. We don't want to take a chance on you getting sick, Aunt Maria. We . . . I need you too much."

Reluctantly, she nodded and returned to perch on a stool by the window where she could observe all.

Robb groaned and thrashed. His face blanched until his skin stretched across his cheekbones, almost transparent.

"Great Mother, help me. Help him," she prayed.

Again and again Faelle and his helpers drew off tainted water, replacing it with clean. Hours seemed to pass. And then, finally, with ten bucketsful awaiting transport to the open ocean, the next one came through almost clear. And the next cleaner still.

Robb's breathing grew fainter, more rapid. She watched his pulse throb visibly at his neck. Labored. They were running out of time. Another dose of the hellebore. Faelle seemed to read her mind as he reached for the vial of her dangerous brew.

Another three buckets and all trace of rusty black disappeared.

She drew one long steady inhalation, let it go completely, and drew in more air. Then at Faelle's nod she poured double-distilled beta arrack into the tub.

Robb screamed and jerked violently.

She flinched. "Hush now," she whispered to him, even though she knew he had slipped too far into his fever coma to hear her. "The worst is over."

The nurses lifted Robb free of the tub and wrapped him in clean towels. She poured more liquor over the original chafing, now merely pink with all traces of the red streaks faded to little more than a memory, all the while murmuring soothing phrases. All of them meaningless.

"There is nothing more we can do other than watch and wait. We leave now," Faelle said softly. He clasped his hands in front of him and bowed to Maria. Then he clasped his brother in a tight hug before he backed away and disappeared.

"Thank you," she said jerkily. Exhaustion flooded through her after the release of tension. Still she sat by Robb's bed. "A loose wrapping of thick towels, I think. If there is more poison, it needs a path to leave the body. Tight binding will only keep it in." That required no thought. She knew how to wrap and tie a bandage. She'd done it often enough with her nephews when they were little and rambunctious.

Toskellar fetched fresh, dry linens himself, for both the bed and the patient.

"Wa . . . water," Robb choked. The first coherent thing he'd said since returning from the farm.

"And water you shall have. Just a bit at first." She dribbled a few drops from a spoon between his cracked lips. He sucked it up and swallowed without help. Another few drops went down just as easily. She followed that up with a bit more of the medicine she'd concocted. He nearly spat out the bitterness but she gave him more water.

"You'll mend now, dear magician. I need you well and hale. Amazonia needs you vigorous and decisive if we are to end Lokeen's tyranny before Rejiia steals the city out from under us."

※

"What do we do with it?" Souska asked Lily as they stared at the cup of hideous black goo they'd drained out of the headman's foot. They'd capped the cup with clay then placed it inside a metal pot with a lid. Still they had to stand back a minimum of ten paces from where it rested next to the midden to avoid the stench of rotten magic.

"Master Marcus and Mistress Maigret would want a CloseSeer to examine it, study it, find an antidote," Lily replied, cocking her head to one side, as if she could see better from a sideways angle. Her gaze shifted from the pot to the hilltop and back again. A faint smile, something akin to satisfaction, crossed her face. "We have sent Death chasing other prey today."

"Do you know someone with the CloseSeer talent?" Souska tried viewing the small pot from the same angle. She thought, possibly, she could see a black aura around the cup, but that could be just a shadow.

Lily shrugged. "I don't even know if such a talent exists. But if we have FarSeers to warn us of danger coming from afar, why not CloseSeers to warn us of dangers too small to see?"

"If such a talent exists, then Master Marcus must know of it. Perhaps we should send it to him," Souska offered.

"Can you do that?"

"No."

"Neither can I. But we can't just dump it. It will spread and poison the land or the water or even the air if we burn it. I think we need another pot and lid around it."

"We need help," Souska admitted. Except that neither of them was very good at the summons spell. "Why are you on journey, Lily? You don't have the skills to be a full magician."

"Da had a chore for me to do." She clamped her mouth shut and firmed her jaw.

"You must have completed the chore or you wouldn't be out here by yourself. You should have gone back to the University to learn more."

"My twin is at the University. Part of my chore was to learn to cope on my own without her."

Souska didn't know how to answer that. She'd heard about the twins. Lillian had strength and a nurturing nature. Valeria had a great magical talent, akin to her awesome brother Glenndon, but was physically frail and kept her emotions tied close to her heart, not letting anyone know what she thought. Together, Val performed magic, and Lily gave her the strength to do it. Lily found the people who needed help and gave them love. Val gave them the help and then retreated into herself. Separate, they were both diminished.

There was more to this story. Souska didn't expect to hear it now. Maybe not ever.

"So what do we do with the poison?"

"Can you contact Lukan and have him relay the message to Mistress Maigret? Then she can summon us. We can both answer a summons better than we can send."

Souska thought longingly about talking to Lukan again, seeing his face in her scrying bowl, hearing his voice talk her through whatever magical problem she couldn't figure out on her own.

A journey is about learning, he'd told her before he left.

"I think we have to try to summon Mistress Maigret," she said on a deep sigh. "It's not the easy way, but it's the proper way."

"I know," Lily agreed. "I need to start the call. I have to

know if I can really do it now or if it was Death lending me talent and strength."

"What does that mean?" Souska backed away a bit, gaze rooted to the flowing white spot on Lily's forehead. *Death had touched her, but left her living.* Why? What did it mean?

Five minutes later Maigret's drawn face, eyes heavy and red rimmed, appeared in the glass inside the bowl of water with a candle flame lighting the whole. "Your communications skills have improved, Lily," she said in a flat voice. "But you must try to light the candle with magic. It improves the quality of the images."

"Yes, Mistress. I hadn't the time or the energy to expend," Souska apologized for them both. They'd only accomplished this much by holding hands and drawing strength from each other. She didn't like the signs of distress on her mentor's face. The flat voice seemed the only way she could speak without breaking into tears. Or hysterics.

"Have you also made progress with the disease?"

"Yes, Mistress. Of those who survived, all but one have shaken off the fever. They rebuild strength, and we've changed their medicine to foxglove to maintain a steady heartbeat. We'll wean them off that drug within a day or two." Lily said. She sounded more firm and confident than her quivering chin belied. Perhaps a fuzzy image was the best course this time.

"So why have you summoned me?"

"We have a bit of a problem." Quickly Souska outlined the procedure to cure the last man felled by the Krakatrice fever. "What do we do with it?" She tried not to wail or cry, but that was almost as much effort as maintaining the spell. Maigret's image wavered in the glass.

"Where is it now?" Maigret demanded. A spark of interest glinted in her eyes, pushing aside some of the signs of her grief and weariness.

"In a triple-covered clay and metal pot beside the midden. We thought the smell of rotting things might mask the smell of rotten magic."

"Good thinking. But you must put it inside a fourth bowl and cover that as well. If there are any Krakatrice roaming that our hunting teams have not found, the smell will attract them."

"Yes, Mistress," Lily replied. Her breathing came easier, and her jaw firmed.

"And . . . I will have to consult with others. Perhaps the dragons know."

"Mistress Maigret, the dragons do not seem interested in our plight. Krystaal refused my request for food to keep this village from starving once we'd burned the fields to rid the land of the miasma."

"Oh?"

Souska didn't know quite how to continue.

"I'm told the dragons are busy elsewhere. Let me consult with the other masters. Stand by your glass an hour after sunset. I should have an answer by then." The glass went black, then cleared, becoming an inert tool devoid of magic to make it useful.

Souska sat back on her heels and calmed her heartbeat and her breathing. "I have to tell Lukan."

Lily merely cocked an eyebrow at her. "I'm going to check on Stanil." She left without another word.

Souska extinguished the candle and lifted the glass free of the water. Then she started the spell again, keeping the image of Lukan firmly in her mind. Light the candle—she had to dip the wick into the hearth embers inside the hut to manage that. Deep concentration, steady breathing, grounding herself in the Kardia until she felt the magnetic pole tug at her back. Then she dropped the tiny shard of glass gently into the water and positioned the candle flame to reflect properly onto the glass and water.

In her mind she followed the flame across hill and vale, helped it leap across the ocean to Amazonia and then watched it search for Lukan.

Nothing.

She found nothing but blackness and the reek of rotten magic.

CHAPTER 35

*L*OKEEN SCREAMS AND holds his head in his hands, pressing fingertips into his temple so fiercely I can see his nails drawing blood and bruises spreading. "My babies are dying. All of them. Fire and storm kill them. Where did this catastrophe come from? Oh, my poor babies."

I prod him impatiently, pretending to soothe him. "Look out the window, my darling. Look across the courtyard to the dungeons. They are whole and strong. Your snakes thrive."

"What is this waking dream?" he asks, looking bewildered. "So real."

"You fell asleep and dreamed," I reply. "Nothing more than your fears preying upon your mind."

"No. No, no. It is real. My pets here in the castle are restless, disturbed, upset. They need . . . they need blood. Lots and lots of fresh blood."

"They need more than fresh blood. They need royal blood. Feed them the dwarf. Or your son."

"Which son?"

"Your choice, they are both useless."

"Captain, have the guards round up all the followers of Helvess, including Faelle. Send them into the dungeons. Feed them one by one to my babies. Let them know their punishment for their sins of sexual perversion."

"Yes, Your Majesty!" My captain slams his clenched fist against his heart in eager agreement.

I catch his eye. We will glory for many days in the blood-bath to come.

When my captain is gone, I send Geon to follow and make certain the chore is done correctly. His ruthlessness and loyalty to me are unquestioned. He accepts pain along with sex. My captain would rather give pain. I can foresee a time when he challenges my authority, if not my power.

Robb knew that he dreamed. He drifted through a blacker than black landscape slashed by undulating streams of light. The colors twisted and coiled, entwined, and braided with each other, like berry vines gone wild. A dim green beam that might once have been the color of deep water at the end of the Bay but now dimmed to gray pulsed slowly, laboriously, then rapidly as if in panic, kept circling and circling him. He wanted to reach out and touch it. Every time he tried to grab it with hands that were not really there, it slipped away. Elusive. Taunting.

A bright orange and red coil came closer and closer. It throbbed with anger, trying to beat at him. It too never quite reached him.

"Only a dream," he told himself. The words echoed in his mind, but not his ears.

(Is it only a dream?) someone, something, asked. He should know that voice. His memory became as slippery as the green band of light that grew fuzzy along the edges.

"If not a dream, then where am I? Why do I feel nothing, no pain, no fever, no despair? Only loneliness."

The orange and red streamer brightened and nudged him. He thought of Maigret. A smile blossomed inside his mind that smelled of flowers and herbs and clean laundry drying on a fresh mountain breeze. He felt as if he should reach out and hug the light.

(Where should a magician be when not inside himself?)

the voice asked. It sounded like . . . a lot like Jaylor, but not quite, more like old Baamin, Jaylor's master and predecessor as head of the University. Someone had told him that Jaylor had died. Brevelan too.

That saddened him greatly, almost as much as the loneliness. Bright orange and red nudged him again.

Maigret. She lived. And so did their two young sons.

The green shed some of the gray and brown that muddied its color. The edges firmed, with only a little fuzz.

(*If you can see your own life umbilical, then you have not yet died.*) A new voice, feminine he thought, chimed through his mind like delicate bells made of finest glass. Precious glass that could only be made by dragon fire burning impurities out of the sand.

His mind conjured an image of crystals suspended in the sunlight and shooting prisms in every direction.

"Am I talking to dragons?"

(*Who else would speak to you in the void?*) the chuckling female voice asked.

"The void." His mind went numb. "The void is a transition place between life and death."

(*Or a resting place when life is too difficult to bear.*) This came from another voice, one he was certain he'd never heard before. A combination of many voices, a marriage of male and female, young and old, soprano, alto, tenor, and bass all braided together. He thought of slender grapevines woven into bridal crowns.

"I'm not afraid to die. But I would like to see my Maigret and our sons one more time."

(*Is that what you desire most in the universe?*)

"Yes." If he had a body, he thought he'd cry, cry for all the lost moments of love for his wife and children.

(*Then live. But you must choose to fight hard to regain your life and health. Death is the easy course. Life is difficult.*)

"But to live is to love. Death is a . . . a void."

(*Then choose love and fight for it.*)

The vines of light dimmed. The blackness eased.

Pain engulfed every muscle and joint in his body. He nearly wept for joy that the grinding aches and stabs meant he lived. He had a chance to see Maigret again. And the boys.

More sensations intruded on his awareness. Candlelight brushed his closed eyes. A soft mattress beneath him. A warm blanket covered him. Coolness touched his face.

And his staff rested beneath his left hand while his right cradled his glass.

He lived and he had the tools to become whole again.

"Great Mother bless you," Lady Maria gasped. "The fever has broken and your heart beats a normal rhythm."

Maria tended his illness. Not Maigret. Sadness and loneliness engulfed him once more.

But he lived. He had a chance to go home. But he had to fight for it. The dragons said he had to fight.

If it took every morsel of his strength and will, he would fight to go home again to his family.

What is wrong with Lokeen? He seems complacent, eager to fall into my spells and obey my slightest whim. Like when I asked for the lives of the dwarf and his son. And then, when most inconvenient, he defies me. The two people who stand in my way still live. He won't even arrest them. It is as if he breaks holes through the bubble of love and lust I weave around him.

He promised me the lives of the followers of Helvess. I could not bend them to my will, so I will use the energy of their miserable deaths to fuel my power. Lokeen's guilt over the execution of his son will also lend me power.

But what is this? The temple is empty! All of the outcasts have fled, melted into the populace of the city. Nowhere to be found. Power drains from me in disappointment.

A doubt wiggles into my mind. Did Geon move ahead of my captain and warn them?

No. Impossible. He is not talented enough. But he is smart enough to go his own way without telling me. I must watch the watcher.

I feel as if I am an apprentice again, a raw beginner who must learn every spell by rote and then bend my will to make them work. The lash of a whip does not stir Lokeen. A kiss lulls his obstinacy but does not break it.

So while he sits at his desk and reads reports and letters, while he signs his name and seals it with hot, sea-green wax, I watch quietly from across the room. I choose a straight and hard chair for this chore. I do not want comfort. I want a constant reminder of what I am about. Geon stands behind me. My captain stands beside Lokeen. Bette drifts around the room in seemingly lazy circles, widdershins, pretending to bring order to the chaotic room. She arranges scrolls into new patterns, then scatters them. She dusts a piece of furniture then blows on the rag, sending minute bits fluttering around the room to find new resting places.

All this touches the edge of my awareness. I lean forward, perched on the edge of my chair, relishing the crease in my bottom and the ache in my lower back. These small pains aid in my concentration. As my eyes cross and lose focus, I look inward until the world dims and tilts. Then the object of my inspection jumps into clear view, an island of bright reality in a gray world that has no meaning.

Lokeen has no aura!

Why?

I can see my magic woven around him in tiny threads of red magic. Black holes mar the beauty of my carefully constructed tapestry. The weaving is complete. I did not leave those holes. The ripped threads of enscorcelment dangle weakly around the holes. Inside the holes.

If Lokeen had broken through my spells the threads would have burst outward.

They collapsed inward from a mighty thrust.

Wait! The loose threads are not rigid, they soften and un-ravel as I watch. They bleed black sludge. They BLEED!

Some other magician has tainted my magic. Someone stronger than me has a tighter control over Lokeen than I.

I must learn who. Quickly. I must bring him—the holes have a feeling of masculine precision rather than feminine rage—into my coven. I must learn his secrets. I will be the strongest magician in Amazonia. Anyone stronger must be absorbed or eliminated.

I am in the mood for elimination. A bloody execution will give me power and remove my rival.

If I were a follower of Helvess, where would I hide?

Lukan swam upward through thick layers of sleep. He knew he had slept and awakened numerous times. He knew he had dreamed. Which was the dream and which memory?

A chill invaded his joints. Moisture dripped down his face. He must be awake. He'd never dreamed rain before. But he'd slept under weeping skies often enough. Then a deep ache from hip to toes and back again on his left leg crept into his awareness. He needed to shift his hips, roll over, flex the knee; move something to relieve the pain that grew sharper with every heartbeat.

"No." A heavy hand squeezed his shoulder. "You have to remain still a little longer."

"Wha . . . ?" His voice cracked and cut off. Had he truly swallowed a bucket of desert dust, or did he merely need water? His tongue flicked across his lips involuntarily. Dry. Rough and flaking. He encountered an irregular protrusion that tasted like . . . like copper.

Blood.

Even as he acknowledged the bruise where he'd bitten deep and drawn blood, he noticed the soft drizzle dissolving the dried blood and soothing his parched mouth.

"You've had a fever," Chess said. He sounded far away, then close, and then far away again. His voice wavered with uncertainty.

"What happened?" Lukan ground out. His voice caught twice while uttering two words, but he got them out.

"You killed the snake. It bit you during the death throes."

"I remember that. Not after." He swallowed, fighting to get moisture into his mouth and throat. Nothing worked. In the end he left his tongue hanging out and let the drizzle coat it.

"Gerta and Juan carried you to the knoll where we left the steeds. They returned to the city. He looks for a way to return home to Coronnan and report to Glenndon and Marcus. She said she'd be missed," Chess said in an even tone. The boy shifted from behind Lukan to kneel beside him. Worry lines had turned him from the inquisitive boy, just touching his teens when he left the University, to a wizened creature Lukan couldn't identify.

"The slave? How? Do you trust him." Lukan tried shifting his body again, but he knew he had to keep his head firmly anchored to the Kardia. Flashing colors and blinding glare pressed against his eyes. Just blinking hurt. Was this akin to the devastating headaches Da had suffered before his heart burst and killed him?

"Juan and I joined in a summons to Glenndon. I saw his aura. I delved into his mind. He is trustworthy and loyal to the University. He took my steed. Last I saw, he galloped down the road as if Simurgh himself was on his tail."

"Ever notice how few red dragons fly with the nimbus? They totally reject any connection to the rogue dragon," Lukan slurred. Someone had told him that. Long ago. He couldn't remember, who, where, or when, just that it had seemed important at the time.

"I'm supposed to keep you here until you are coherent and can stand on your own . . . well maybe not your own, but supported by your staff," Chess continued as he looked longingly to the west.

Was he carefully avoiding looking east, toward the snake farm?

"The Krakatrice?" Lukan asked, really wishing for a

long drink of water. The rain just wasn't enough. In his desperation he turned his head to the east and saw only Chess' knee where he knelt on the ground.

"Dead."

"You're sure?"

"The . . . the dragons are still flying patrols, flaming any that poke their noses out of dark hidey-holes."

Lukan strained to look up for a glimpse of a dragon wing. *I flew with the dragons. It wasn't all a fever dream.* The sense of lightness and freedom, wind blowing his hair away from his face, flooded his memory. He almost cried that his body anchored him to the Kardia and a tree sheltered him from the gray sky.

"If you can sit up a bit, I'm supposed to give you water," Chess said.

"That would be good." Lukan squirmed onto his elbows, bracing himself for more pain and for his head to start spinning. The rising sun stabbed his eyes, and his leg ached abominably. Other than that he didn't feel too bad. Not great, but like he just needed a little more time to become mobile.

Half a skin of water later his headache faded to an unpleasant memory. As long as he didn't twist his neck too far or fast.

"Time to inspect the damage," he grumbled, slowly bending his left knee to bring his wound closer.

"Um . . ." Chess stayed his hands from pulling up his ripped clothing. "It's not pretty."

"I didn't expect beautiful embroidery along the knife slash." Resolutely he shrugged off Chess' restraint and bent so he could hold his leg closer to his body.

The scent of rotten magic made him rear his head back. That sent his senses spinning. He bit his lip again to anchor himself. That set off a new series of cracks and blood drops.

"Breathe," Chess reminded him, clamping a solid hand on his back.

"Working in the smithy has built up some muscle in you," he mumbled. *I'm rambling. Still feverish.*

"I had to grow strong. I have to rescue Master Robb," Chess said with more determination than Lukan could remember.

"What did Gerta say about us getting back to the city?" Lukan asked. He didn't move his leg, knowing he had to look but not quite ready to know how bad it was, how much the Krakatrice had robbed him of.

"She said she'd scout out the castle, figure out the best way to get the master out, if . . . if he's still alive." Chess gulped.

"He didn't look good when we saw him. Was that only two days ago?"

"There's more. The king has a passel of those snakes in the dungeon. We have to kill them before we can rescue the master."

"How?"

"Fire and water. Just like we did here."

"We had help from the dragons here. They burst the bubble of magic around the snakes. If the king even hears a rumor of a dragon he's going to panic and send his men to hunt them. Kind of hard to sneak a dragon into the city."

"Dragons are nearly invisible . . ."

"They can't squeeze into the castle and sneak into the dungeon. We're on our own." Lukan leaned forward, cradling his head in his hands. "These people have been fighting the snakes for a thousand years. They have to have some kind of weapon hidden away. Even if it is only folklore now." He breathed deeply and surveyed the landscape as dawn light crept forward. "We should survey the wreckage to make sure no snakes survived. Maybe salvage some food and an extra steed."

"The fire and the dragons were quite thorough," Chess said, still not looking over his shoulder toward the smoldering ruins.

Lukan took another deep breath to gather the courage
to move. That's when he saw the hunk of flesh missing from
his calf and spewed all the water he'd just drunk, gagging
and gagging like he wouldn't stop until he'd turned himself
inside out.

CHAPTER 36

ROBB DREAMED OF someone singing. A mournful tune of a lost love and deep regret. A light baritone, skilled, and . . . beautiful beyond imagining. He needed to cry and mourn along with that voice.

Then he recognized a name. Lillian. The singer's sweet and gentle Lily turned into an assassin by the evils of a rogue magician. Samlan.

Bits and pieces of stories he'd heard over the moons of his imprisonment fell into place. Skeller, the bard who was really a prince, had said he'd seen the light of life drain from Samlan as his knife twisted in the magician's heart. But he had not wielded the knife, Lily had.

Robb could not imagine one of Jaylor's twin daughters performing such a deed. Valeria, perhaps. But Lily? More robust than Val, the twin with the weaker talent resembled her mother—not only in coloring but temperament. Both were strong empaths, sharing both good and bad emotions in others, instinctively understanding ailments in mind and body. Neither one could bear to eat meat.

So how could Lily have murdered Samlan?

Robb didn't understand any more than Skeller did.

The song broke off on a sob and a discordant note from an abused harp. A rustle of movement, and quiet. The unnatural quiet of the sick room, people hovering outside, waiting to see if the patient lived or died. He'd sat many such vigils with Maigret over the years. If he reached out just a little, he should be able to envelop her hand in his and give her the comfort she needed, knowing that she could do nothing more. The will to live or die lay with the patient, not her skill as a healer.

His fingertips brushed across his staff as he stretched with his hand, mind, and will to find his wife.

A hand landed heavily atop his.

Not Maigret. He knew that instinctively.

His eyes flew open in alarm.

"Who?" he demanded of the man whose scarred face filled his vision. The skin on the right side had been pocked and burned by acid. His right eye was an empty socket of scar tissue, no lashes or brow remained. The left eye, dark brown, burned with a strange hunger, or anger, Robb couldn't decide which. A permanent grimace of pain had twisted his mouth and frozen it in place.

For answer the stranger's hand clamped tighter on Robb's, squeezing until bones began to shift. "I'll have the staff. Give it easily and no more harm will come to you," he said. Educated tones overlay a rough street accent.

Movement behind the stranger threatened to draw Robb's attention away from the man.

"Hurry, Geon. We 'ave ta git out of 'ere afore *she* discovers us," a woman said. She totally lacked even a pretense of sophistication in her voice.

Robb yanked his hand and staff back across the top of his body and squeezed his other hand tighter on the glass. A faint tingle of magic caressed his skin. Contact should have given him more power than that.

But he was inside the castle. The Krakatrice drained magic from everything in order to maintain their protective bubble.

The man, Geon, bared his teeth in his version of a grin as he clamped down on the wood that had twisted with every spell Robb had channeled through it over the last fifteen years. Perhaps the grain had begun to straighten in places from lack of use during his time of confinement. Not much. It still held much of Robb's essence, and his power, even if he couldn't tap it at the moment.

"Yiieee!" Geon screamed and lurched away, holding his hand tightly against his chest.

"Quiet y' fool," the woman hissed.

"Didn't anyone ever tell you that a staff has to be earned? It has to be given to you freely by the trees on Sacred Isle. You cannot cut a staff from a tree. Nor can you steal one from a magician!" Robb snarled as he swung his legs off the low cot that had been his sickbed for too long. He grasped the staff tightly between two knots in the comfortable place his hand had worn over the years. He and the staff *fit* each other.

"That isn't recorded in any of the books . . ." Geon protested.

Robb pounded the butt of the staff against the rush covered wooden floor. The sound echoed around the room, and vibrations massaged his bare feet.

"Didn't anyone ever tell you that coven magic is centered upon pain," Geon sneered. "We draw power from pain, both given and received. We thrive on chaos. The Krakatrice feed us magic—like to like—while they drain it from you." He held forth his reddened hand. Cracks gouged the inside of his knuckle joints. Blisters popped up on the pads of his palms where he'd gripped the staff.

He reached again, his hand actually trembling with pain. All the while his mouth twisted upward showing his pointed teeth. "Give me your staff," he demanded.

"What can you do to me that Lokeen and his pet snakes have not done already?" Robb replied. He drummed the staff against the floor, letting the musical cadence of wood against wood feed his soles with energy.

The woman approached from the corner, holding a long kitchen knife forward, as if she intended to butcher a boar for cooking. "I can dismember you piece by piece," she said.

Clearly she was the more dangerous of the pair, reacting without thought of consequences.

Keeping his eyes on the woman, Robb swept the staff out and up, catching the butt behind Geon's knees and then the top under his chin. The man grunted as he stumbled backward, jerking right and left for balance. He flailed with both hands, trying desperately to grab something, anything for balance. His right hand found the back of Maria's empty chair. He jerked the damaged skin away with a shout of pain and continued his desperate attempt to keep from falling.

For good measure Robb grabbed his staff with both hands and rammed it into the man's groin. Geon collapsed to the floor, doubled over and groaning. His good eye rolled upward as he fainted.

"I'll kill you for that!" the woman screeched. She shifted to an overhand grip on the knife and dashed forward.

Balancing on one leg, Robb shifted his staff into a wide swing against her arm. The snap of her breaking bone was almost as loud as the door banging open and his own thud onto the floor.

"What is the meaning of this!" Gerta demanded as she kicked the knife across the floor, out of everyone's reach.

"They tried to steal my staff," Robb said stiffly. His burst of energy drained from him like a receding tide. He wondered how he was going to get up far enough to collapse onto the cot.

"Not a good idea, I'd say," Gerta continued, surveying the scene. "Even without magic, you are a rather intimidating man," she said and bowed slightly in respect.

"I think they were trying to escape from their mistress and wanted my staff as a weapon against her," Robb panted. His head started to spin. He'd been abed too long, and now his body rebelled against the sudden action.

"You don't think they were stealing it *for* Princess Rejiia?" Gerta asked.

Robb shook his head, then regretted it as the walls faded in and out and he lost touch with his sense of up and down.

A feral smile touched Gerta's face. "I think we can accommodate their goal of depriving the princess of their support and power in her magic. But they won't be walking free anytime soon. It's the dungeon for them. Separate cells, close to the snake pit."

Four more women in palace guard uniforms marched in and dragged the prisoners upright, barely noting their screams of pain and wails of despair. In seconds they'd all departed, leaving Robb on the floor and Gerta standing over him with hands on her hips. "I suppose after your magnificent display of defending yourself without magic you are now too weak to care for yourself?"

"Something like that," Robb admitted. He tried to get his legs beneath him but they felt like unwhipped egg whites.

Badger and Scurry appeared at a gesture from Gerta. Badger wiggled behind Robb and got his hands beneath his armpits. Scurry grabbed his ankles. Together they lifted and swung Robb back onto his bed.

Robb patted his staff as he nestled it alongside himself again and made certain his glass still hid amongst the covers.

He was asleep before the door closed; dreams of burning pain and gaping emptiness plagued his mind.

Souska felt the warm, moist wind before she heard the rush of angry air in the treetops. Instinctively she braced herself for thunder.

Across the field where she and Lily helped harvest the scanty grain and dwarfed tuber crops, Lily smiled and lifted her face with closed eyes.

A dragon roared a greeting. No name or telepathic communication followed. At least nothing she could sense.

"Lily knew they were coming before I did," Souska grumbled. "She welcomes them while the villagers cringe in fear." Souska wondered what she'd done to offend the dragons.

Stanil looked up with a frown, worrying his lip with his

teeth. Fatigue and worry added deep lines to his still-pale face. He was too young for the job of headman, not more than early twenties. Who else was there to take the responsibility? Then he continued scything the grain stalks, limping painfully forward in grim determination. He couldn't wear a boot yet, so Souska had wrapped layers of raw wool and cloth over his bandage. He had to be hurting from his barely healed foot wound and fever. And yet he continued with the hard, grim work of bringing in whatever harvest he could.

Souska followed behind him, tying the fallen grasses into slender sheaves. She had to move slowly so she didn't overtake him.

She had finally remembered he had a name. As did the women coming behind her, loading the sheaves into baskets to carry to the thresher. Lanette and Barbo.

Lily knew them all, had learned their names the first day she came here. She could name the dead as well as the living. She'd shared each death. In some ways she lost a bit of herself with each passing. Death had touched her in more ways than one. With each passing she grew stronger, almost as if she gained wisdom and maturity from each one.

Souska didn't want to know their names until she knew they'd live. Stanil would live.

The dragon came into view, a shimmer of crystalline light tipped in blue that shaded toward the green of deep water. A bit of silver still clung to the tips of the spinal horns.

(Taeler here!) the dragon proclaimed with exuberance.

The remnants of silver meant he was still quite young. This might be his first solo outing away from the lair. The same age as Krystaal?

Lily started to run to meet him, then paused, returned for her staff, and raced toward where he landed on the meadow to the west of the village. Normally two dozen sheep would graze there, but they'd been moved farther south to avoid any possible contamination from the plague.

Souska adjusted her broad-brimmed straw hat and followed Lily more sedately. Barbo stepped up to take over the chore of binding. They didn't really need two gatherers. The crop was too scanty to require more than one. They'd easily finish the harvest tomorrow. Two days of moderate work with a scant ten men and eight women with only a dozen children in tow when it should take ten days of hard labor by a full village of twenty-five or thirty adults and a dozen or more children.

She should have felt dismay, or worry, or something. Instead emptiness surrounded her. As if she'd been stripped of all but the ability to move from one task to the next.

A tiny bit of relief niggled at her back brain. They hadn't had any new cases of the plague since Stanil, nearly a week ago. Maybe, just maybe, it had run its course.

A young man in medium blue journey leathers slid down from the back of Taeler. He left his staff tucked between two thick horns at the base of the dragon's neck.

"Journeyman," Souska decided from the color of his uniform and the presence of a staff.

Then another blast of wind from the east sent her hat flying. A second dragon circled the village and descended toward the same meadow.

"It's getting crowded here," Souska said.

(Krystaal here,) the all-color/no-color dragon said, somewhat meekly. She touched down on the other side of the meadow. No rider graced her back, but it looked like several sacks of grain, tubers, and seeds had been tied between the biggest spinal horns. A closer look revealed a few more of the sacks on Taeler's back.

Souska's knees nearly gave out. "They didn't forget us," she cried. Tears burned behind her eyelids. "We'll survive the winter. Thank you, Krystaal. Thank you." She wanted to run to the dragon and stroke her long muzzle but couldn't seem to make her legs work.

A growing babble from the harvesters told her that the villagers had noted the supplies as well.

"Linder!" Lily called with nearly as much excitement as the dragon had exhibited. She threw herself into the man's wide-open arms. He grabbed her around the waist and spun her around. "Lily, what have you been up to that has got the entire University bounding to do your bidding?"

No mention of Souska and her part in healing the villagers, calling a dragon and requesting food, knowing how to cut the infection from Stanil. No idea that Souska's tasting of the dirt had proved more informative and beneficial than Lily's blind acceptance of the dragon's *wrong* pronouncement.

"Souska figured it out," Lily said, laughing.

"So I have heard," Linder said, setting Lily back on the ground. "You must be Souska," he added, giving her a brief bow. "I am to fetch from you a pot of noxious something and return it to Mistress Maigret as soon as possible."

"It's over by the midden." Lily waved north and west of their location. The wind rarely blew from that direction.

"What is Mistress Maigret going to do with it?" Souska asked. She had no solution to the problem herself.

"Bait," Linder replied on a grin. "Or at least most of it. The Krakatrice hunters will set out a bit of it to see if we can draw in any surviving snakes. Some of it, the mistress insists, she'll keep to study, see if she can make an . . . an . . . anti something out of it."

"Antidote," Lily supplied the missing word.

"Or a vaccine for the snake hunters," Souska added.

Lily shuddered at that idea. Hadn't they listened to that lesson taught by Master Marcus last year? He wanted the healers to find ways to give the general populace who didn't have access to magical healers a tiny bit of a disease, to make them slightly sick. They'd recover quickly but have the immunity to that disease for a long time. Possibly a lifetime.

Souska liked that idea. She didn't trust magical healers if they listened to dragons who didn't know everything.

Linder just looked blank. Then he shrugged and turned back to his dragon. He began untying the sacks of grain.

Lily took the first bag from him, still laughing. Souska went over to Krystaal and began releasing the sacks. The knots were sturdy and twisted and did not yield easily. "Can you crouch down a little, Krystaal, so I can reach these better?" she asked as she indulged in running her hand down the sleek fur of the huge animal.

Krystaal turned her head away and promptly plopped down onto her belly, legs tucked neatly beneath her.

She'd announced herself properly but had not directed any more communication into Souska's mind.

"What's wrong, Krystaal?" Souska asked quietly so that Lily and Linder could not hear over their own jabbering.

(I am not worthy.)

"Nonsense. You are a perfectly normal dragon."

(I spoke too soon with not enough information.)

Ah, so the dragons did know that the solution the female dragon had given them was incomplete and potentially disastrous.

(Female dragons are not as numerous as males. So we are made to feel special. I believed myself too special to listen to my wiser elders.) She closed her eyes and hung her head so that the long, spiral forehead horn nearly touched the ground.

"I forgive you, Krystaal. I understand. I'm not much better when it comes to magic."

(You could have been harmed. The village could have been destroyed. You saved them. Not I. It was my duty to save you and I failed.)

"We all worked together. You told us fire and salt. We thought we had to burn and then sow salt. But we need to burn the fields after harvest, not before, and scrape up the extra salt, not add more. Your words set me thinking along the right path."

(Is that enough?)

"For now." Souska gave the dragon hide an extra vigorous rub, then set about loosening the knots.

"May I help?" Stanil asked, hovering a good ten paces away from the dragon.

"Yes, thank you," Souska replied. The headman didn't move.

"Oh, yes, I forgot I have to introduce you. Krystaal, this is Stanil, headman of the village. Stanil, this is Krystaal, a young female of the nimbus of dragons."

Stanil bowed his head in respectful greeting before taking those ten hesitant steps forward. He made a show of putting weight on his bandaged foot, but he still limped and pain clouded his eyes.

"She won't eat you. Or flame you. She's my friend."

The dragon lifted her head from her depressed slump and turned her big all color/no color eyes on the newcomer. *(Krystaal here. Welcome, Stanil.)*

"Did . . . did she . . . just speak to me?" Stanil's eyes opened wide in wonder.

"Yes, she did." Souska suppressed a giggle. Then she paused, surprised that she actually felt the little bubble of mirth. Warmth and the need to reach out and touch her friends filled her. Suddenly she felt as if she belonged here, wanted to become part of the village community, to learn everyone's name and share with them.

Hesitantly she laced her fingers with Stanil's and guided his hand to scratch Krystaal's muzzle where she knew it itched. "Announce yourself," she whispered.

"Um . . . Stanil here, Krystaal. Welcome to our village." He looked away from the dragon long enough to capture Souska's gaze. "*Our* home."

Souska couldn't look away from him. *Our home.* Did that mean he welcomed her as well as the dragon? Offered to let her stay?

"Magic," Stanil whispered as he stroked the silky coat on the dragon. "I can feel the tingle of magic in her fur."

"Yes, the magic of friendship," Souska agreed.

Lily laughed again. Her entire being seemed to have brightened as she and Linder shared memories and gossip about mutual acquaintances. They'd grown up together, had much in common. Linder passed along a message from Lily's twin. They didn't seem to notice or need Souska.

But Stanil did. And Krystaal did. They needed her. No one at the University did.

CHAPTER 37

"THIS CASTLE NO longer welcomes me," I mutter to my captain as we patrol the curtain wall after moonset. "Something has changed."

"I agree," he replies. His eyes shift nervously as he counts the guards on watch. "Twenty-five. As I scheduled. We always have twenty-five on the walls. At all times."

"Why do you question their presence?" I too grow alarmed. Something is very wrong with these guards. They each turn and salute as we pass. Yet . . . yet they keep their faces lowered. Is it respect that they will not meet their leader's gaze directly? Or is it fear?

Neither. I cannot smell fear in them.

"I know every man in the palace guard. I selected each one for this duty. So why will they not meet my eye?" He has spent too much time with me of late rather than seeing to his duties. I needed to force the bond between us, so that he looked to me rather than his king or his comrades-in-arms. Temporary, I thought. But to what detriment?

I look ahead, behind, and across the forecourt. Every uniform is the same. They are all tall and broad shouldered. They all carry their weapons with easy familiarity.

My heart skips a beat in recognition.

"They do not look to you as leader," I whisper, seeking an exit. Any exit. This place is no longer safe.

"They must . . ."

"They are not your men. They are Lady Maria's women," I hiss, dragging him toward a tower door that should lead to the interior of the castle, or at least down to the forecourt.

My captain gasps in recognition. Finally he realizes the danger of these women turning on him in the name of their lady. Their dwarf!

How can they take oaths of loyalty to a misshapen crone of no beauty and no authority?

They should fear us. I am beautiful and dangerous. My captain is strong and handsome, a proven leader.

They have no fear of us. Only disdain.

We could order them directly into the Krakatrice pens. Or could we? Have they replaced all of the men here?

I must flee. I have misjudged this place and these people. They cannot help me. They cannot feed me power. And I cannot find Geon and Bette anywhere. They have deserted me! I will punish them when I find them. But I have not the time to search. I must flee. Now.

My gaze drifts to the port. There are ships there. Many of them. They all display different flags, different designs. I point them out to my captain.

"I agree. We leave now."

"And what of your king, my fiancé?"

"A useless fool who no longer listens to anyone but his poisonous pets in the dungeon. How safe will anyone be when he turns them loose? That last ship in line flies the flag of Venez. We buy passage on it within the hour and sail on the morning tide."

Bette and Geon can rot in this foul place. I must save myself and my captain.

Lily looked across the evening fire toward the crest of the hill. Sparks popped and normal green flames licked the wood merrily. The villagers *talked* to each other. The listless meal preparation and the silent but hasty gulping of thin, bland stews had given way to thoughtful additions of herbs and enthusiastic chatter while each person savored their food.

"I'm no longer needed here, Linder," she said quietly to the journeyman. He'd brought the requested supplies, sent the poisonous pot back to Maigret and . . . and lingered beside her.

"Then come back to the University with me," he said succinctly, gaze circling the villagers and not meeting hers.

She felt his slight embarrassment and attraction. Her own emotions stayed bland, welcoming his friendship but not needing to explore a deeper relationship with him. Her heart belonged to Skeller.

She acknowledged it and held it close within her, cherishing the tiny flame of love.

And now that Death had touched her and left her living she considered the possibility of living. More than that. She needed to embrace life and love, while accepting death as part of the natural cycle.

"The time is not right for that either," she replied. "There are other villages suffering from this plague. They need me now."

"Mistress Maigret has dispatched every healer and herbalist she can to seek out those afflicted villages and aid them with *your* cure and fresh supplies."

"Not my cure. Souska is the one who knew how to mix it and use it properly."

"But you were the one to ask for the ingredients. Yours is the name whispered among the Healing Halls."

"Then take Souska back with you. She's the one who should get credit."

"If she wants it." Linder tilted his head toward where the girl sat a little distant from the companionable group around the fire, talking quietly to Stanil.

Lily didn't need to hear their words or search for an aura to know that their life energies reached toward each other.

"I'm not certain I like that. He's twenty-two, she but fifteen."

"So? Age means little when hearts and minds align."

So it did. Skeller looked at the backside of twenty-four, while her seventeenth name day was still many moons distant.

"I heard that Lady Graciella wanted to join the healers in seeking out afflicted villages, but she is too close to her term—big as a hut and waddling more than walking. Her mother sent her back to the University. Seems only her husband wants her, but he's not been heard from since the flood." Linder shifted subjects as he shifted himself a little closer to Lily.

"I'm happy that she thrives. We never did grow close while traveling together. She has a wall around her, protecting her from emotional involvement—even with her baby."

"Wouldn't know about that. But Lady Ariiell and your sister seem to have reached friendship."

Is that true, Val? Lily reached out with her mind toward her twin, something she'd avoided for too long. A gentle warmth of love filled Lily. She and Val didn't need words, just the knowledge that the other lived and thrived.

The death of Samlan by Lily's hand was something she did not want to share with Val, did not want to taint her with guilt and despair and losing a bit of her soul to . . . Death.

But Death had given it back to her, or taken away her guilt with that burning cold touch.

"Why is there a glowing spot on your forehead, Lily?" Linder asked, taking back that little bit of space between them.

Automatically Lily touched the cold spot. She found the skin slightly rippled, like a frostbite scar. That little circle of skin had died but lingered rather than sloughing off and letting new, healthy tissue grow over it. As she lowered her exploring fingertip she caught a glimpse of color through the flames. Narrowing her eyes and peering closer, Souska's green aura leaped into view. It blended and mingled nicely with Stanil's paler green and brown.

Lily leaned back so that the flames no longer interrupted her view. The auras vanished. She leaned forward again and watched others, knowing each surviving villager by name and where they belonged in the community. Again the flames allowed her to see more — Barbo had conceived and didn't like the idea, she'd lost two children to the disease and still felt guilty for surviving. Stanil worried about the health of the doe goat that was bloating from improperly chewed food. Another man wondered if he dared plow up another field to plant winter wheat. And Souska . . . Souska exchanged her previous anger and fear for contentment.

A smile crept across Lily's face and brightened her vision a tiny bit.

"This is a gift," she said quietly. "And a curse. I need a longer journey to discover its purpose."

"Don't stay away too long."

"As long as I need to. That's the purpose of a journey."

"Lukan here. Verdii?" Lukan called into the distance with his voice, his mind, and his heart. "Please, Verdii, if you are anywhere near, answer me," he pleaded.

His head still felt vacant between his ears, and his wound sent fiery darts outward in all directions. He'd like nothing more than to sit here for a long, long time, but knew he couldn't.

He had to finish this.

(Verdii here,) the dragon said. He sounded a bit subdued, no longer finding mirth in every situation. Yesterday's business had been hard and grim for all of them.

"My friend, I cannot walk to the ruins to make sure there are no more Krakatrice and no more eggs, or men to gather them from the wild. Can you show the place to me, through your eyes?"

(Yes.) Short. Curt. Reluctant.

"Please, Verdii. I have to know before I can return to the city and find a way to eliminate your ancient enemy once and for all." Anxiety itched along his spine. It nearly propelled him to his feet. He needed to pace, he needed to see what was happening.

He needed up. Up in the top of the tree or the roof of the corner building that looked almost intact. From up he could breathe cleanly. Up he could think. Up he could remove himself from the details of life that constricted him.

But the pain in his leg kept him immobile.

"Please, Verdii, help me do what I cannot do alone."

A huge weight seemed to lift from his chest. He couldn't do everything alone. He shouldn't do everything alone.

If only Da had learned that earlier, he might not have become a victim of his own strength, lost his sight and his life to the draining forces of the massive magic he insisted upon controlling by himself.

"I am not my Da. Nor am I my brother Glenndon. I need only live up to my potential, not their expectations, and I need help. Chess, can you give me a hand and help me stand?"

"Gladly," the boy said and lent him a strong arm and broad shoulder.

Lukan's head tried to spin away into darkness. He held on until it settled. A better perspective on the ruins. Not good enough.

(Close your eyes and join your mind to mine,) Verdii whispered.

Chess complied quite readily. Lukan followed suit. He breathed deeply and allowed his thoughts to drift until Verdii caught them.

Together, the three of them (Lukan sensed Chess' tight reddish brown aura unfolding into a mellow rust) rose up and up and up as the dragon soared toward the cloud layer and scanned the desert landscape that shaded into green from the new moisture.

Lukan saw the square created by the wood and mud-brick buildings and newly swollen creeks. He saw red clay roof tiles scattered and broken. He smelled the almost sweet charred wood beneath the acrid stench of rotten magic. Death and destruction.

His heart ached.

Something moved.

"Closer, Verdii. I need to see more details."

"I don't think we want to, Lukan. It's awful," Chess gulped.

"I have to know what we have wrought. I have to know that we succeeded completely, no matter how awful, before we continue on to the next chore."

(For that lesson I will give you what you need.)

A vertigo-inducing dive. The ground grew closer and closer. Wind pressed tightly against his face, biting his cheeks with a moist chill. Making his eyes burn with churned dust and ash.

His stomach flopped at the instant change in perspective.

Then he saw it. A slender tendril of black slithering out from under a much larger snake body. An infant. A baby.

A baby that would feed on the carcass of its dead relatives and grow large and strong on death.

Another Krakatrice that would grow into a monster that fed on human blood and poisoned the land.

Then he noticed the six nubs, three on each side of the spine, that would grow into the huge leathery wings of a matriarch. The potential mother of a new crop of destruction. A matriarch to guide all the males.

"Flame her, Verdii."

The dragon released a long tongue of bright green flame. The baby snake shriveled and screamed, tried to retreat to the safety of the dead carcass.

Verdii was relentless and sent more flame that ignited the fats within the snake flesh, offering an inferno instead of shelter to the baby.

It died with a last screech that made Lukan's ears ring.

Another screech, longer, louder, farther away, much,

much farther away. The grieving protest of all the male Krakatrice in the city reverberated around his brain and across the whole land.

He didn't think he'd ever leave that sound behind, no matter how far he fled.

CHAPTER 38

ROBB STUMPED ABOUT his room, leaning heavily upon his staff for support. He healed. But his heart still beat arrhythmically when he did anything other than lie still. He didn't have time to be an invalid. Things happened too quickly in other parts of the castle. Some sort of storm or war was moving rapidly among the people of Amazonia.

"The fever has left you completely," Maria said with approval. A frowning female nearly as tall and broad as Robb hovered at the doorway of his cell.

"You were with my boys when they came to me in the dungeon," he said bluntly, facing Gerta. She reminded him a lot of Maigret in their youth, before the boys were born. Before maturity and responsibility gave her an excuse to trade in her trews and weapons for matronly skirts and a stillroom with enough herbs and potions to kill or heal a continent. Many of those exotic herbs and recipes came from Mabastion, the Big Continent. Much of it still unexplored.

"I would hardly call Lukan or His Highness a boy," the woman snorted.

"Maybe not. But I trained Lukan, and Chess. They will always be boys to me. I do not know your prince."

"Aunt Maria!" Said prince skidded to a halt on the landing outside. "Aunt Maria, you've got to stop them." He looked harried and drawn. Toskellar, the prince who had forsaken his heritage to become a bard. Now he was back, with a heart aching for one of Jaylor's daughters.

Robb thought he could do something about that, but not from here. He took three more awkward steps, determined to build up his strength as quickly as possible. The young prince's anxiety told him he didn't have a lot of time before the castle erupted in a major crisis.

"Slow down and breathe, Toskellar," Maria ordered. There was a new firmness in the set of her chin and the angle of her back.

"You have to stop Princess Rejiia and Captain . . . Captain Stavro. They are preparing to flee the city."

"Rejiia!" Robb roared rather louder than he thought wise. "When did that conniving bitch become a princess? She's barely a lady, daughter of an outlawed and exiled lord."

The prince dismissed his protest with a wave. "Don't you see, Aunt Maria, they are fleeing like rats off a sinking ship. They know something . . ."

"They know my women have replaced many of Stavro's men. They know that Lokeen's days as king are numbered," the grim female said, as if reciting a routine report of what she'd seen on patrol.

"Where will they go?" Maria asked. "If they leave, then the king has two less allies to fight for him."

Robb caught the prince's eye. "Are there other city-states with a grudge against Lokeen, or even just a lust for power?"

The young man nodded.

"The captain of the guard and a strong rogue magician could sway them to attack while you are vulnerable," Robb said quietly.

"What can I do? I have no authority. I have no strength . . ." Maria wailed, wringing her hands. All traces of her earlier pride and determination evaporated.

"You have *us*, my lady," Gerta said. She toyed with the

grips of both her knives, one long, one short. He bet she had other weapons hidden on her person.

She wasn't like Maigret at all. She was much more ruthless.

Suddenly Robb didn't want to be on the receiving end of that woman's wrath.

Toskellar cringed a bit too as he took another step into the room, away from the Amazon. She was one of the legendary warriors for whom this city had been named. Robb wondered that Lokeen had dared depose them.

Only he hadn't deposed them. Just shifted them aside for a while with the power of his snakes to back him up.

He prayed that Lukan had succeeded in wiping out the farm.

But they still had a full nest of the monsters in the dungeons.

"Lady Maria," he said gently. "Have Gerta and her warriors capture the captain and the witch and put them in separate cells in the dungeon, near the snake pen. There is a bubble of magic around the snakes that drains a magician of power. Let them wallow in the stench and the evaporation of their strength."

"Can I do that?" The lady turned bleak eyes up to him. Ordering meals and laundry and the cleaning were easy for her. Taking charge of politics was quite another thing.

"You have to. There is no one else who can. This is the first step to stopping Lokeen's tyranny," he replied gently. "Your nephew and your warriors will back you up. There is no one else with the authority of heritage to do it. You *must*."

She looked around the room, out the window, into every face, seeking another solution, trying to defer to others. Her moment of decision came as a visible straightening of her neck and a clearer gaze. "Very well. What must I do?"

"Put it in writing, and sign it. That way Lokeen can't countermand the order," Robb said.

The prince nodded vigorously in agreement.

Gerta, or should he say Captain Gerta, dipped her chin once, decisively.

"You can't do this to me. I am the king's betrothed!" I yell at the four women disguised as soldiers. They do not blink, they do not flinch, nor do they falter in their steady march through the corridors of the castle. One leads, opening doors with a huge ring of iron keys. A second woman follows, prodding my back with a spearpoint. One on each side of me holds my arms above very heavy manacles in a grip that will leave bruises.

I cannot doubt that any one of them will kill me before I can raise enough power to throw them off.

I am so outraged I forget to draw strength from the pain.

I am out of practice. Then I see that four more women have captured my captain. He wears iron manacles on wrists and feet that drag him down.

"Where are you taking us?" I demand.

"The dungeon, where you belong," the woman behind me sneers.

The dungeon. Part of me recoils in abject fear. I have been in prison before. The prison of a cat body and stripped of my magic. For fifteen years I had to live by my wits, evading large predators, escaping human kicks, eating stolen scraps, rodents, and carrion.

I will not be subject to imprisonment of any kind again.

"You will be right next to the foul snakes, living with their stench day and night," the woman in front says as she unlocks a small but heavy door, bound in iron. The entrance to the dungeon. I know it well.

"You ... you can't feed us to the snakes. The king will not allow it," my captain protests. He is not so strong and brave or attractive to me anymore. His weakness robs him of beauty.

If we are separated I cannot draw upon his fear and pain to gain power over locks. But the snakes feed me. They will give me the means to escape the dungeon.

What I will do afterward I do not know. Yet. But I will think of something. Something that will destroy this miserable city-state and their backward government and their disdain of magic. I will triumph even if it means if I have to bring down the entire castle stone by stone.

Lukan balanced upon his staff and stared at the grazing steed. Somehow he had to transfer himself from the ground into the saddle. So far he'd managed to stand and rest a tiny bit of his weight on the ball of his left foot. Mostly he leaned on the staff and relied upon his intact right leg to keep him upright.

This was the disguise of a crippled beggar he'd worn to court. Only it wasn't a disguise anymore. He shuddered at the thought that he'd invited this wound by pretending.

"Maybe if you grabbed the pommel and hoisted your whole body across the saddle, then shifted your legs around," Chess offered. He stood near the steed's head, ready to grab the reins the moment Lukan tried to mount.

"Doesn't look as if there's enough room in the saddle for both of us," Lukan grumbled, stalling.

"I can climb behind the saddle."

"It won't be comfortable, and we've a long way to go. I'm not sure this steed is sturdy enough to carry both of us all the way to the city."

"I can walk beside you," Chess replied, relentless in his efforts to get them moving and back to the city so they could release Robb.

"I'd gladly walk if I could. But I can't. So I guess I have to take your suggestion. Hold him tight." Lukan hopped to the steed's side. It sidled away the same distance as Lukan moved. He could foresee an endless dance in a big circle.

Just then the glass in his pocket vibrated strongly, nearly visible through the fabric of his trews. Grateful for the reprieve he dropped to the ground and pulled the little circle of glass free. A bright swirl of gold and green twisted and coiled within the circle. Glenndon.

His heart both sank in disappointment that he needed his brother's help and rose in gratitude that his brother bothered to call to offer help.

The glass continued to bounce in his hand with some urgency.

No bowl of water, no candle. He licked the glass, a quick and dirty trick useful only in dire emergencies.

"What have you been up to, little brother?" Glenndon asked, almost before his face came into view.

"What I'm supposed to be doing, journeying." What else could he say?

"Only you could find the only magician in all of Mabastion, a spy of Da's sent there years ago when he first noticed Samlan taking long leaves of absence."

"Huh?"

"The slave who summoned me along with Robb's apprentice."

"Oh. Juan. He's a spy for the University. He said something. I wasn't. . ."

"He told me that he's been too afraid to mention his true mission to anyone, even another magician. He was too afraid to work magic even when he could. And he couldn't until you broke the protective bubble around the snake farm."

"Yeah. About that . . ."

"Juan also told me that you are in trouble. Wounded."

"That is sort of a problem."

"You've got to get away from the area contaminated by the snakes. Quickly."

"Not exactly viable."

"Listen closely, Lukan. Lily discovered that a plague infests the land anywhere the snakes have been in large numbers. She and her assistant have found a remedy, not a cure. All the drugs do is reduce the fever and keep the heart strong and steady until your body heals naturally. You've got to get away."

"Already had the fever. Came on after your spy cut a goodly chunk out of my calf."

"Oh."

Glenndon's face faded but his magical signature continued to twine and twist into knots in the glass. He hadn't gone away or ended the spell, only paused to think.

"Can you work any magic at all?" Glenndon surged into the glass again, almost close enough to step through it from his distant post.

"Not sure."

Chess snapped his fingers and brought a nice flame to his palm. The steed neighed and stepped back, as far away as it could get from the fire while on the short rein.

"We've got access to magic now that the Krakatrice are all gone and the dragons are patrolling the area," Lukan confirmed to his brother.

"Then I suggest you gather your strength and use the transport spell to get back to the city."

Chess' eyes grew wide as he shook his head in fear.

"Just stay away from those snakes. They are almost as nasty dead as they are alive," Glenndon continued. He hadn't seen Chess' reaction.

"Um . . . Glenndon, did Juan tell you what we found in the castle? The castle where Robb is held prisoner and my friend Skeller is trying to yank the reins of government away from his father the tyrant who sent the Krakatrice eggs to Coronnan?"

"Uh, no. I don't think he's been in the city for a couple of years. How he survived the farm without succumbing to the plague I don't know."

"We have to go back and rescue Master Robb," Chess insisted quite loudly, as if he knew he had to put some extra push into his words for Glenndon to hear them within the spell.

"I'm coming to help," Glenndon said curtly. His colors began retreating from the glass.

"No, Glenndon. You can't," Lukan protested loudly. The rush of worry for his brother surprised him. He'd nurtured anger toward him for so long he'd forgotten what it felt like to care . . . to love his older brother. Warm emotions washed through him, memories of their childhood. Barely a year apart in age, they had been as close to each other as the twins Lily and Val.

"Lukan, you need help. You are wounded. The fate of two continents is at stake . . ."

"You are King Darville's heir. You dare not risk it!"

"I have to."

"No, you don't. Look, you could probably make all this go away with a flick of your finger. But, just like Da, you have to trust someone else for a change. Taking the entire burden of magic onto his shoulders alone all the time is what killed Da—that and probably using the Tambootie and lingering in the void a time or two. All of those are things you do too. You have a Tambootie wood staff, for Stargods sake. And you treat the void like a second home. I'm not going to lose you too!"

"Lukan . . ."

"You are valuable, big brother. You were always Da's favorite. The gifted one. The dragon's golden child. I'm merely a second son. A tagalong, easily forgotten and over-looked. You can't come. Chess and I can manage. We have to. You have to stay there."

"Lukan, you are *not* expendable," Glenndon insisted. "Not to me. I don't want to lose you, little brother. I need to keep you safe."

"Thanks, big brother. I love you too. But a journey is about facing dangers and finding new solutions. If we can get back to the castle, I think I know what to do. Maybe my friend Verdii will drop us off onto a tower roof."

"Use the transport spell. I grant you permission and authority to do so. I don't care if it is forbidden to journeymen on journey. Use it. And . . . and stay safe."

"I'll contact you as soon as we get this all settled."

"Summon me every hour so that I know you are safe," Glenndon insisted. "I won't rest easy until you do."

"I'll summon you when it's all over." Lukan closed the spell by wiping the lingering moisture on the glass away with the palm of his hand.

"Okay, Chess. We release the steed and let him find his own way home. You and I will take a shortcut."

"Um, how about I ride the steed back to the stable and you use the transport spell on yourself?"

Lukan shook his head. "I need you to hold me up when we land. I'm aiming for the parapet at the top of the watchtower. I scouted it before we left. We're in this together, and I think the masters will gladly grant you a staff when we finish this." He closed his eyes and gathered his energy as he built an image of the castle parapet in his mind, layer by layer, stone by stone, adding color, texture, and the smell of the sea. Chess' hands slipped around his waist, holding him up and sharing the image Lukan built. Together they moved from here to there, barely pausing to acknowledge the void and the dragons in their passage.

CHAPTER 39

MARIA PAUSED TO wipe her finger across the surface of a small table outside Lokeen's private study. Servants used it to place trays of food and drink before knocking and opening the door. And they hadn't dusted it.

She made a mental note to reprimand those responsible. As she turned she noted that Robb had almost caught up with her. She didn't think anyone walked slower than she, but he managed. He'd only been on his feet a few hours since rising from his sickbed.

"You should rest," she said quietly as he pushed himself two more steps and paused, leaning heavily on his staff and panting. Sweat dotted his brow and he looked pale. Not as pale as when the fever had grabbed hold of his heart, but still not well.

"I," pant, "need," pant "to build my strength."

"I know. But if you push yourself too far, too fast, you will relapse and lengthen your recovery."

A ghost of a smile drifted across his face. "I seem to remember giving that same lecture to my wife when she had the milk fever after Stevie was born."

"You miss them terribly, don't you?" She sighed deeply, letting go a little bit more of the daydream that this man might learn to love her. He looked so very happy when he thought of his family that she couldn't deny him that little bit of joy in this dire and gloomy castle.

"Yes, I miss them. They are my life."

"Maria! Maria, what have you done?" Lokeen shouted from inside his study. "The Krakatrice are grieving and scream for the loss . . . I'm not sure what they mourn. Captain Stavro doesn't respond. What have you done?"

Maria straightened her spine as much as she could—easier now with Toskellar's adjustment to her boot.

"You don't have to go in there, Maria," Robb whispered. He too stood up from his heavy slouch against his staff.

"Yes, I do. I have to face him, sooner or later. Best we get this over with."

"Not until Lukan and Chess get back and we know for certain what happened at the farm. I suspect that the death of the nest at the farm is what has upset the nest in the dungeon."

"We know what happened. Gerta gave me a complete report, including the news that your journeyman was bitten by a Krakatrice. He's not likely to live." She rested a gentle hand on his arm. "Gerta has been back for three days. We've had no word of Lukan and Chess. Rejiia and the captain have been in the dungeon for a day and a half. We can't wait any longer to confront Lokeen."

"You're right. But you can't do this alone." Robb lifted one hand and beckoned toward the shadows hovering at the end of the corridor. Gerta stepped forward flanked by three women and two men, the guards who had been so faithful in protecting Robb. He called them Badger and Scurry. The names Robb had given them fit, regardless of what their mothers called them.

"Maria!" Lokeen stomped to the door, his footsteps echoing off the wooden floors despite the rich rugs covering them. Then he flung the door open so hard it bounced and reverberated against the outside wall. "Where are Rejiia and Stavro? Why are the Krakatrice so unsettled?" Then he looked at the assembly in the passage. "Why is *that man* out of the dungeon?" Anger pushed high color from his neck up past his ears, making a vein in his temple throb visibly.

"I am supervising some moderate exercise to help your magician recover from his illness," Maria said firmly, not blinking or stammering as her rapidly pounding heart wanted her to do. Only the knowledge that to fail now, or to quail, would end in her complete humiliation and possible death at the hands of her brother-in-law kept her upright.

"I don't need Master Robb anymore. Throw him back into the dungeon until I decide it's time to execute him. Maybe his blood will settle my pets." Lokeen waved the crowd away and turned to retreat into his private sanctuary. "I have Rejiia now. She can do more and better magic and isn't limited by these castle walls. Send her to me."

Maria grew cold from the inside out.

"You no longer have your betrothed, Your Majesty," Robb said evenly.

"What?" Lokeen roared, whipping around to face them once more.

"Lady Rejiia and Stavro, your captain of the guard, have eloped, Your Majesty," Gerta informed him.

"You are lying. My Rejiia would never do that. She loves me! Guards, arrest this woman."

No one moved. Maria counted her breaths, making sure they remained slow and steady though her knees trembled.

"I said, arrest her! Arrest that woman. She's an imposter. She has no place in the castle. Nor do any of those other women I see walking around in uniform and carrying weapons. Guards, get rid of them!"

No one moved. If anything, Scurry and Badger retreated a bit, allowing the women to stand forward. Frederico and his sister Frella appeared and stood fast beside the men. Jacko and Jimbo added their numbers to the solid wall of support for Maria.

"What have you done, Maria? You are responsible for betraying me. I'll throw you to the Krakatrice first." The last came out on a long hiss.

"I don't think so, brother-in-law," Maria replied.

The color drained from Lokeen's face. He took one step back, reaching to pull the door closed behind him. As if he'd be safe in the study.

"Lord Lokeen, I believe your tenure as regent of Amazonia is ended," Toskellar said, appearing behind him.

The king jerked his head back and forth between his son and his sister-in-law. "Wh ... where did you come from?" Lokeen looked truly frightened.

"Surely you remember, my lord. The entire castle is riddled with secret passages and hidden rooms. Escape routes to the harbor and into the hills. Isn't that part of the definition of being a castle?" the prince quirked the left side of his mouth up in a sarcastic grin that did not reach his eyes. "I know every inch of the back ways in and out. I'm surprised you don't."

"But ... but ..." Lokeen blustered.

"Oh, but you didn't grow up here. You came here as my mother's husband. You assumed you were safe and secure from the first moment you crossed the threshold. You had no need to explore. Unlike your sons, who saw the way you leeched authority from Mother at every turn. The way you hurt her, and intimidated her when she resisted your orders to disband the women warrior troops. The way you ignored her when you severed one of our most sacred laws and made executions not only legal, but the norm. We saw, and we knew the time would come when we would have to escape you."

"You have to agree with me. You returned," Lokeen protested. "Fear alone keeps people from succumbing to their base natures and breaking every moral and ethical law that defines civilization. The people have to fear their rulers or they will rebel. We'd have chaos in the streets if the people did not fear me."

"Strange, we never did before," Toskellar said, rubbing his chin in deep thought. "Tell me, Master Magician Robb, is there chaos in Coronnan? I hear your people love their king and honor him in every way. But they do not fear him."

Robb nodded. His mouth twitched as if suppressing laughter.

"Lord Lokeen, husband of my late sister," Maria began the ritual words she'd memorized long ago and never thought she'd have the opportunity or the courage to use. "Five years and more have passed since the untimely death of my sister, our queen. Your term of regency has passed. Since my sister bore no daughter to succeed her as queen of Amazonia, I hereby assume the regency until Prince Toskellar marries a woman of suitable lineage, or a natural leader arises from the ranks of the Women Warriors."

"You can't do this! The people will never tolerate a twisted and deformed dwarf as their queen," Lokeen sneered.

"I disagree, my lord," Gerta said, hand on the grip of her sword. "As the newly elected leader of the Women Warriors and captain of the Castle Guard, I declare my allegiance to the Lady Maria."

Lokeen leaped sideways and began running.

Robb flipped his staff and tripped him. He sprawled on the floor, his elegant robe hiked up to expose his skinny legs.

The stone walls shook.

Maria felt as if the floor had dropped out from under her. Her precarious balance sent her stumbling backward. Both Gerta and Toskellar rushed to her side. Robb steadied her.

When she righted herself, Lokeen was gone.

The Krakatrice slither inside their prison restlessly. They poke and probe, desperately seeking an escape. No longer are they content to exist, fat and lazy, satiated on the fresh blood and human flesh the king feeds them. They have taken over his mind and his will so that he exists only to please them.

In this state they do not freely give me power. I have to work at sending a sliver of my mind into their cell, penetrate the protective bubble that surrounds every scaly, black inch of them, and establish a flow of magic from them to me.

For a day and a half I have worked at building this rapport. They do not easily trust me. They trust no one. They see humans as food. Magicians as a special treat. Royals are almost as fine a delicacy as magicians. Lokeen, they inform me, is not truly royal. Merely a tool.

I, on the other hand, am both royal, though distantly so, and a magician.

They want my blood. They have no need to give me power that I might use against them.

I have to demonstrate my good intentions.

Slowly, carefully, I search the emotions of the people around me. They are nearly as restless as the Krakatrice, uneasy. Some are frightened. Some are determined despite risks.

A man's mind flares with panic as a garrote tightens about his throat. I snatch the energy from his choking—for some strange reason I cannot fathom, he does not die. Another man flails and falls. His landing knocks the wind from his lungs but does not kill him. I add his fear to my store.

And another, and another. One by one the male guards and soldiers disappear. Strong, logical women replace them. They assume places that were once theirs and denied them too long. They exude satisfaction. I cannot use satisfaction. It is no more useful than the complacency of satiation.

I must find the displaced men and feed upon their fear. I sense a physical binding. Then they move too far away for me to bring them into my circle of power.

Stavro sleeps heavily, as if drugged. A wise move on the part of our captors.

Do I have the strength to continue my tasks? I would if I had some Tambootie, but my satchel of potions has been stolen from me.

I must work without it. I have no choice. I will die if I face prolonged captivity again.

And so I clench my fist as tight as I can and slam it into the unyielding stones of my walls.

Sharp fire lances through my veins. Pain brightens in my mind. I husband the strength fractured fingers give me. I suck the blood from broken knuckles. My belly warms. My eyes see more clearly.

Power tingles along my spine.

A weakness in the mortar between two stones above the low door becomes obvious. The door is so low I had to nearly bend double to enter the room. Easily, I reach up to caress the stone and the crumbling mortar. I dig at it with my damaged hand. The additional pain keeps my power alive.

The stone vibrates beneath my touch. It is not just any stone. It is a crucial piece in holding up the foundation walls beneath the weight of the stone castle above. A keystone.

Slowly I stretch my being into the stone, feeling the way it needs decades to accept the responsibility of holding so much weight together. Centuries to forget the pain of being cleaved from its parent wall of granite. Millennia to cool after flowing as part of the elemental fire at the core of Kardia Hodos. It is a living part of the world.

I need its patience. It needs me to take away the memory of fire and chisel.

I step backward. The stone tries to follow me, scraping away from its fellows, inch by inch.

Hours I work with the stone.

Hours of standing in one position put a strain on my feet and back. I relish the pain.

And then, at last the stone works free of the wall and drops to meet different fellows on the floor. It has left a hole that brings in no new light. The hole leads only to another cell. An empty one.

No escape. But the stone sends vibrations to my feet. I easily interpret them. Its recent mates are adrift without its support. The stone to the left of the hole breaks free with more ease. The one beside it easier still.

Then a dozen stones tremble and shift.

The entire wall collapses into a pile of rubble.

The ceiling sags.

The Krakatrice scream in fear that they will be crushed as the entire dungeon shakes.

"Escape while you can!" I yell at them. "Slither free and wreak chaos on your captors." I fully intend to do the same.

CHAPTER 40

LUKAN WOBBLED AS the flat roof of the tallest tower formed beneath his feet. He needed to open his eyes and find out why.

Not yet, his mind and a dragon warned him. The magnetic pole, far away to the south, tugged at his back, begging him to turn and face it. Filtered sunlight glared beneath a cloud cover to stab his closed eyes. His boots muted the rough stones beneath his feet.

A fresh sea breeze brought the scent of a wide-open ocean, pushing away the acrid odors of humanity packed into a city.

Chess' strong arm still encircled his waist and kept him from giving in to the pain and weakness in his left leg.

And then the roof wobbled. Not much. *Kardia quake?* he asked himself and the dragons. He'd known those tiny tremors in the land all his life in the mountains. But this . . . this felt different.

"Are we there yet?" Chess whispered from beside him.

"Seems so," Lukan replied, finally daring to open his eyes and confirm that the parapet they stood upon was the same one he'd visualized.

A loud boom came from below, somewhere near the courtyard. The stones beneath them trembled again.

"That isn't normal," Chess nearly screamed, clinging

tightly to Lukan and keeping his eyes shut, so firmly his face scrunched into a mask of lines and wrinkles.

"No, it isn't normal. And we need to get off this tower!" The thought of hoisting up the trapdoor—he knew from experience it was heavy and the hinges stiff and rusty—and then negotiating the narrow spiral staircase downward sent Lukan's innards roiling.

"It might be easier if you sit and scoot down," Chess suggested. His gaze tracked Lukan's to the iron ring in the wooden square. Cautiously he loosed his grip on Lukan and bent to lift the portal. With barely a grunt he heaved and the heavy trap swung upward on a loud screech of protest. Those hinges really needed a good lashing with grease.

Chess looked up in alarm at the noise.

From the wails and chattering coming from a myriad of people in the courtyard, Lukan didn't think anyone noticed. He peeked over the crenellated wall. Hundreds of people, noble and servant alike, poured out of the buildings from every doorway, and a few windows. They jabbered questions he couldn't decipher beyond the lift of tone at the end of the utterances.

And then to his horror a lone female appeared in a doorway he knew led to the dungeon. Long black hair flowed freely to her hips. A wide stripe of silver ran from her temple to the tips. Her rich gown of black and silver brocade appeared rumpled, dirty, and torn at the shoulder seams. *Rejiia.*

She looked up and caught his gaze. A predatory smile creased her face. *You are next, little magician. I will enjoy watching you die slowly and in great pain.*

"The Kraks already started the job," Lukan muttered in reply.

"Speaking of Kraks," Chess said hesitantly from beside him. He pointed to a place in the low wing above the dungeons where the walls and roof seemed to sag. Five large Krakatrice slithered through a hole in the wall. Each was nearly twice Lukan's height in length and as big around as his thigh. Their eyes gleamed red. And even at this distance he saw venom glistening on their bared fangs.

"Now would be a good time for the dragons to show up," Chess said.

"Now would be a good time for my leg to heal and my magic to return."

"Someone just teleported in," Robb said as he righted his balance.

"Lukan?" Skeller asked, holding his aunt by the elbows to keep her upright. She looked dazed, eyes glassy and unfocused, balance askew. Robb could barely hear the prince over the screams of chaos coming from all parts of the castle.

He sniffed the air for a stronger hint than the actinic taste on the tip of his tongue. "Up," he said.

"That will be Lukan," Skeller confirmed.

"Up," Robb mused. The trembling of the walls and floor stopped. He looked around to see who remained to help.

Gerta dashed to the window inside Lokeen's study. "Far wing damaged, on the edge of collapsing. Rejiia free of the dungeon, and . . ." she gulped. "And five big black snakes oozing free of some rubble at the far end of the barracks above the dungeon."

"And yet Lukan managed to transport in. That means that the protective bubble around the Krakatrice doesn't extend as far as . . . wherever he landed. Skeller, I have to get up to the roof. The highest tower of the keep." Of course he had to go up. All the times he'd hunted Krakatrice a-dragonback should have told him he needed to go up, not just away, to regain his magic.

Skeller released Maria as her eyes cleared and she found her balance. "Follow me."

"Robb, you do not have the strength . . ." Maria protested, resting a tiny hand on his arm.

"I have to find the strength. I'll rest later." He gently removed her hand and walked as steadily as he could in Skeller's wake, leaning on the staff a lot more than he wanted to.

"Here, eat this, you're going to need it. Fuel." Skeller thrust a hunk of bread piled high with cheese into his free hand. Then he grabbed a goblet of wine from the side table near Lokeen's desk, looked at Robb's hands, one filled with food, the other with staff. "I'll carry this for you."

"Lukan will need . . ."

"Bringing more food behind you," Gerta announced. "Been told all my life, the easiest way to control a magician is to keep him hungry. Never made sense until now," she grumbled.

"Lokeen?" Robb asked around his first mouthful of sustenance. He hadn't realized how hungry he was until the bread near melted on his tongue.

"My people are hunting him." With one hand Gerta grabbed the entire tray of food left for the former king. With the other she freed her sword and held it in front of her. "Let me go up the stairs first."

"Wait," Maria commanded from the corridor. "If the snakes are free, there is something you must have."

Gerta's gaze shifted from Maria to both Robb and Skeller. "They can't use it," she said. "And I have no training with a spear."

"A male can use the sacred Spearhead if I give it to him with my blessing," Maria said sternly.

"Then follow us as you can," Gerta said and thrust aside a tapestry to reveal a dark and twisting staircase. "You want up. This is the way."

"Skeller, can you sing without your harp?" Robb asked. His mind churned with ideas returning again and again to some, discarding others.

"Of course," he snorted. "Any bard worth his salt can sing unaccompanied."

"Can you sing a lullaby and aim it directly at the snakes?"

"Never tried aiming a song. My style is more a broadcast, like an oversized fishnet to catch a single shark."

"That may have to be enough. Think about singing an arrow ... or a spear." Robb took another bite preparing for the arduous task of climbing up five stories to the top of the tower keep. His knees grew limp. "I don't think I can make it up there."

Maria tried to brush aside the guard at the treasury. A man, left over from Lokeen's rearrangement of security. He stood with feet braced and hand on the grip of his sword, as if expecting another quake.

"I can't allow you in there, my lady." His sword suddenly appeared in front of her, barring the door.

"Out of my way," Maria ordered. Anger warred with confusion. As chatelaine of the castle no one had ever questioned her right to enter the treasury. Now she was ... she had become regent by default. She borrowed a look of indignation from her older sister.

The man bit his lip but his sword did not waver. "Stand aside. You dare question a female of the royal house?"

"King Lokeen ..."

"Lord Lokeen is king no longer."

"Who, my lady? Who replaces him?"

"I do." There, she'd said it. Did that make it so?

"She said, 'Stand aside,' soldier. Now do it!" a female said sternly.

Maria turned her head a tiny bit and caught a glimpse of Frella in a palace uniform. Gerta must have sent her. She decided her best course was to ignore the man and leave him to the tall woman with a long sword and dagger.

She reached for the latch. The man's sword lowered so that the edge rested across her wrist. "My king said you were not to enter. You stole the magician's staff and glass. You will steal nothing more."

"Then join your king in the dungeon with his pet snakes," the woman snarled. The tip of her dagger pushed against his throat apple.

Maria depressed the latch and ducked beneath them. She knew precisely where the Spearhead, almost forgotten, wrapped in silk, rested ignominiously in the midst of broken pottery shards on a shelf just to the left of the door. She grabbed it and turned to leave.

A glint of light from the corridor caught the metallic body of the goddess. Maria paused to bow in reverence. "Protect us this day in battle," she whispered the ritual prayer handed down for generations.

A scream, a whoosh of air. A metallic thud. A small throwing knife quivered where it stuck in the rotund belly of the goddess.

"Duck!" Frella yelled.

Maria dropped to the floor, grimacing at the pain in her hip. The new boot had made walking so much easier she had almost forgotten a lifetime of pain.

More scuffles and thuds, the clash of blades.

Maria clenched the Spearhead, its obsidian edges pressed through six layers of silk to crease her palm.

Without thinking, she rolled to her feet, tugging the silk wrappings free as she moved. Then she raised the Spearhead high and surged forward. Momentum carried her. She stumbled again over Frella's legs where she sprawled awkwardly on the floor stones. Lokeen's man knelt atop her, knees pressing hard to her middle. She gasped as she writhed, trying to dislodge him. He brought the edge of his blade across her neck. She stilled.

He drew a deep breath.

Maria lunged and plunged the obsidian into the man's back. It slid easily between his ribs. Blood spurted. He reared his head back in surprise then slumped, hands limp.

"Your Majesty, gracious thanks," Frella whispered as she wriggled out from under the man's corpse.

"I'm . . . I'm not . . . your queen. Only regent," Maria gasped, hands before her mouth, trying desperately to keep from choking up hot, foul, burning bile.

She'd killed the man. She'd *killed* him.

"Majesty you are. You proved yourself worthy of the crown. Frella at your service." The woman rose to her feet and bowed deeply. "May I have the honor of escorting you and the Spearhead of Destiny to the battle?"

"Yes, you may." Maria wrapped the silk around the Spearhead. Her personal guard tugged it free of its victim and presented it back to her with another formal bow.

Maria accepted it and began the trek toward the tower.

"Your Majesty?" the guard asked quietly from a proper two steps behind. "Your Majesty, will the spell still be intact on the obsidian? It's just that I worry that since it has now been used to take a life the . . . the . . . that once it drew blood, the magic died."

Maria almost stumbled in surprise. "I . . . I hope that killing a mere man has not damaged it. This is the only weapon that can penetrate the magic bubble around the Krakatrice."

Loud screams from the forecourt diverted her trek. "I'll never make it up those steps in time. You, Frella, you have to take it to the magician. Present it to him with my blessing. Make sure you say the words properly. Gift it to him with the queen's blessing."

"With honor, Your Majesty. In the meantime, I advise that you wait in the throne room. It is near an escape tunnel. I'll send guards to protect you. They will be led by Hannah. I trust her." Frella took off at a run.

CHAPTER 41

ROBB FOUND A window in the throne room overlooking the forecourt. He threw open the shutters and leaned out. No glass hindered his view of five midsized Krakatrice oozing out of a crack in the wall at the end of the dungeon wing, near the corner that joined the curtain wall facing the city and overlooking the harbor.

His attention rested on Rejiia as she climbed over a pile of rubble to take a stand near the middle of the open space.

Rejjia, the source of many of his nightmares fifteen years ago, when he'd been a journeyman and she the most feared woman in all Coronnan. Until her own magic backlashed and she became her own totem animal, a black cat with one white ear. He'd know her anywhere.

She raised her arms level with her shoulders and spat crackling energy from all of her fingers. Ancient mortar between building stones began to crumble all around the courtyard. Her body trembled with the massive amount of power she channeled. Her eyes grew completely black, no trace of colored pupil or white surround.

Robb recoiled in instinctive fear of the woman who demanded absolute obedience from her minions. She wanted to be a goddess. Nothing less. By whatever means she could tap.

Right now, she tapped the magic of the Krakatrice and made it her own.

But ... the bubble of magic around the giant snakes shrank. He had enough magic at his fingertips to see the shimmering black aura. That meant she drained them. Pain and fear fed her powers. Very like the food the Krakatrice needed.

Robb's question was: did they give it to her freely?

The biggest of the black males reared his head and hissed at her, venom dripping from his fangs. Rejiia ignored him.

Why didn't he attack? Perhaps something else had weakened the bubble, allowing her to tap into it.

Rejiia caught Robb's gaze. A compulsion for him to come to her, bring to her all his secrets and all of his power and knowledge wiggled into his brain. She promised him more. All he had to do was join her in an ecstasy of pain.

He turned away, heading toward the door and the exit to the courtyard.

The heartbeat he broke eye contact the compulsion snapped into revulsion.

His stomach nearly revolted at her demands.

Pounding footsteps descending the tower reminded him of his duty.

"Master Robb," Gerta panted, slightly out of breath from her rapid climb to the top of the tower and even more rapid descent. "Lukan and Chess prepare to throw fire at the snakes and try to channel storm clouds to dump rain on them."

"Yes, good. That will help. But I fear that these Krakatrice are older and tougher than any we have fought before without the help of the dragons. Fire and water will slow them down. We need more to kill them. We have to break the magic bubble around them. It fades on its own, but one taste of blood will renew it. Only obsidian weapons, *enchanted* obsidian weapons, will penetrate thick hide and pierce vital organs."

"It's not obsidian, but this is the finest steel with a keen edge." She drew her sword and brandished it for his inspection. "I made it myself. I know the strength within."

"In ancient times, blacksmiths were considered akin to magicians because they could transform lumps of raw iron into magnificent weapons and tools." An idea wiggled from the back of his mind. He had access to a little magic. Not much, and he feared it would evaporate if the snakes tasted blood. "Perhaps I can help."

He clutched his staff with both hands and raised the tip until it rested upon the proffered blade. "If I do nothing else this day to turn the tide of battle, I give this blade the power to overcome the evil emitted by the Krakatrice." Power welled up through his entire body, tapping resources he'd forgotten he had. He forced it to concentrate into a single outlet. His hands glowed blue with supernatural light. Then he pushed and pushed and pushed it down through the staff, letting the natural wood grain, so attuned to him and his magical signature, amplify it, hone it, force it into the steel until the sword itself shared the blue light and then absorbed it all from him.

He dropped the staff tip to the floor and let it support his weight. His head felt as though it spun in full circles. Or was it the room that whirled around him?

His stomach growled.

"Eat this!" Gerta thrust more bread and meat and cheese into his hand. "Eat until you can eat no more. That's your only source of energy right now. From this window you can see the entire field of action. Direct me as you can. I will listen for your voice and blank out the siren song of the sorceress and the Krakatrice." And she was gone, shouting orders to her Amazons, the glint of battle lighting her eyes.

"Chess, you have to throw small fireballs," Lukan said, swallowing his anxiety. The boy was nervous enough watching the snakes spread out around the courtyard with Rejiia standing smack-dab in the middle. The line of slithering black encircled her, almost as if . . . allowing her to direct them.

A female. Next best thing to a matriarch. Verdii had flamed the only living female Krakatrice. Could they be looking to Rejiia as one of their own.

"Stargods! We are out of time."

He gulped back his own fears. He'd seen the way Rejiia wove spells of enthrallment. He knew the seductive nature of her power.

"I resisted you aboard ship. I resisted you at Lokeen's dance. I can resist you now." He tried to bring forth the gentle image of little Souska to his mind's eye. Souska was just a flimsy shadow of raw dependence.

All he could imagine as a foil to Rejiia was Gerta, her strong features set in determination, ready to face this battle with courage, honor, and duty.

The forces that bonded all of the University magicians together. The forces that had pushed Samlan to go rogue. That man hadn't wanted to work with other magicians. He wanted to command them and would not accept another's authority.

In a way Lukan's father, Jaylor, had also rejected the community of magicians with his need to do it all himself, because once he was the only one of them who could think beyond rigid ritual. Later because he always knew better, always needed to do it himself to make sure it was done right. His strength had killed him.

Lukan firmed his resolve and shifted his balance so that he could stand beside Chess and work with him to aim those little fireballs correctly.

"See the little triangle of smooth skin at the base of the Krak's skull, Chess? Channel your eyesight to find the spot for real. Block out all the distractions to the side. Focus. Don't let your gaze drift right or left. *Don't.*"

Chess focused his eyes once more. "I can only see red eyes and dripping venom." His voice wavered in uncertainty.

"That's their enthrallment. Yank your gaze away from their eyes. Look at the far horizon where gray sky meets gray sea." Lukan felt Chess comply. He himself avoided looking outward. He needed to see the vulnerable spot himself.

"Now look at the tail, follow the spine upward. It's a curving line as it twists its body to glide forward. Follow the spine. See how the scales move and shimmer in the light. Count the scales. Focus on the spine. Upward, higher, higher yet. There! Notice how the scales ripple outward from a single spot. *See it!* See it in your eyes, in your mind, and in your heart."

"Yes. I see it," Chess chanted almost as if controlled by a spell in Lukan's voice.

"Aim your little fireballs right there."

Chess lifted his hand, palm upward and curved. The weak and watery sunlight concentrated there, glowing, growing; igniting!

"Not so big. You need little ones."

A look of confusion creased Chess' brow. "Small ones."

The ball of fire in his hand reduced in size by half.

"Now throw it. Guide it. Bring the triangle to the fire, bind them together."

Chess drew his arm back and threw the ball with all the power built into his shoulder from moons of work in the smithy.

Fire exploded outward into an array of cascading sparks as it struck an invisible wall encasing the snakes.

Rejiia smiled and turned her focus upward, directly at Lukan.

Lullaby. Why do I hear only a lullaby in the back of my mind? Soothing. Surrounded by someone who cares for me, who will keep me warm and safe.

No one ever sang a lullaby to me before. My mother didn't care. My father forbade my nurse to sing them. He said I needed to grow up tough and independent, not coddled, not cuddled, never loved . . .

The singer belies that. The singer makes me want to abandon everything I have worked for while I suck my thumb and curl up into a sleepy ball.

Abandon . . .

Never! I scream in my mind and to the singer. I am above this. I am in control here. The Krakatrice look to me for guidance. I determine their targets.

Easy targets. Those loathsome Amazon Warriors sway on their feet, half-asleep. Food for my Krakatrice. Fools for even trying to subdue me.

But my lovely black snakes do not respond to my commands. They rear their heads and sway to the lilting melody. Their eyes droop. They want only sleep.

I cannot allow this. I need my snakes. I need them awake and aggressive.

I raise my arms once more and concentrate all of my formidable power into my fingertips. When I can contain it no longer I lash out with all of my anger and thirst for vengeance. I need destruction, murder and mayhem to fuel my power. Raw energy shoots unnatural red flame. Two women try to lift their swords to catch the lightning. But the lullaby makes them listless. The swords are heavy.

I fell them with a jolt of magic that flings them backward until they land flat on the stones, their heads cracking audibly. They lay there with jaws agape and eyes glazing.

I block off the lullaby from my mind as I once pushed away the pain of magical ritual. Outside distractions do not penetrate my mind. I am focused on revenge. I will destroy this castle and everyone in it. Now where are the magicians who are set to oppose me?

I laugh long and loud, for I have power, and as long as my Krakatrice are with me, the other magicians cannot use theirs.

What is this? A change in the music? An invigorating marching tune that sounds like energetic footfalls. It is determined and triumphant. I can almost hear the words of the refrain, "How many of them can we make die!"

The shift in cadence allows my snakes to awaken. They do

*not understand this kind of music. Marching feet mean noth-
ing to them.*

*Not so the women warriors. They take heart and shout
together their strange warbling war cries as they swing and
twist their weapons with a willful rhythm. And now they are
joined by men. Men who should follow me out of pure lust.
They raise their weapons with new vigor and advance upon
me. An entire army of them.*

*And ... and the castle gates swing open to reveal another
army. The followers of Helvess have returned in triumph
with butcher knives and pitchforks and hammers, mundane
tools they will turn into weapons to fell me. Useless, mundane
tools. I do not fear them.*

*Still, I must put all of my strength into the shield of magic
that keeps people and weapons away from me and my
snakes.*

*Where are my helpers? Why has my coven deserted me?
My Captain Stravro and even Lokeen are nowhere in sight.*

*I see Geon and Bette crawling from the dungeons, slink-
ing behind great stones, hidden from sight of the Amazons,
but not from me. I command them to join me, to add their
magic to my own.*

*They ignore me and tumble behind another half wall. The
magic shield prevents me from sensing where they go. He
leads. She follows. As always.*

*Very well, I can do this on my own. I do not want their
help. I do not want their help.*

*I will deal with this on my own. As I have always been
alone. And always will be. No wonder the lullaby did not
affect me. I never needed or wanted one. Comfort is for the
lazy and powerless. And I am neither.*

*My supposed followers will learn that when I deal with
them as the traitorous wretches deserve.*

How many of them can I make die?

CHAPTER 42

"H... how do we penetrate the bubble?" Chess asked as he sagged against the stone parapet. Apparently controlling fire took more energy than just flinging it about.

He batted listlessly at stray sparks that backlashed toward them.

Or was it Skeller's lullaby that drained him of energy. Lukan could barely hear it over the din below them.

But the soothing melody did make his leg hurt a little less.

Rapid footsteps slapped against the stone steps leading to this roof. Lukan shook off some lingering lethargy and limped to the side of the trapdoor. Then balancing on his right leg he lifted his staff in both hands, ready to swing it into someone's head.

"Master Magician?" a feminine voice squeaked.

Lukan checked his swing and had to spin around to maintain his balance. Flailing, he fought to ground his staff. The tip skidded on the slates of the conical roof rising above the walkway. Instinctively he touched his left foot to the ground and instantly regretted it.

Fire as hot as Chess' conjuring lanced in all directions from his wound. When it hit his hip he lost all strength.

Small but strong hands grasped his arm and held him tight until he found his feet.

"Thank you," he grunted.

"Where is the magician?" the woman asked. She wore a palace uniform and stood tall and proud, very like Gerta. Stunning.

"I am Journeyman Magician Lukan," he said, trying to infuse his voice with confidence.

"You will have to do. Queen Maria asked me, Sergeant Frella of the Amazon Warriors, to gift to you the Spearhead of Destiny with her blessing." She thrust a silk wrapped lump into his free hand.

"Spearhead?"

"Of Destiny?" Chess echoed.

"It . . . it is a legacy from the first Amazons who fought the Krakatrice and carved out this city from nothing. Only a woman can use it unless it is gifted to a man by a true Amazon. Queen Maria has proved herself worthy." She bowed and dropped back through the trapdoor. Her boots slapped the stones with as much speed and eagerness to leave as she had come.

"Thank you, Sergeant Frella of the Amazons," Lukan called after her. *Magnificent.* All of the women here were magnificent.

"Spearhead," he mused.

"To kill Krakatrice!" Chess said eagerly.

"Obsidian!" Lukan shouted in triumph as he tore off the protective silk.

The music in the background shifted, became a lively marching tune, a prelude to battle, filled with energy and enthusiasm and righteousness.

"How many of them can we make die!" Skeller shouted into the wind, making certain his voice carried to all corners of the castle.

Renewed sounds of battle rose from the forecourt. Shouts of aggression. Screams of pain. The clang of metal against stone.

Chaos.

Rejiia and the Krakatrice thrived on chaos and riotous emotions.

Only Lukan could bring order.

"Quickly, I need twine, thread. Rope. Something to secure the Spearhead to my staff." His mind raced and settled on a strip of cloth from the hem of his tunic or his shirt. The shirt; finer cloth than the blue leather tunic. Stargods only knew the fine linen his mother had woven and sewn for him was ragged and filthy enough to rip apart for other uses.

"Here." Chess thrust a ball of string into his hand.

"What?"

"From the pack. I packed bits of odds and ends before we left the city. Never know what you're going to need. Master Robb taught me that."

Lukan shrugged and looped a slipknot over the obsidian and the staff, then wrapped, pulling as tightly as he could. When he thought the two tools had become one weapon, he wiggled the blade. It didn't move. So he tied a secure knot and let Chess cut the cord with a utility knife.

"Okay," he said on a deep inhale. He used the breath to trigger the first stage of a trance. He'd need all the help he could find.

"How many of them can we make die?" shouted an army of men and women below.

Barely noticing the pain in his leg, he limped back to the wall overlooking the courtyard. He focused all of his senses on the Spearhead. Just as his Da had taught him. He drew strength from his memories, from his family, from his love for them and theirs for him. He bound all that up in his connection to the staff, and through that to the obsidian. Volcanic glass from the heart of Kardia Hodos. Fire and Kardia. He needed water and air. Nothing for it, he ran his fingertip over the knocked edge. A drop of blood welled up. He smeared it on the point. Then he breathed on the whole.

One more step. He had to turn widdershins and pay homage to south, west, east, and north. Awkwardly he turned a full circle, making a quick but reverent bow at each point of the compass.

"Speed my quest to the triangle from which radiates all scales of magic and death. Penetrate the evil; make it vulnerable."

He peered over the crenellated stone wall, sorting through the images of warriors, men and women all in palace uniforms, slashing and hacking at the snakes to no avail. Their weapons bounced off the magic wall of protection. And Gerta led the fray, facing down the largest of the five snakes. Five of them, all bigger than any strays he'd trained to kill. None of them as big as legend said they could grow. But one of them . . . The one facing Gerta . . .

All the other snakes mimicked its actions, half a heartbeat behind.

Rejiia focused her control on that one big one.

They looked to her as they would a matriarch with six wings. Lukan was almost surprised Rejiia hadn't sprouted bat-like protuberances from her spine.

He centered his vision on the big, black snake's head, nearly as long as his torso. The monster opened his mouth wide, hand-sized fangs dripping venom. Red eyes gleaming with hunger and malice.

Lukan drew back his arm, grip flexible on his staff, Spearhead ready. He affirmed his connection to the wood, the essential magical tool gifted to him by the trees of Sacred Isle. His thoughts and soul twisted with the wood grain in a braid from tip to butt, clean and smooth. Chanting a prayer to the Stargods, begging help from all four elements and cardinal directions, he cast his weapon, keeping his gaze affixed on that vulnerable triangle at the base of the Krakatrice skull. "Guide my weapon," he whispered. His mind remained half inside the spear, half on the monster below.

A part of him continued twisting with the staff, flying fast, diving, carving a path through the wind that resisted him. Dropping, dropping faster and faster, the triangle firmly in his sight. The ghost of his body remained rigid on the roof while his essence found his target. Magic sparks pricked his surface and flashed into premature death. He thrust them aside.

Black snakeskin bent beneath his point and threatened to push him back out. He concentrated deeper, deeper, and deeper yet. The skin parted, unable to protect itself against that magically charged glass point sharpened and honed by elemental fire from elemental Kardia, empowered by a magician's blood and blessed breath.

Cold, cold snake blood washed over him, engulfed him, threatened to drown him.

A sharp pinch to his arm jerked him back into his body. But his vision remained in the courtyard. Gerta rammed her glowing blue sword deep into the Krakatrice's open mouth, all the way to the hilt. Half of her leather-clad arm disappeared beyond the deadly fangs. As she drew back her weapon, the light of life drained from the snake's red eyes. She raised her blade above her head, heedless of the gore dripping back on her helmet. A wild ululation of victory rippled from her throat and echoed around the courtyard.

> *Axes flash, broadswords swing,*
> *Shining armor's piercing ring*
> *Horses run with polished shield,*
> *Fight those bastards till they yield*
> *Midnight mare and blood-red roan,*
> *Fight to keep this land your own*
> *Sound the horn and call the cry,*
> *How Many of Them Can We Make Die!*

"Weapons. We need more weapons," Robb said, pounding his fist against the stone windowsill. Outside he watched as only Gerta's glowing blue sword made a dent in the shimmering magical wall surrounding the snakes. Nothing penetrated that wall.

"We have weapons aplenty, but what have you done with the Spearhead?" Maria asked from behind him.

He whirled, unaware that she had joined him. Badger and Scurry stood warily on either side of her.

"We need enchanted weapons," he replied, then added, "I don't have a spearhead."

"Can you work the enchantment?" Maria asked, concerned about the fate of her weapon but ready to help in any way she could. With a gesture she sent her two guards to raid the armory. Badger went. Scurry stayed.

"I . . . I don't know. I have little strength left. No reserves . . ." But Skeller's music sent tingles of new energy up and down his spine, made his feet and fingers itch for action. The lullaby had done more harm than good. But this tune . . . This one changed the tide of battle.

The bard might not claim to be a magician, but he was certainly wielding his music with the same effectiveness as a staff even without the aid of the harp that might be his equivalent of a staff.

He caught a flash of movement out of the corner of his eyes and whirled to face this new threat.

A spear, vibrating with an eerie blue and red light with an inner layer of more natural green fire flashed from above. It pierced that shimmer in the air and dove deep into the back of the skull of the largest Krakatrice.

Instantly, the heavy weight of magic dampening fell from his body, as if he'd shed a wet blanket. Sounds and scents slammed into his awareness. His eyes found new details, firmer outlines, and brighter colors all around him.

And he felt . . . tingles against his skin. Dragon magic begging him to gather it close and store it in that special place behind his heart. He stood straighter, taller, strength flooding in to replace the pall of illness and deprivation. His heart beat strong and true for the first time in days.

He dragged in fresh air and almost gagged on the smell of rotten magic mingling with death.

"I found spears," Badger said breathlessly as he returned

with at least two dozen long shafts tipped with iron clutched in his arms.

"Not obsidian, but it will have to do." With the help of the two guards he lined up all of the spears on the floor, the tips pointed south toward the closest magnetic pole.

Maria retreated to the throne and climbed awkwardly into the seat. She curled her legs beneath her and observed with a new confidence and authority. In the shifting and fracturing light from the windows, she looked almost . . . almost beautiful.

Robb returned his attention to the spears. His renewed vigor wouldn't last long. Already a vacancy at the back of his neck began to nibble away at his clarity. He'd have to ration the magic he poured into the weapons.

First he knelt on the floor with the South Pole tugging at his back while he faced the iron speartips. No sense in expending extra energy staying upright. Besides, if he collapsed at the end he'd have a shorter distance to fall flat on his face.

Before he could think better of his plan he closed his eyes and spread his arms before him, palms down, fingers splayed. His hands trembled too much. He didn't need to see it to know it.

"I need a lit candle, a basin of water and you two close enough to breathe on the spell," he called to Scurry and Badger. He heard them bustle about.

"Will a pitcher of wine do for the water?" Badger asked.

"Close enough, maybe better since it holds the essence of the Kardia from the grapes as well. Set it down in front of me."

"Found a torch in the passageway," Scurry said.

"Better. Hold it parallel to the ground, over the speartips." Robb drew on years of practice and gathered the essence of three of the four elements into his cupped hands. They shone in his mind's eye, eager to do his bidding.

"Together the four of us must draw a deep breath and hold it. Don't let it go until I do. Watch me closely."

He drew air deeply into his lungs, letting it fill every crevice of his body. "Release!" he shouted to his companions as he opened his hands and spread the elements onto the speartips.

Natural green fire pulsed from the metal. "Take them quickly to the warriors. The spell won't last long."

"Sir, we vowed to protect Queen Maria and not leave her side," Badger protested.

"The only way to protect her is to get those spears to her warriors." Robb sagged, bracing himself with hands flat on the floor. His lungs felt ripped apart and his heart beat too rapidly again—as it had during the worst of his fever. He closed his eyes to stop the black splotches from enveloping him. Bright splotches replaced them behind his closed eyelids.

He couldn't fight it any longer. He had to give in to the pain, the fatigue, the loneliness. He'd done what he had to do.

He prayed it was enough as he slid to the floor. "Maigret, I love you," he whispered as blackness engulfed him.

CHAPTER 43

"THE DRAGONS ARE back," Chess crowed. To prove it, he raised his arm high and hurled a small, elongated ball of fire into the battle. He pinched a tiny bit of the writhing flames between thumb and forefinger, forcing the ball to stretch and stretch into an arrow.

"Verdii?" Lukan looked upward as tingles raced from his upturned head down through his body, directly to his wounded leg. Blood pounded against the loose bandage. He looked to make sure it didn't soak through the layers of linen and ooze down his leg. Clean. His leg remained clean despite the twisting of flesh that felt like—maybe, hopefully—his flesh knitting together and rebuilding some of the lost tissue.

(Some, not all. Even your best healers with our aid cannot repair all the damage,) Verdii said. *(A limp will always mark you. Take it as a badge of honor.)*

A little bit of the heaviness in his heart lifted. Not all. Rather than fully face his permanent handicap he turned his attention back to the battle below.

Rejiia still commanded the center of the forecourt. She flung up an arm and blocked Chess' fiery arrow. It shattered against her protection.

But the sparks flew outward in a perfect circle landing, on the remaining snakes.

The smell of burning poisonous flesh seared Lukan's nose.

The wall beneath his hand shook. Rejiia turned a full circle, widdershins. Two stones, each a yard long and half that wide and thick, flew from the pile of rubble in the corners of the far wall.

Thud, thud. They struck the tower barely a yard below Lukan's hands.

The next one will not miss, Rejiia assured him. An ugly smile cracked her face.

"I need my staff!" As he said the words, the shaft of wood still buried in the neck of the largest snake quivered. Lukan braced himself at this sign of life from the monster.

But the Krakatrice was dead. The ripple of muscle spread outward from the obsidian blade. The staff, *his* staff, had responded to his need.

"Return," he said on a long exhale. "Return to my hand as you left it."

The wood wiggled and twisted free of the tough hide. "Come," Lukan pleaded. He didn't think he should order his staff. It was as much a part of his magic as his mind. It channeled his power, and the braided signature in the grain defined him. "Return to me, where you belong," he continued his litany.

The moment he saw the staff lift free of the snake he felt it slap against his open hand. His fist closed around it without a thought.

Chess loosed another bolt of magical lightning. Again it shattered and sprayed against Rejiia's wall, but this time a few of the sparks landed upon her tattered and filthy gown.

She screeched in outrage. Two more stones flew wildly from the pile. Without her firm control they landed harmlessly on the already dead Krakatrice, breaking its spine. She whirled her circle again and again. She stopped, facing Lukan, her skirts continuing to float outward for several heartbeats more.

If she saw two soldiers distributing spears with elemental fire swelling the iron tips, she paid them no attention. Gerta directed her Amazons to throw them into the mouths of the three remaining monsters. The blue glow on her sword had dimmed but it still contained a little lethal magic.

Rejiia conjured a ball of unnatural red fire, as large as any Chess had brought to bear. Her lips moved, commanding the alien flames to seek and destroy.

Lukan and Chess ducked behind the parapet.

"Robb's alive and throwing magic! Only he could enchant those spears and Gerta's blade," they said together.

"But so is Rejiia," Chess reminded Lukan.

"With dragon magic filling the air, we're stronger together than apart. We have to join him," Lukan gasped, crawling toward the trapdoor.

Red fire flew over the top of them and struck the slate roof at the center of the tower. The sparks lingered a few heartbeats, trying to feed on the stone. They died of starvation.

Lukan froze with his left hand clasping the metal ring embedded in the wooden planks. Three live Krakatrice. One dead.

Where was the fifth?

He looked over his shoulder to Chess. "Count," he mouthed.

Chess' fingers flicked open from his fist. Four.

"Where?" he whispered.

Something strange and cold passed from the iron ring into Lukan's hand. He heard and felt a vibration that was different from flying stones hitting the structure. Different. Worse.

His staff quivered in his hand. The obsidian tip was still bound to it, still available as a weapon.

Silently he rose to his knees and directed Chess to grasp the latch from the side.

Praying fervently to the Stargods, to the dragons, to the ghosts of his parents, he raised the staff over his head, speartip aimed at the portal.

Chess mouthed his count. One. Two. Three.

He heaved the door open.

Lukan plunged the spear down, directly into the gaping maw of the fifth Krakatrice.

Obsidian easily pierced the soft palate, met resistance against bone. Volcanic glass, honed to the sharpest edge imaginable, sliced and penetrated deeper. Lukan pressed harder against the shaft, taking good care to stay away from those venomous fangs.

The staff broke through the bone and tore into the brain.

He yanked his staff clear. A gush of blood and brain matter followed. He rolled quickly to the side to avoid the splatter. "Not again. I'm not coming in contact with that poison again," he muttered as he dragged himself to his feet.

"How are we going to get around that thing?" Chess asked.

"Ah, it's just a little one. No longer than I am tall. Barely as big around as my upper arm," Lukan brandished his staff in a show of bravado he didn't really feel. He must be giddy with dragon magic flooding his system after so long an absence.

Or maybe he was just tired and in pain. He could use a good meal. The tray Gerta had left with them was empty. Not even crumbs remained. They'd only find more food below.

But first they had to get past the Krakatrice. The last one. He hoped.

The tower shook again. Rejiia still up to her old tricks.

Maria dropped off the throne. Pain jolted up her leg and lodged in her twisted hip. She didn't care. She had to help Robb.

A dozen shuffling steps later she knelt beside the man who had helped turn the tide of battle against Lokeen and his pets. A niggling reminder that no one had seen the king since his escape. Hours ago? No, she thought only a few minutes, perhaps half an hour, had passed since the first tremor. From the reports and shouts outside, she thought that Rejiia had dislodged some keystones in the dungeon that had shaken the entire castle, but damaged only the barracks and dungeon wing.

"Robb?" she asked, placing her fingertips against his neck pulse. A faint flutter like a butterfly on the wing. His chest didn't move. She pressed her ear against his mouth. No air. "Breathe, Master Robb. Great Mother, you must breathe. You must live." She pounded her fist against his chest, aware just how tiny her hand was and how feeble her blow.

She pounded harder with all her might. "Breathe, *S'murghit*. Breathe!" Another blow that ached all the way to her shoulder.

He groaned. His chest rose and fell. Rose and fell. But still his eyes remained closed, his face slack and unresponsive.

"Don't die on me, Robb," she pleaded. "I couldn't bear it if you died trying to help save my land from Lokeen and his monsters." A tear trembled on her eyelid, tipped over and trickled down her cheek. She didn't care.

"I'll live," he said on a harsh wheeze. Then he lapsed back into unconsciousness.

But he breathed. And his heart beat more steadily.

She sank back onto her bottom and worked her legs around to a more comfortable position, likely stuck there until Badger and Scurry returned to help her up. Gently she gathered Robb's long-fingered hand into both of her own and cradled it in her lap.

"Traitors, both of you!" Lokeen screamed. He thrust aside the tapestry on the interior wall that Maria knew led to an escape tunnel.

Maria dropped Robb's hand. He groaned again and shifted his body uncomfortably.

"You are the traitor, Lokeen. Traitor to our most sacred traditions, traitor to the land, traitor to my sister's memory," she said flatly as she scooted around to put as much of her body between the deposed king and the magician as she could.

"I decree that you both die. This instant." He raised his right hand, brandishing a dagger as long as his forearm. Blood dripped from the blade onto the crossguard.

Death and destruction all around me. I drink in the fragrance of power. But nothing fills me. The Krakatrice are all dead. Even the one I sent to dispatch the magician. They took their power with them when they passed from this life, sharing none of the glory with me.

I have only my own anger to fuel me now. Of that I have plenty. I may die this day, but others will die with me. Lokeen among them. Geon, Bette, and Stavro, who all deserted me. But first I will kill the magicians. All of them. Including the dastardly bard who still sings his cursed battle music.

They are inside the castle. They have no escape and they cannot hide from me.

Once they'd sidled past the Krakatrice corpse, Lukan opted to sit on the winding staircase and scoot downward. Awkward and slow. But it took pressure off his wound and gave him the opportunity to listen to the castle and find pockets of people hiding, or battling, or conspiring. Narrow tubes containing staircases between the walls funneled sounds nicely.

They reached a landing with an arrow-slit window overlooking the courtyard. He paused to peek out. They'd come down nearly three full stories. Only two more to go.

"We have to hurry. Rejiia is coming!" he hissed to Chess who followed him.

The younger magician leaned over to survey the courtyard. "She's batting aside armed warriors as if they were flies. She swats the air and they bowl over backward, landing flat. Can't tell if they're dead or just had the wind knocked out of them."

"Her eyes are still black. Really black. We can't let her loose in the castle." Lukan pushed himself down and around as fast as his arms would let him. *Stargods* he needed food. And sleep. "I don't know if I'm up to this," he confessed to himself.

(Verdii here. You have to be.)

"Yeah, yeah, I know. Glenndon could handle this with his eyes closed and his mind on placating a difficult diplomat. But I'm not Glenndon. I never will be. And truth be told, I don't think I want to be."

(Good. Now do your duty. We will help as we can.)

Energizing tingles ran up and down Lukan's spine. He drank in the dragons' gift of magic and power, storing as much as he could, letting it replenish his expended reserves. Almost instantly he felt bigger, stronger. Capable.

"Thank you," he called up into the air, at the last second remembering to keep his voice soft so it would not carry to other parts of the castle.

The staircase branched at this landing. One led left, to the king's study, the way they'd come up. The other led to another room where heated voices originated. He headed that way.

At the last step he braced himself with the staff, careful to keep the obsidian Spearhead upward and damage free, and against the wall. Once on his feet, he gingerly balanced himself on his right leg, touching only the ball of his left foot to the stones. Almost painlessly, he opened the tapestry that concealed the staircase two finger-widths from the wall.

"Robb's down. Maria stands over him like a mother saber cat protecting a cub. Lokeen approaches with a bloody dagger. Skeller just slid to a halt at the doorway. Sounds like Gerta and her crew are pounding up the primary entrance from the courtyard."

"Where's Rejiia? She's the most dangerous at this point," Chess reminded him.

"I can't . . . wait a minute. She's . . . she's in the left-hand corner, on the wrong angle for clear sight. She's focused on Lokeen."

"Fancy this, finding all my enemies in one room," Rejiia cooed. She raised her arms. Energy, black and raw and angry, crackled down her arms to her fingertips. "But where are my servants? I thought for certain you'd need their help, Lokeen."

"I killed them!" Lokeen brandished his gory dagger. The blood had congealed and started to turn dark. "All three of them. I slit their throats and enjoyed it," he sneered. "You should have been there, my love."

"You killed them! My followers, my coven. How dare you. Their lives belonged to me. Only I have the right to kill them!" With her last word she released her anger in a steady flow of magic.

Black fire engulfed the former king in a burning web, shrouding him like a living fishnet. Then it squeezed and tightened, strangling him. Crushing him. Burning flesh from bone, deeper and tighter it pressed.

A long shadowy figure rose up behind him with another dagger held high. He rammed it into Lokeen's back. A hideous snarl of a smile flashed across his acid-scarred face. Then he faded into the darkness. One more shadow among many.

Lukan didn't think Rejiia had seen Geon.

For still Rejiia poured magic into destroying Lokeen, long after the last scream squawked from his charred lungs.

None of her anger dissipated.

Lukan stared, agape at the senselessness of her continued outpouring of power. He didn't think he had ever been or ever could be that angry.

A question formed in the back of his mind. The dragons demanded he look deeper within himself.

"Right. I was nearly that angry when I learned that King Darville is Glenndon's father and not Jaylor, the man we both called Da. I grew angrier that Glenndon was summoned to court, leaving me alone to figure it all out by myself. I carried that anger deep in my heart for many moons. But no longer. I'm not going to waste time and energy nursing hurts that were never really there at all."

As Lokeen's body crumbled to ash, Rejiia whirled to face the tableau at the center of the room.

Only a few heartbeats had passed since she first entered. Everyone else seemed frozen in shock at the outrage of her murder of a king; no matter how insane, a former king deserved better than that. A trial in a court of law before execution, if nothing else.

"And now for you, Master Magician Robb," Rejiia snarled, gathering more power from her seemingly endless supply of anger. "I shall have your life in return for all the years you and your kind imprisoned me. You were the one who used your staff to backlash my spell. You and you alone are responsible!"

She raised her arms again. Black fire crackled anew from her heart outward to every tip of her body.

"No!" Chess yelled, pulling the tapestry that concealed them completely back.

Rejiia faltered half a heartbeat.

Lukan cast his staff and the Spearhead of Destiny directly into her heart.

The black fire withdrew to the obsidian and funneled outward along the twining grain of the wood.

Rejiia gasped, pulling inward. Convulsively she grabbed at the staff only to thrust her hands away again with an agonizing screech. Her palms nearly glowed green with the fire of an alien touch upon the staff.

"You can't do this to me," she said, surprised. Blood gushed from her mouth. Her eyes turned back to their normal midnight blue surrounded by white. Then the life poured out of her.

She collapsed into a pool of her own blood, normal red blood. The black of her magic died with her.

Lukan sat down hard, fully aware that he'd just taken the life of a person.

He had to force himself to breathe. "How much worse did my empathic sister Lily feel when she took the life of Samlan?"

CHAPTER 44

"SEND ME HOME, please," Robb croaked. He raised his palm a few inches from the floor in entreaty. All he could manage.

"Master Robb, you live!" Maria sank down beside him. She lifted his much too heavy hand into her lap and cradled it lovingly.

"Home. Please," he managed a few more words around his dry throat. "I would die beside my wife. I need to hug my sons one more time."

"If you aren't dead yet, chances are good you'll live," Lukan said matter-of-factly as he stumped toward him from the cover of the tapestry. He yanked his staff from Rejiia's cooling body. Then he examined the Spearhead curiously.

Gerta approached him, hand out. "The Spearhead of Destiny, please." She didn't like to pretty up her sentences much.

"I think I'm glad to be rid of this," Lukan said on a shrug, flashing her as big a smile as he could. *Stargods*, she was gorgeous, with the full dignity of an honorable battle draping her like a fine fur cloak. He fished a small utility knife from his boot and used it to slice through the binding on the Spearhead. "I don't like using my staff as a weapon." He let the obsidian point drop into Gerta's hand, complete with its gory coating.

"The battle is over," Maria said. "Now we can rebuild Amazonia in honor of the traditions our ancestors gave us." She lifted her voice so that all assembled could hear.

"Majesty, permission to dispose of the Krakatrice corpses, however the magicians think safest," Gerta requested, on a bow to Maria.

Robb tried to smile in satisfaction. Somehow he'd known that facing a true crisis would force Maria to come into her own.

"Master Robb?" the new queen turned to Robb, still holding his hand.

"Salt them heavily, burn them to ashes. But stay upwind of the fire," Lukan answered for him. "And sweep the residue into lidded containers. Then dump the remains as deep into the desert as you can. We don't know how much poison remains in them. But we do know that eating the meat is deadly."

Robb nodded his agreement, too weak to speak more.

"We have wagons. With wheels," Skeller said proudly. "We can manage this better than you could with your primitive sledges." He winked and smiled at Lukan.

"I would value your help and advice, Master Robb," Maria said quietly. Her eyes seemed to bore into his mind. But he felt none of the tingle of a telepathic message. Her magic was more subtle, healing and organizing, and finding another's strengths. She'd make a good queen.

"Majesty, I have nothing left to give you. You have Gerta and her Amazons. You have Skeller and his wisdom, even if it is disguised as music. You have your other nephew." He nodded toward the doorway where the red-clad healer and his followers assembled, crumpled, dirty, exhausted, and triumphant. "You have less need of me than I do to go home to die." He turned his face away and closed his eyes.

"I guess I have to do this," Lukan said. He sounded weary as he approached Robb, his staff grounding each of his steps. "Chess, you'll have to give me the strength for the spell. I haven't much left." He sat at Robb's head, legs stretched along either side of him.

"Um . . ." Chess hesitated. "I'm not overly fond of using a transport spell."

Robb could almost see him tracing a rune pattern with his toe. The sigil wouldn't help him much, except to stall. The boy had talent and imagination—perhaps too much imagination, since he always found the worst possible end to whatever he did.

"Courage, Chess," Robb whispered. "I brought you with me because I knew you had courage, if you just looked deep enough for it."

A moment of silence. Robb knew the boy would chew his lip, shuffle his feet, unconsciously seeking a ley line, and finally look up with a determined chin and a disapproving grimace across his face.

"I'll give you strength, Lukan. But I'm not going with you. If he hasn't found passage home already, I'll find Juan—the slave who helped us at the farm and contacted Glenndon to tell him about your injury—and then . . . and then we'll take ship to Coronnan City. I'll report to Master Marcus at the University."

"Agreed," Lukan said on a weary sigh. "Juan needs to come home too. Best if you make sure he gets there, friend." He began the deep breathing ritual required for any major spell. Chess placed his hands on Lukan's shoulders and matched the rhythm of inhale and exhale.

Robb found his own breathing relaxed into the familiar pattern. But his skittering heart could not settle. "Good-bye, Maria. I thank you for your care and kindness," he whispered while keeping a measured cadence. "I'll honor my promise to send a magical healer to you."

"Thank you, Master Robb, for giving me a reason to find my courage." She raised his fingers to her lips, then placed his hand over his heart. Skeller offered her a hand up to stand and back away from the circle of magic that began to flow around Robb and Lukan.

"Lukan, say hello to Lily for me," Skeller said just as the blackness of the void engulfed them.

Maigret, I'm coming.

(Come, come, come. You are needed now!) Krystaal burst into view above the fields of the unnamed village. Her command sank into Souska's mind with the weight of dread.

"What is happening?" Lily called back from her place beside the thresher. She continued to flay dozens of sheaves of barley on a wide tarp. A goodly pile of seeds had built up at the sides as she separated them from the stalks.

(You are needed at home. I am come to take you there.)

Lily handed off her flail to another woman who wasted no time continuing the work. Storm clouds built to the south, and they needed to get this vital work done before the first rains of autumn damaged the grain.

A third woman worked at keeping a new crop of fluster-hens from eating all the grain before it could be properly stored for winter. Orderly routine returned to this tiny village. The routine of life and continuance.

Souska found herself retreating behind Stanil, to where they worked at cutting tuber tops to plant in a newly worked field. The late-growing plant would produce new roots big enough for eating by early spring when the rest of their supplies dwindled and the remaining people had to resort to short rations.

"Come on, Susu. Grab your pack, we've got to go," Lily said as she passed Souska on her way to their hut.

"You've been packed for days," Souska said, as much to herself as her companion. "You're ready to move on. I . . . I'm . . . I don't know what I am."

"You don't have to go," Stanil said quietly. "We need you here. You are welcome here."

Lily stopped short and stared at Souska. "This is important. Maigret wouldn't have sent a dragon for us if it weren't."

"I . . . I am useless at the University," Souska replied,

studying the ground at her feet and seeing new shoots of grass and fireweed in the burned fields, a sure sign that life returned to the land.

"No, you aren't," Lily protested.

"Yes, I am. But I know what to do here. I know how to help my friends without magic. My place is here." Resolution brightened her mind and filled her with courage.

Stanil's hand reached for hers, holding it tightly. "She's staying with us," he told Lily. "She's staying with me."

Lukan accepted the bone-chilling cold of the void as just one more thing to endure before he could rest. He'd barely registered the sight of dozens of bright umbilicals snaking around him when sunlight warmed his face and soft grass cradled his backside. He sighed in relief.

Then the weight of Robb's head in his lap and the comforting smoothness of his staff in his hand reminded him of the urgency behind the transport spell.

His master was dying. He'd tasked his heart too much, too soon after enduring the fever.

"We're home," Lukan whispered. "Truly home."

Even as he said it he felt the rush of air from a dragon backwinging in order to land in a tight place. He looked up to see a juvenile female with silver still tipping her all color/no color wings and horns. His sister Lily slid off the dragon's back at first touchdown, while long claws clasped chunks of grass for balance.

"What have you done this time?" Lily asked as she slung her pack off her shoulder and began rummaging around inside for . . . for whatever Lily thought she needed.

Thought was beyond Lukan at this point. He just needed to sit a while longer and let his body rediscover where and when he was.

But he knew deep inside him that something was different with Lily. Thinner, quieter, more confident. And . . . and a small white circle glowed brilliant white on her forehead.

"Robb!" Maigret bellowed from the top of the steps to the Forest University. She pelted down them with her apprentice, Linda, close on her heels. Within a heartbeat a dozen others appeared out of nowhere, all converging on the center of the master's circle in the open forecourt of the three wings of the wooden building.

Moist, temperate air caressed Lukan's nose, bringing him the familiar scents of harvest, grass, and everblue trees.

"Home," Robb said with some surprise. "We're home." He roused a little, lifting his head and smiling at sight of his wife.

Strong hands lifted Robb free of Lukan's grip. Someone clucked in disapproval at sight of the crude bandage on Lukan's leg. Moments later he found himself lying flat on a cot in the infirmary. He surmised that Maigret had taken Robb back to their quarters where she could tend to him herself. The last he'd seen of them, she was raining kisses on his face while inspecting the rest of him with her hands, seeking the source of his illness and injury.

A healer Lukan did not know cleared the room to work his magic. Seconds later, Lukan dipped into deep sleep, from drugs or magic, he didn't care.

"Val?" Lily asked hesitantly as she stepped inside the family cabin. The only home she had ever known smelled different. The scents of rising bread, baking yampions, and fresh rushes on the floor still rose to greet her. But the spices and herbs were different. The perfume of three different women permeated the air. None of them Mama.

Lily's twin rose from the rocking chair Da had built for Mama. She held a bit of knitting in her hands. For the first time . . . ever . . . her red-gold hair shone in the firelight with health and vigor. Her skin, though still pale, had more color, and the lavender shadows around her eyes had faded.

"Lily!" Val dropped her handwork and rushed to embrace her twin. Her fingers clutched with new strength.

A flood of love passed between them, doing more to re-store Lily than food or a return home, which didn't seem like home anymore, ever could.

"Come, sit, rest. Supper is almost ready," Val said, urging Lily toward the settle on the far wall. "Take off those boots, not enough leather left in them to cover a book let alone your feet." She knelt in front of Lily and yanked the offend-ing gear off her feet.

Gratefully, Lily sighed and wiggled her toes against the dirt floor. That at least felt natural and familiar. Val helping her, urging her to rest and eat was . . . the opposite of normal.

Another woman emerged from the inner bedroom with Jule and Sharl clinging to her skirts. Tall and willowy, ethe-really blonde, with a decisive glint in her eye. "Good to have you back, Lily," Ariiell said. "Gracie's just started her labor. I suspect she'll birth before dawn."

"But she won't be returning to her husband any time soon," Val said. "He was never found after the flood, her mother doesn't want her, and the castle isn't safe as long as Krej lives, even if he is just an old man telling stories by the fire. Gracie needs to stay with us. We'll raise her babe to-gether."

"You aren't a vague wisp of guilt hiding behind insanity anymore," Lily said quietly to Ariiell.

Ariiell just grinned. Then she urged the children for-ward. "It's only been a few moons, surely you remember your big sister," she said.

Sharl hastened to climb onto the settle beside Lily, still a six-year-old bundle of curiosity, but she'd learned a few manners over the course of the summer. "You look more like Val than before," she whispered.

Lily hugged her tight and opened her other arm to invite three-year-old Jule to join them. He came more slowly, eyes huge, examining her from head to toe and back again be-fore deciding she was familiar. Lily felt his reluctance.

"You've made a nice life for yourselves here," Lily said. "Comfortable."

Val nodded and blushed. "We are happy together. We fit."

"I never thought I'd enjoy cooking," Ariiell admitted as she bent to stir whatever concoction simmered in the pot over the hearth.

"And I have found a talent in creating things out of yarn and thread," Val almost crowed.

And I don't belong here any more.

CHAPTER 45

A LONG TIME later, Lukan woke to find much of his pain and fatigue evaporated and Lily sitting on the end of his cot.

"Maigret wants to promote you to master and give you a medal," she said with a trace of humor. "She says that you are a natural teacher and belong here working with the apprentices. She doesn't think you are fit to journey anymore, either."

Lukan groaned, remembering that the dragons had diagnosed a permanent limp. Not a handicap, but a badge of honor. "What's going on outside?"

"You've slept two and a half days," Lily said.

"I think I needed to."

"You'll always walk with a limp, but the healers have cleared you of infection and rebuilt some of the muscle in your calf. Not all of it. That snakebite was deep and the venom spread quickly."

"I know."

"So, are you up to attending the bonfire and homecoming celebration?"

"I don't know. Am I?"

"Robb is coming. He's confined to a chair, and Maigret won't let him out of her sight, but he'll be there."

"Will he recover from the bad heart?"

Lily shrugged again. "I can't see Death in his aura. Doesn't mean she won't find him. Just not for a while yet." The glowing white dot on her forehead pulsed.

He shied away from that ominous portent. What was it? What did it mean? And why had gentle Lily been gifted with that . . . that . . . whatever it was?

"That sounds like something new happening in your magic," he choked out.

"It's been a strange year."

"Did . . . did Death give you that?" He pointed at the glowing white spot.

"Death and I have become intimates, almost friends," she whispered. "I understand better the purpose of Death, when to push her aside and when to welcome her."

"Mama and Da?"

"Together, as they should be. Death has sent them on to whatever awaits us. They were ready to go, as long as they could go together."

They sat in silence a moment, not quite needing to cry, together and separately.

"Don't become too friendly with Death. I'm not ready to go with her yet." He paused a long moment while he assessed his body and mind. He didn't hurt, and everything seemed intact. "I would like to see Val again. And the little ones," he admitted.

"Good. They are outside waiting for you to wake up. Lukan, I . . . I spent some time with my twin."

"And?"

"And it's not the same. I love her, our minds link just as firmly as they ever did . . . but . . ."

"But you have grown. You both have. You no longer need each other to survive. You've finally realized that you are two separate people, not two halves of one whole." Lukan itched to move. Slowly, testing every inch of his body, he levered himself to sit upright. It took a moment for his head to settle. Gripping his staff, which lay alongside him, helped. Several new braids had begun to form near the top, smaller companions to the initial one that spiraled down the shaft, leaving a clear, smooth indentation for his hand. He smiled, knowing that this tool of magic was truly his now. They belonged together as much as ... as much as Robb belonged here, home with his wife and sons.

Then, with a gush of air and noise, Val and the little ones rushed in. They hugged and chattered at him. He barely heard or understood their words, only needing to hold them close a moment and marvel at how they had all grown.

"There's a party," Jule whispered to Lukan as if imparting a great secret.

"Then I guess we need to go greet everyone and eat special cake," he whispered back. With a lot of help from Lily and Val, Lukan managed to stand on one wobbly leg and debate setting his other foot to the ground.

"Lean on me, big brother," Lily said.

"Half the world leans on you, little sister."

She shrugged, and they made their slow way out to the center courtyard. The children raced ahead into the noisy crowd gathered around a bonfire. Robb sat there, enthroned in a high-backed bath chair with wheels. Maigret stood behind him with one hand possessively on his shoulder. He clutched that hand with his own, with desperation, as if he were afraid that if he let go, she would disappear into the smoke from the fire.

Apprentice Linda bustled around, organizing food and beer, music and dancing, as if born to the chore. Well, she was.

Then a new gust of displaced air shimmered beside the encircling trees. A swirl of bright gold coalesced into the figure of a tall man with broad shoulders and blond hair pulled into a tight four-strand queue.

Glenndon.

All activity and noise ceased abruptly.

Glenndon stepped forward as if accepting the silent reverence as his due. But beneath his elegant brocade tunic, his shoulders twitched with unease.

Lukan had to chuckle. "A timely entrance, big brother," he called.

Glenndon visibly relaxed and hastened to his side. "How are you, little brother?" He pulled Lukan into a backslapping hug.

Lukan shrugged and leaned upon his staff. He'd automatically put most of his weight on his right leg when he paused in his limping gait toward the gathering.

Glenndon took a moment to hug each of his sisters then offered Lukan an arm to assist him. Val ran ahead the twenty paces to roust two senior apprentices from a camp chair and claim it for Lukan. The two tall boys acquiesced but not before demanding a kiss from Val as payment. Laughingly she bestowed a quick caress to their cheeks and shooed them away.

"Is that truly Val?" Glenndon asked in amazement.

"My twin has come into her own," Lily confirmed, not so eager to rush forward.

"And you?" Glenndon surveyed her with half-closed eyes, checking her aura as well as for outward symptoms of weakness.

"I am still working toward that," Lily said. "We each thrive in our own way now."

Linda appeared before them. She'd donned her formal pale blue robe and twisted her thick multicolored hair onto the top of her head and secured it with a long silver pen. Ink stains on her fingertips and a smear of woodsmoke on the tip of her nose had changed the elegant princess into a thoughtful administrator. Obviously she'd shouldered many of Maigret's duties while her mistress tended to her husband and family.

Linda reached up, kissed her brother's cheek, and clasped elbows with Lukan in greeting. "Glenndon, M'ma and P'pa? My sisters?"

"All well and safe."

They progressed toward the group as the youngest apprentices began handing around trenchers piled high with meat, fresh bread, and uncooked greens drenched in vinegar and oil.

"I can't stay long," Glenndon admitted as he picked delicately at his meal.

Lukan shoveled food into his mouth with his fingers. "I'm not surprised," he replied. "You don't really belong here any more than I do."

"Nor I," Lily said.

They ate in silence, only half-listening to tall tales and wild songs.

Very quickly they finished their meals and rose from their places. Lukan took a moment to greet Robb. Silent words passed between them.

"I know. Do what you need to do," Robb said.

"I need to take a healer to Queen Maria, and some of Lily's potions to cure that Krak-cursed plague," Lukan said.

Robb nodded. Two heartbeats later Maigret added her own approval. "We can send a healer. Don't worry about it. You will come back? And stay in touch, Master Lukan?" she asked.

"Not a master yet," Lukan said on a blush.

But Glenndon slapped his back in congratulation. "See, you are better at something than I am, and Da. Youngest master on record."

Lukan nodded a half acceptance as he backed away. Lily and Glenndon followed closely.

"I can't stay here, Lukan," Lily said proudly. "There's too much work for me still out there." She gestured vaguely beyond the confines of the University and her pack half-concealed beneath a saber fern.

"I know."

She looked at him strangely. "Give me two minutes to pack."

Val appeared beside him with a shoulder pack stuffed full with clothes and journey food. "Lily and I talked. I figured you'd want to leave again." She kissed his cheek as he shrugged into the pack, half-balanced by Glenndon's hand on his back.

"I . . . I have a lot of the world left to explore, Val. Lily, meet me in Amazonia when you can. Skeller is waiting for you." A long silence of agreement followed.

Val and Lily embraced one more time before Val returned to the party around the bonfire. She lifted her voice in a rousing song of celebration, sounding a lot like Mama.

"Lily, Skeller still loves you," Lukan said.

"And I him." She blushed prettily, the creamy skin of her face nearly matching her red-gold hair. "But I'm not ready yet to commit my life to him. I've learned to live with myself, alone in my mind. I've more learning to do. I've a relationship with Death I need to explore, and her gifts to understand."

Lukan reared back, almost shocked. But who was he to question strange relationships with elemental forces. "I don't think Skeller's ready to leave his aunt to rule Amazonia alone. Yet. By the time you journey in that direction, he might be."

"Journey. I like the sound of that word. We are journeymen, after all."

"Lukan's a master now, whether or not he wants to admit it," Glenndon added. "I have to get home. Come with me. Both of you."

"For a time," Lily said.

"I'd like to meet your other sisters," Lukan said. "But I've got an entire world to explore. I'm free to live my own life away from the shadow of older, more powerful, better-respected magicians. And so are you, Lily. How soon can we leave?"

"How about now?" Glenndon draped an arm around the shoulder of each of them and enfolded them in a transport spell that lingered in the void only a little longer than necessary.

EPILOGUE

I AM NOT so easy to kill. Samlan tried. He threw acid in my face and dumped me into the ocean. I survived. Lokeen stabbed me in the back. But he missed my heart. I returned the favor and didn't miss. I will survive.

I am done with attempting to learn magic from masters. They are all so consumed with their own power that they use me and then betray me.

Never again. I will learn and I will study. Hanassa, the city of outlaws, rogues, and Rovers, hidden deep within a burned-out volcano, calls to me. There I will find ancient libraries. And I know not to trust anyone. They all lie. I will do this on my own. I will bide my time and wait until I am ready.

And when I am ready I will have my revenge on those who have ignored me, or will betray me. I am no one's pawn.